Black Clouds over the Isle of Gods

Black Clouds over the Isle of Gods

and Other Modern Indonesian Short Stories

Translated and Edited by

David M.E. Roskies

An East Gate Book

M.E. Sharpe
Armonk, New York
London, England

An East Gate Book

Library of Congress Cataloging-in-Publication Data

Black clouds over the Isle of Gods and other modern Indonesian short stories / translated
and edited by David M. E. Roskies.
p. cm.
ISBN 0-7656-0032-3 (cloth : alk. paper).—ISBN 0-7656-0033-1 (pbk. : alk. paper)
1. Short stories, Indonesian—Translations into English.
2. Indonesia fiction—20th century.
I. Roskies, David M. E.
PL5088.B57   1997
899′.221301802—dc21
97-1658
CIP

Printed in the United States of America

The paper used in this publication meets the minimum requirements of the
American National Standard for Information Sciences—
Permanence of Paper for Printed Library Materials,
ANSI Z 39.48-1984.

BM (c)   10   9   8   7   6   5   4   3   2   1
BM (p)   10   9   8   7   6   5   4   3   2   1

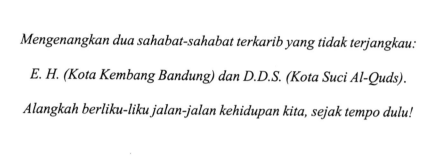

Mengenangkan dua sahabat-sahabat terkarib yang tidak terjangkau:

E. H. (Kota Kembang Bandung) dan D.D.S. (Kota Suci Al-Quds).

Alangkah berliku-liku jalan-jalan kehidupan kita, sejak tempo dulu!

Contents

Acknowledgments

Kind thanks are owed to the authors and to the editors for permission to translate; to Pak Julius Sadtono and Mrs. Gloria Poejoesardomo, former colleagues in Singapore, for having answered several queries; and to the publisher's copyeditor, Nora Cavin, for intelligent redaction. Rebecca Poston made a number of useful suggestions.

Sources

"Pertemuan," by Nasjah Djamin, "Eksentrik," by Asnelly Luthan, "Bertarung Dengan Banteng," by F. Rahardi, "Garong Garong," by Taufiq Ismail, and "Sebelum Yang Terakhir" by Satyagraha Hoerip have all been collected in *Cerita Pendek Indonesia*, a three-volume collection edited by Satyagraha Hoerip (Jakarta: Gramedia Penerbit PT, 1986); the English translations herein have been made with the editor's permission. This collection is also the provenance of "Anak" by Budi Darma and "Mendiang" by S. N. Ratmana.

"Yang Menyewakan Diri" first appeared in Pramoedya Ananta Toer's *Cerita Dari Blora: kumpulan cerita pendek* (Jakarta: Balai Pustaka, 1952), and has subsequently been reprinted without change in a volume bearing the same title (Kuala Lumpur: Wira Karya, 1989), from which the present translation has been made. Permission granted by William Morrow and Co. of New York.

"Dompet" was originally published in Putu Wijaya's collection *Gres* (Jakarta: PN Balai Pustaka, 1982).

"Perjalanan" first appeared in Nh. Dini's collection *Segi dan Garis* (Jakarta: PT Dunia Pustaka Jaya, 1983), and has been translated with the author's permission.

"Mega Hitam Pula Kayangan" first appeared in Putu Oka Sukanta's *Luh Galuh: kumpulan cerita pendek/kurzgeschichten* (Jakarta: Goethe Institut, 1987).

"Tukang Potret" by Prasetyohadi was first published in *Paradoks Kilas Balik: sayembara cerpen Kincir emas,* 1988 edited by Ray S. Anitya Dyanoe et al. (Jakarta: Pustaka Sinar Harapan, 1980).

"Topihelm" first appeared in A. A. Navis's collection *Robohnya Surau Kami: eight tjeritapendek pilihan* (Bukittinggi and Jakarta: n.v. Nusantara, 1956); permission to reprint with emendation has been given by the editors of the *Review of Indonesian and Malayan Affairs,* in which a version appeared (25, no. 1, 1992).

"Belitan Nasib" by Achdiat Karta Mihardja first appeared in *Keretakan Dan Ketegangan* (Jakarta: Perpustakaan Perguruan Kementerian Pendidikan dan Kebudayaan, 1956), and was translated in *Indonesia,* the journal of Cornell University's Modern Indonesia Project (no. 30, April 1991). Permission to reproduce with revisions has been granted by the editors.

"Heiho," "Sanyo," and "Jawa Baru" by Idrus first appeared in Idrus's collection *Dari Ave Maria Ke Jalan Lain ke Roma* (Jakarta: Balai Pustaka, 1948); the translations slightly adapt versions first prepared for Yayasan Lontar in Jakarta and are published with its permission.

"Kena Jaring" by Rahmat Ali first appeared in *Sayembara Kincir Emas* (Jakarta: Sinar Harapan/Radio Nederlands Weldenroep, 1975).

Introduction

This little book is neither a survey nor a scholarly study. It serves a different and altogether more modest purpose: to offer the general reader and the Indonesia enthusiast a range of stories from a vast, complex, and intoxicatingly interesting country. It goes without saying that the subjects, character, and merit of the selections vary. But in its own way each communicates something of Indonesia's distinctive and manifold life; and each, in its own way, is entertaining.

Generally speaking, the short story is the least forgiving of forms. Ideally it should echo, should expand across its economy; in short, it should be enormous. Novels, Henry James's "loose, baggy monsters," are easily forgotten. Stories, irrespective of their provenance, stay in the mind; a really good story creates its own self and subject, in a way peculiar to itself. In Indonesia particularly, the short story enjoys the further advantage of being by far the favored prose form. It is not difficult to understand why this should be so. A novel-consuming public lives in cities and has leisure time to fill, cash to spare, a modicum of privacy—and electric light to read by. Impoverished, for the most part; deprived of educational opportunities until very late in the Dutch colonial period; living in dense agglomerations in rural surroundings, the majority of people in what used to be known as the Netherlands East Indies were illiterate. Those who weren't were disinclined to buy bound volumes, and still less to read them for pleasure; in any case, apart from the fact that their traditional culture was largely visual and oral, they hadn't the means. Relative to absolute numbers, the reading and book-buying public in the colonial Indies was minuscule. Publishing on an industrial scale and in the sense taken for granted in Atlantic societies was in its infancy and catered to the needs of small European and Eurasian minorities.

Little wonder, then, that an increasingly lively provincial and metropolitan press, often nationalist in orientation, served to transmit and disseminate such literature for and by Malay speakers as did, despite all odds, come to be written. Newspapers cost little, were communal in character, and were often read communally, out loud. Here there was every guarantee of reaching a larger audience. Since the foundation of the republic in 1945 things have of course changed out of all recognition; literacy is widespread (though one out of four Indonesians still cannot read), and in the major cities publishers, large and small, are no longer in short supply. But it remains the case that the author of a short work of fiction will tend in the first instance to seek an outlet in dailies like *Kompas* (published in Jakarta) or *Jawa Pos* (appearing in Surabaya), or in literary journals like *Basis* (in Yogyarkarta) or *Horison*. Being, as he or she so often is, a journalist, and with time to write therefore at a premium, there is a need to reach a wide audience with maximum ease. The literati are a fragment of this audience; the majority is made up of housewives, lecturers, secondary school teachers and pupils, government employees, and the like. Writers of short stories, in Indonesia as elsewhere, are in the challenging position of having their work cut out and of building on a tradition of popular reception by means other than bound and printed books.

The variety of Bahasa Indonesia they and their readers speak is, broadly, the dialect of the urban bourgeoisie, the intelligentsia, the print, visual, and broadcast media, the instruments of government, the professional stratum. It serves as the carrier of all formal and semiformal communication. It is sometimes held to be a relatively easy language to master. If we are talking about internalizing the ground rules of functional grammar and acquiring a command of what lay opinion often deems a limited range of received forms of expression, this may be so. Whether as a demotic, designed for use in barter, a vernacular of which no more than a rudimentary grasp is desirable, or a vehicle of imaginative expression characterized by simplicity, the Indonesian language may appear to a listener not yet inward with to to fall well short of anything resembling the complexity and range of its European counterparts.

But, as is so often the case, appearances deceive. The diction of Indonesian, for one thing, is formidably supple. Vocabulary no less so: this is true even of speech at the level of daily life. Both feed off a plurality of sources. There are the regional languages of the vast archipelago: Acehnese, Makassarese, Sundanese, Sumatran Minangkabau,

Coastal Malay, "Betawi," or Jakarta Malay, to name the more important of the total 583. Preeminently, Javanese, which is not only the everyday spoken language of Central and East Java but for a long time was also an important language of learning and literature among the Sundanese, Madurese, Balinese, and Sasak. Other sources are tributary. Sanskrit was the vehicle for religious values, and for the expression of philosophical concepts and political ideas; Arabic, the language of formal worship and prayer; Chinese, of commercial terminology. Also to be reckoned with are trace elements of the main imperial languages, Dutch and Portuguese, a superficial but discernible influence of American English, excrescences like Bahasa Prokem, the slang of well-to-do or miscreant Jakarta youth, and last but not least, internal sublanguages like bureaucratic jargon, newspaper argot, and the argot of the civil service *apparat.* Where the penetration of the state into civil society has been as deep as it has been wide, such jargon flourishes. But here too, things are not what they seem. Officialese in Indonesia, while it may seem oppressive to an outsider is, when seen from the inside, a source of amusement that invites satire, subversion, mockery—anything, in fact, rather than passive, somber acceptance. The observer of Indonesian life must look not so much at surface or undergrowth as at their dense entangling nexus.

So, contrary to one widespread misconception, here is a language every bit as intriguing in origin and as many-sided in vernacular character and formal register as many European tongues and as any other modern Asian one, with a literature that at its very best can be absorbing to read and is never less than interesting. But there is no sense taking this latter claim for granted. Readers, instead, are invited to see for themselves, in the pages that follow.

As languages go, Bahasa Indonesia is still in its first youth, both a cause and an effect of the drive toward autonomy within new nations in the making, in Asia as well as in Europe, in the first quarter of this century. Its certificate of birth gives 1928: year of the famous *Sumpah Pemuda* or Oath of Youth, enjoining all inhabitants of what was then Tropical Holland to favor modernized Malay over Dutch as the medium of national self-identification for indigenes. The still-evolving character of Indonesian and the youth of many of its contemporary speakers—most of the country's population is twenty-five or younger—accounts to a considerable extent for its elastic qualities, and for its extraordinary effervescence of expression. But its plasticity of form and liveliness of idiom, especially the spoken idiom, have antecedent causes. The Malay of which it is a projection served in centuries gone by as a lingua franca: a vehicle for trade and raid, for the conduct of diplomacy and of court life since the days of the seventh-century Srivijaya and fourteenth-century Majapahit empires. If its character is as pungent and allusive as it is, its word-hoard so motley, this may be because Indonesia—more precisely, Java—has for so long been one of the great emporia of the world as well as the seat of successive dynasties known for their material splendor and spiritual accomplishment. A cultural crossroads, it has been at one and the same time home to monumental civilizations of its own, and promiscuously open to outside influence. Our dealings, then, are with one of the world's more important lingua francae, whose sources are many and venerable, a language powerfully receptive to all manner of stimuli from overseas. While importance is seldom a function of size, it is nonetheless worth noting that the number of speakers of Bahasa Indonesia, belonging as they do to hundreds of distinct clans, peoples, and localities, now stands at getting on for 200,000,000. The numbers are fewer if you take the speech of home and hearth as your yardstick rather than that of school and radio, but on any reckoning they are still massive.

Anyone proposing to transfer this language into English has taken on quite a lot. Your dealings are with a sophisticated creole, once employed throughout much of insular Southeast Asia, as far north as the region—once, the kingdom—of Champa in Cambodia and as far west as Zamboanga in the southern Philippines, but a creole that has since mutated into a capacious national language and one of which comparatively few Europeans, resident or otherwise, have an expert command. How best to act as a go-between? You are working with words and concepts that fail to coincide across the two languages, with rhetorical effects that don't match up. You are always trying to steer a course between the rocks of a too-literal rendition and a fanciful recreation. Veer in one direction, and you risk winding up with lifelessly correct prose straitjacketed in translationese. Move too sharply in the other, and what results may have sailed clear of the intended meaning, to the point where it comes to correspond to little on the page that was there to start with.

Obviously there's more than one way to chart a course through such treacherous waters. The one opted for here involves sitting light to the original: keeping faith with the tone and essence of the Indonesian while attempting—one can do no more—to find plausible equivalents in one's own dialect of English. To translate is *not,* as is sometimes said, invariably to traduce, but creatively to transform. The object in reimagining any language is to enable it to travel far, and readers with it. At the same time there has to be imposed what one might call the fidelity test. By this I mean the test of whether the translation has retained the spirit or essence of the original. Would the author of the original work recognize the translation as being his work, and would he be proud of the result? That is one question a facing text might have settled. But publishers and translators live in the real world and are bound by its constraints. Readers will therefore have to make up their own minds as to whether the character of the originals has been retained while being conveyed from one context to another. The proof of this pudding is in the eating. A good appetite is, needless to say, assumed—who, having set foot anywhere in these 13,600 islands spread over three million square miles of ocean, wouldn't be hungry?

But to argue for such ease of access is to stir up a hornet's nest of controversy. There is a romantic view which holds that the mentalities encountered during contact, casual or prolonged, in print or in the flesh, with an "exotic" country like Indonesia must—try as one may— remain opaque to a Western understanding, precisely because that understanding is Western, not indigenous. But this, as well as gloomy, is a shallow and tendentious line to take. It is prompted by an exaggerated regard, verging on a kind of superstition, for the impenetrability of alien societies. And it can be every bit as patronizing as the callowness and insensitivity it seeks to reproach. Intelligent travelers will confirm what the best scholarship has always known: namely, that an inquisitive attitude sustained by a modicum of intuitive sympathy is not only possible but desirable—always allowing, of course, for the inevitable difficulties. The chief difficulty is the fact that our view of foreign landscapes will in some ways remain forever colored by the actualities of who we are and where we're coming from. As outsiders looking in on Indonesia, or any other non-Western society, we are looking perforce through a smoked glass. But this doesn't mean that we can see nothing. What we, as (let's say mainly) Europeans bring to the encounter with Indonesia is finally neither more nor less than what we might expect to bring to the rendezvous with any community other than our own. In terms of imaginative effort this may be asking a lot, but it is not unreasonable. In the end, there are tourists and there are tourists.

Readers of this book, I have ventured to suppose, belong to the second category. The real foundations of modern Indonesian life are what interest them: the forces at work within the component parts of the modern state. About those forces a great deal has of course been written. Here it must suffice to mention contradictions which the camcorder range finder, focusing on externals, will never pick up. It is, for instance, recognized that notwithstanding its membership in OPEC, its self-sufficiency in basic foodstuffs, and the wide availability of health and education services at every level of society, Indonesia is still a very poor country when judged by the conventional yardstick of per capita GDP. According to *Tempo,* Indonesia's equivalent of *Newsweek* ("Kemiskinan Kita," 15 May 1993), almost 27 million people, or more than a fifth of its population, are underemployed or living below the poverty line. At the same time, the rise of a prosperous middle sector—which embraces a number of heterogeneous groups whose common denominator is regular consumption of newspapers and magazines and other media—is one of the more striking features of Indonesia today, and a feature hard to miss. The casual observer cannot fail to notice the increase in private-vehicle ownership, the mushrooming of posh housing estates on the outskirts of the towns, the abundance of new supermarkets and shopping malls. Not to mention the number of professionals, clerks, and business managers, with disposable income and all the accoutrements of a late twentieth-century style of life, now recruited to the ranks of the working population. (Both phenomena are closely related to the deregulation that began in the mid 1980s and has been growing apace since.)

Precisely what is one supposed to make of such contradictory facts? The answer is far from clear. What *is* clear is that "facts" as contradictory as these seldom speak for themselves. They have to be spoken for, represented, given form if they are to be rendered intelligible, if a construction is to be placed on them. Nowhere, I think, is this more likely to happen than in the wonderful lies of fiction.

An awareness of this contradiction on the part of contemporary Indonesian authors doesn't, as the foregoing may seem to suggest, automatically make theirs a literature of crude protest. Far from it. It does, however, make for a quality of *engagement.* Unavoidably, this body of writing is in the strict sense of the word *interested.* For whom am I writing? In whose behalf? By way of intervening in what sort of family quarrel? In defense of which side, in what conflict? Of their own accord the stories in this book are committed to asking such aboriginal questions, in the very act of amusing or diverting.

This will come as no surprise. The modern republic was born in violence, and postindependence Indonesian fiction has correspondingly been the product of stress at the base. The historical "moments" in which this fiction is embedded and to which, by fascinatingly devious routes, its narratives recur, are two: the national revolution of 1945-49, a transforming and transformative event following the Proclamation of the Republic of Indonesia by Sukarno and Hatta and followed by war, within the Republic as well as with the former Dutch imperial power, and the suffering and dislocation war brings; and the watershed formed by the military putsch of some fifteen years later. This must rate as one of the twentieth century's more extensive atrocities and certainly as the worst episode of political violence in Indonesian history. The Revolution and the 1965 coup represent historical breaks with an unacceptable past; and modern Indonesia's imagination of itself—the popular imagination as well as the authorized narration of the nation—has been haunted by both events. The shock waves sent forth from these episodes continue to reverberate through the country's life and letters. Both areas are profoundly conditioned not only by the *Revolusi*—a truism, of course—but by what has become known by the chilling acronym GESTAPU (*Gerakan Tigapuluh September*). Bitter anticolonial struggle accompanied by mass action and the exhilaration of *Kemandirian,* of standing on one's own two feet, had given rise to hopes for a *negara yang makmur dan adil,* a prosperous and just state; had, indeed, been engendered out of such turmoil. This, however, Sukarno, contending with hyperinflation, regional rebellion, and the failure of constitutional democracy, was unable to bring into being. The regime of President Suharto, who seized the reins of power in what, looking backward, can only be described as a civil war long in progress, has brought about stability and prosperity. But it has done so at a felt cost, in control and invigilation, and in the *dirigisme* reflected in big things and small, not least in carefully supervised elections, a controlled parliamentary process, the repression of dissidents, and the resulting dissatisfaction, however inchoate, among the middle classes as well as the intelligentsia.

If the New Order, as it has styled itself, has aimed to create a disciplined machinery of state capable of reaching down to the village level, it has also had to contend with centrifugal tendencies at work in national life. Many such tendencies have a long pedigree; space being at a premium here, no more than a few can be mentioned. There is devotional Islam, set against the individualism characteristic of westernized metropolitan life. Consumerist materialism and instrumental values generally vie with ascetic worldviews. Optimistic rationality is to be found contending with determinist philosophies. In their always unsolemn and often startling way, the stories in this anthology meditate, and mediate, these tensions.

They, in turn, operate at the very base of contemporary Indonesian life. The travel agent's cliché says that the Indonesian nation-state is characterized by extraordinary local variety and is above all a colorful amalgam. But that same cliché omits to mention that the amalgam, as well as colorful, is also fissile: an unstable alloy of *daerah* (region) and *propinsi* (province), *bangsa* (people) and *ummat* (community), compounded of different collective memories, ethnicities, sensibilities. To take the peripheries, for example; so different in these respects is Aceh, at the tip of Sumatra, from Timor, in the country's far east, that misgivings about Javanese hegemony are, on some assessments, all that serve to weld them together. Those who take this line overstate the case, no doubt. But the overstatement may serve as a reminder of how hard-won is the coherence of the whole structure, how delicate the edifice. While "Indonesianness" is, thanks to so zestful a national language, real enough, and while the Indonesian Republic is far from being at risk of dissolution—as it was in 1958 and 1965, for example—the nation's motto *"Bhinneka Ika Tunggal"*—"Out of Many, One"—remains a consummation devoutly to be wished for rather than an indisputable description of what is the case

As with politics, so with economics. One can argue the toss as to how far divisions have been exacerbated since the early 1970s by programs designed to foster a climate of consumption and investment from abroad. But there's little doubt that a central division between haves and have-nots has grown lately in reaction indirectly to the push from above to industrialize. In the foreground, in the cities on Java— the whole island now well on the way to comprising a single conurbation, with consequent and ever increasing pressure on land and population—are the *orang gelandangan,* or street people, often to be found sleeping rough on broken pavement stones or else eking out a precarious existence from hand to mouth in urban kampungs or in encroaching shantytowns. In the background, a carefully orchestrated environment of lower inflation, reduced current-account deficit, and higher nonoil income has taken shape, benefiting, in the first instance, a nouveau riche ensconced in the comfortable suburbs. Certainly the social costs have come to be judged worth bearing by those with their hands on the tiller; they are seen as the price of entrance to the international club of high growth. There are those who, marshaling statistics to support the claim, assert that a trickle-down effect is at work, that things are far from as fraught as they may seem or as might be supposed, given the acknowledged magnitude of the problem. But a contrary school maintains that while no one is actually starving, there is still a very long way to go.

More recently, other problems have supervened: The dual role of *dwifungsi* of the Indonesian armed forces, ABRI; should the armed forces still be involved in politics as well as maintaining internal security? What ought to be the response to a new middle class's demands for greater freedom of expression and more open political arrangements? Workers are getting restive; what to do about their dissatisfaction with subsistence wages, the single government trade union in which membership is compulsory, and an industrial relations policy that discountenances strikes? These are but three of the questions of the day, often raised and discussed at length in, for example, the lively pages of *Tempo* magazine—latterly on-line, the print version having been banned for alleged subversiveness. What can't possibly be gainsaid, and what the least amount of time spent in Jakarta or the hinterland of Java or in the Outer Islands will confirm, are the immense changes—and, yes, the prodigious achievements, the absolute improvements—that have taken place in the thirty years since President Suharto's assumption of power following the 1965 coup d'état.

The literary record at its most articulate can provide a purchase on all of this, an inside view that isn't accessible by other means. But, granting that Indonesian literature at its best is, like any other, intriguing in its own right and indispensable as a point of entry to culture and society, one is bound to ask, What is the internal ratio of good to bad? The short answer is: pretty low. The ruck is prolix, boring, uncreative. The exceptions to this rule are not easy to get hold of, even if you know—or think you know—where to look. Translations into English of modern Indonesian writing are dated or out of print. They are not always up to scratch, and the texts themselves are of indifferent quality. This is so in Europe and North America, and elsewhere too, Australasia not excepted. The situation, though not exactly hopeless, is in marked contrast with that of twentieth-century China, India, and Japan: wide-ranging anthologies of short fiction from these countries are not hard to come by. In assembling this volume I have hoped to fill a void, with the understanding that no anthology can aspire to representative or canonical status—or rather, aspire is pretty well all it *can* do. Better to say that I've plumped, from the word go and quite shamelessly, for those works I liked more than others, and which I fancied my readers may like as well. I've taken their curiosity about Indonesia for granted, as I have the curiosity of those who see the advantage of being better informed about a country that is home to the world's largest Muslim community and is its fourth most populous nation. Southeast Asia's most powerful state—powerful both in economic terms and geopolitically—is going to become harder to patronize and impossible to ignore in time to come, were one of a mind to do so.

As to the stories themselves, it's worth remembering that they were not, in the first instance anyhow, meant for export but are arguments behind closed doors, so to speak, a kind of intramural conversation on which friends and neighbors may delight to eavesdrop. In so doing it's possible to discover something about the circumstances, public and private, of men and women in Indonesia in recent years, and the pressures that attend them. I say "in recent years" since, with several exceptions, the texts chosen belong to the period dating from the late 1960s to the present day. The Japanese occupation of 1942-45 and the Revolution itself are represented, to be sure. In the main, however, the collection spans the crisis in national life marked by the bloody collapse of Sukarno's Old Order and the subsequent rise and consolidation of a regime committed to "development." This regime has been poised to move Indonesia into the van in the region, mainly by granting more freedom to the private sector. At what human price is a question hotly debated at home as well as abroad. It's untendentiously posed by more than one story here; that is to say, in ways that are latent not patent.

It can't be emphasized too strongly that this book, far from being intended for professionals, is written for readers who are assumed to be amateurs, in the complimentary sense of that misunderstood word. As amateurs, they are also assumed to be keen to know something about the backgrounds and contexts of the authors represented here.

This presumptive hunger I have tried to appease by means of the Notes and Comments grouped at the back; the comments are offered as food for thought, to be taken or left. There is as well a glossary, mainly of Indonesian and Dutch terms, and there are Suggestions for Further Reading. All of these may serve to whet the appetite of readers new to Indonesia, an appetite which with any luck this book, in a very small way, will have helped both to provoke and to satisfy.

DMER
Jakarta 1995

Black Clouds over the Isle of Gods

Three Tales From the Occupation

by Idrus

Heiho

K artono was hard at work. He was bending over, doing a creditable imitation of a Japanese, his midriff pressing up against the desk. He was an office clerk, but the work was more than he could bear. As for his ever getting a rise in pay, forget it. He'd been going at it for three years, there wasn't a day he wasn't plugging away. But was any of this acknowledged by his superiors? Dream on.

A few months back he'd put his name down as a *heiho** recruit and had had his physical. Whenever anyone asked, he'd say he was keen to do his bit to defend the Fatherland.

He glanced up, in some surprise. The boy from the post office had come round, bringing some letters before going off to make his deliveries. Kartono's surprise was the greater when he opened one of them to learn that his application had been accepted. He'd to present himself at the *heiho* barracks that very day.

He was over the moon. Friends proffered their congratulations, for all the world as if he were a bridegroom. He beamed with joy. He went around saying, "Miarti . . . Miarti . . ." to himself, muttering his wife's name over and over. As he did so his brow would

---

*Indonesian auxiliaries recruited to the Japanese Imperial Army during the Occupation, 1942–45.

furrow like an old woman's cheek. He scratched his head like a monkey searching for lice.

His boss was glad for him. "You're a hard worker, Kartono. I do believe you'll be even more useful to our beloved country as a *heiho*. Just wait here a moment, will you . . . there's a testimonial I want to give you. You deserve it after all your diligence."

Knitting his brow once again, Kartono replied, "Thanks, sir, but I'd be ever so grateful if you could manage to have it written in Japanese."

Now this boss of his was no nationalist. He was your ordinary chap, a man for whom such things as putting food on his family's table and money in the bank came first. As he'd once put it, he kept to the straight and narrow: no risks, not for him. But when he heard what Kartono was asking, he all but hit the roof.

"If it's a letter written in Japanese you're after, why the heck are you working in my office?" he yelled at the top of his voice. "Do I have to bust a gut to learn Japanese on top of everything else, just to write a bleeding testimonial letter for you? Brain fever, that's what you patriotic chaps are all suffering from! Tropical malaria, I shouldn't wonder. You're living in cloud-cuckoo-land, Kartono. . . . To be blunt, I'm beginning to ask myself whether it's worth even losing my temper with your sort. A bunch of apes, that's what you all are, all you're good for is pulling the wool over people's eyes. You see your friends finding a cushy berth thanks to some testimonial or other in Japanese, and what do you do, you want one too, don't you! Monkey see, monkey do. Look, I can't speak a word of Japanese, but just supposing I did, supposing I wrote in that chicken scrawl of theirs saying that you, Kartono, were a pig's arse. Now, would you be any the wiser? Tell me that!"

To this Kartono calmly replied, "There's no call for you to fly off the handle, sir. The idea wasn't for you to do it yourself. After all, there's Supadi here; he's just finished an advance course in Japanese."

The boss, to all appearances, was finding it hard to get a grip on himself. He spat out his words; spewed out, they might have been Japanese written characters. "Now look here, Kartono, don't give me this bullshit about advanced-level Japanese. For all I care it might as well be advanced-level coconut climbing. You want a testimonial letter? Fine. But in one hundred percent Indonesian. And if you don't like it you can take a running jump, for all I care. You're not a *heiho* yet, Kartono. I'm not afraid of you—not yet anyway!"

"Lose your temper if you like, sir," Kartono gently replied. "I was only asking, that's all. You can say yes or no, just as you please. I'll be perfectly happy with a letter written in Indonesian."

Arriving at the barracks, he was handed his uniform and told to take off the clothes he'd worn to work and put it on. "Excuse me, sir, but don't we get underwear too?" he asked, turning to a *heiho* who happened to be standing there.

"That was our suggestion too. But the Japs said there's no need. Fast workers, that's what we *heihos* have to be. A production line, that's what it's got to be like and, well, he made like a fountain and just laughed. So there you are, I'm afraid: no underwear!"

Kartono joined in the laughter. But when he donned his uniform his lower parts started to itch like crazy. It felt like tiny ants were crawling into every pore.

"It starts off like that," the *heiho* said. "You'll get used to it, though. We don't even mind the stink anymore. Now, you go on home, kiss the wife and kiddies good-bye, and see that you're back here at eight o'clock sharp—or else."

His shoes were a tight fit; he'd not taken two steps when the skin of his heel began rubbing off. It was all he could do to walk straight, and his foot, the one with the rubbed-raw heel, would scrape along the ground as he went.

"Look at that *heiho,* Mat," said a father out for a walk with his child. "You've got to hand it to those Japs, they certainly know what they're doing when they make a point of recruiting these yokels. This one here doesn't even know how to wear shoes."

"But Dad, how can he," the child replied, smiling, "when his big toe's swollen? Look how puffed up it is, like a fan when you open it wide."

"I tell you, son, it's a sight for sore eyes. Back when the Dutch were running the place," the old man laughingly observed, "it was the educated types that got all the attention. Under the Japanese, it's the country bumpkins who matter. Oh, they're a clever lot all right, the Japs. Country folk are so much easier to get fired up.

"Actually they're every bit as clever as the Dutch," he went on as if anxious to qualify his own observations. "Six of one and half a dozen of the other, when you come down to it, that's what I mean. It's like Bung Karno says ... what *does* he say, Mat? You know, 'divide and conquer, *vida dan pera*'— at least I *think* that's how it goes."

"You do like talking posh and using foreign languages, Dad, don't you," little Achmad said. "Anyhow, Bung Karno only said it the other day, and here you can't even remember. Funny, isn't it Dad, how fast we forget words that we hate. That awful woman, for instance; you wouldn't by some chance remember her name, would you?"

The father went red in the face. Mortified, he stroked his white-washer's mop of a mustache. "Don't you dare speak to me like that! Show some respect! You may be a big boy but I'm still your father. Don't you talk to me about an 'awful woman.' In all my life I've had dealings with her on no more than three occasions, and then only on account of your mother's being such a shrew. You dare bring this home and I'll give you what for!"

"Come on, Dad, take it easy. All I was getting at was that the things we tend to forget about are the things we find hateful, and in no time at all."

"That's not true either. What about your mother, how come I've never forgotten her name?"

"Oh, really, Dad," Achmad said plaintively, his voice hoarse. "Why use such language when there's a better way of putting it? 'Scoundrel'—isn't that a better word for the likes of them? Dutch scoundrels, Japanese scoundrels, Indonesian—"

"Stupid, clever, what difference does it make," his father agreed between fits of coughing. "I've got to hand it to you, Mat. You're dead right, best to go easy. What it boils down to is that they're two buttocks of one bum!"

Kartono arrived home. Miarti was shooting him a sour look. "Ti, look, Ti!" he gaily cried out nevertheless.

"See what?" she replied, livid. "That monkey suit you're wearing? You think I fancy you becoming a *heiho*, do you? Frankly I'd rather be dead! And what if you get killed? Who's going to bring you back to me, eh? The Japs?"

This came as a shock. He'd honestly thought she'd be tickled pink. "But Miarti, you do see, don't you, that I want to do my bit for the Fatherland?"

"Fatherland? Where's this 'Fatherland' of yours, eh? Tell me that! Have you any idea whatsoever what the word *heiho* means, you nincompoop? A domestic houseboy, that's what it means!"

"Miarti, you don't understand. It's you I was thinking of, not myself! Our country's issued an appeal to all her sons. You've got it all wrong, you've got to realize the times we're living in!"

"Times! I don't give a damn about 'the times.' But if you think I'm going to let you join the *heiho,* well you can jolly well think again! Now, it's up to you; you can throw that monkey suit of yours into the dustbin, or else you can give me a divorce and do as you bloody well please. It's your choice."

"Miarti . . . " Kartono heaved a deep sigh, as a pregnant woman might, and wrinkled up his brow. For a long time he said nothing. Then "Right you are, Miarti," he blurted out like a child confessing to some wrongdoing. I can't very well go, can I, if you're having none of it. Still, what's done is done, Miarti. Fact is, if I'm not back in barracks by eight sharp they'll have my head on a plate. Anyway, I thought you'd be chuffed. That's why I kept it secret from you."

She thought the matter over. Several tears rolled down her cheeks as pity for her Kartono filled her heart. "What's done is done, indeed," she said slowly. "How can I say no? Go on then, off with you."

Now that came as a surprise. He was even, if you want to know, a wee bit disappointed. He'd rather thought she'd balk to the bitter end. So with a heavy heart, he said, "I can see you don't love me, Miarti, otherwise you wouldn't be letting me go."

Sharp at eight Kartono was back in barracks. Eight months later he had met his death in Burma. Miarti, meantime, was four months pregnant. By her "second" husband.

Sanyo

The fried-peanut vendor, Kadir his name was, sat under the radio loudspeaker that had been rigged up in the village square, his basket full of hot peanuts and his pocket empty. Overhead an oil lamp flickered, like some beacon far out to sea. You could hardly breathe in the stifling air. There were no takers that night; it was the ice-cream man who was drawing them.

He'd been sitting there like some sort of watchman for the past two hours, itching to talk. The loudspeaker blared at him, a brittle jewel, calling on people to offer themselves for appointment as *sanyos.**
Kadir could make neither head nor tail of it, it was like the radio was a foreigner, so far as he was concerned. A foreigner from outside Java,

---

* Advisors attached to administrative departments during the occupation.

squat as a tribesman from upcountry, skin yellow, the color of turmeric, bloodthirsty as a tiger.

With great effort he managed to get his tongue round a few words, as if someone were listening.

Sanyo, sanyo. What on earth was that supposed to mean? *San . . .* that means three in Japanese, doesn't it?

He considered the matter. "Oh, what's the use anyway," he burst out suddenly, "no sense brooding on it is there, if no one's buying today. Bother this *sanyo,* whatever it means. I'm willing to bet that's the reason why business is so bad."

The popsicle vendor came up to him wearing a wide-brimmed peasant's hat, his clothes in tatters. He was shirtless, his body half white and half black, like the flowers adorning a gown you'd wear to a ball. They'll come running when they get a load of that, ten to one, Kadir thought to himself.

He was no mind reader, the ice-lolly man, he wasn't to know what might be running through Kadir's head. "Give us some peanuts, *bang!* two cents' worth," he said with a laugh.

Kadir looked him up and down. "You can't get any for two cents, not nowadays," he said contemptuously. "*Sanyo*'s the reason, I'll wager. Don't ask me why!"

"Oh come on, be a sport. Just a wee bit, *bang.* Anything to dull the hunger pangs. Popsicles are all I've had to eat lately."

Kadir's heart went out to him. He sorted through his stock, selecting a few small peanuts and handing them over. In return the lolly man gave him two banknotes charred with dirt. The nuts disappeared into his maw, one at a time. "What's with all these empty ones?" he remarked, irritated.

"What do you mean, 'all these'?" Kadir came back at this, surprised. "I've given you just four, haven't I?"

"You're from . . . where did you say?" the lolly man wanted to know.

"Bogor. I manage a visit back once a month. I serve as a *kumico* there."

This brought him up short. He'd always been scared to death of the *kumico.* In his kampung he'd always played safe and given the man a lolly a day—he was afraid he'd be docked his daily portion of rice, otherwise. "So who's been taking your place while you're in Jakarta, Mr. Kumico, sir, if you don't mind my asking?" This in soft tones, and respectfully.

Kadir rather took to hearing himself being called sir. "Binu, my son," he replied cockily. "He's just finished school in our village. He's the one with the brains in the family. Me, I can't even read or write. When I get wind of cigarettes being handed out at Bogor, that's when I go back, not otherwise. Not to flog them at black-market rates, mind you. You won't catch me selling them under the counter."

"Mr. Kumico, sir, tell me, do you . . . you don't suppose I've got any chance of becoming a *kumico* too? Or not."

Kadir scrunched up his face. "Couldn't say really. Used to be a cinch. But it's got harder now. Still, I seem to recall having heard over this radio here in the square that they're taking on new ones. But you can bet it'll be harder to get in." This was delivered in what was meant to be a fair imitation of Saiko Sikikan, OC Java Forces, Imperial Japanese Army.

"Mr. Kumico, sir. This *sanyo,* what's it mean anyway?"

"Search me. People these days use big words for the most trivial things."

Someone wearing a pajama top and undershorts, his hair all in a tangle, had drawn nigh. The man was short in the thigh; looking at him, you thought of a stalk of *padi* rice. "Let's have three cents' worth," he said.

The lolly man took out three ices and gave them to him.

"You nitwit," the man said crossly, "not popsicles. Peanuts, that's what I meant!"

"Thing is, sir, them lollies, they cost three cents," Kadir replied slowly.

But the man was up on his high horse. "Give it here, or else. There're more *sanyos* about these days than ever, or haven't you heard? If you don't hop to it, I'll report you!"

Kadir quivered with fear. He chose a few very small peanuts and gave them to the man. "Please, sir," he said, plucking up his courage, "this *sanyo* they're talking about, what's it mean exactly, if you don't mind my asking?"

"A big boss, Indonesian," was the man's reply as he cracked one peanut open. "A guy"—cracking open another, only to find that it held nothing— "with a head that's totally empty. Like this!" And flinging the husk angrily at Kadir, off he went, grumbling to himself.

"You can be sure I'll know what this word *sanyo* means from now on," Kadir said, turning to the lolly man. "He's put the fear of God in me, that he has. This *sanyo,* he can turn out to be anyone you care to mention, a black marketeer for instance. You never can tell, not in advance!"

"It's a hard life these days. In all ways," sighed the lolly man, glancing down at his own figure. "We're getting as thin as these here popsicles. And smaller by the day too. In the end we'll melt away into water, until we're finally flung aside, like them wooden sticks!"

"I don't know about that," was Kadir's reply. "If you ask me, we're like the ices on the stick, no difference really when you come to think about it. We're bitten into, licked, slurped up. Comes to the same thing."

"Well, you know the saying, there's more than one path to go by, when you're headed for the mosque. Choose your poison."

The radio in the square was playing music. Japanese songs, Kadir suspected; you could catch the words *and with spirit!* somewhere in the middle of it all.

"Wasn't that nice!" Kadir said, applauding. "An updated *keroncong,* probably."

They were both startled to see someone standing there before them, asking for "a pennyworth of peanuts, *bang!*"

Quick as a wink Kadir reached for a piece of paper and wrapped the nuts up in them, gladly giving them to his customer. "Mind if I ask you something, sir?"

"Ask away."

"What I'd like to ask you is this, sir. This . . . this *sanyo* everyone's talking about, does it mean black marketeer?"

"Well, I never! Insulting Dai Nippon the emperor, like that! Have you *any* idea who that is? I know what you are, you're a spy. Right then, off we go then to the police station, you miserable scoundrel, you!"

The New Java

Your tears having run dry now, there'd be little you could do other than sigh heavily in complaint. You'd moan on about the sheer bloody difficulty of getting by. Three rupiah for one liter of rice, 25 cents for a measly packet of *gado-gado!* Life was tough, that's what people would say whenever they got to talking, as they did of nothing else, about rice. And they laid the blame for it squarely on Japan.

Shortages? Don't give me that! I mean, if there's one thing Java's famous for, it's rice, isn't it. There's been nothing like this for as long as anyone can remember.

The Japs, the Dutch, they're six of one and half a dozen of the other, I tell you, they strip us bare. No, they're worse than the Dutch, they do us down while muttering honeyed words.

You'd long since stopped pricking up your ears at such talk. It was all par for the course, now.

In the city thoroughfares, on the pavement in front of restaurants, for that matter wherever you cared to look, you'd see people half naked and practically at death's door. They'd be begging for food in the streets, food for humans, though they'd do dogfood justice too if it came to that. You'd see them sprawled in the middle of the road, everyone crowding round, somebody wondering out loud, "What's he lying there for?" only to be told that the fellow had been "looking for something to eat, poor devil."

You'd see this young man sitting stark naked by a tree stump. He might have been a horse or some such beast, judging by the state he was in. He'd do his best to cover himself up as people went by, but with only two hands at his disposal he'd have scant success. Girls would look at him, tittering to one another, as if it were the funniest thing in the world. He wouldn't be up to walking, and as for begging, he'd rather have died of shame. There he'd sit, leaning against the block of wood, day in day out, summoning the courage to be up and about when night fell and not one minute before. Not once would he take his eyes off the nearby river. He'd hurry on down upon catching sight of a dead chicken or a human corpse drifting past, he'd go up close to the riverbank and he'd . . . he'd go to bed. He'd be for it too, in due course. Nothing to do with malnutrition. It would be the result, rather, of gorging on, well, on dead bodies.

The whores, too, would be dying of hunger in droves; trade was slack. Young girls by the thousands would queue up to sign on as prostitutes, they'd do anything for money, anything to buy rice for their loved ones. Hordes of men would chase them, in turn. A matter of time before the girls would start dropping like flies. Now that they'd lost their bloom, potential clients had lost interest. Bees searching for pollen were steering well clear of these particular flowers.

Nor would there be any escape for those boys who still had shirts on their backs. They'd gone pale from wanking off: anything, anything at all to still the pangs of hunger! Their number too would soon be up. Masturbating too much, that's what did it for them, the doctors agreed.

The papers would be choc-a-bloc with news from the front, but about what you could see in front of your very eyes they'd have no comment to make. From what they were saying, you'd never guess these things had happened in Jakarta and elsewhere. Reporters would be sent out on their rounds, but their copy, when edited and published, would be all about the Wonderful Prosperity Enjoyed by All and Sundry.

Rice had gone fearfully short, you'd be allocated no more than a fifth of a liter per day, while the Japs now, they'd get five whole liters. Any leftovers and these would be handed to their housegirls and houseboys. They'd be in clover—that is, until they learned that their new-found wealth had been dearly bought, their womenfolk representing the going price. And should ever the Japs tire of sporting with them, well then, these servants could, if they so wished, crawl off into some corner and starve to death, for all the Japs cared!

The *Jawa Hokokai* would organize these monster rallies, during which questions would be put by the Japanese, with those present obliged to answer pat for all the world like some primary school classroom. Were the government's commands being carried out to the letter? The harvest: was it being reaped exactly as instructed? That's what they'd want to know. You'd think long and hard, as if these questions were real posers; anybody speaking up would have his work cut out for him answering with any degree of precision.

The man in the street would find that it was all he could do to make ends meet. Those replying to the questions the Japs would put made no bones about that. "There's got to be a change up top, the people in charge can't have the foggiest idea of how things are for the likes of us." "How the heck *can* they," somebody would titter, sotto voce, from behind, "with their bellies all puffed up from eating those little rice-balls they love to gorge themselves on!"

On day two of the mass meeting, the Japs would throw more questions at their captive audience. And at the end of this dialogue of the deaf, they'd advise their listeners that only matters strictly relating to what had been asked would be entertained as topics for discussion. They might have been shouting into the wind, for all the good it seemed to have done them, those people who only the day before had taken their courage in their hands and come out with it all.

A gunny-sack of rice would go for four rupiah, in Malang. The powers that be had need of the sacks, they'd use them for fetching rice to Japan itself, whereas the common folk, they'd need them to cover their nakedness.

Coffee would run short in Jakarta, but out in Bantam they were positively drowning in it. Not that they too weren't dying of hunger: after all, for keeping body and soul together, coffee wasn't exactly what the doctor ordered.

Bandung would find its street packed with Indo-Dutch women—all selling their bodies.

Life was a bitch, everyone, everywhere, would grouse, but nobody had the guts to speak out. A representative of the government had just returned from a circuit of Java and had tabled a report of his findings. Night after night the radio would announce that while things might indeed be tough, nobody was complaining, a stiff upper lip was the order of the day, and this, the radio would blare on, was a Sign of Indomitable Spirit on the Part of the People. And, winding up, it would state that the Japanese government had been duly impressed by the whole-hearted commitment shown by all the peoples of Java.

Tokyo, to be sure, was far to the north, a heck of a distance from Java itself, but when the call came to send rice, distance had proved no object. The telegraph operators would get at it, and what do you know, two days later rice would be shipped out by air, in planes that would be put to use both for kamikaze attacks and for this noble purpose.

Every day, down in the Noorwijk district of Jakarta, you'd see these little urchins lining up to go off to church. Pale as ghosts they'd be, their bodies stick figures from lack of proper food.

You'd have to moonlight to make ends meet, in flagrant breach of standing instructions. But not the Japs. Oh no. They'd other ways of making money on the sly. The authorities would force the kampung folk to surrender up all their ironmongery to them, but when the stuff would fall into the hands of Japanese civilians, what would they do but fence it back to the occupation on the black market, and at prices to match. The rates fetched for this went through the ceiling.

It would be desperately hard going, in Jakarta, in Surabaya, in Plered, you name it. In despair, you'd raise your hands skyward, imploring heaven, beseeching the Almighty for a livelihood, as if for some strange reason He'd neglected to make provision. Year in, year out the padi rice had ripened, year in, year out it had been hulled . . . could the whole thing be *His* fault?

For Hire

(Yang Menyewakan Diri)

by Pramoedya Ananta Toer

I was all of four. That's if my memory's anything to go by. I'd
known the family for quite some time too: old man Leman and his
missus, Leman, Siah, Nyamidin, and Sidin.

Every time I'd come round, at nine in the morning, they'd still be in.
They hadn't yet left for work. I'd hunker down at old man Leman's
feet. Without my saying anything he'd twig what I'd be after, and I'd
be handed the dregs of his coffee to drink. Both of us would laugh,
Granny Leman chiming in. And when I'd ask, "Where's Siah, Grandad?" pat would come the answer: "Still sleeping."

"But *I've* got up!"

It amused him no end to hear how chuffed I was with myself.

"Siah's a lazybones," I'd hear him say, at pains not to wound my
pride.

"Where's Leman, Granny?"

"Down by the river, bathing."

"And Nyamidin, Grandad?"

"Not back yet. Doing night duty, at the guardhouse. You know the
guardhouse near the cemetery? That's where he sleeps."

"You mean, he hasn't woken up yet?"

"Shouldn't think so. He'll be knackered, doing the rounds at night."

Every so often there'd be a potato to eat, or some cooked cassava.
When nothing else was on offer to tickle my fancy, I'd run along
home, to tell all to Mother. It was a safe bet. Her slanting eyes riveted

14

to my features, her voice would be loud in reproach. "If I've told you once I've told you a million times," she'd say, index finger lifted to her nose, "you're *not* to go round there. Making a nuisance of yourself, you are, to people at work."

"But, they aren't working."

"How can they, with you going round."

"But, Siah's still sleeping. So are the others."

"Which is precisely why you're not to go over." This with her finger down now and resting in her lap. Her voice, tense with purpose, softened. "That slug-a-bed, she's ill, something to do with her eyes. I'll bet anything it's contagious. You go over there often and you'll catch it, you wait and see."

I'd never heard advice like that before. And I went back there when the sun was standing high in the sky, repeating what Mother had said. Granddad Leman replied calmly enough and in all sincerity, "I'm a slacker, I am. Even if I were hardworking, what would I work at?" he said, laughing through his nose. "Ain't got no *sawah*. Or a *ladang*. Not even a hoe. Just a machete. I sharpen it every day." His eyes went to a grindstone squatting there in the center of the room, clean, its surface glinting. "If I'm asked to swap places with him on night duty, I get two and a half cents. If I haven't got a machete as sharp as that, nobody's going to bother."

His voice was filled with a melancholy music. I loved listening to it.

"Go on," I demanded.

Granddad Leman would seldom refuse. He'd repeat himself, taking his time. It made no difference if I was a bit slow to pick up on his peculiar expressions, I could get them off by heart. At home, if Mother wasn't around, I'd often recite these words to myself. Their wistful music would resonate, though the words would be coming out of my mouth, not his.

But Mother said to me, "Show me a lazy sod and I'll show you a glutton," and, "A pain in the arse, for a lot of people!" After that, I'd seldom repeat old man Leman's words to myself again. Why I stopped doing this I couldn't rightly say. But there was something in Mother's words that smacked of a gauntlet being flung down at the both of us.

For a long while I didn't go round to the Leman household. Finally, one day, I did, to ask, "Where's Siah?"

The old man fixed me with his look. Granny Leman slowly cleared her throat. The two of them made no reply. This had been my standard question on arrival. But this time old man Leman said, "She's gone—gone to Palembang."

"Is that far from here, Grandad?"

"You might say so. Overseas. You have to go by boat."

"What's she gone away for, Grandad?"

"To make money. Later on when she comes back she'll bring gold coins, you'll see," Granny Leman rejoined. Contempt for herself was etched into her face.

"Times are harder, nowadays," the old man remarked, unprompted. "Lots of *priyayi* have come down in the world."

I got this off by rote, so as to be able to apprise Mother or Dad. I was feeling pretty fraught before delivering the news. That afternoon, as Father sat round on the bench in the garden, I marched straight up to him. I was just going to break the news when he got in first with a question. "You were asking to be sent to school, a while back. Are you still interested?"

Interested? I was beside myself for joy. " 'Course I am!" I shouted. "When's it going to be, Dad?"

"Tomorrow."

This turn of events made me clean forget the news I'd had from old man Leman. The following morning was going to be my first day at school. I was, as I say, all of four. I was painfully aware of how this meant no more morning coffee with Grandad Leman. Apart from holidays, or at the weekend, there was precious little opportunity for me to wander around at will of a morning. I'd made loads of new friends at school, was getting news from all round the country, and was learning something new every day.

On the way home from school I would sometimes find Grandpa Leman waiting for me in front of the house, to give me a kite he'd have just made. But the surprising thing was, I could never fly it or otherwise play around with it. Not like the other kids. It wasn't long before I vented my rage on the thing, ripping it apart, breaking it into bits.

More than six months must have passed before I went round to Grandpa Leman's. At last the great day arrived: the beginning of school holidays, which put paid to Mother's vetoing my doing just as I liked.

One day during the break, when I was at play with my friends in the middle of the road, a *dokar* drew to a halt in front of Grandpa

Leman's. As if at a signal, the children all charged into his house, keen to hear the latest news and hoping to be given goodies to eat.

I caught sight of Siah sitting on the *bale* alongside a middle-aged man in a black jacket. On seeing me, she smiled and, getting up, came over.

"It's been ages since we last met. I've missed you!" she said, laughing.

Gold teeth. I could see that clearly enough. The pin fastening her *kebaya* was made of eighteen-karat gold reals, strung on a gold chain.

"Are you . . . are you rich now?" I asked.

A candid smile was the answer.

"D'you think I could have one of those reals?" was my next question.

She shook her head ever so gently.

"When you grow up, then you can get your own," she said in a seductive voice before plying me with goodies.

Sitting on the chair, old man Leman was chatting away amicably enough with a man with gold teeth like Siah's. I was surprised at how polite he was. Granny Leman was busy in the kitchen putting up water to boil.

With Siah home, I'd often go round to the house. She'd gripping stories to tell, about elephants, tigers, sacks of money, bags of gold. She taught me to make animal sounds. At home I'd go over the latest news I'd managed to pick up, which I'd also give out to anyone at school who cared to listen. Afterward, I'd feel as though a great weight had been lifted from me.

The holidays over, I could only go round after school. Often enough I'd find that Siah was not yet up and about but still asleep, even though it was midday. Which is how I came one day to notice that the man with the gold teeth had gone.

"Where's he gone to, *kek?*"

"Away," came the uneasy answer.

"But wherever to?"

"Search me."

"And Siah? She's going to follow him, then?"

He shook his head. Very, very slowly.

"She is going to come back, isn't she, *kek?*"

Granny Leman poked her head round from the kitchen. "I'm praying to heaven she never does come back. She can go drown, for all I care!"

"Where, *nek?*"

"The deep blue sea!"

I thought to myself, Siah's probably left for Palembang, but I bit my tongue. I could see. They looked so cast down, these two old folk.

"It's been ever so long since I last saw Leman. Where can he have gone to, *kek?*"

He fetched a great sigh; then, dejectedly, he let drop.

"Lots of *priyayi* are coming down in the world, nowadays. They don't call on Leman anymore, to ask him to mend the fence or the WC. When I want to swap shifts, I don't get paid. I'm old now, time I was paid for doing guard duty. Leman's gone off to look for money elsewhere."

"Where to, *kek?*"

"To Cimahi. Gone for a soldier."

"He'll be dressed in black when he comes back, won't he, *kek?*"

"If you want to know what I think, he isn't going to come back. He's gone, that's what I think, he's gone and forgotten all about *kakek* and *nenek.*"

"Way back, there were lots of soldiers who didn't come back," Granny put in. "Spandri—you know, the one who's been pensioned off—he said that the fighting in Aceh's over and done with. Says there's no more work for soldiers, it's just parade-ground drill and target practice."

I thought of the squads of Dutch *veldpolitie* heading off to their drill grounds across the river for gunnery practice every Wednesday and Saturday. They looked so splendid, large of build, their rifles slung high across their backs.

"And Nyamidin, *kek?*"

"These days, he's working the *sawah* on his own. Money's very hard to come by now. That's why he's gone off. God knows where. No one's playing fair by him anymore."

"You mean, he wasn't happy here?"

"When you've got money, you're laughing. Doesn't matter where you live. But when you're broke, when money's tight, that's another story altogether." He coughed slightly, exactly why it was hard to tell. "You'd best ask no more questions." He bowed his head; down it came, until it touched the table. His features seemed to lose definition, surrounded as they were by his shock of graying hair, the white interspersed among the black. I took my leave without his looking up.

Naturally I told mother and dad all about it. They were all ears, though they pretended they weren't listening. This made me feel ill-at-ease with myself, though I was at a loss to explain why.

"Had your bath?" asked my Dad, cutting me off in mid sentence.

The question was enough to send me scurrying off toward the bathroom. I stared blankly at the walls while bathing. This washroom, I thought to myself all at once, why, it's ten times nicer than the one at Kek Leman's. I wonder why?

Father looked sunk in thought. When he answered, it was with a ghost of a smile, feigning laughter. I couldn't make him out.

I saw at once that Mother couldn't either. So I put the question to her.

She frowned; then, assuming her normal expression, she looked straight at me. "Well, what have you to say for yourself? Have you learnt to read by now?" No question could be more unwelcome!

Confused, I said nothing. Mother rose and, taking me by the hand, led me out to the *pendopo*. Crikey, my schoolwork! My ears instantly flamed red as she gave me what for. "You're *not* to go round there ever again," she commanded. "You do, and I'll . . . "—this was a new one—"I'll have your guts for garters, just you wait and see!" At this, my tears dried.

I didn't go round. Not after. But a year's time had gone by and there I was, still stuck in grade one. My physical growth was much the same as my intellectual growth—stunted. "Plant manure," that's what I'd get called when we'd play games. Allowed to tag along, but far from being one of the gang. There was one time I'd taken part in a game of hide-and-seek and we'd been hiding behind old man Leman's house when I caught a voice I'd never heard before. A man's voice, no two ways about it. "D'you want it or don't you?" it said, heavy with threat.

"We daren't, *ndoro*. We may be poor but we're honest."

"Five rupiahs?"

"We daren't, *ndoro*."

"Six rupiahs, then.

"Okay, seven," he continued. "I see that machete of yours's pretty sharp. One hack and Bob's your uncle.

"Seven and a half," not letting up. "Ten, and that's final. Can't say fairer than that."

I was only listening with one ear. When we crawled out on our haunches from our hidey-hole, I saw a *priyayi* leave old man Leman's house. He wore a *kain* of excellent batik, glittering slippers, a headdress after the manner of Solo, and a jacket fastened with silver buttons. But this too scarcely registered. Two or three days later I saw another man, but this aroused no curiosity either.

Then came the night I won't forget. Not if I live to be a hundred.

Father and Mother were sitting around in the courtyard with me and my younger brother. Everything gleamed brilliantly in the moonlight.

All of a sudden the moon was shrouded by a thick pall of darkness. Thunder started to rumble, faintly at first, then loud; lightning started to flicker. We went indoors to eat supper. Outside, warning gongs called from every part of the village.

"Those gongs, why've they started to sound just now, do you suppose?" Mother asked.

"The kampung headman's here."

Silently we listened.

"It's the *titir* beat. Someone's been murdered," Father said, getting up. "You stay put. I'll go and see, in just a minute."

He looked panic-stricken. I hadn't the foggiest notion what was going on. Though I pressed her over and over to explain, Mother said nothing. Her eyes roved about, wandering from one dark corner to another. The oil lamp in the middle of the table burnt low. My little brother had been asleep since seven o'clock.

Father came back a quarter of an hour later, his face contorted.

"What's happened?" Mother assailed him.

"Oh, old man Leman," he replied, taking a seat. "Good job he used a hammer. The man he hit managed somehow to make it to the headman's."

"Not Grandad Leman, surely? That old duffer?"

Father nodded.

"What are they going to do with him now?"

"Beat the living daylights out of him, I shouldn't wonder. It's a good thing, though, he didn't use his machete."

"Why the hammer?" Mother asked.

"When they questioned him, all he said was 'The machete, *ndoro*. Don't take it. It's all I've got. I couldn't use it to commit treason. So I used a hammer.' "

"Dad, what's going on?" I asked. But Father ignored my question.

"I just can't believe the old devil's as wicked as all that," Mother said.

"Makes perfect sense. Hasn't been in his right mind for as long as anybody can remember."

We ate on, in silence. But all I could think about was the business with Grandpa Leman. The entire town, that night, all its citizenry, was in the grip of a desultory, flickering anxiety.

In the morning, the past night's murder was common knowledge. Word was, he'd been locked away. I would find myself hanging about the jail, on the off chance of his having been detailed to carry buckets of night soil down to the river, like all the other prisoners. But he never turned up. I'd go off to school, memories of him crowding all else aside.

Three months later it was put about that old man Leman had been sent to prison for seven months and given hard labor at Malang. "That hunch of yours was spot on," Father commented to Mother. "It ain't him that's the culprit. He got ten rupiahs from somebody or other for doing what he did."

I tried to tell them about the way the *priyayi* who had come to Kek Leman's house had leant heavily on him, but they paid no heed to my tale. There was nothing for it but to keep entirely to myself the story that was running round like mad inside me. The story I just *had* to get off my chest, to tell someone—anyone.

My opinion of old man Leman took quite a knocking once I'd heard the news that he'd tried to do someone in. All too often thinking back about him would give me the shivers. Night and day.

Something else disconcerting happened on the eve of the old man's return home. We'd been playing ball in the middle of the road when off in distance there appeared a figure trudging wearily along, dressed in black from head to toe. But the tramp wasn't important enough to distract us. You can imagine my surprise then, when suddenly, hey presto, there she was, bang in front of me. The tramp lady, of only a moment ago! Close by, she was a squalid sight, all bent, having to use a cane to stand upright. I arranged my features into a smile.

"Have you forgotten all about me?" she asked.

It was her gold teeth, that's what did it for me—Siah! My memory of her linked up with what I knew about the old man, and I lost my cool. I let out a scream and ran hell for leather home. Three or four times I must have looked behind me, only to see the figure of Siah still standing there, hunched over, watching.

I was dying to let everyone know about my afternoon's experiences. But I didn't breathe a word, not to anyone. That night it was more than I could do to keep my mind on my homework. Mother's boxing my ear, even her pinching me, wasn't enough to make me keep my nose to the grindstone.

"It's a wonder you don't get stupider than you already are!" she cried out, vexed. The next thing I knew, I was being hauled off to the bathroom, my feet were being washed, I was being slung along on her hip and flung into bed. "What did I do to get such a moron for a son?" she said, despondent.

But the mental picture of Siah and memories of Kek Leman overcame my fear of being pinched or of having my ears boxed. When I saw her like that, her head bowed in sadness, I found the courage in me to pipe up.

"I'm scared, Mother."

"Scared of what?"

"Siah. She's come and asked me round to talk. I'm scared of being hit with a hammer by Kek Leman."

"Go to sleep," Mother softly said, stroking my forehead and hair. "There's nothing to be scared of."

"I'm frightened."

"Want to sleep in my bed, do you?"

I did, and that night I slept securely, her arms about me.

The next morning I heard that Siah's gold reals were all gone. All the gold she had left was stuck to her teeth. Once I saw her go down to the river to bathe, and the way she carried herself wasn't in the least like it used to be. It was as if there was this big, invisible pillow between her legs. Didn't matter where she'd go, you'd always see her draped in black.

"Why hasn't Sidin ever come back to her parents' house, *bu?*" I asked, as the news about Siah spread like wildfire.

"I'm glad you asked. Sidin's a hard worker. Bought a home of her own, she has. It's obvious to anyone *she's* not going to work herself to the bone for lazy folk. You could say the same about me. And mind, if you turn out to be a lazybones, you won't see *me* cooking your meals for you, that you won't!"

That shut me up.

Months passed, the days flitting by in quick succession. Nek Leman now could often be seen outside her house. Her wandering off to her neighbors' when mealtimes came round was no secret. Siah seldom put in an appearance, save to go down to the river to bathe.

Once I was in the middle of lunch when Mother remarked to Dad, "Nek Leman's just come over."

"Given her advice, have you?"

"Yes."

"You're wasting your breath on the likes of her. Just let her have money or rice and tell her to piss off. There's no one here can cure her laziness."

I just didn't have the guts to pipe up with my two cents' worth.

The seven months up, old man Leman came back to his house, never to leave it. He beavered away every day, making baskets and other stuff out of coconut fiber. He'd keep himself to himself, coming along when invited to a *selamatan* but making no attempt at small talk whatsoever and slipping off home when it was over. Once a week he took the things he'd made to the market. Granny Leman had long since stopped doing rounds of the neighbors at mealtimes.

Every so often I'd see the old man busy with his plaiting out of doors. On seeing me he'd offer no greeting but just get on with finishing the job. And when he'd turn to examine his handiwork, you could see he hadn't a single black hair left. It had gone white. All of it.

A Twist of Fate
(Belitan Nasib)

by Achdiat Karta Mihardja

The sun had been blazing down for three hours: it was growing pleasantly warm. Its rays slanted down through the glass skylights, passing through windows and through doors flung wide, spilling into a courtroom packed to the gills with people. In the forecourt of the ancient building, folk who hadn't managed to find a seat within were warming themselves in the sun. Here and there they clustered together, talking excitedly amongst themselves.

Leaning back against a flagstaff, a lanky fellow dressed in gray and flashing gold teeth was chuckling to himself. "Seven years," he was saying, "you wait and see, seven at the outside." His raucous voice grated on the ear. In the normal way of work he was a printshop foreman. So saying, he shot a glance to his left toward another fellow, lankier than he, who laughed in retort, shaking his head in disagreement.

"Five years," he rejoined. "Five years I'll bet you anything, no more, no less. More than that'll be unfair—too stiff. Any less he'll be let off too light." And he rattled off several articles from the Criminal Code, which he'd got off by heart. As a bush lawyer, Hadji Tahir was known to be a pretty crafty fellow. To the gamblers, these citations of his from the Criminal Code had an air of credibility, so that if you were set on winning, you acted accordingly and laid odds on for five years.

Morning sang out, the trees were full of birds. The scent of flowers wafted along the length of fence lining the curb. A hill breeze blew, making the leaves sway and rustle and bringing a refreshing tingle to

24

people's faces. Government proclamations long since gone yellow were coming loose from their boards. Now and again they fluttered listlessly.

People continued to crowd forward in droves, in a bid to enter the courtyard. Cigarette hawkers, each lugging a thermos almost as thick as his own midriff, carried trays crammed with packets in front of their bellies; ice-block vendors, their bins filled almost to the brim, moved nimbly among the members of the public, crying their wares above the crowd, which hummed steadily away like rain in a downpour.

All of which gave Anwar the barber food for thought. He was squatting in a corner off to the left of the garage, musing to himself. He gazed upon the people gathered together in restless motion. His cheeks puffed out, his lips sucked in as he took a deep drag on a cheroot stub the length of a thumb. How come murders always draw the crowds? he wondered. As though the thought were inscribed on his furrowed brow, Parta the village teacher suddenly turned to him.

"Ain't that something, *bung*. I mean, look how keen they are. Extraordinary. Look at those kampung folk, all stocked up on rice and *ketupat* from home. But wait a sec, come to think of it, you can see why, can't you? A murder like this, the victim the local strongman, and the culprit an ordinary farmer? Nothing to write home about if it weren't for all this hullabaloo."

Anwar squinted out of the corner of his eye at the stranger but made no reply. He carried on his struggle with his cheroot, thinking, Now, you take the slaughter of a water buffalo or cow, or a goat, or a chicken. Happens every day. Why doesn't *that* catch everybody's interest?

The strongman whom Guru Parta had in mind was none other than Hadji Misbach, a repeat offender of whom all the people of Panjing-kiran and its surrounds were terrified, much the way you'd be terrified by a tiger or a bogeyman. He was known as far as the town itself as a first-class scoundrel, and even within the town precincts he'd been responsible for many sleepless nights. This Hadji was familiar to one and all. He was burly and tall, invariably rigged out in black from head to toe. Two fingers were gone from his left hand, the price of a machete fight with one of his enemies.

Suarma, his killer, was a simple peasant farmer, a taciturn chap renowned for his patience. It wasn't his way to quarrel or argue with his betters. Not once had he given serious offense to anybody. It was just as Parta the teacher had said: "He wouldn't say boo to a goose!"

Indeed, catching wind of the killing, people shook their heads incredulously. Impossible! they thought. They could scarcely believe it. Only Anwar the barber wasn't surprised. Why on earth not? he thought. *Agar-agar* when it gets eaten by an ant often spells the creature's doom. Where people are concerned, what isn't possible? Why the surprise? In life anything can happen!

Suddenly, like baby chicks summoned by the mother hen, everyone in the courtyard was astir, rushing to the doors and windows, pressing against one other, elbowing one another aside. Those at the back rose up on tiptoe, craning their necks to see over their fellows, who stood together jam-packed. In walked Suarma, fetters clinking with every step he took. The officer escorting him looked the sort you didn't want to tangle with. His long machete extended straight downward, his mustache a straight bar across his round mug.

Suarma sat himself down, bowing low in deference to the magistrate in his black robe, who sat foursquare, head lowered behind the baize table. To the left and to the right of him sat the clerks and other members of the court, also arrayed in black. All were retired officials. They looked like they were dozing off. So did the *penghulu negeri,* with his red turban perched atop his head and in his hand a copy of the Koran. Straight across from the magistrate, at the far end of the table to the right, sat the prosecutor, looking young for his years. His eyes roved all over the place: he looked raring to go.

Near the prosecutor counsel for the defense was busy wiping his spectacles clean. Now and then he glanced at the public. What a wimp he looked, in the presence of these august figures. His rumpled yellowing shorts and his checked *kain* with its faded squares made the oddest contrast with the black and the green. Every so often the chairman of the court session would give him the once-over. Suarma kept his head down, eyes fixed on his toes, feet splayed wide upon the floor. He seemed unfazed. Neither his tousled hair nor his unkempt mustache and beard gave an impression of inward disturbance. Every so often a gleam of intelligence darted forth from his eyes, striking through the fog of incomprehension enveloping his sunburnt features. Twenty-eight, and looking for all the world as if he were pushing forty.

In an earlier session of the court deliberately convened *in camera,* Suarma had given in full his account of events. What it came down to was this: There'd been two earlier occasions when Hadji Misbach had been banished, in punishment for murder. The first time was to

Sawahlunto for six years, for having killed Asnawi, a rice trader, a merchant in a small way. He'd been cut down near a bridge one day at dusk as he was hurrying homeward from market on his gammy leg. He'd been relieved of all his money, his gold rings were taken off him, and his corpse unceremoniously thrown into the river like you'd fling aside a banana tree-truck. It had fallen *kerplop* into a fast-running current, which bore it away downstream.

The second time, Hadji Misbach was exiled to Nusa Kambangan for eight years. An old gent had been the victim then. Pak Ibro was done in for refusing to hand over his goat. This was at a time when Misbach was hot to wed a young girl, daughter of a mosque official of Kampung Pasirhuni, over whom he'd lost his head.

So long as Misbach was kept well away from the area, everyone breathed easy. Farmers could wield their picks lightheartedly and were merry come harvesttime. They'd pluck the strings of their lutes of an evening, play on their bamboo flutes, a weight off their minds.

But with Misbach on the loose again it was back to square one. The sky had caved in, your breath lodged in your chest. Once again, the kampung turned into a no-go area. Everyone was gripped with fear. Say you owned two goats; just supposing Misbach had a yen for one, you didn't dare refuse and would offer one in homage. If he were walking along and happened to catch sight of some almost ripe bananas on a tree, he'd lop them down without so much as a by-your-leave from the owner of the grove. When hunger struck, he'd just go into any old house he happened to be passing, make straight for the kitchen, and gobble up whatever rice happened to be around; if none had been cooked, he would pound the table demanding to be served— and hands atremble, you'd start cooking. Come harvesttime and he'd go the rounds from one *sawah* to another, two henchmen wielding heavy knives and bamboo carrying poles in tow. And every *sawah* owner knew precisely what they were for. Anything trapped had no chance to grow to full size—and we're not talking about otters—what with this Hadji as fond as he was of pondfish, especially goldfish. Most especially those female goldfish. You know, the ones whose innards are bulging with roe.

So the short of it was that with the return of Hadji, the kampung resembled nothing so much as a lush garden whose greenery had suddenly gone all faded and withered. Fear and hatred sat on every countenance. Everyone wore a melancholy, listless look. In the end there was none so brave as to stand up to this callous rascal. No one had the guts to report him to the police. If I report him, they argued, he'll get several weeks at the outside, and what's a prison sentence anyway for the likes of him? He'll only get more boastful, more arrogant. Each time he comes out of jail it's like he's passed some new, higher-level examination. And the consequences for Yours Truly? So it went. They'd recall the fate of Pak Ibro, or of Dimjati. Remember that young fellow, the one Misbach left deaf in one ear, with his teeth knocked down his throat? Now there's a case in point. Misbach had thrashed Dimjati to within an inch of his life after his accusations had landed the strongman in prison for a month.

There were many who, besides themselves with terror, sought other means to save their skin. Ijon, for example, a tobacco dealer whose wife had once been propositioned by Misbach, was a real bootlicker. He'd only to run across Misbach in the street and he'd move well to the side, bowing and scraping as he went. He'd always be the one to laugh loudest whenever Misbach would be having his little joke. He'd nod obsequiously whenever Misbach commanded him to do this or do that. And as if all that weren't enough, a couple of kilos of tobacco would wend their way every week from his house to Misbach's—just so long as he leaves my wife alone! But in his heart of hearts he prayed for Misbach to be run over by a car or clobbered by a falling coconut. Please God make him ill with smoking, at least! Djaja, whose wife was also a looker, chose another route, hightailing it to the big smoke.

The whole district was scared clean out of its wits.

One fine day Suarma came in from the field with a load of firewood on his shoulders and three outsize eels dangling loosely from one hand. Munah, Munah with that fair skin of hers, would presently clean them for cooking. Bathed now, and having recited the afternoon prayer, Suarma sat himself down alongside her beside the hearth, arms round both knees. Munah kept the fire going. She was younger than Suarma by ten years, and with her fresh countenance and slender but well-proportioned figure was rated one of the prettiest women in the kampung.

There'd been a time when the subdistrict head had taken a keen interest in her, only to fall back once it was clear that his higher-up, the district chief, was keen on her too. Later, however, the district chief shrank back too. He couldn't bear the innuendoes which people were starting to put about: "Big scissors, little scissors—ripe fruit on the branch. Big cat, little cat—tussling over the thigh of a goat." And you didn't get any prize for guessing who the big cat was and who the little! Predictably a third cat had turned up on the scene.

As was his wont, Suarma rehearsed the day's doings at work. Slicing away at the chili pepper and onion for the eel, Munah was rapt. Her face was reddish-yellow as she blew on the coals, forehead, giving way to an aquiline nose, a kissable mouth, and an adorable chin. A sight most lovely to behold to Suarma, observing her from the side. At such times he'd be seized with joy at having so lovely and faithful a woman for a wife.

"Earlier this afternoon," he said, getting into his stride, "just when they were starting to beat the prayer drum at the mosque, I caught sight of a frog being swallowed up by a field snake. You should have heard it croak, the poor little thing! It was obvious it was badly hurt, and scared to death. Its voice became weaker, until it stopped. I swear it sounded like a human voice crying for help. Begging for help, with death so near. And the funny thing about this, Munah, is, I remember having dreamt about exactly such an event. Can't say quite when but it was crystal clear and just like this one. And what's odder still was that, in this dream my thoughts were the same. The voice was just like a human being's, pleading for help, as if there were still time to escape. Go figure!"

Munah, who set little store by superstition, listened but thought the whole thing was no big deal. A frog swallowed by a snake—so what? What was so remarkable about that? A *snake* swallowed by a *frog*— now *that* was news and might signify something, she reflected. But Suarma's thoughts ran along different lines. What had happened had made an enormous impression on him. Though he didn't say as much to Munah, he thought, Why did what I see match my dream exactly? I mean, *exactly?*

That's when the hammering on the door started. Someone was demanding to be let in. Suarma ran to open it, only to find Misbach standing there before him, one foot planted on the threshold. In he charged without first asking permission, stooping to enter as the door was too low for his massive frame. The bamboo floorboards cracked and snapped under his tread as, without further ado, he strode across to the brazier. "I'm starving," he said. "What's for supper?" There was no mistaking the question for anything but a command, and they hopped to it. Misbach's stomach was crying out for food, which made him very impatient, so that he harried them to get the food ready, and pronto. Munah, for her part, rushed about, hands shaking, shoving more wood into the flames.

Soon the food was ready. Misbach fell to. He sat down cross-legged in front of a full bowl of rice, a pan of cooked eel, a bowl of *sambal,* and several plates of other side dishes. Rolling up the sleeves of his black shirt, he tucked in. He'd a hearty appetite—as he kept on announcing—and thrusted ball after ball of rice into the spices. The sweat ran down his face, glinting on his nose and chin, as he ate the fiery *sambal.* His nose and eyes streamed. It was his habit, when taking his pleasure, to emit a growl of contentment, a sound somewhere between that of an angry cat and a duck's quack.

He'd treated himself to dinner there three days earlier: On that occasion Kukut, Munah's pet chicken, still brooding, had to have its throat slit. Her thighs had had to be roasted to a turn and sprinkled with soy sauce, into which a little lime juice had been mixed. He'd thought that a pretty good meal, all told. But this—man, this was hard to beat!

Munah and Suarma watched him wolfing the rice down and polishing off the cooked eel. Prepared to wait on him hand and foot, did he but give the word, they listened to him smacking his lips and going *gr-r-r* at the back of this throat. The meal over, he wanted coffee and some scorched cassava, which he ate with red sugar. "Dee-licious!" he said. "Must be my lucky day." Another growl of contentment.

At last, having eaten and drunk his fill, he lay himself down on a mat in front of the fireplace. He stretched out, his thick body plump and long like that of the black caterpillar in the fable of Lenggankajana that Sundanese folk like to recount. He'd placed his machete close by.

Suarma and Munah bore off the plates and saucers, together with the remains of the meal. They'd been starving but had no appetite. Not any more. It wasn't just that it was distasteful to eat with Misbach in front of them; they were none too keen on eating their uninvited guest's leftovers. Anyway, bitterly watching him go at it, their desire to eat had dried up.

All the while, Misbach would be shooting glances in Munah's direction with those beady eyes of his. The shape of her well-developed limbs. That saffron skin of hers glimmering under her thin *kebaya.* They set his blood racing through his body. Munah had but to pass close by and he'd feel his pulse surge, his throat contract with lust, his head pound. He'd have given his right arm to see through that flimsy kebaya. Then came the moment when he ordered Munah to massage him. Her heart thumped; the next moment she felt as if it had ceased to beat. Every-thing seemed to have gone black. This was soon succeeded by a wave of disgust that produced a tightness in her chest, and vertigo. Never before had she massaged any man save her own husband. Deep within she balked, rebelling.

"Get a move on and massage me!" snapped Misbach, eyes ablaze. Munah quaked with fright.

Seeing her hanging back, glancing reluctantly at her husband as if seeking his permission, Misbach took grave offense at this and, with-out warning, fetched Suarma so hard a blow to the head with a piece of kindling that the poor fellow sank senseless to the ground. Munah gave a scream, but the burly Misbach pounced on the delectable little thing, as might a lion on a goat. She shuddered with terror, her whole body going all limp and helpless.

It wasn't long before Suarma came to, his eyelids fluttering open ever so slowly. Hazy and unsteady as it was at first, his vision soon cleared. Hearing that loud growling and seeing what was happening before his very eyes, he felt the room start to spin like an aircraft propeller. There was a whistling and roaring in his ears. He forgot about everything else, and lightning quick his hands laid hold of the machete lying near Misbach. Gripped by rage, he hacked at the stout Hadji, chopping him to pieces.

This was Suarma's version of events, as told to the magistrate in camera. Having thus delivered himself of the story, he broke down, sobbing like a child.

Everyone by now was positively throbbing in anticipation of the verdict, which at any moment now was going to be handed down. Suarma seemed cool as a cucumber, prepared to take what was coming with equanimity. He hunched over, waiting for it. The magistrate began to speak. Tense with waiting, the whole courtroom fell still.

Then from the public gallery there came an astonished buzzing. Rustling softly like a swollen stream, it reverberated outward through windows and doors. Whoever wasn't already standing leapt to his feet. They were bowled over upon hearing the magistrate's "Not guilty." He'd spoken clearly enough. There was no ambiguity about what he'd said.

Not guilty? You've got to be kidding! Not a soul could credit it. A sensational case like this and you say not guilty? In disbelief they shook their heads. But as for Suarma, he seemed not to have fully taken in what had happened. He was off in his own world, floating somewhere between dreaming and waking. As if he believed and doubted, at one and the same time. For a while he just sat there, head bowed, eyes roaming nervously about, face about as expressive as a child's marble. Surprise gave way to amazement, amazement quickly gave way to delight, and there was a murmured "thank God" from the crowd. They were as grateful to the magistrate who'd just set Suarma free as they were to Suarma himself for having released them from the utmost terror. Delirious with joy, they were intent on staging a big *selamatan* in the kampung, in Suarma's honor.

Released from custody, however, Suarma seemed to have changed beyond all recognition. He'd been transformed, into someone his kampung friends didn't know quite what to make of. Where formerly he'd been fond of company, now it was as if he wanted to avoid everyone. He'd always be off on his own. Previously, he'd usually stop in at the mosque to pray on the way home from his *sawah*. Now he'd make straight for his house, not taking the *desa* footpath but the one that cut through the graveyard.

Everyone was surprised; tongues began to wag. But when all was said and done, Munah felt depressed. She sensed that something was missing, something the value of which couldn't be assessed—her inmost happiness. For Suarma was a changed man with her too. Her husband's good cheer and warmth, as formerly expressed in fond smiles and in happy laughter intended specially for her, for his Munah, all this had gone. Instead there was this chill melancholy, and a flat blankness.

In the end, Munah too was plunged into gloom. She wasn't her old self, the girl whose laughter and banter brought sunshine into careworn kampung lives. No longer was she a *dalang,* telling stories, amusing others so as to cheer them up, especially her husband, her husband whom she loved so. She'd become a sort of gong, resonating only when sounded. Things at home got worse, turning cold, oppressively cold, as if the breeze had ceased to blow, as if the sun's rays no longer poured in.

The result was that people started avoiding the house like the plague. They had a high old time wondering about the changes wrought in these two; they speculated till the cows came home. If only they knew! What had really happened was that the freedom the magistrate had granted Suarma was nothing of the sort.

All he had to do was run into someone and immediately he'd feel as if they were mocking him, despising him, making a laughingstock of him. There was the time he'd been passing by the edge of a waterspout under a *waru* tree. Some women were busy bathing and washing clothes. They laughed as they did so, chaffing and bantering. At once Suarma quickened his step, half running, feeling his ears going red, before breaking into a full gallop, spurred by something which sliced searingly through his heart. The more he'd go off on his own, withdraw into his shell, the more people seemed to be laughing at him behind his back. The more lurid, too, were the pictures conjured by his imagination. Inside he was burning up—incinerating!

One day he found Munah throwing up and gone white in the face. She complained of feeling out of sorts, of having lost her appetite; at the same time she had this craving for spicy and for sour foods. The longer Suarma's imagination worked overtime, the more obsessed he grew. On one occasion Munah asked for a massage, saying she had a terrific headache. But Suarma refused point blank. Indeed, it was all he could do to stop himself fetching his wife a slap. Holding his breath, he stormed out of the house, leaving Munah prostrate on the couch all alone, her head splitting.

By the time Munah had reached the end of the eight months Suarma was in a fine state, keyed up like he'd never been before. But not for long. At long last he came to a firm decision. That's it! I've had it. To hell with the *adat!* he thought. I'll be damned if I'm going to give a *selamatan!* The die was cast. When she found out, Munah first smiled to herself round the corners of her mouth. Softly she said, "If that's your decision, *kakak*, so be it. I was thinking to myself only the other day that we've got to tighten our belts. Your clothes are in a state, and there are those repairs we've been meaning to do as well."

He wasn't to know that later, all alone down by the pool, Munah cried her heart out.

Surprise bred astonishment, astonishment conjecture. This in turn led to ever more questions. But the more this happened the more put-upon Suarma felt inside. One day, when he just couldn't take it anymore, he put the question frankly to Munah.

When she heard her husband's question she went into hysterics, collapsing in a sobbing heap. But at least she realized now what lay behind it all. She understood why her husband had undergone a sea change. She replied with matching candor and in no uncertain terms. She laid to rest every one of Suarma's suspicions, every one of his burgeoning doubts. She crossed her heart and hoped to die. May God blacken all the days of my life if I'm not telling you the truth!

So everything suddenly stopped spinning for Suarma. The clouds lifted, a load was taken off his shoulders. He was coming back to life, he was happy again. But, it soon became apparent, all this was little more than a bright ripple on the surface of waters which, in their depths, remained as turbid as ever. Slowly but surely a gray mist descended again, drawing a curtain over his features. He'd only to chance upon someone for ugly images to loom up yet again in his imagination. He'd hear people laughing at him. Poking fun at him. *Humiliating him.*

So it came about that when his son was born, Suarma could contain himself no longer and, running to seize a cleaver, laid about him in a frenzy. The baby's mother too was slashed all over and finally cut to pieces. Only afterward did he run for it, blood all over his arms, his face, his clothes.

And now, as when he'd chopped Hadji Misbach to pieces, Suarma hurries to surrender himself to the police.

He's breathing deep now. Long and deep. The sergeant's standing there. He feels so, so *free.* . . .

The Helmet
(Topihelm)

by A.A. Navis

Judging from the respect shown toward the helmet set atop Tuan
O.M.'s head, you'd have thought all was well down at the railway
workshops in the small town of Padangpanjang. A pipsqueak the man
may have been; standing ten feet tall by virtue of his hat, he was, you
might have said, crowned with the power he wielded as lathe foreman.
"Helmet" was the sobriquet given to him by his men. Gunarso was
what his own Dad called him. For his part, he preferred the appellation
Raden Mas, in token of his noble Javanese pedigree.

Whence his authority. So awesome was it that if the men were
standing about in groups in the workshop passing the time of day,
someone had merely to whisper, "Psst! Here comes Helmet!" and,
whirling round, they'd set to work with a will.

Downright ridiculous, that's what it was. You'd be standing there,
passing the time of day, and apropos of nothing in particular, someone
would make reference to Helmet and off they'd scuttle helter-skelter to
their workbenches, there to make great show of working away for all
the world as if they had only just been taking a breather. Like a column
of ants disturbed, they were. You'd then hear barking laughter and
know you'd been caught with your pants down. It got so bad you'd fair
jump out of your skin at that whispered "Psst! It's Helmet!"

One fine day, however, this persiflage did for the chief engineer.
Cut him down to size, it did. Turned him back into a plain old stoker.
As per usual, it had fallen to two chaps to see to the cleaning of the

underside of a locomotive. Now, since this particular engine was positioned above a long pit, they were forced to work standing upright, cleaning all round underneath. Once he'd levered himself down into the hole to carry out his inspection, the engineer, a burly chap dubbed "King Kong" by all the clerks and operatives, couldn't prise himself out again. At first he gave his usual running commentary. The longer it went on the funnier it was to listen to, until he had them all splitting their sides. Hearing laughter, men working in other parts of the shop dropped what they were doing to scramble down into the pit.

While our friend was talking a blue streak, accompanying himself with comic gestures and movements, Tuan O.M., quite unknown to him, was standing beside the locomotive, eavesdropping all quiet like. Catching sight of his shoes and brown shirt through the spokes of the locomotive's wheels and turning cold with fear, one of the men standing in the pit gave out, "Psst! Helmet!"

Not knowing whether to believe their ears or not and frankly caring less, they were instantly at it hammer and tongs. Some scoured the wheels, others cleaned the connecting rods, still others banged away at whatever seemed worth banging away at. But our engineer, seeing how terrified they all were by the rumor going the rounds, chortled quietly to himself. They were a scream!

"Hey, you lot. What're you frightened of? Of Helmet?" he mocked. "What makes you so scared of *him,* that runt? Why, it's *me,* King Kong here, that you should be scared of, not Helmet, that short-arsed monkey. Bah! Just let him show his face here and I'll break his neck, like a gorilla breaks a monkey's. My God you're the living end you are, all of you! You hear 'Psst! It's Helmet!' and you're scared shitless. Just let King Kong here have a go at him, mates, just let me have a go—"

Somebody cleared his throat—an "ahem" that was, alas, all too well known. That's when the engineer, looking over in the direction of the sound, caught sight of the man through the interstices of the locomotive's wheels. And that's when all his brave talk dried up. Normally you'd have wet yourself to see how discombobulated King Kong was by the sight of "the monkey." Not this time. He'd hardly a chance to collect his wits before Tuan O.M. turned on his heel. Dutifully they all clambered out of the locomotive bay, every man slinking off to his post.

No sooner had the engineer managed to regain his composure than the summons arrived. And now it was King Kong who had been made a monkey of!

So went the story. At all events, from that moment onward, Tuan O.M. no longer bothered to wear his helmet. Was it because it was getting old? Or because wearing it had turned him into a laughing-stock? Your guess is as good as mine.

Anyhow, from this point on the headpiece lost its mystique. Lost it, that's to say, from the moment Pak Kari started to sport it. The change-over coincided with a momentous event for Tuan O.M. and his family. He'd bought the hat three years earlier in Semarang in Central Java, upon learning he was to be transferred to the little Sumatran town of Padangpanjang. (The sobriquet clung to him long after the thing had been hung up on the hatrack, up until his transfer to Bandung.)

They'd been so busy packing up Raden Mas Gunarso's furniture that the battered hat was in serious danger of being left behind. Only when the house stood bare and empty did Nyonya Gunarso's eyes almost pop out of her head to see it hanging precariously on a nail on the wall.

"What's this doing left behind, Pap?" the woman said. "You might as well wear it. Shame to throw it out."

"Oh come off it, will you. Imagine someone as distinguished as myself wearing a hat like this onto the ship. I'd die of shame."

"What, may I ask, do you propose to do with it, then? Everything's been packed up, and the boxes carted off to the railway station."

Tuan O.M. cast a sidelong glance at his crew, who were helping him pack up. He knew them all well, the brakemen. Whom in all fairness to give it to? That was when he'd clapped eyes on Pak Kari, and something in the old man's heart came to life.

"Mightn't it be better to give it to one of them instead of chucking it out?" Tuan O.M. said in a ruminative sort of way.

Agog, Pak Kari gazed into the woman's eyes, as if it was under-stood between himself and her that the hat was meant for him. But all she said was, "First see whom it fits best."

He cast another glance at the brakemen; their blood, he knew, was racing with the hope of getting hold of this hat. They each took it in turns to try it on for size. And wouldn't you know, by chance, by pure chance, it fit Pak Kari's head perfectly—him a runt and all, same as Tuan O.M. So by rights it was his.

He was grinning sheepishly from sheer joy at this stroke of good fortune when the woman blurted out, "You know, Kari, you look really spiffy. But mind you don't give yourself airs at my man in your turn!"

Laughter ringing in his ears, Pak Kari felt his body borne aloft, as high as the roof, and swelling to the size of an elephant's.

Tuan O.M., I'll grant you, may have taken good care of his helmet, but he hadn't a patch on Pak Kari. *He* couldn't even bring himself to let it get the slightest bit wet. When the thing was on his head his pride knew no bounds. He'd smirk with self-satisfaction on catching sight of himself, by-accident-on-purpose, in some shop-front plate glass on his way to work. As for his mates, there was no getting round the ridicule the man's outlandish behavior was drawing. His higher-ups, too, were getting browned off; of late he'd been slacking on the job. To hear him tell it, though, all the jeering and annoyance were the result of envy, plain and simple. After all, who else had a hat quite like his?

From the day he became its proud possessor he was christened Gunarso, not "Helmet," the moniker Tuan O.M. had found himself saddled with. Unlike Tuan O.M., however, who took no pleasure in his nickname, Pak Kari rejoiced in his. Come to that, there were times aplenty when he positively felt he *was* Gunarso.

He'd been a railway brakeman since the age of eighteen. The first-born child of elderly parents, even as a boy he'd had a fair idea of what the work involved: rising at the crack of dawn, reporting at the station before half past four, coming home at half past eight at night. Being so short and weedy, he felt inferior; he also had to be more patient than was his nature. Which was just as well: ever since coming into posses-sion of the helmet, Pak Kari's composure had been most sorely tried.

Padangpanjang is a sodden little place of a town. Hat off, Pak Kari saw no point in cursing the rain; hat on, there was no shutting him up. The drizzle, you see, had compelled him to wear the thing in a way he felt was quite improper. On top of which, he had become the frequent butt of his friends' teasing. He'd be at prayer only to find that some of his mates had nicked off with the hat, which would leave the old man searching high and low for it, greatly cast down and feeling on the whole hugely put out.

There came a day when all the brakemen were given a certain kind of official headgear, and Pak Kari, in consequence, was indescribably sick at heart. Mulishly, he refused to don the official hat that the others were now wearing in the field. Only when the boss threatened to dock his wages did Pak Kari put it on—over the helmet, which stayed glued fast to his head. The instant he was off duty, however, off the official headgear came. Lucky for him, the ruling didn't last long. The people at HQ who decided such things hadn't a clue what sort of hat was really suitable for railway brakemen. Which is by way of explaining how Pak Kari, ever long-suffering, triumphed again.

His victory, to be sure, was long in the making. From the moment he took to wearing it, the hat not only put paid to his authority but drew hoots and jeers. Once achieved, however, his victory enabled him to come gloriously into own, and he was rendered proof against the taunts of his mates.

It came about like this. Pak Kari and other brakemen had been traveling from Kayutanam to Padangpanjang. The railway track followed the length of the precipitous Anai Valley; each and every carriage had therefore to be guarded by a brakeman. Getting on for Anai, however, as the track climbed uphill, two-thirds of the brakemen up and went "BD," to use their own term, as in *"buiten dienst,"* or off duty. This meant sitting at their ease atop the railway carriages or else snoozing on the long benches, provided passengers were few.

Pak Kari lay stretched out along the railway carriage seat, his helmet covering his face. Fast asleep, he was dreaming that he'd really and truly become Tuan O.M., feared by everyone under him.

As he returned from work—in the dream—what was his wife's surprise when she saw that he'd actually become Tuan O.M. But not only that, his wife had apparently metamorphosed into the lovely Nyonya Gunarso, no less. No wonder that he clasped the woman to his breast. But as he shifted in his sleep down fell the hat onto the carriage floor.

At that very moment another brakeman passed by and—by accident as it seemed—gave the hat a kick, sending it flying. Jolted from sleep by the motion of the carriage only to see his headpiece airborne, Pak Kari went haring off after it. His mates, however, were not content to leave it at that—the hat was now being tossed from hand to hand, and Pak Kari lurched after it from one person to the next, like some small child. Everyone, the passengers not least, was in stitches. But Pak Kari, temper flaring, drew his knife and made to stab at whoever had the nerve to turn his hat once more into an object of ridicule.

And that is how the helmet recovered its authority. Nobody had the guts to trifle with it ever again.

But one ill-omened day Pak Kari set out with the first train to Kayutanam on official business. Rain had been coming down in torrents all night long. The early morning freshness still lingered, the track had gone all slippery, and the engine strained as usual to pull tens of charcoal-laden carriages. The train was in constant danger of slipping back and would have done so had the brakemen not taken particular care.

Pak Kari, in charge of the last carriage, had his hands full. The brakes were in very good working order, so good in fact that the wheel no longer turned round. This was exceedingly dangerous—the carriage could leap the track. The engineer blew the locomotive whistle every second, as if to ask, is the brake still working? And for the umpteenth time Pak Kari would apply the brake. But for the umpteenth time the wheel of his carriage would drag along the track, only to be released once more by the brake. And so on, endlessly.

The brakemen were in the habit, whenever the brake played them up, of sitting astride the railing and gripping the handles. When the carriage wheels no longer appeared to be turning, they'd release the brake ever so slightly, checking to see what state the wheels might be in. Which was precisely what he, Pak Kari, had been doing from the moment the train had left Padangpanjang station.

What with him all engrossed in swaying from the balustrade handle and sitting astride the ladder, when the train made its way across an arched bridge it didn't dawn on him until the very last second to pull his body back to avoid colliding with the arch.

The train had no sooner drawn into a small station, Kandang Ampat, than everyone realized that Pak Kari was no longer at his post. A brakeman said he'd been spotted just before the train had passed over the bridge they'd only just crossed. All hell promptly broke loose—a few years ago a brakeman who'd hung by the railing had been struck by the iron arch of the very same bridge and had fallen to his death in the river below, the brakeman added helpfully. Was this a repeat performance? All hearts were seized with foreboding.

The engineer in charge of the charcoal train decided to wait a few minutes before sending a party in search of Pak Kari's body. Several brakemen were ordered to walk along the banks of the River Anai; you never know, the corpse might have been swept upstream. The engineer blew the locomotive's whistle nonstop, as if signaling to Pak Kari's body that they were out looking for it. All eyes were fixed on the river, which flowed the length of the track. But this was no easy job; the sun had yet to rise and illuminate the valley.

But a kilometer or so toward that object of universal fear and trepidation, the bridge, who should they come upon but the man himself—alive! Far from having been crushed, still less become a corpse as they'd all feared, there he was, sauntering along the embankment, cool as a cucumber. They rounded on him. When Pak Kari reached the station the engineer summoned him up into the locomotive cabin. Hopping mad, he was.

"Why in blazes did you get off?" he snarled. "How the hell am I supposed to explain this?"

Pak Kari just stood there speechless, head bowed as if to say *mea culpa, mea maxima culpa.*

"Supposing you'd died, like old Buyung did—*then* what? I'd be held responsible. But you didn't die, did you? Come to think of it, what are you doing still alive?"

Pak Kari still stood there in absolute silence.

"You deaf as well as dumb? Answer me! How come you're not dead?"

Still no reply.

"That's it. That's bloody *it.* I've had it," the engineer said. "You've got to go."

Blanched and quaking with cold, Pak Kari cringed at the news that he was going to be sacked. He was desperate to set matters straight, but unable to find his tongue, he just stood there, head sunk further onto his chest.

"Answer me! Why did you leave your place?" snarled the engineer.

"It was the hat—the hat, it just—it just fell off. Hit the side of the bridge," Pak Kari managed to stammer.

"Hang on a sec—I'm starting to get it. This here hat falls off and you leave your place, eh? All because of this here hat? Because of this here hat I've got to hold up the train's departure. And *why,* may I ask, was it this here hat which fell? Why not you? Nice sense of humor we've got, haven't we?"

The engineer carefully eyed the hat atop Pak Kari's head. "*I* see," he said at last. "Just because of this here hat, this precious family heirloom of a hat. Here, let's have a good look at it"—and he yanked it off Pak Kari's head.

"Oh me oh my, your hat's all wet, isn't it? Crying shame!"

"Yes sir. It fell down into the water. Good thing it fell near the riverbank and not into the middle," Pak Kari said, set somewhat at ease by the look of regret on the engineer's face and the distressed tone of his voice.

"Crying shame!" the engineer repeated, slowly shaking his head from side to side, as if deeply moved, his tongue clucking in sympathy. "Water touches your hat and it gets all wet. What would you say would happen if it caught fire?" Saying which, he opened the furnace door and flung the hat into the burning flames. Then he looked sorrowfully at Pak Kari, who was aghast. "Ah, that hat of yours, good job it's just an ordinary hat after all. Water makes it wet, fire burns it." And then before Pak Kari could quite credit what he'd seen, "*Ayo!* Back to your place, and be quick about it too, you scoundrel!" the engineer snapped.

Soaked to the skin though he was from the day's adventure in the highlands, Pak Kari no longer felt chilled; he felt, on the contrary, warm—deep down within him was a blazing inferno. This affair of his helmet having been incinerated, it wasn't to be forgiven and forgotten just like that. Oh no. But what to do? At the moment, he didn't quite know. All he could do was stand there mutely, exhibiting as always that almost limitless patience of his.

Days came, days went. Everyone had quite forgotten the incident of Pak Kari's helmet. That he had sported Tuan O.M.'s helmet and the way it had struck fear into them all, they couldn't even remember. As for Pak Kari's having been christened Gunarso on account of it—this too they'd forgotten. Forgotten that once he'd wanted to run amok. That he'd once abandoned his post at the furthermost railway carriage because that blessed hat had fallen onto the arch of the bridge.

One fine day, there he was, absorbed in scraping slag off the locomotive in Kayutanam station, when what should he see but a foreman wearing a helmet. Damn him if it wasn't exactly like the one that had gone up in smoke in the very same furnace he'd just been cleaning out! His gaze shifted to the furnace, and he could just about see his old hat dancing round, flung this way and that by the flames that blazed there. Then he pictured his own face beneath the dancing, bobbing helmet; his was every bit as imposing a countenance as that of Tuan O.M. And that's when his thoughts led him back to a certain incident that had occurred at Tuan O.M.'s house.

He'd been working at the time, with no provision for time off. Notwithstanding this he'd been ordered by Tuan O.M. to help with chopping wood at the lathe foreman's home, something he usually did on his day off. Hacking away at the wood, he'd heard Nyonya Gunarso's cries coming from the bathroom. He hurried inside to find the woman seated on the bathroom floor rubbing her neck in pain; it was obvious she had slipped and fallen. What to do? He gazed long and blankly on the woman in her plight. But when she asked him to help her his confusion grew worse—in fact, he was acutely embarrassed. He was aching to hold this lovely woman, and she the boss's wife, no less!

Finally, however, he plucked up the courage to help the woman to her feet, at a complete loss as to what next to do. Turns out he needn't have worried: reaching out to hold her, stroking the woman's back, he knew right away that he was in for a good time. He was led by her to her room and made to lie down on the bed. Afterward, he felt that, runt though he was, he was the very man fated by God to serve as the lover of the boss's wife. Just his luck too that the boss was a shorty like him, the pair of them had given this beautiful woman something to remember. These thoughts, together with the woman's winning ways, gradually gave rise to love for her. The kind that drives a man wild, enslaving him to his wildest fancies.

As for the helmet, the hat given him by Tuan O.M. earlier when he'd thought to take his leave—it was, Pak Kari now felt sure, both sign and symbol of his sacred love for Nyonya Gunarso. It was nothing less than God's will—if He hadn't willed it, what was that hat doing perched atop Pak Kari's head?

Tuan O.M., its original owner, had convinced him that little folk like himself were not brought into this world merely to have ridicule and humiliation heaped on them. Pak Kari now saw Tuan O.M.'s superiority, the reason King Kong was taken down a peg, as a triumph for all little people, and as a personal coup too. How potent Tuan O.M. had felt with the hat—seemingly the equal of Queen Wilhelmina's crown—on his head. And this hat had at long last passed into Pak Kari's keeping—Tuan Gunarso's crown!

Again he thought of the helmet singed to ashes in the flames of the furnace. And as he did so the flame of vengeance was suddenly rekindled within him. He wanted to take revenge right there and then. He quite forgot himself, he, a mere railway brakeman, impotent, his body dwarfish, stunted, quite forgot himself. One thing, and one thing only, obsessed him: vengeance, burning within, a bright, blazing fire. And God Himself surely willed the engineer to walk in at that very instant to check Pak Kari's work. No sooner had the fellow started to grope about for the handle to the furnace door, the better to climb up the locomotive ladder, than Pak Kari flung straight at him a shovelful of glowing charcoal dregs that he'd only just removed. It struck the luckless engineer smack in the face, leaving him, as it was meant to leave him, worse than useless from that instant on, a creature of no further value to anyone. Darkness and boredom have since been his lot—all he's got left, in fact, apart from his pension of forty-five rupiahs per month.

Beaming with satisfaction, Pak Kari contemplated the helmet, looking at it as if keen to tell it that a debt owed had been repaid, in spades.

Nobody blamed him. Freakish bad luck—that's what it seemed. Nor did he blame himself, well though he knew that the "accident" was nothing of the sort. . . .

The Encounter
(Pertemuan)

by Nasjah Djamin

It was raining stair-rods when the second beer I'd ordered was opened. A bevy of patrons entered, seven in all, three men, four women. Jalan Malioboro was left behind, glinting blackly under its curtain of rain. It had just gone a quarter past eight, on a pitch-black night. Fat chance of anyone else coming into the Chinese restaurant on a pouring night like this! Since I'd sat down a little while back, no more than two men had been drinking, over in the corner by the cashier. A grand total of ten patrons now.

The seventh of them had just walked up to the big table and was chatting away; laughter boomed. A whiff of expensive perfume drifted through the room. Certainly not made in Indonesia, that's for sure, was my first thought. Their gear, their very figures—you wouldn't believe the sheen they gave off. Not Yogya folk, I'll tell you that. Through the sodden, murky night you could just make out their number plates: Jakarta. One gent, bespectacled, middle-aged, sat facing me; another sat with his back to me, with the glittering women between. The first man was tall and long in the leg, hair turning gray. I felt reduced in their presence, more precisely by their woven clothes, their imported shirts, ties, footwear. My faded drill trousers, my shirt with its washed-out colors, my decrepit shoes, all at once looked so crummy cheek by

---

Note: For translation of the many Dutch terms in this story, see Glossary, passim and p. 193 in "Notes and Comments on the Stories and Authors."

jowl with the glitter of the big table over there. Forget it, I thought, all indignant, it's not as if they own the place. I'd come into some money that morning, and damned if I wasn't going to sit there drinking it pleasantly away. What caught my attention, though, wasn't the group as such but one member of it: a good-looking woman wearing glasses, who sat facing my corner. The wife of one of them, no doubt. I'd made up my mind to take no notice of the big table or of Gorgeous with her oh-so-softly sparkling smile. I just sat there, all quiet like, holding open the magazine I'd bought earlier. But, me and my bad luck, my eyes would forever flit back to her face. Every time I gazed at her, or stole a sidelong glance, Gorgeous, by chance as it were, would catch my look. I cursed myself for a thief caught red-handed: that smile, those eyes, those movements. Wherever did they invent such loveliness? This world's meant for those who've got what it takes, not for the likes of me, isolated over in my corner and sunk in discontent. Their voices, shot through with Dutch, twittered on as they ate and drank. One thing's clear, that lot had all had the chance to go overseas, was my bitter inward remark. They were bandying about memories of the grand times they'd all had abroad.

"I always feel so *lost*," the bespectacled man said, laughing. "Just let my feet touch home and already I'm pining for Paris or Venice. I detest London, its peasoupers, the heavy colds you catch there!"

"You've been to London, let's see, how many times is it?"

"Three, *mevrouw*."

"Bingo!" interjected the large fellow. "Yes, *mevrouw, het is waar wat hij zegt! O dat ondragelijk heimweegevoel!* He's dead right. Oh that incredible homesickness! Don't I just know what he's talking about. Whenever I'm in Paris or on the Riviera, I long for Indonesia. *Anything* from home seems precious, a sentimental *keroncong* even. But I've only to come back to my own country and what do I do but start hankering for Paris, its museums—the Louvre especially. I positively ache for the theaters, the Eiffel Tower."

To dispel my irritation I whistled slowly to myself. Gorgeous, when I shot a glance at her, just acknowledged it with that smile of hers, all the while propping up her chin on her hands as she followed the conversation, eyes brimful with astonishment. Don't even *think* about it, I said to myself. You're not in the same league. Their chatter about their time overseas was so dreary. Gorgeous, though, seldom spoke, just sat there listening, and me riveted to my seat, though heaven knows I was anxious to get the hell out of the restaurant. I'd catch her eyes repeatedly, but the little game had begun to get on my wick. On hers, too. Better, far better, to curl up in your corner and pretend they'd all dropped dead. I fingered a vein in my temple. It was taut. Drink's gone to my head, I thought. My eyes had begun to droop shut.

How long I'd put them out of sight and mind I can't rightly say. Outside, the rain continued to thrum. All at once a chair scraped the floor and Daddy Long Legs was heard to say, "Excuse me, *dames en heeren, Ik geloof,* ladies and gentlemen, allow me. "

Bit by bit his features began to swim into my now woozy perspective. There he stood, in front of me. That white hat. The laugh. Instantly I was jolted upright, going all stiff and cold. I nodded a wordless reply as he bade me good evening, begging permission to take a seat at my table.

"Forgotten who I am, have you?" he asked.

"Not much chance of that now, is there," I replied indifferently.

"Yes, it's you all right," he went on. "Why just a second ago, my wife was nudging me, did I know that fellow over in the corner sitting all by himself, the one who can't take his eyes off her? Yes, it's you. How many years has it been?"

I said nothing. My hatred, going all the way back to the old days, flared up unbidden. He was my old HIS teacher in the years just before the Japanese. Halim Harpan his name was, a graduate of HIK and a man who was *gelijkgesteld,* on a footing of equality, with the Hollanders in those days.

His wife was a Dutch woman of Indo extraction.

"Yes," he said, "this is my new wife. We got married last year. You remember my former *mevrouw,* don't you. She passed away ten years ago."

Again, "You're *quite* sure you've not forgotten me?"

"Quite sure," I replied, trying to sound convincing. "You haven't changed one bit, sir."

Hearing himself addressed as sir, he fell tensely silent. Then, "Oh come now, Patih, don't 'sir' me."

I laughed, feeling like an ass.

"Sorry. Back then I called you *meneer.* Now . . . oh all right then, I'll just say Bapak Halim."

"Yes, we're neither of us spring chickens," he said. "You're all grown up, and me, I'll be pensioned off soon, and one fine day, *flup!*

I'll be gone. But I'm tickled pink that one of my former students has made it. I seem to recall having read somewhere that you've become a name to conjure with in the art world."

At that, I just smiled stupidly.

"Not grubbing for a living still, are you? A middle-level civil servant at the very least, I should hope."

He fell suddenly silent as he caught sight of my drill trousers and worn shirt. What could be going through his head, I asked myself. The old days came flooding back, when our school would march in procession on 31 August to celebrate the birthday of Queen Wilhelmina. I was his poorest pupil, going shoeless, my shirt full of patches. Meneer Halim would blow his top with me.

"Tomorrow you're to wear shoes. With rubber soles!"

"Haven't got any, *meneer*."

"And *why,* may I ask, haven't you got any? Don't come the bashful kid from some *desa* classroom! You're not in some unlicensed Malay school, you know!"

So, because I really couldn't afford to buy shoes, and loath as he was to hear his school referred to as a "wild" school, he extracted a few coins, offering them to me to cover the necessary. I was in grade seven then, and, what with my being his cleverest pupil, he'd pinned his hopes to my passing the *examen* in order to enter the MULO. Not to mention the fact that as the newly appointed head teacher at an HIS subsidized by the Netherlands Indies government, not just any old "wild" school, he'd a reputation to look after. I did, in fact, go forward at last to sit the government high school entry exam. But the whole thing left a flat taste in the mouth. The gift of the fifty cents especially was what made my self-confidence go through the floor, at a time when it had been at rock bottom to start with. If, say, he'd given it to me not to preserve his standing as a *gelijkgesteld* "inlander," if he'd done so without trying to pass himself off as some sort of Dutchman dealing with the "natives," then you can be pretty sure there would have been none of this feeling of having had my face rubbed in it. But after the business of the shoes, I'd come to hate him.

I said, smiling, "Oh, I never did graduate MULO, you know. I'm an ordinary civil servant now, on the same level as SR."

"Never!" he said. "Well, one thing's clear, you've let down the school side. So tell me, what were you up to when the Japs were here?"

"Oh, the usual," I said. "*Kinrohosi,* black marketeering. Then going off to wherever there was fighting, during the Revolution. After the formation of the RIS, I entered a government service. Now I'm here."

"Not some low-level clerk, surely?" he asked, shaking his head in disbelief.

I laughed. "I never did graduate HIK, not like some people I know. Anyhow, I'm happy just as I am. For the time being."

Then he came out with it. "Patih," he said slowly, "I'm in a position to help. Do you want to become a clerk in my office?"

"Thanks all the same."

He watched me silently, studying me like that for some time. At some deeper level he was challenging me with that look of his.

"You're turning me down. Why?"

"No reason, except that I'm not so keen on the idea. You must be pretty high up. Head of department at the very least," I added, with forced jauntiness.

He just stared at me without taking in the remark, not batting an eyelash. When at last he spoke, it was with head bowed.

"I can feel you still hating me, Patih, wanting to get your own back."

I laughed softly, shaking my head.

"Let's let bygones be bygones," he said.

To be perfectly honest, I'd forgotten all about him, but his having turned up there that night, so extravagantly, out of the blue, had given rise to feelings of profound disquiet. A man like Pak Halim Harpan accommodated, trimmed to changing circumstance with such speed, and so easily. And it's this suiting yourself to circumstances that they call living! How to Succeed in Life. God knows quite how, but when the Japanese took over he and his half-Dutch wife managed to keep themselves well out of harm's way.

No detention camp for him. Oh no. Meneer Harpan—Halim *de* Harpan, as he was known to his Dutch cronies—fetched up as a *sensei,* Mr. Teacher Halim Harpan, if you please, though not *gelijkgesteld* with the Japanese, oh no, not by a long shot. The Japanese soldiers had sworn at him too, called him a swine, beaten him. He fetched up an enthusiastic Japanese language teacher, dutifully performing the *kerei* ceremony every morning in the direction of the rising sun. His every gesture, his very walk, was lent a dragging quality by his heavy jackboots. He out-Japped the Japs themselves when it came to twisting his tongue round their gibberish. He shaved his head, the better to wear a Japanese soldier's *bosi*. School for me in those days was a nonstarter: I went round in the footsteps of a Japanese artist. Then, quite suddenly, Japan surrendered, revolution broke out, Dutch and British soldiers started to land and to occupy our cities, and Meneer Halim took the view that the time had come to dust off and resurrect that *gelijkgesteld* status which had been trampled underfoot by the Japanese. Like other *pemuda* at the time, I took part in the fighting against the Japanese and then the British Ghurka troops, engaging in sabotage of Dutch barracks, attacking without questioning orders and with a song in my heart, as if I was setting off for a party.

"You tried to kill me once. Remember, Patih?"

"Alas, I failed. That time."

"Not only aren't you sorry, you're still feeling vengeful. Aren't you?"

I laughed it off. "No, Pak Halim. I'm not the vindictive type. But if ever a Time of Readiness should be declared again, I wouldn't hesitate to kill."

"Still a hotheaded ex-*pemuda,* aren't we," he said, brought up short by this.

"Ex, maybe. Extremist, no," I corrected him. "A young disturber-of-the-peace, or bandit, as the Dutch used to say. And still am—provided it's convictions I'm fighting for, and the truth of the land of our birth."

Head still bowed, he took out a cigarette, offering me one. I declined. That's how we'd confronted each other, back then.

In the Time of Readiness I'd come round to his house at night on an errand—to murder him. He'd been keen to refurbish his status, with an eye to the Dutch forces and the NICA then landing, anxious to find a foothold amidst the ruckus the *pemuda* were kicking up, fighting for revolution and independence with those sharpened bamboo spears of theirs. Tuan Halim and his wife chummed up to the Dutch NICA. My unit commander ordered me to make contact every so often with the former HIS teacher, to find out where he stood vis-à-vis the Revolution. Twice I went round, the first time alone.

Tuan Halim tittered scornfully at me.

"You stupid *pemudas!* Fighting the Dutch with bamboo spears! *Merdeka* you want, is it? Where are your rifles? Where're you going to get 'em? You're my student, and I'll have you know you're going to die in vain, fighting the Dutch!"

"So Meneer Halim doesn't hold with the Revolution or with Bung Karno?" I asked.

"Too right I don't. We haven't a hope against the Dutch!"

"If that's what you think, *meneer,* on your head be it."

He laughed raucously. "What's it to be then? I'm going to be killed by a *pemuda* extremist, am I? Tell you what I'll do, I'm going to call the KNIL to clear you lot away. You and your bamboo spears!"

I made my report to my commander, to the effect that Meneer Halim was pro-Dutch. He came along with me the second time I paid a call. The answer was the same as before; if anything, more upsetting. Our commander was moved to laugh out loud. All at once he socked one at Meneer Halim, and kept on letting him have it. "Having me on, are you?" he bellowed. Then, snickering, "We've got a lot of time for Meneer Halim the teacher, but none at all for an inlander who can't wait to turn himself into a black Dutchman."

That day, during a meeting at our quarters, it was decided that Meneer Halim had to be liquidated. That very night. That was the plan of action. I was detailed to go in first to meet him, to try to knock some sense into that thick skull of his for the last time. If he persisted in being pigheaded I was to indicate as much. My comrades, armed with their sharpened bamboo spears, would take up positions round his house. That night I set out, a sharp knife at my waist. None of us had guns, with the exception of our commander, who had a Mauser which he'd taken off a Japanese officer.

"So, Patih," Meneer Halim said, as I sat down. "Come to bump me off, have you?"

"Yes," was my firm reply.

He was seated behind his writing desk, laughing. "What, with your bare hands?" he asked, glancing at his watch several times. "Seven minutes to go before seven P.M.!"

"I've come once again to ask you, are you going to throw your lot in with the Revolution, or are you going to go over to the Dutch?" He just chuckled, leaving me seething. My hand crept down to feel for my knife. But he burst out suddenly, "That's enough playing around!" He sat there at his writing table pointing a Colt at me. "Patih, you dolt! Throw down that knife of yours. A pistol's faster than a knife, or didn't you know that?"

When still I refused to budge, he counted to three. Quickly I placed the knife on the desk. I'd failed, and I was crestfallen. And he wasn't even allowing me to stand up—no chance of my signaling to the comrades outside.

"See that clock there? Still a few minutes to go. At seven sharp a KNIL truck's coming round to pick me up. You just sit quietly over there. Don't think I don't know your fanatic friends have surrounded the house." From afar came the sound of a truck. He smiled happily.

"Here they come. Now let's see how brave you all are, with those bamboo spears of yours!"

The truck ground to a halt in front of the house. Outside all was quiet, as the NICA men took up position. My comrades outside scattered to the four winds.

"Game's up," he said. Chuckling cynically, he picked my knife up off the desk and tossed it into the corner, replacing the Colt in his trouser pocket. Soldiers' footsteps were at the door. My mind was all in a whirl. The minute they walk through that door it's curtains for me, I thought. Without warning I leapt at Meneer Halim, only to find myself hurled into a corner by a punch.

"Take a good look. You want *merdeka,* I'll give you *merdeka!*"

What with his having fallen upon me, raining down blows on my head and chest, it was all I could do to catch my breath. Pulverized, splattered with blood, I was dragged back to my chair and made to sit down.

"I'm no murderer!" I said. "I wasn't going to kill you!"

That's when the NICA soldiers burst in, with his wife the Dutch half-caste in tow.

"Well, well, what have we here? One of them *pemuda* fanatics? Tie him up!"

But Meneer Halim only said, "Leave him be! He's one of my former students. We were practicing boxing. I landed a knockout punch!"

They all laughed, and after they'd gone, bearing away Meneer Halim and his missus, I was rescued by my comrades, who came panting up into the house. All this had happened during the first month of the outbreak of revolution.

"Best not to recall times past," Pak Halim said. "We've all got our own lives to get on with."

"Yes," I said, slowly, "so we have. Life's full of irony, like some painful and unjust dream."

He looked at me, finally saying, "Everybody makes mistakes, screws things up. When you realize where you've gone wrong, you'll be the better for it."

"That's as may be. But when it comès to the crunch you get two sorts of people. There's Jesus Christ, who cares about things, who acts conscientiously and out of conviction. And there's Judas. No prizes for guessing which one was crucified." I shot him a black look: he still thought the world of himself. All at once the poem "Kerawang Bekasi" came to mind. I remembered my comrades who'd fallen in battle, hearing the voices of those who'd cried, "I'm not yet dead!" or "*Merdeka!*" at the top of their lungs, fists clenched. They were at rest now in the Heroes' Cemetery, their white bones scattered. They had offered up their most precious possessions, their bodies, bones, heart, spirit, soul.

I stole a sidelong glance at Gorgeous, Halim Harpan's young bride, softly glittering there. Lucky bastard. He knows how to go for the main chance. Doesn't take any risks. The good life, and landing feet first.

All of a sudden I was seized by a gust of feeling. Memory came, and with memory scalding tears. I looked at the woven shirt, the tie, the fingers, wrinkled but richly oiled, the hands still unsullied by mud, blood, by expense of spirit! Hands which for so long had done nothing but take, laying hold of the best of everything. I swigged down the dregs of my beer. Again that tedious question of his, reverberating: "Patih, do you still hate me? Still want to get your own back?"

I laughed. "No point, is there, talking about revenge. Why on earth should I want to? You see, I gave the best part of my life to the past when I took part in an orgy of spirit and flame. I'm alive, Fate hasn't come knocking, and I'm doing my utmost to make a go of my life in a free Indonesia."

For a long while he remained silent, those be-ringed fingers of his drumming slowly, edgily, on the counter. Without looking up he said slowly, "What do you say to my earlier proposal? Fancy moving to my department? If you like, I could send you overseas to study. If you like."

"Thanks all the same."

I stood up. He looked me up and down. The feeling of pity which pierced my heart seemed to have struck an answering chord; then, gazing down, he caught sight of my battered shoes. I was reminded of that business of the fifty cents. I laughed inwardly.

"These days I'm able to afford shoes, thank you very much, Pak Halim."

A nod: touché. His face had a hurt, defensive look. I had this urge to lash out at him right there and then, but seeing him like this, I hadn't the heart. He was old, too old for tomorrow. Takers like him, they're ten a penny.

"My best to your wife," I said, smiling. She really *was* a looker!

He'd hardly managed to open his mouth when I was shaking hands by way of farewell. I laid money down on the table for my two bottles of beer and left him standing there, flabbergasted. Time to be making a move.

The rain was still pelting as I made my way along the edge of the pavement fronting the shops. My heart was light, wide open. No vindictiveness. No regrets about anyone or anything. Deep down, though, the tears were coming on like the nighttime downpour.

The Last Train But One
(Sebelum Yang Terakhir)

by Satyagraha Hoerip

We'd said our farewells, "we" being Dr. Macro and wife, with their twelve kids in tow, and myself and my kid brother. The whistle shrieked again, and the two of us flung our valises onto the platform of our carriage and managed to hop aboard.

The train, getting off to a slow start at first, picked up speed so fast there was no chance to wave good-bye from the platform. The family had taken their leave as if they had all the time in the world. Indeed, it was all they could do to stop their littlest one, who couldn't understand a word of what was going on, from wandering off after two German shepherds, a male and a female.

The train had a forlorn air about it. We met not a soul, though it might have been that our fellow passengers had all gone into their cabins. The doors too had all been shut, making it easier for us to find our compartment. We heaved our valises straight up onto the luggage racks, my kid brother flinging wide the windows. But with the wind gusting strongly, I asked him to shut it right away, and to do so as tightly as possible. We'd been up talking till dawn at Dr. Macro's, about God, devils, things marvelous and strange, war and peace and whatnot. So we tried to get some shut-eye, straightaway.

My kid brother stretched out on his back on one seat, legs sticking out toward the window. I followed suit on the opposite bench, except that I lay down with my head beneath the window. The rolling motion of the train sent us right off into a deep slumber, the wheels going clickety-clack. The locomotive whistle shrieked now and again as we sailed off into dreamland.

God knows how long we'd been snoring away, but when the conductor came rapping on the door, I got up to open it. He asked me, ever so friendly and polite, to show our tickets. We handed them over to him, ever so friendly and polite. My kid brother'd slept dead to the world; he looked as if he'd relished his snooze.

" 'Fraid there's been some mistake, gentlemen," said the conductor. He'd taken a long hard look at our tickets and, appearing not to think twice about it, was about to motion to the ticket puncher. The latter, clearly new at the job, was going about his duties like greased lightning. "You gentlemen must have mistaken this train for the one following. This here isn't the last train. There's one to come still."

He made his point calmly enough, but blow me if it didn't set me well and truly on edge. What felt like a cold sweat—could it be it actually *was* a cold sweat—had, quite without warning, sprouted on my forehead and started to trickle down my back. Both hands started to tremble. It wouldn't surprise me if I'd turned as white as a sheet.

"But . . . the porter, *he* didn't say a word to us when we ran through the gate. Also—"

"Well, he wouldn't, would he, sir," he replied smartly, but by no means discourteously. "This train's bound for the same destination. Thing is, it takes a different route. It's going to follow a very roundabout sort of route. I daresay you'll think it'll be going nowhere in particular. Might even seem like the journey's never going to end. Well, how about it, sir? Think you're up to it?"

I cracked a forced smile. A cynic, I thought to myself. Or at the very least a conductor with a far-out sense of humor. A train that just goes on and on and on, never stopping. Can you beat it?

"What's it to be then, sir?" he demanded, his patience suddenly wearing thin. "I see you're a friendly sort. Stiff upper lip and all that. Put your trust in God, take a positive view of life. But see here, I haven't got all day. Save that smile of yours for another day, will you; just tell me what I need to know!"

Instead of flying off the handle, I merely nodded. He nodded back, and at long last our tickets were punched. Then off he went, swaying in rhythm to the rolling of the carriage, but as he turned to go, I was struck by surprise—seized with alarm would be more like it. That face of his now: could it really be as flat and smooth as all that? It was almost completely without depth, the lips and nose practically flush with the surface. I was suddenly annoyed with myself. What sort of fool was I, not to have noticed before?

Needless to say, I suppressed my doubts. My eyes were bleary with sleep, but that wasn't the reason why. It was a matter of my having remonstrated with myself. This train conductor now, I told myself, here's a man who's come across any number of passengers in the course of work, children included. Someone who can safely be assumed to have been at it for a good long while. Could such a person have a mug like the one that had started to give me the shivers? Devil take it! I said to myself. You and your cockeyed way of looking at things.

I lay down again just as before, making sure not to wake my kid brother, who was once more sound asleep. He looked, I must say, the very picture of ardent adolescence, out like a light though he was. The train's swaying motion soon sent me back to sleep as well, but a sleep penetrated by the noise of wheels going clickety-clack, and the occasional shrill whistle of the locomotive. Back I sailed to dreamland, where Dr. Macro and family turned up. We had our conversation about mysticism, God, devils, the works. Being a dream, it was confused and irrational.

There was no telling how much time had actually gone by, but all the while I felt ravenous. My belly growled with hunger. I woke with a start several times, to cast a sidelong glance at my younger brother sleeping the sleep of the just. Not much point, was there, inviting him along to the dining car.

This happened more than once. At last I couldn't stand it. I nerved myself to rouse him and in the process found myself fully alert.

Wait a minute. What the hell was going on? Was this for real?

You could have knocked me down with a feather. When I moved my arms and legs about, stretching my muscles, I couldn't credit it. I knew things had come to a pass, but could they be *that* bad? It all felt so . . . so broken, mixed up, as if it were past praying for. I was aghast. Surprised? That's putting it mildly.

Drifting off to sleep for the second time, I had caught sight of the conductor's face, now gone totally flat and smooth. Devoid of any curvature, it lacked all protuberance. And now, as I woke for the second time, my younger brother, seventeen years my junior, had suddenly changed out of all recognition. His skin, or at any rate that part of it not covered by clothing, had gone all wrinkled with age. His jet-black hair had turned gray. He'd always carried that body of his so handsomely—now he looked aged, decrepit.

I was overcome by the urge to shriek. *Don't!* screamed my brain. I stopped my mouth with my left hand, rubbing my eyes in utter disbelief. Hold on, my brain protested, this sort of thing just doesn't *happen*—this is carrying things too far! Taken by surprise, my heart broken at the sight of him. I heaved with dry sobs.

I've gone mad, I kept saying to myself in mute protest. Someone's cast a spell. Maybe this compartment's spooked. Or maybe someone's played a joke in bad taste on us while we lay sleeping.

"Yusaak!" I managed to bellow out at long last. "Yusaak!"

He seemed to hear me. Moving his limbs with considerable difficulty, he succeeded with great effort in opening his eyes and, still blinking, looked directly at me. My God, but he really *was* an old man now, far gone in years! His eyes no longer shone like those of a strapping young man; they were the dull eyes of an elderly gent. The eyes of my late grandfather, no less.

"Wha . . . what's going on?" he asked, in the quavering voice of the very aged.

At first I found it hard to speak for the tumult within. A million feelings, all vying for expression, were roiling about inside me. My inmost self felt like it was being sliced to bits by some enchanted blade. Finally I managed to speak, blurting out the first thing coming to mind:

"Sak—your skin. Just look at it!"

He did so, casting his eyes down over it before glancing at me and saying in that croaking voice of his, "Ye-es. And? Wait a sec . . . who *are* you anyway?"

Who was I? As God's my witness, I just couldn't fathom any of this. This was lunacy, all of it. I wasn't going to put up with it. I was aware of my lips moving slowly, knew for a fact that once again I was choking on sobs.

What was the point of saying anything, with him like this right in front of me? What, finally, was the point of *doing* anything? When it came down to it, I'd been defeated. And I hadn't even put up a fight. Some sort of black magic had won the day, that much was clear. All opposition was in vain.

"It's like . . . like, I used to know you, once. Somewhere," he presently remarked. His voice, the way he moved his forefinger, the set of his whole body—everything about him smacked of age and decrepitude.

I stared at him, unable to tear my eyes away. Some people, I daresay, would tell you to get the hell out if you tried a stunt like that on
them. But with nothing to lose anymore, I got up, and, with a violent
motion, flung open the door to the compartment, to stand stupidly at
the threshold. All quiet, the length of the corridor. Empty, deserted.
The doors to the other compartments remained shut. God, but I was
aching to kick them in! What I wouldn't have given to see the faces of
the other passengers. Anything to see their mugs one after another, as
the doors opened.

Fighting for balance against the to-and-fro rocking of the railway
car, I clung to the side. The great thing was to keep walking. To keep
steady. I couldn't wait to get my hands on that damned conductor,
down at the other end.

For what seemed like an age I staggered forward, flung this way and
that by the rattling and rolling of the railway car. You can't begin to
imagine what it was like. It might have indeed been every bit as awful
as it seemed at the time—on the other hand, I can't rule out my having
lost my marbles. That was the question. For if there was one thing I
was sure of, it was that I was at a total loss as to what was going on.

I rapped frantically on the door of the compartment at the far end.
The gentleman on the other side of it took no notice, caught up as he
seemed to be in enjoying the landscape racing past his window. Judging from his uniform, and to my unbounded relief, I could see he was
none other than the conductor I'd encountered earlier.

"Conductor, excuse me," I hailed him, in a voice suddenly gone all
strangled.

"Something the matter? Oh it's you, sir. Need some help, do you?"
he enquired, shifting his body round completely to face me.

I swear he really did have a face as flat and as smooth as the
concrete wall of a new house that's about to get a lick of paint. His
features were those of a very aged man. Nose so flat it looked like the
two nostrils had been drilled above the wrinkled upper lip as a mere
afterthought. His skin, too, was wrinkled, his hair completely gray.
And the voice was as cracked and unsteady as my younger brother's.

"You remember me, don't you, I'm from—"

"Course I do," was the indifferent reply. "Chap that's boarded the
wrong train, isn't it? Need my help, do you, sir?" he asked, a coy smile
forming on his lips.

This amiability of his stunned me into silence. So did his elephant's memory. Only a minute ago my younger brother had been totally unable to recognize me.

My just standing there speechless might have been the reason he felt obliged to totter over to me. "So, am I right or what? From the word go, I've been telling you and your kind, haven't I, that you've boarded the wrong train. If I've told you once I've told you ten times, this isn't the last train, the one you've bought the ticket for. You're dead right, this train, it'll get you there in the end, just like the one you really want to take, but *this* one's goes by way of—but hang it all, you've suspected as much, haven't you, sir?"

I was still dumbstruck. All of a sudden, though, I desperately wanted him to carry on talking, about any subject under the sun. He could curse me up and down if he liked. Anything, just so long as he accounted for the goings-on in this wretched railway car. Surely the old gent could, if he chose, draw back the veil to disclose his secret, in part if not in full.

"Do go on talking!" I must have pleaded; he just continued wordlessly looking me up and down. I became aware that I was whimpering in terror at him. Devil take the man. "Come on, you, speak!" I said. "TALK!"

All he did was smile. At last, bored with inspecting me from top to toe, he nodded, his hands moving every which way before my face. His mouth was working, every bit like that of some carping female.

"God, but you're the limit!" he finally said. "Why just a second ago there you were giving me the impression that here was someone who had what it takes, someone resolute and God-fearing, and that you, sir, felt lighthearted and cheerful on that account. So how do you come. . . . "

He didn't bother to finish his sentence; it hung in the air, wide open to any number of possible interpretations on my part. He just went back to staring at me, smiling all the while, as if engrossed in scrutinizing some strange exotic object.

"You know," he burst out, before resuming his former attitude of long-suffering patience, "you're really something, you are, sir! You're just as you were ages ago. My word, but you're well-preserved!"

Now he was really laughing merrily, tittering to himself. He bowed respectfully, so that what with that long hank of gray hair of his drooping down right in front of me, it was all I could do not to fly at him with both hands and give him what for, or at least box his ears.

"You're the absolute limit! The genuine article," he blurted out, in earnest admiration. "A terrific chap, that you are, sir. *You're* not going to knuckle under to Time and Space, not you. Now that's what I call a man!"

I wasn't taken in by his flattery, I swear I wasn't. But if there was one thing that pulled me up short it was his repeated use of phrases like "when Time began," "when it all started," "in the beginning." My misgivings grew. What *could* the fellow be driving at?

"You wouldn't by any chance be bound for Eternity all on your own, would you, sir? To meet your Maker, I mean?" he proceeded to ask, stepping back, looking somewhat spellbound. Those old man's eyes of his narrowed to slits. They were filled with admiration, and as I judged it to be, filled with pathos too.

This made me unexpectedly happy. I volunteered a smile, nodding and—though I can't think where the idea for such a ruse came from—addressing him in a voice which I made sure sounded authoritative, with body language to match. "You bastard, you've only just found out, haven't you?" Contrary to my every expectation he fell back and went stock still; he made no movement I could see, none whatsoever.

I quickly shut the door, breaking into a run as I set off in search of the compartment my brother and I had occupied. The corridor was as deserted as ever. Eerily quiet it was. The railway carriage seemed all of a sudden far too long. Indeed, it seemed to have no end.

But wasn't I meant to find it, given that the number had been stamped onto the upper half of our tickets? I'd half a mind to wait it out there until such time as this mystery, this piece of insanity, might be cleared up.

But it never was. And that's how I've come to be walking, stumbling, tottering, fighting to retain my balance against the shaking of the railway carriage, which gets more intense with each passing moment. Sometimes the shaking stops, just like that. That's when I'm able to find my feet a little more steadily. But I'm beset with countless temptations. They come in all sizes and shapes. They pile up, they vie with one another. For how long, you say? Your guess is as good as mine.

Dearly Departed
(Mendiang)

by S.N. Ratmana

The coffin—*tebelo*'s the local word for it—lay there in the middle of the floor. The dressers had all been shifted back up against the walls and hung about in white *kain*. An altar stood by, its apparatus and the sacrificial offerings ready. The mourners—there must have been about one hundred of them—were seated, each facing a table groaning with food. I took my place among them, the only one to have entered the room without making the ritual genuflection. Which explains why those already seated had greeted me with astonished stares. They didn't, however, take long to resume their look of blank indifference. After a pause they fell to talking again, in a lingo I couldn't follow.

Lost in thought, I surveyed the room, hoping to find a familiar face. Worse luck! I couldn't even see the deceased's husband. My every attempt to start up conversation was coldly rebuffed by those around me; I wondered if they had decided, mistakenly, that the only reason I was there was to tuck into the funeral meats along with them. I hadn't, if you really want to know, the slightest wish so much as to touch any of the food on offer. I fell silent, sinking back into thought, going over and over the record of the deceased, or that part of it anyway which I happened to be familiar with.

Then, unannounced, a man appeared from a back room, dressed in mourning in a *kain* of unbleached cotton and wearing a headpiece made of the same. This had to be the deceased's spouse. Getting up, I went over to him, holding out my hand and offering too suitable expressions of condolence. He took my hand hesitantly, his eyes alone showing how dismayed he felt.

"Is Wati really dead?" I asked him.

The man with the slanting eyes nodded in doleful affirmation.

"I used to be her teacher."

"I see." There was no other reaction. He stood there mutely for what seemed ages—he seemed to have forgotten me.

"Do you suppose I might see her face, just for one minute?" I asked.

"Whatever for?"

I was getting confused. What more was I supposed to do, to prove my bona fides? "Her . . . ah . . . her parents, aren't they here? What about her other relations?"

A shake of the head.

What was I to make of this? Nevertheless, standing there before the grieving husband I held my ground. I was determined to have another go at expressing my sympathy.

"May I ask when's the burial?"

"Next week."

"Oh."

I fought down a sudden urge to scream. I felt a fool, amongst all these folk. Every move I made, every word I uttered was making me scurry for cover into the kind of clumsiness you take refuge in when you're at a total loss as to what to do or say. Or so it seemed. Pretty soon I was making my excuses.

Never, not in all my born days, had I imagined that Wati would meet her end while still so young! She was not even eighteen. I could make even less sense of the fact, if fact it was, that her mortal remains were being handled with such mystifying pomp. How they'd fetched up here, amongst a people not her own, was a further mystery.

She'd been a student of mine, ten years back, in the second form in high school. A bit of an oddball, so far out neither her schoolmates nor her teachers knew what to make of her, and that included me. She was nothing to write home about so far as looks went. Features all bunched together in her face, build stocky and running to fat. No doubt this accounted for a certain mannishness about her.

One day we found ourselves assigned another member of staff, a gymnastics teacher. A young guy, not yet married. Attractive, and with a really sympatico way of speaking. Marman, his name was. He'd been there for hardly a month when Wati fell head over heels in love with him. It was an accident waiting to happen. The setup was such that you'd have to report to this teacher's quarters on your way to school, and again on your way home. Pretty soon Wati was at her lover's every afternoon, sometimes spending the night there as well. Marman was clueless about how to handle this. He bent over backward to avoid having to meet Wati. She for her part was a dab at dreaming up all sorts of ways to be at the side of the dashing schoolmaster. Things were reaching the point where she was round to his quarters every afternoon. In the love-struck pupil would march, not even bothering to knock, to take up her watch in front of the bedroom of the sleeping Marman, where she waited patiently for him to come out. His mother, who by special dispensation was staying with him, hit the ceiling; giving the girl the sharp side of her tongue, she sent Wati packing. But in spite of everything she'd no shame, and as for her friends' ridicule, well, they could just take a running jump. Cozying up to Marman, that was the name of her game. Wild horses couldn't stop her.

It was only when he'd up and married a pretty teacher, a graduate of another school, it was only then and not before that Wati cried off. She went all moody and taciturn. In due course her schoolwork, which at the best of times had never turned her on, went completely to pot. No chance of her being moved up to the next class at year's end. We could see it coming, all right.

Funnily enough, though, when the teaching year began she wore a sprightly look, not in the least in the dumps about it. Came to school, did her homework, for all the world as if nothing had happened. We were pleased as punch by this. Everyone was hoping her failure in love had led to a greater emotional maturity, that thanks to it all she was at last becoming an adult. But it's a long and winding road, isn't it, the whole business of growing up?

One fine day, first term, it would have been, she came round to my quarters to ask for help, something to do with her lessons. Naturally I did my best to assist—who wouldn't? That afternoon she was back again, jabbering on about things connected with schoolwork. I'd a pretty shrewd idea that this was how it had all started with Marman, with disingenuous queries about homework and such like. My suspicions grew. She'd come round to my lodgings every afternoon, for no other reason it seemed than to make conversation, and about nothing very particular. Often I'd try to get round meeting her; I'd leave a message to the effect that I was out or having a snooze. But she was a determined young lady, our Wati. Once when, as would often happen, she hadn't run across me during the day, she came round at *magrib* time. I'd just finished doing the *shalat* and was making to go out onto the front veranda when there she was, already come into the forecourt of the house. This time there was nowhere to hide. I had to confront her. She burbled on, giving every sign of being at her ease, you'd think she was chatting to her own friends, about her hobbies, movies she'd seen, favorite dishes, and all the rest of it. I'd think to myself as she went rabbiting on, if this young lady's got any sense at all she'd be busy getting on with her lessons for tomorrow, but the idea seems never to have crossed her mind. It began to sicken me, listening to her gabbing away there.

Having reached the point of wanting to puke, I got up. "I've got quite a lot to be doing tonight. School exercises to correct, you know."

"Oh but it can wait, can't it, *pak*. I do so want to talk to you!"

"Look, Wati, I'm terribly sorry but I just haven't got the time."

I was about to step back into the inner room, when, abruptly getting up, she blocked my passage, and very niftily too, one arm extended across the doorframe. I blinked, practically giggling with disbelief.

"Oh come on!" she said. "It's not as if it's even late. And me with no friends and all."

"Wati!" I cried. "Do you realize whose house you happen to be in?"

"In Bapak Ratmana's, where else?"

"I suppose you think it's perfectly in order for you and me to be together like this, don't you. Go on, get along with you now!"

"Nothing doing. I don't want to be left all to myself. Be a sport, *pak*, keep me company, do!"

Talk about vexed. This was the living end! Had it been my own house I was living in, I'd have given her a slap across that little bunched-together face of hers. But I was acutely conscious of being a lodger. Instead I fixed her with a baleful stare, the idea being to get her to stop this willful behavior of hers.

"Come one, give us a smile—there, that's ever so much better! Now don't be cross at Wati."

When I glanced over at the inner room I caught sight of a face, a member of the household peering out. I tell you, I could have died from shame!

"If you've got things to be getting on with, sir, that's fine, don't let me stop you. But could you walk me home later? It's not far, you know. Please, sir. Can you bear to see me going home all by myself, so late and all? Can you, honestly?"

"Whose idea was it for you to come here at this hour?"

"It was still light when I left home."

Her arm was still outstretched, her hand clamped to the doorframe. She'd swung round to show her back to the "audience" looking on from within. I could see that some of them were in stitches, while others were looking distinctly bemused. Finally I caved in and walked her back.

"Right, you win, this time. But in future I'll be damned if I'm going to be at your beck and call. Is that clear?"

She grinned sourly.

She was still talking away to beat the band as we walked along, me keeping a resentful silence. As we neared our destination I said to her, "The next time you've got the cheek to come round to my house, watch out or I'll douse you with water, you see if I don't. I'm not joking!"

This elicited no comment.

Turning on my heel, I headed home before her family could open the door for her. Once there, I found myself bombarded with questions. But I wasn't about to oblige. No way.

Next time you've got the cheek to come here, mind or I'll give you a soaking!—a bucketful of words, tantamount to my slamming the door in her face.

A week later, more or less, and it seemed I'd worked myself loose of the nuisance Wati's forever coming round was starting to pose. In school she'd look right through me. I thought, She's learnt her lesson, no two ways about it. But I couldn't have been more wrong. One afternoon, it must have been around one in the afternoon, our neighbor's *pembantu* came banging on the door to say there was a visitor looking for me. Further enquiries revealed that it was none other than Wati. I needed a minute to think this one over. The servant girl had already let the cat out of the bag by saying I was at home and not asleep. If I'd meant what I'd said, then what I ought to do was go out to meet Wati with a pail of water and drench her. But was that really called for? At last, tearing off a strip of paper from a packet of mosquito repellent, I scribbled *Must rest this afternoon. Go home!* asking the girl to hand it to our distinguished visitor and taking good care to get a pail of water ready to douse her with if push should come to shove. But she'd gone home, it seemed. I could rest easy.

That was the last time she showed up on my doorstep. At school too she kept her distance from me, taking care to give me a wide berth even when, as happened once, her friends engaged me in casual conversation. In class she'd gone all coy, lowering her head when her eyes happened to meet mine. But did that spell the end of her attempt to get intimate? You may well ask. There'd be these letters, practically every week. Screeds, some of them sixteen notebook pages long. Must have taken her three hours working flat out to write one, I'd reflect. And what do you imagine they were about? I'll tell you; a sort of true confessions, all self-analysis to do, surprise surprise, with that old love affair of hers. Though I hadn't the slightest interest in replying, strangely enough I couldn't stop myself from reading them.

My teacher's heart couldn't help but go out to her. Plucking up my courage, I went and laid the wretched affair before our headmaster. He'd the advantage of years and would be able to help. Or so I hoped.

"Let me see then. If I understand you correctly, my young friend, you're trying to get me to . . . to do what, exactly?"

A tough one, that.

"Her parents have been round to see me," he went on. "Fact is, they've asked me to get in touch with you. Seems she never stops asking all about *adik* here. I've said you're a young and dedicated teacher, that you're devoted to your work and a *santri* Muslim to boot." This was delivered with a chortle. "I mean, all of that's true, isn't it? Oh for heaven's sake, she's not a bad sort is she, that girl? Good family, that's clear. Dad's a retired *wedana,* brothers hold heaps of important positions. She's the youngest. What do you make of it, *dik?*" he asked, grimacing wryly. "My feeling's this: if anyone can help her, it's you, and nobody else."

It made me want to spew, hearing that. I had this urge to make a rude retort and would have done so too, had he not been the headmaster and a good deal older to boot. A letdown, that's what he's made me out to be!

Meanwhile, Wati's letters kept streaming in. Through the post they came, every one of them. Letters which I vividly remember, the last in the series filled as it was with her disappointment in me. Among much else, this is what she'd written:

> *I can't figure out why men can never be bothered to look at me. Maybe 'cause I'm not beautiful. Is that it? But then, other girls, they're even*

less beautiful, and they've got lovers. How do you explain that? Seven times I've been in love, and not once has the man ever reciprocated my feelings. Spontaneously reciprocated, I mean. All they do is belittle me, and hurt my feelings. Am I just supposed to sit around twiddling my thumbs and waiting for Number Eight? Oh no. You won't catch me hoping and praying. No, when I fall in love, I don't fancy taking a back seat, not like some girls I know. I seize the initiative. I make waves! If I fall for a man, I'll go for him. I'll ask him over, I'll invite him to see a movie, I'll buy him cigarettes, shoes, what have you, if it comes to that. No point being passive, is there, specially when it's me that needs him. But when a man falls for me, that's a different story altogether. It's up to him to make the first move, if he wants to get close, that is. My feeling, though, is that there's no such man. The seventh guy I was in love with, he was a good man, laid-back, the quiet type. An educated man, a teacher. And not at all what you'd call good-looking. (How's it I always fall for men who aren't so handsome?) But in the end he let me down. He humiliated me, he did everything in his power to hurt me. That's why I'm through with men. They're brutes, every single one of them. Selfish to the core. All they want is to turn you into their slave. But there's no escaping the truth—I need them. God, how I need those sheep in wolves' clothing, 'cause I'm a woman. Would you like to take a wild guess who's Number Seven on my list? It's you, Bapak, you and nobody else!

I burnt this straightaway the instant I'd read it, same as I'd burnt all the others. I didn't doubt that this letter would be the last. None followed, and she'd stopped showing her face in class. Left school, it seems, offering no explanation. I'd heard the headmaster had been in touch with her parents. The reply he'd got seemed to suggest she'd left for keeps. No ifs, ands, or buts. What with there being hundreds of students, Wati was soon history. But five months hadn't gone by and again she'd become the talk of the town amongst staff. We'd had word—rumors, to be precise—that she'd become a call girl working out of the big hotels. Of all the teachers I expect I was the one hit hardest by this bit of news. My mind went back to that last letter of hers. That's when a question began to form: this ugly thing she was said to have done, could it have been the result of some *subsequent* despair? Because if so, then with a bit of luck I was off the hook. In that case I wasn't one of those men responsible for the poor girl's having lost her footing, for making her leave the straight and narrow.

Whatever the case, more pressing matters soon banished the whole thing to the back of my mind. I'm not particularly sentimental, but as it turned out, Wati's tale was far from being over and done with. One day, down with flu, I found myself at the doctor's, waiting my turn to be examined along with lots of other patients. There was a vacant seat next to this woman whose face looked drained of color. She sat rapt in conversation with a man whose skin was yellow. Having nothing better to do while waiting to be called, I was glancing idly at one of the magazines laid out in the waiting room. When I put the one I'd finished back in its place, the woman sitting beside me piped up:

"You're not still teaching high school, *Bapak*, are you?"

"I am indeed. Might I ask how you knew that?" We stared at each other.

"Oh, Wa—"

"Yes, it's me! And this is my husband. Let me introduce you."

I rose to shake hands and had hardly taken my seat again when the door to the surgery opened and one of the nurses sang out:

"*Nyonya* Oey Hoo Lam!"

"That's me," Wati replied.

The yellow-skinned gent accompanied her inside. I'd been taken aback and couldn't help thinking about the encounter. Surprised? You could have knocked me down with a feather! And it had all happened so quickly! I'd heard nothing about Wati for the better part of six months, then out of the blue she pops up right under my nose, albeit for a brief instant, and unless I'm mistaken, much had happened to her in the interim. Her skin wasn't bad, not like it used to be, she'd got more slender and her hair had been crimped. In fact she looked altogether prettier than she'd been when a student of mine. But that husband of hers now, what was she doing married to such an old fart? That's what really floored me. Forty-five plus if he was a day. Oey Hoo Lam his name was, too.

When the pair emerged it was to manage hardly more than a nod in my direction before walking—in a daze, I thought—out to the *becak* waiting in the courtyard. Can't quite say why, but their way of walking pleased me no end. They looked such a couple! I began to think that the word going round of Wati's having become a call girl may have disposed me to think ill of my former student. There was no denying she'd become a respectable married lady now. For the umpteenth time I recalled that last letter of hers. This Oey Hoo Lam, I reflected, was *that* Number Eight? I was glad for her.

I forgot all about Wati soon enough, the more so as I'd married and had had a child. I was, it seemed, called upon to put the whole question of this woman and all thoughts of her on the back burner. Ditto the love affairs she'd been caught up in. Only, I couldn't help knowing that she was living as the wife of the owner of a shoe shop, in the high street of our town. That's how I knew—I'd pass by it, almost daily. Not that I shopped there myself. It's just that I'd often stop to watch her or her husband waiting on customers. Make of this what you will, came a day and something happened which forced my hand, compelling me to face up squarely to the whole question of Wati. It started with my having caught sight of a bunch of people crowding round the shop. Then one fine day I noticed a bit of white *kain* hanging down from the door, signifying a death in the family.

My first impulse was just to walk past, as usual, but second thought led me to inquire of someone near the door, "May I ask who's passed away?"

"*Nyonya* Oey Hoo Lam."

"She has? How?"

"Giving birth."

"The baby's safe?"

"Dead too."

"When did this happen?"

But he'd nipped back in; had to see to something, and quick I suppose. I stood there by the threshold for a few minutes, lost in thought. Then I went in. Inside it all felt very queer and looked very outlandish. The feeling of gaucheness which took hold of me was positively overwhelming. Yet I found myself thinking clearly.

My former student's corpse lay stretched out before me in the coffin they call a *tebelo*. Last respects were being paid her in a weird and striking ceremony, with neither father nor mother present, nor any close relations. And you didn't see any of her old friends there either, not a single one. It was hardly as if they would have had to come from out of town.

I bowed my head. Inside, I was shattered. Standing there, I asked myself, And you? What do you think *your* chances are of ending up in an early grave, like Wati here? What was the likelihood of my remains being left unattended, like some corpse left to molder on a battlefield after a fight to the finish? It's a possibility, all right. You can't rule anything out.

Matias Akankari

by Gerson Poyk

Matias Akankari was brought forth out of the forests of Irian Barat by a paratrooper, who, having landed atop the jungle canopy one night, fell dangling from a tall tree. By dint of prodigious effort he had managed to work himself free, and, dusting himself off, set off in search of his comrades. Before rendezvousing with them, whom should he happen upon but Matias, an Irianese male afflicted with some sort of disease. A dose of medicine and, the gods be praised, he was cured. Shame he couldn't speak a word of Indonesian. Still, he'd served as a reliable enough guide, leading the paratrooper out of hair-raising danger and effecting his return safe and sound to Jakarta.

And there you have it in a nutshell: the history of the encounter with Matias.

In due course he was carted off by this paratrooper to Jakarta. Unlike other folk from Jakarta who'd served in Irian Barat and who staggered home burdened with television sets, fridges, and all manner of luxury goods left behind by the Dutch, our paratrooper brought back his friend, his comrade in suffering, whom he'd not forgotten.

But this Matias now. He wasn't just any old luxury item. A meal for this guy amounted to almost three platefuls, so that in the course of one day he managed to put away nine helpings. The paratrooper, speaking as a military man, was flabbergasted. Where in heaven's name was he supposed to find the money to subsidize such extravagance?

He came up at last with a brilliant idea: he'd kit Matias out in elegant, costly clothes, which he'd bought in Irian Barat. Matias found himself rigged out in a woolen suit, a shirt and tie, and imported shoes.

71

In a borrowed Russian-built Gaz the pair of them zoomed off toward the busy city center. Scarcely three days had passed, and already Matias had settled into the capital, all agog at the brilliant neon and the city lights. He was bowled over, too, by the lamps, the towering build-ings, the dense jungle of humanity, not a single one of whom was in the least bit like him. Blinking his eyes, he yanked his head about now this way and now that, lest some enticing prospect be missed in the course of the car's rapid progress through the streets.

On reaching Senen shopping district, the two of them stopped off to see a film; it was Matias Akankari's first time ever. Which explains why his attention was glued to the silver screen—so glued to it that when the paratrooper up and left just like that, Matias didn't notice a thing.

"Just for the hell of it," the paratrooper remarked to a mate of his who happened to be watching the movie with them, "I'm going to leave Matias here on his own while he's all eyes. I'd give my right arm to see how a savage makes out in the big city. Why, you never know, I might even write a book about it and hit the jackpot!" he said, laughing as he jumped into the Gaz sedan and skedaddled off.

The film ended and Matias looked all about him, his heart already hammering against his ribs. But as he couldn't speak a word of In-donesian, not a sound came out of his mouth. He scanned the crowd in search of his friend, his eyes red in his black face. But all in vain! He was borne along in the flux; outside the cinema, his heart began to thump even faster.

The one thing he had come to count upon—the paratrooper, whom he'd met with in the midst of the thick, welcoming forest—had well and truly vanished. There he was, smack in the middle of a jungle of electric lights and human bodies, of *becak,* motorized trishaws, and cars—a place, in short, nothing like as calm or as friendly as the rain forest. And so, aimlessly drifting, he wandered on by himself.

Suddenly a loudspeaker blared—now here was something he'd en-countered in Irian Barat, when the VIPs from Jakarta would turn up. But he was damned if he could understand one word. He edged closer, if for no other reason than that his heart was stirred by memories of the great open space in his village. But whereas back home you'd find lots of folk like him swarming round this harshly squawking thingummyjig, listening to their local language, the people here were not in the least like him, and he could make neither head nor tail of their speech.

Ever so slowly he made his way to the heart of the circle, to see what all the fuss was. "Must be a friend of that guy I ran into back home," he said to himself in his own tongue. What he needed was somebody to take him home, to a house where there'd be an *atap,* a bed, three square meals daily. What he needed was a patron.

It was in this condition, suspended as he was between hope and fear, that a helping hand arrived in the person of a refined, hospitable lady, gaily chattering at him and wearing a look that made his heart pound happily. A flick of her hand and forefinger and *becaks* drew up, and the next thing he knew the two of them were heading off toward a part of town he'd never been to before.

No sooner had he entered the woman's bedroom then he was in the arms of the exquisite creature, with that pert figure of hers. And that, precisely, was where Matias, with that squat little body of his, came to grief. There wasn't a thing he could do about it. He'd been in need of a friend, a home, a little island where he could find a haven, and boy had he discovered it! That night he was in heaven, lying there fast asleep beside the woman who had offered him such hospitality. On waking in the morning, he found a table prepared with food and drink next to the bed.

Breakfast eaten, it was action stations again. But still he couldn't get it up. At which point, one ritual quite new to him over and done with another started.

Seated opposite the girl, Matias felt himself to be a spectator at some pantomime. His mouth gaped, an age seemed to pass, and it was only when the girl thrust some pieces of paper before him, her finger pointing accusingly at Matias' chest and then at her own, that the penny dropped.

Matias shook his hands and head in an effort to get the girl to grasp the fact that he simply didn't have that sort of paper. Except for the clothes he stood up in, he possessed nothing at all. But the girl grabbed hold of Matias's jacket, stabbing his chest with her finger. Understanding full well what this meant, he stripped off his jacket and gave it to her.

After this carry-on, the refined little creature began to comport herself in a vulgar manner. She dragged Matias toward the door and unceremoniously shoved him out. Having slammed the door in his face, the girl breathed easy.

He jerked around, this way and that, but among the people around him there wasn't a soul he knew. He felt as if he'd been flung into a jungle that was nothing like as welcoming as the one in West Irian.

Taking his time, he hiked along. To walk for several hours in a city like Jakarta is no joke when you're used to getting round on wheels, but for Matias this was all in a day's work. He was accustomed to going by foot for days on end through the friendly jungle.

Come late afternoon and his journey had brought him to a church. The only way he could purge himself of the sin he had never meant to commit but had committed for one whole night with the girl who had taken him in was to go into the church and beg forgiveness from Jesus Christ. So in he went, to kneel devoutly. Leaving the church, he found that day had turned to night. He sat down outside and thought of his kampung.

There, in the far remoteness of his jungle fastness, he'd go to church wearing his penis sheath, milling about as a member of the clan group, singing his head off in front of the minister. Ever since he was little he'd been part of the clan. Practically every one of its members was illiterate, but songs in church are pretty much like those sung any-where, you can get them by heart easily enough. Once Matias had raised such a stink he'd got himself expelled from this penis-sheath clan. What he did was this: when the members of the clan stood in front of the minister and the community was gearing up to sing, Matias, who had been at the very front, flaunted his penis sheath, which was constructed so as to seem to resemble a flute. He played the hymn on it, getting all the members of the clan to listen raptly before the whole lot of them burst into laughter that shattered the solemnity of the occasion. The upshot? The minister lost his temper with him, and with other members of the clan. Matias was cast forth from its midst without further ado. From that day on his flute went with him every-where. His hand now reached into his shirt and drew it forth. Slowly he began to play on it.

It was getting late. A young man came sauntering toward him, a map dangling from one hand. From a distance he appeared to be walk-ing on air, but as he approached, Matias could see that the sole of one of this man's shoes had worked itself loose; he was having to lift his foot high off the ground, then to place it firmly down, so that he seemed to be floating along. In he went to the church, only to come out again before long.

"This church stays open twenty-four hours, not like others in this city," he said, taking a seat alongside Matias, whose clothes were far more impressive than his own. Matias still had on his long-sleeved foreign-made shirt, his tie, and his woolen trousers. This young chap's were hand-me-downs.

The young man, blithely unaware that Matias knew no Indonesian and couldn't understand a word he said, addressed him without beating round the bush. "God but I've been having one hell of a time walking round this town. The sole of my shoe's as rough as a monitor lizard's tongue. Would you believe I've got a degree but haven't been able to find a job?" he said, pointing to the lizard- tongue's sole of his shoe.

Matias, seeing this, undid his own shoe.

"It's been murder, wearing these shoes," he said as he gave it to this unemployed university graduate. "In the rain forest and in the jungle undergrowth I never needed to wear shoes, and the place was full of thorns and brambles. The only time my feet actually started to bleed was after I started wearing shoes. Here, you're welcome to them!" Matias said in his Irianese tongue. All his interlocutor heard was gibberish, all he saw was the new shoe being taken off and put on his foot.

From the portico of the church the two of them headed for Banteng Square, in the city center. There they went to sleep in companionable silence under the statue commemorating the liberation of West New Guinea. They slept the sleep of the just that night. Waking before dawn, the graduate abandoned Matias. He'd been afraid to rouse him, lest the pair of them would have to carry on together. What a sight they'd make. He'd left a letter in Matias's pocket.

Matias awoke to find his friend had done a bunk. He caught sight of a bit of paper in his pocket and extracted it, but, quite unable to read, he merely turned it round in his hands every which way before crumpling it up and flinging it aside. Then he went back to sleep on the chill tiles, caressed by the wind off Banteng Square.

Waking, he found that day had turned to night. Though his belly growled with hunger, he found the strength to continue walking and made for an area favored by vagrants. There, what should he happen upon but a woman in the very act of giving birth on some paper. He remembered that Our Lord Himself was born on in the hay and swaddled in nappies: he'd come upon another Christ, one born on paper! It rained the whole time the easy birth was taking place—a good thing the vagrant woman had a plastic covering. But underneath this plastic *atap* there was nothing but paper. Matias peeled off everything he was wrapped in, handing it to the woman. "I can't thank you enough!" she said.

Then he donned his native dress, putting on his penis sheath while the rain pelted down. And when he'd rendered every possible assistance to the woman, off he went in the downpour.

As he reached Jalan Thamrin, the main thoroughfare, a street flanked with office blocks, and Hotel Indonesia hove into view, he was floored. The drivers of the cars whizzing past in the rain seemed obliged either to stop or else to pass by slowly, the better to take a good look at him. Inside one car cruising by, Matias saw a creature much like himself; a black man. He wore a suit, a stunningly beautiful girl in tow. The car drew up alongside, its passengers peering out at him. Thinking that here were folk who looked just like him, Matias made an all-out effort to lunge forward as the car drove off and clung to the rear of the vehicle. It picked up speed, but he held on for dear life. The car tooled along toward Hotel Indonesia, finally dropping off one of its swarthy passengers—an American Negro. Talk about getting it all wrong!

A crowd of uniformed people stood hugger-mugger round him. Observing their movements, so like those of hunters bent on trapping some animal, Matias took flight into the cascading rain.

They were none too keen to set off in pursuit and get soaked, but all the same a bit later Matias found himself being tailed by a man in an overcoat. As the man gave chase Matias, naturally, shot off, swift as an arrow. He veered into a multistoried building and dashed helter-skelter into a narrow room, the open door of which now suddenly clanged shut. It turned out to be a lift; it soared skyward, and when it stopped, the door opened onto a dim room with a floodlit platform at its center. On the platform were naked women wearing loincloths just like Matias's, except that his had a penis sheath. And strike him dead if the dances these women were performing weren't the same, give or take a few steps, as those performed in the great open space in the center of his village! Leaping onto the stage wearing his penis sheath he began to dance alongside the women. Applause burst forth from the audience seated in the shadows.

Thus it was that Matias's peregrinations came to an end. It was splashed all over the front pages of the daily newspapers and he was reunited with his paratrooper "master." This time Matias had struck paydirt. He was given funds to travel home to his village, where everybody was on tenterhooks waiting to hear his story.

To hear him tell it, what passed for "high class" in Jakarta was the same as what you'd find in Irian Barat. Right down to the loincloths.

A Journey
(Perjalanan)

by Nh. Dini

This city's hot and dusty: not my sort of place, at all. In the cool season it's plagued by rain falling for three or four days on end. Then you get puddles in the street. In other parts of town it's black and dirty, the color of mud. No matter what the color of the water, the upshot's always the same: traffic slows to a halt, motor vehicles grind to a standstill, things reach the point where law and order starts breaking down. And there's no telling how many tempers get frayed, how many folk lose patience altogether. You get people screaming their heads off from behind their steering wheels, to the accompaniment of the raucous voices of *becak* drivers busting their guts to push forward their cargo. From behind another steering wheel there'll be some European gent cursing up and down: his car, a gleaming blue, scratched by motorcyclists brushing past. You get verbal set-tos, cars stretching back in a long line, their horns blasting. And hanging over it all, a gray, lowering sky. No doubt about it, flooding in Jakarta's nothing compared to the flooding in this little town of mine. Here you'll find people sailing and fishing. Children merrily draw up water before it reaches door level. Working with my uncle, Father starts to make ready a warm space in the corner of the rice barn for the pigpens, and stalls for oxen, ducks, and chickens. If the water rises to a dangerous level, the domestic beasts can be led away to safety up the ladder.

Mother starts to fret the moment the first drops of rain begin to fall.

She bustles about, ordering us to lend a hand. And around we run, trying to put the two-legged creatures into their pens. They're so little, so squat. The water often rises very quickly, swallowing up these animals of ours in no time at all. Ducks are the last to be lifted clear to safety. They're so happy just swimming about, heedless of the swift current. The whole thing's like nothing so much as a family outing. It's very like a festive occasion, cheerful in all sorts of ways, everyone in a terrific mood.

But I've had done with this town of mine, down by the bank of that river.

Now my place of work, my center of business, is here. Before I came I'd often hear any number of not terribly encouraging things said about the people here and the difficulty of making ends meet. But this never worried me. Large towns have so many different groups with strange manners and politics, but alongside these oddnesses you meet with strokes of good luck and enjoy certain advantages you don't have in provincial cities. I'd weighed this all up carefully. My parents had voiced no objection to my going; on the contrary, they were proud of the work I'd managed to find for myself.

I was late getting up, having slept right through the alarm; I'd stayed up late dancing in the company of friends from work. Some male friends with cash to spare had invited me to what was considered to be the top restaurant in town, an invitation I couldn't turn down. And we danced and joked far into the night, until the small hours. I woke to the sound of a car engine juddering away, its driver stepping on the gas again and again. That's how it is, in my line of work. No chance of us keeping regular hours. It all depends on the car's time of arrival and departure. If, like me, you've trouble falling asleep, you don't want to be disturbed by a company chauffeur. I do my best, though, to be civil to them. Once or twice, when coming home from a trip overseas, I give them brand-name cigarettes; sometimes, at New Year's, I make them a present of a very expensive razor. I keep in mind who's received something and who hasn't, as I can hardly buy gifts for the lot of them. By means of such small-time smuggling, I keep them sweet. That morning, too, I leapt unconcerned out of bed, stepping out to light the lamp in the garden next door; this was the signal that I was just about to come out. But I took the time to wash up first and then hurriedly got dressed in my uniform. I'm supposed to grace the airport terminal building pretty early; that's our normal routine, if you must know. On reporting to the flight section, we vanish into the powder room, where we do up our hair. I've got to look after all this quickly and properly. And ever since I'd had my hair cut short, I'd felt all the freer, in so many ways. Especially when on duty, like now.

On the tarmac were men dressed all in white, each holding up his hand and pointing thumb and index finger forward. The right propeller started to turn, regularly as current was fed to it, then more rapidly. The men next extended their middle fingers only, and the left propeller churned to life, slicing through the morning wind off the sea. A few seconds later other members of the ground crew removed the blocks from the wheels of the aircraft and the metal bird was in motion, hurling itself the length of the tarmac in the direction of the takeoff line, obedient to instructions from the control tower.

We began that day's journey with the usual offerings: parti-colored peppermints, aromatic water, sweet diluted coffee with bread and jam or an omelet. The morning papers were always eagerly snatched up, the airline never supplying them in sufficient quantity. Whenever there'd be any critical allusion to this or that shortcoming from the passengers, I'd just show a fine indifference, smiling all the while, of course. What did I care? My higher-ups were busy raking it in on the side and couldn't be bothered to attend to the needs of the public, still less to carry out their duties conscientiously. Most of them, in fact, ought to have handed in their resignations. As for me, I work away at my job, and that's that. I'm not some office type paid just to uphold the firm's good name. I was paid to do my job. That was enough, thank you very much.

The aircraft made straight for Central Java. In the back were just two empty seats. Most of the passengers were civil servants, university lecturers, or military men. There were several Chinese businessmen; no doubt *they* were able to afford the fare. The passenger in the seat next to the empty one seemed somehow familiar to me. He had smiled a lot at me since I'd first taken notice of him. When the work let up a bit, he came over to the galley to address me.

"You wouldn't happen to be from Makassar, would you?"

I'd half a mind to answer without beating about the bush. But all I said was, "What gives you that idea?"

"I've a good friend from there. Kampung Hulu Latimojong."

I studied the man's face intently. Could I have met him before? In my line of work, anything's possible. He might well have been a passenger several times on my plane.

"Who is your friend?"

The passenger told me his friend's name.

"Why, he's my brother!"

When I was little, Johan would often come round, together with my brother's other friends. But he would eat at our house, and sleep over, more often than most. Often he'd lend a helping hand with whatever work Father had given us to do. I was still very young at the time. I didn't really remember what he looked like.

After the meeting that day, Johan would often ring or come round to take me out to dinner. I could hardly refuse an offer like that, especially coming from a friend of the family. And he'd so many stories to tell. He said he often carried me piggyback when I was little. When Father was testing out the motorboat in the river, Johan would be the first to get into it. These were stories which never grew stale, reminding me as they did of my hometown. It wasn't as if I'd go out with Johan only; I'd still go out dancing or to a restaurant with other friends from work quite often. Birthday celebrations almost always finished in the early hours of the morning. But with Johan, going out was always a different experience for me. A few friends dropped broad hints that I was forgetting myself of late, living with my head in the clouds. They poked fun at me or made sly allusions—perhaps I was falling in love. But was that really the case?

Deep down I tried to avoid the knowledge that I just felt close to Johan. Not in love, that's for sure. So why was it my heart started to pound when he gazed at me with his eyes half shut, as if sizing me up? That was the sort of thing that really did it for me. He was well set up, and nice-looking. At the time the way things were, among all of us friends from work, you'd often get a fair bit of touching and caressing, depending on how each of us felt about the matter. There'd be nothing in the least bit strange about our putting our arms round waists or shoulders. But with Johan I could feel something akin to a live ember in my breast when he'd fasten his mouth to my shoulder while we were dancing together. There was a huge difference in age between us. Maybe this is what people meant when they talked of a fully mature man. Could this be the reason I felt so absorbed by him? Or was it because Johan is from the same kampung as I and is familiar with practically everything I love? All the while I turned these things over in my mind, we continued to go out together often. I became bold and willingly received his caresses, his fondling and kisses, which held me fast with their tremendous passion. There was the time he invited me to stay the night at his pied-à-terre, an annex he'd rented for use when in town. Rather fetching it was, crammed with all manner of expensive things which every woman—every wife—dreams of. An icebox, a cooking range and stove, a radio, phonograph records, a wardrobe and rattan chairs charmingly set about with pillows. It was in his house that Johan tried to get me to go to bed with him. It wasn't as if I had to refuse. Relations between men and women in our district were free, the younger generation thought nothing of following their inclinations. And I really wanted the night to be brought to consummation. Yet I said no. The following morning, I even apologized. I really wanted to know what that "event" would feel like—wanted it, in a way that was more like a wild animal's than a woman's. It was that night, I think, that I grew conscious of the fact that I loved Johan and wished us two to become man and wife. This, for me, represented the peak of perfection, for in my mind I was planning out a splendid wedding ceremony in church. I wanted to be dressed all in white, to be surrounded by my family, admired. That's practically every girl's dream. So, by turning him down, I felt I loved him all the more. Johan for his part began to sense my hope; he continued to go out with me and to be my intimate friend. I began to receive promises from him which satisfied my deepest longings, unformed as these were. On several occasions he persisted in trying to have sex with me, but still I turned him down, delicately and full of love.

I awoke the next day in my hotel room.

The plane had been out of commission the night before and couldn't leave for Nusa Tenggara. Passengers and aircrew hung about for a long time at the airfield, until at last word came that the flight had been put off until the next day.

I glanced at the clock on the table. It was still early, so I continued to lie there. My thoughts went inevitably toward Johan—isn't that just like love? You can't tear your thoughts away from the person you love for anything in the world. Was I really going to marry him after all? He wasn't short of money, business doing well. He owned a car. He was saying things in conversation about a house in the country, a place I approved of, over on Jakarta's south side. Supposing Johan weren't well-to-do, would I be in love with him? I dismissed the question: daft!

After breakfasting with two aircrew, I said I was hopping into town to do a bit of shopping. There wasn't anything I wanted particularly to buy, but I was never one for being cooped up in some hotel. Departure was set for five o'clock that day.

The copilot wanted to go into town with me, so we hailed a *becak* and headed off for the shopping precinct. There we popped in and out of the Chinese emporia, stopping at last beside a *warung* and then wandering along the pavement, looking at the things laid out for display in the shop windows.

Suddenly I was stopped dead in my tracks. Through the shop-front plate glass I saw Johan in the store, and with him two little boys. They were absorbed in conversation, gesturing animatedly. They started for the door, and as they came out I heard Johan say, "Father will buy it for you in Jakarta next week; these ones here aren't that good. Come on, get a move on now, Mother's waiting in the car."

Johan took each of them by the hand as they made ready to cross the road.

Then I saw one car among the many other vehicles. As they crossed, I quickly turned my face toward the shop window. "One of our regular passengers," remarked the copilot.

"Where?" I asked, feigning ignorance.

"There, just a second ago, in the Mercedes."

"Do you know him?"

"Oh yes, we often fly together."

"That's his wife?"

"His first wife. Dutch by birth. A real white lady. Good-looking, isn't she?"

I felt myself growing more insensible by the minute. Thick-wittedly, I asked, "His first wife?"

"Yes, the second's Sundanese. You don't mean to say you can't tell! He's from Sulawesi too. Used to be a Christian but converted to Islam, 'cause he wanted to marry again."

I made no rejoinder, nor bothered to ask any further questions. It was glaringly obvious to me now. The only thing was, how had this colleague of mine come to be better acquainted with Johan than I was? I'd known him for the better part of a year, we'd become friends, gone out together, albeit our intimacy was unconsummated.

"Looks as if you know a fair bit about our passengers," I said pointedly.

"Oh, that's just talk among men on the job or at the airfield. Some of my mates are from your district. That gentleman especially, the one who's a frequent flyer with us—now there's a customer for you. Word is, when he goes overseas, he invites the aircrew to some pretty wild nightspots."

Isn't that just typical? The person who's most intimately concerned doesn't even suspect the truth; I'd been blind to this entire business. And I hadn't a clue as to who Johan really was. To be sure, there were plenty of colleagues who came from the same district as myself. But would you know, our conversation didn't once touch on the matter of Johan after that. Was I now supposed to languish and droop, on account of what I'd just learnt? Must I think I'd made a great mistake? I just didn't know. What I did know, and know clearly, was that Johan was not content with having just one woman. He had the means to get what he wanted, women of any sort, from no matter where. And he needed two wives, as his personal property. Two families as well, I shouldn't wonder. Was he planning a family around me? Flattering when you think about it, the first an Indo, the second a Sundanese, maybe a third hailing from the very same kampung as Johan himself! A collection which was hardly likely to end with me. Proving for the umpteenth time the common view that men have it all over women. In affairs of the heart, Johan had made use of religion, moving on from one belief to the other—the point being to do exactly as he pleased.

I'd no wish to make a great tragedy of all this. The thing that's important to me is a person's character. As for my own, it isn't the sort to let me sink into melancholy, or despair, or even anything that might smack of pessimism.

There's a long day ahead still. And with it, perhaps, the chance that I'll find love, and the family life I so crave.

Stop Thief!
(Garong Garong)

by Taufiq Ismail

"Well well well. So you're the gentleman's been broken into, are you?" the income tax official behind the wicket asked, reading through the form that had just been filled out.

" 'Fraid so, *pak,*" the clerk replied.

"And how, may I ask, did that happen?"

"Mmm . . . what do you mean 'how did that happen?' "

"You deaf? I said: how did you come to be broken into?"

"Oh, I see. Well . . ." answered the clerk, a bit doubtful.

The other, reading the form, slurped at his hot tea; in it there floated a jasmine leaf. "Let me see now. If I understand you correctly, your house was broken into by thieves yesterday." The clock said nine A.M. "Someone's TV set you were looking after, fifteen grams of gold jewelry, an electric iron . . . that's the lot then, is it?"

The clerk heard this all right, but his thoughts had wandered back to the notary public's office where he worked. He'd been with them for seven years, and during all that time he'd only once taken two weeks' leave. Today was day two.

". . . nabbed, you say, by thieves armed with pistols, a Sten gun, and a Bren."

The clerk groped round in his pocket for a cigarette. Dead stony broke!

"Now let me see," the tax officer said, eyes traveling down another list. "If you'll give me just a minute. . . . " Up above, the fan whirred lazily round, while he affixed some stamp or other. "That'll be four hundred and fifty rupiahs."

"But, that TV, it was my brother-in-law's. Here, *pak,* I've got the papers to prove it!" said the clerk, fumbling in his back pocket.

"Four hundred and fifty rupiahs," the official curtly said, taking another sip of his jasmine-laced tea.

The clerk forked the money over, whereupon the official bid him sign again; this time it was for the Thieving Tax, down in the lower right-hand corner. "Thanks, *pak,*" the clerk said, bowing deferentially.

"That's the way it goes," was the reply.

In front of the tax office he'd stopped to buy three cigarettes, which cost three ringgit. A big drum boomed rhythmically, *rrp, rrp, rp, rp,* it went. A line of cars patiently waiting stretching out tens of meters back was creeping along behind the parade at a weary snail's pace. Vehicles approaching couldn't drive at speed either, trying as they were to keep to the road. The main artery of the *kapubaten* capital was packed this morning with vegetable trucks, buses crammed with office workers, sedans, heavy vehicles, ambulances, *becaks,* trucks bearing livestock, motorcycles, and jeeps. Bicycles threaded their way amongst the lot.

Pulling on his cigarette, the clerk stood there at the corner surrounded by the crowd of people watching the traffic. Rag-and-bone men, old-age pensioners, the unemployed, street people, beggars, all feasted their eyes on the parade. The marchers in the drum band had formed into platoons replete with trumpets and flutes.

A kid with a sheaf of calendars hanging from his shoulders went by. "What year have you got there?" a potential customer was wanting to know.

"This year, last year, it's all the same, ma'am," the young fellow replied. "Point is, d'you want to buy or don't you?"

The woman looked miffed.

"Mind your language, sonny boy!" chided a pensioner in dark glasses. "Show some respect for your elders."

The drum band was marching on: *rrp, rrp, ram-a-tam-tam.*

"So, what's it to be, *bu.* You buying or not?" the fourteen-and-a-half-year-old kid asked, slipping his wares off his shoulder and exhibiting them one by one in front of everybody.

"If next year's the same as this one's, what's the use of buying last year's calendar?" asked an unemployed guy who was using an umbrella for a cane.

"If this year's the same as the ones past, what's the use of buying next year's?" the *cingcao* peddler put in.

"Yeah, well, the pictures, that's what makes the difference, *pak,*" the kid pointed out, making his pitch. "Last year's different from this year's. Instead of panoramas, now you get these nice paintings. And in color too, *bu.* From overseas. Here, look, see for yourself. Terrific, isn't it? Pinups, too, pretty girls. Lovely stuff!" He was hoping against hope someone would buy.

The drum band played on. Rows of hobnailed boots scraped on the asphalt.

Suddenly, from behind the parade, there came a long whistle. Everyone turned to look. A man ran up at a trot, carrying a stretcher, with some of his mates following on behind; they drew up behind a white ambulance. The platoons bringing up the rear were still busy showing off their skill at marching in formation and turning on a dime, as the trumpeters' and flautists' corps played a *marche militaire.* What with all the fuss, the traffic was now gridlocked. People were standing on the roofs of pickups, sedans, and trucks, on mounds of cauliflower, on bicycle panniers to have a better view. A pasty-faced, heavily pregnant woman was emerging from the back door of the ambulance on a stretcher. Shaking from side to side and weeping tears of pain, she was carried out onto the pavement.

The onlookers emitted high-pitched whistles and clapped their hands for joy. The drum-band majorette, a kid of fourteen in a white uniform with gold braid, flung her baton upward, giving the crowd four twirls, not missing a trick, catching it as it fell to earth.

Two men advanced in front of the stretcher, clearing a path through the crowd on the pavement.

"Make way, make way there for a pregnant lady!"

Her face contorted in agony from labor pains, she squirmed and writhed where she lay. Another man was running along behind.

The drum-band's music corps was playing "Colonel Bogey," little kids shrieking with pleasure and whistling along. Office and shop workers hung out of the windows of the buildings lining the street, looking on gratified at the spectacle.

"What's the occasion?" a pensioner wondered.

"National Children's Day," a clerk replied.

"Oh, quite. Silly me! Smoke?"

"Haaallttt!"

The party of stretcher bearers stopped suddenly behind the man clearing a path through the crowds thronging the pavement.

"Where's the husband?"

No reply. His glance fell upon the chap bringing up the rear.

"Well, actually, I'm—"

"Give us a fag first, mate," the leader demanded in menacing tones.

Stammering with nervousness, his victim turned his pockets inside out, as, brokenly, the woman moaned, "*Aduuu, Aduuu . . . gustiii, gustii!*"

"Ain't got none, *pak,*" he said, in dismay.

"Pay for one, then—cash. Cash. Let's see it first!"

The man extracted three fifty-cent coins. "This do?" he said, adding another, just to be on the safe side.

"That's the way it goes!" said the leader of the stretcher-bearing party, as once more they hoisted the woman aloft.

"Oh God, please God, please . . ." she groaned.

The leader was using the wooden butt of his rifle to beat a path through the people thronging the pavement, crying, "Make way, make way, pregnant lady!"

The spectators bellowed their disappointment as the leader of the majorettes, having twirled her baton upward three times, fumbled it— down it fell, to bounce and roll onto the pavement.

"What's it to be then, Tante?" the fourteen-and-a-half-year-old calendar peddler asked hopefully. "Aren't you buying any?"

"You don't get any takers for these calendars now, my lad," she said. "Nowadays they've got these watches that can tell the date, day of the week, plus the—" She broke off, staring at her empty wrist. "My watch! Where's it gone to? Who's pinched it?"

She cast furtive looks round, eyes popping. Everyone had heard her scream. "Who's pinched it? Watch thieves! Stop thief, I say!"

They all started looking high and low, round the pavement, on the roofs of the jeeps, on the tops of the vegetable trucks, everyone, from the detachment of soldiers to the drummers to the people in the shop and office windows. Everybody who'd been wearing a watch clutched at his or her wrist—every single watch had vanished into thin air.

"Bandits!"

"Thieves!"

All gone! Fobs, table clocks, wall clocks. The clocks on all the clock towers in the city. All the watchsmiths were shut; their workshops had disappeared. All the almanacs gone, calendars vanished, daily diaries blotted out. It was as if everything had petrified, turned into some skeletal tableau. The wind too had dropped.

The fourteen-and-a-half-year-old Calendar Kid was sobbing his heart out: his merchandise, all twenty-three calendars, nine from Japan, had vanished in a twinkling. He was squatting on the pavement, fists pummeling the ground, groaning, "Me living, give it back . . . me future . . . me calendars!"

But then the drum major gave the order to start up, and at once the whole frozen scene sprang to life. Trumpets blared, hobnailed boots scraped along the asphalt, flutes tooted, drums went *rrram-tam-tam, rram-tam-tam-tam*. Batons twirled on high, the Sousa march once more echoing into the void. Traffic, a hungry lizard, crawled forward.

"Sorry, but would you mind telling me what's the occasion?" the pensioner asked, champing on the curved stem of his pipe.

"I've taken two weeks off," the notary public's clerk replied.

"Whatever for?" the black-spectacled old man asked, his eyebrows knit in puzzlement.

"Wouldn't you just know, the first day and what happens, my house gets hit by thieves, and in broad daylight."

"Sort of a Children's Day today, is that it?"

"And this morning, can you beat it, I paid 'only' forty rupiahs thieving tax! 'Only' forty! Hahahah." Standing on the old chap's left, he whispered into his ear, "Ought to have paid more, by rights. Fool of a tax man. Brains in his arse. Fantastic, I tell you. Fan-tastic! Hahahahah."

The clerk doubled up with laughter, quite beside himself; he rolled on the pavement, howling, alongside the kid peddling calendars.

"Should have bought today's paper," the old geezer said to himself, digging away a little in his left ear with his finger, teeth still clamped around his pipe.

"Haalltt!"

The stretcher-bearing party had come to a standstill in the middle of the crowd on the pavement, which had now parted; the woman was jolted forward as the men bearing the stretcher juddered to a stop. Contractions gripped her womb, and, moaning, she cried out to God again.

A man leant against the trunk of a *kenari* tree. He sported a hat made of newsprint, and an empty one-liter butter tin hung from a cord slung around his neck. He felt for the butt of the make-believe pistol at his waist.

"What's the big rush?" he hissed through clenched teeth.

The leader of the group nodded at the stretcher. Paper Hat considered the stretcher and its burden.

"Bun in the oven, have we?"

Taking his own sweet time, he strode confidently round behind the party. "Where's her man then? Where's her License to be Pregnant?"

The man who only a minute ago had been following on behind took fright. "I'm not really—"

"Oh, what the hell," Paper Hat remarked. "It ain't my affair. The point is, though. . . ."

Squatting down on the ground in search of something, the frightened man came upon an empty cartridge casing by the edge of the gutter. Taking out a fifty-rupiah note, he rolled it up very small and stuffed it into the case, which with a clinking sound he put into the tin hanging from Paper Hat's neck.

"Many thanks, *pak,*" the donor said, making a small bow.

"Them's the breaks!" replied Paper Hat. "Right, now beat it!"

And beat it they did, making all speed for the district hospital. Traffic was still creeping forward. The flute squad had moved on to "Cry Out for Joy!" The drum bands were all streaming out toward the parade grounds.

The pensioner was walking along in the direction of an alleyway that branched off the main road of the *kapubaten.* At fifty-seven he moved slowly, feet dragging, back bent. With every tenth step he stopped to take a deep breath. Behind him a row of *kenari* trees lining the pavement, heavy traffic, and the sound of the band playing marching songs.

The sun felt so hot it fried your pate. The pensioner had bought a page of newsprint to use as cover. Turning into a side street in search of shade, he went up the steps of a large building there, setting himself down all agasp in a guest chair on the veranda. After a while his breath began to come more regularly.

The young clerk, having laughed himself silly on the pavement, now lay sleeping face down beside the Calendar Kid. Passersby took care to step round.

The pensioner had started to light his bamboo pipe, having first stuffed its bowl with a fingerful of shag, when from inside the building came the drone of officialdom. Opening the paper he'd just bought, the old man read:

NATIONAL THIEVES POLICY IN NEED OF UPGRADING

QUALITY OF THEFT IN DECLINE: CUSTOMS AND EXCISE

PROPOSED UNITY, UNIFICATION, AND CONCORD AMONGST THIEVES GETS WIDESPREAD SUPPORT!

THEFT OF FOREIGN LOANS TO START SOON

ANTITHEFT RING NABBED RED-HANDED!

Turning to the back pages, he glanced at the adverts on page four:

Need a contraband weapon? Ring 2722404. Everything from Pistols to Anti-Aircraft.

Let us make your day! Learn by correspondence HOW TO BECOME A GARONG WITHOUT REALLY TRYING. We offer:
1. Amateur Theft
2. All-Purpose Theft
3. Military Theft
4. Theft for GOLKAR
5. Spiritual Theft
6. Theft for Students
7. Thieving From Thieves

PUREST SPIRITS CONSULTANCY SERVICE. Offering you expert advice on holdups, extortion, smuggling, highway robbery. We also do blackmail, smuggling, and prostitution. Contact: DPM Advertising. *Sorry*—no go-betweens.

The pensioner drew a breath, long and deep. Whipping off his glasses, he put the *Daily Thief* down on the visitors table.

"Another minor nuisance. No big deal."

The hubbub in the room inside rose.

"Use your head, sir. There's thirty-six of us here. The whole field's being taken over by that lot and you're expecting us to go quietly back to work!"

"Redundancy, oh dear me yes, I'll grant that's a hard nut to crack."

"But you might at least give us a leg up. I mean, what *is* this? Here we are, wanting to meet with the head of manpower allocation, and you say it's no go. Blocked, every way we turn."

"It's not a matter of your being 'blocked.' Head of Manpower's got a lot on his plate."

"For days on end?"

"It's this way, *bung*. When last I spoke to him, Head of Manpower says he's agreeable to you gentlemen taking up your former jobs. That is, until charges are brought against you in court."

"And how are we supposed to do that? Government might at least lay on facilities, equipment. . . ."

From his desk over in a corner of the veranda, the office porter smiled at the pensioner.

"That's some crowd, *pak,* inside there. Been that way since yesterday."

"Who are those guys?"

"Ex-convicts, robbers, purse snatchers, heavies, murderers. You name it, *pak.* Thirty-six of them."

Secretary to head of manpower was to be heard irately pointing out, "Government's agreeable, in principle, to a return to work on your part! And there's an end to it!"

"But *pak!* These guys, they're trying to muscle in."

"That doesn't concern us."

"Facilities, equipment at the very least. On loan, or else on hire."

"*BerDiKari!** Stand on your own two feet! That's what it's all about!"

Traffic along the town's main artery had eased up. The sun hung high in the sky. The drum bands had assembled on the parade grounds. The young clerk and the Calendar Kid were still sprawled face down on the pavement, in the shade of the *kenari* trees. A wedge of sunshine falling through the branches directly above lit up the boy's neck. He opened his eyes a crack and then sat up slowly, rubbing the sleep from them. Spying a cigarette protruding from the clerk's pocket, he grabbed it and lit up, puffing away with pleasure.

He gave the clerk's sleeping form a good shake—and another shake for good measure.

Acronym of "*Berdiri Atas Kaki Sendiri*"—"to stand on our own two feet"— one of former President Sukarno's favorite exhortations in his sloganizing speeches to the masses.

Startled, the clerk sat up too, feeling a bit woozy.

"What year's this?"

"Same as the previous one. And all 'cause they've gone and taken the bread out of me mouth."

The clerk thought this over for a while as he brushed off his shirt and trousers, which were foul with the dirt of the pavement. Then he took out his last cigarette and lit it.

"Could be you're asking the earth for those calendars of yours," he suggested, taking a drag.

"No more than the others. Last year they took the lot as well."

They got up and strolled off.

"You'd be, what, half my age, wouldn't you, and here you are an old hand at smoking."

Here and there the *kenari* leaves rustled and fell, shaken by the wind.

Coming to a building, they turned to go in. The Licensing Authority consisted of wicket upon wicket, all walled in glass. That's where you went if you had to get any sort of license stamped. The two of them went over to the Certificate of Ownership Department, stopping at a counter above which hung a sign reading LICENSE TO HOPE.

The clerical officer stared at them contemptuously.

"Yes?"

"We're, um, we're wanting a form, *pak*."

"Not here. This counter's closed. Been that way for donkey's years. There's a notice over here, by the side. Can't you read?"

They could, and did. Then they went across to a counter in the corner where there were masses of people queuing up, waiting their turn to fill out the form. Overhead a sign read LICENSE TO DREAM. They joined the queue, and a frightfully long queue it was. . . .

The woman's eyes were clamped shut, though she wasn't dreaming. She was struggling to experience to the full the pain of separation. Her lower lips had parted, pushed at by the fiery red creature about to come into existence. She was soaked in sweat, mucus, blood. Her mouth was shut, fists clenching and unclenching. The walls spun round, the floor and ceiling turned upside down. The end of the lamp cord in the middle of the room rose and whirled about, a black dervish. A thousand fireflies flickered in the darkness, turning into blooming flowers of flame. Everywhere you could hear gunfire, explosions dwindling to little tinkling sounds. The shrill of flutes. The tintinnabulation of ear bangles. The clink of metal; creaking hinges; a thousand windows blown open and shut by the wind. The muscles of her buttocks pulsed. Her sinews contracted; it felt like being massaged by fingers full of thorns. The pain came on in the shape of a dragon: black, its head tapered, threatening, with teeth to scare the daylights out of you. The fireflies flickered, going *tink-tink;* her breath came sharp, her hands clasping and unclasping, as the contractions arrived in high waves. They became fiercer by the minute. It was as if some meddling hand had slithered all the way into her womb. Two sharp-nailed fingers squeezed the neck of her uterus, tried to drag it out, contents and all, by main force. Oh how she screamed! A burden was yielding itself up to the pull of gravity. . . .

Eyes shut, the woman in her agony was half dreaming.

"*Aduh* sweet child of mine, *aduh* my sweet, *aduh* . . . " They'd all gathered round on the veranda, *gado-gado* ladies, bewildered *mie bakso* sellers, the hospital's female clerical staff, *delman* drivers, cigarette peddlers. She was no longer conscious of the fact that she was lying flat on a narrow wooden bench, on the veranda of the hospital's maternity ward. She had started to breathe regularly, the pain to subside in small waves. She was smeared with sweat, mucus, blood, and she stank to high heaven. Eyes shut tight, she was half given up to dreaming. The people who were crowding round her had come back from roll call on the parade grounds, bringing her a white bedspread, a cot done up in white, white nappies, a white sash, white powder, a white enamel plate, a white baby's hat, hot milk, white wheat porridge. . . .

Afternoon: silence was dispersing itself into the *kapubaten* capital, the silence of streets, of broiling sunshine, of the waiting room veranda at the hospital maternity ward. The silence of the mosque at noon on a Friday. A light breeze blew, *kenari* leaves rustled, dropping one at a time into the road. The *delman* horses were thoughtfully munching their tapioca mixed with rice bran. Black vultures hang-glided under the broiling sun. Far off, a cow was lowing. Inside the mosque, all was tranquil.

The *khatib*'s voice soared upward; sitting there zonked, the faithful nodded. The sermon was "Be Thou True to Your Own Heart in the First Instance." Seated cross-legged, they were catching forty winks en masse, having mastered the art of sleeping upright, when a tile propped up against a crossbeam fell—the beam gone brittle—*crash!* onto the young clerk's head and shattered to smithereens on the rug.

With a start the clerk awoke. Quickly wiping away a rivulet of saliva from the left corner of his mouth, he gaped at the *khatib,* who, warming to his theme, had now reached Part the Second of his sermon.

Suddenly the clerk jerked forward.

"Allah be praised!" It was none other than the *khatib,* now in full cry, who'd led the thieves that had raided his house yesterday!

He could scarcely believe the sight confronting him.

"So, praise be to Him—"

"Hold it right there!" the clerk cried out.

Waking from their collective snooze, the faithful, every man jack of them, were taken by surprise. This young man, just what did he think he was doing, interrupting the *khatib* like that, and in middle of the sermon too?

Extending a finger in accusation, the clerk rose. "Most honorable *khatib,* yesterday, at this hour precisely, you were busy looting my house, weren't you?"

The place was now well and truly astir.

"Since when does a *khatib* turn to thieving?"

"I daresay it's possible!" was the answer.

"Slanderer!"

"Who *is* this anyway?" the *muezzin* wanted to know.

"You mean he isn't a provincial high court magistrate?" someone shouted.

"A *khatib?* Come on!"

"Or a thief?"

They were all talking at the same time.

"That's no magistrate!" someone else cried out. "That's the public prosecutor, the one that's just been transferred out!"

"Okay, then, a public prosecutor, how does he get to be a *khatib?*"

"Happens all the time!"

"Or a thief?"

"A thief too! There's lots that manage to swing it!"

"*Waaa* . . . " they cried in unison. The mosque was now in pandemonium.

"Hold your horses, *bung!*" someone sympathetic to the *khatib* called out. "A mosque's no place for a showdown."

"That's precisely where we ought to start setting things to rights!"

"He's no public prosecutor!" someone else retorted.

"Who's he supposed to be, then?"

"Bet you anything it's the general who lives near the textile warehouse."

"Since when does a general wind up as a *khatib?*"

"Since always!"

"Or a thief?"

"Why on earth not! I mean, he's only human!"

"But he's got a gun, hasn't he!"

Waaa!

"Now listen, you! Don't you go mixing up religion with politics like that! Politics is a dirty business! This here's a holy place, I'll have you know!" This from one of the *khatib's* supporters.

"I'd have thought a holy mosque's the very place to wash all your dirty linen!" the clerk said.

The worshippers were starting to get to their feet.

"He ain't no public prosecutor, *or* magistrate!"

"Plus he's way too young to be a general!"

"So who in heaven's name *is* he, then?"

"A member of the People's Assembly?"

"Some high-ranking customs officer, I'll wager, living round dockside."

"Fine, then, suppose you tell us how a high-ranking customs officer fetches up as a *khatib.*"

"Or a thief!"

"Why shouldn't he? There's heaps that get rich all of a sudden."

Waaa! Wooo!

"He's a bloody thief, he is!"

The Calendar Kid, who during the whole furor had been sitting under a big ceremonial drum, now grabbed hold of the drum and gave it a gleeful thwack, so that it resounded in time to the shouting.

"You thief!" *Dung, dung-dung dung-dung!*

"You thief!" *Dung dung dung!*

"You thief!" *Dung dung dung!*

The *khatib,* who up till now had held his peace, slowly removed his turban and placed it upside down atop the pulpit. From inside his headgear he produced a pistol, which he pointed right at the young clerk's head.

They all flipped. The Calendar Kid, pissing himself in fear, stopped beating on the drum. Some of the crowd made a dash for the exit, but most weren't that quick off the mark and hit the deck instead. The clerk was crouching down, ears stopped up in sheer fright.

The pistol went off, but the bullets, it turned out, were made of sulphur; kids' stuff.

Leaping to his feet, the clerk went scuttling off after the *khatib,* who, still firing his made-in-Japan popgun, hurdled the windowsill to fall into a Nissan patrol jeep parked in front of the mosque, in which he made his escape. The faithful dashed out into the courtyard, brandishing their fists.

"*Huuu! Huuu! Huuu!* You thief, you. . . . !"

The clerk and the Calendar Kid ran after him until their legs gave out. Then they made their way panting back to the mosque, walking slowly now as the sun began to set in the *kenari* leaves.

The pensioner sighed deeply. "Almost out of pipe tobacco. Shops'll be closed this afternoon. Fat chance of buying any."

"Me, I'm out of fags," the clerk said.

The Calendar Kid was walking along behind, kicking the gravel. Coming to a fence surrounding the primary school, they could hear children singing. They paused to listen.

"May we come in? You'll forgive my asking, but what's the occasion?" queried the pensioner.

"National Children's Day, *pak,*" the Calendar Kid volunteered brightly.

" 'Course it is. Old memory ain't what it used to be."

Inside Hope Street Primary, things were hotting up. A stage stood to the fore, and stands had been set up along the walls; some sort of bazaar seemed to be in progress. Rows of kids in white shorts and socks and black shoes were seated up front, and behind them stood their mums and dads, their teachers, the guests, government officials and their wives. A bevy of flautists was playing "Little Tails," as the children's choir burst into song:

> *Rong Garong Garong Garong*
> My Daddy's now a thief
> Uncle too is now a thief
> All of us kids too, *Hei!*
> *Rong Garong Garong Garong—*

The master of ceremonies, up there at the mike, interrupted with the announcement that the program was about to begin with the bazaar's official opening and would all those present please rise for the National Anthem, sung by the children's chorus of Hope Street Primary. Whereupon, to the accompaniment of the drum-band flute platoon, the choir broke into:

Indonesia, Land of Robbers
My True Homeland stiff with thieves
In the future, I shall plunder
While my *ibu,* she shall seize—"

All at once the song was cut short by a woman's long, heart-rending shriek. Everyone swung round to have a look, asking who on earth was that? She stood at the threshold. Her *kebaya* was worn, the batik ancient. She shambled toward the stage with a shuffling, slightly unsteady gait, clutching to her something wrapped in that *kain* of hers. She skirted the children, the mayor's wife, the general's, the prosecutor's, the judge's, the customs officer's, the lady teachers, their husbands standing all in a row behind. As she went by they all held their noses: phew, what a smell! Did she ever stink of sweat, mucus, blood. On she walked at a crawling pace, ponging of sweat, drops of mucus and blood falling between her feet. Up she climbed onto the stage.

"A very good afternoon to you, sweet little children of mine."

"Good afternoon, miss!" they replied in chorus.

"How well you all sing. Your voices, they're *so* moving. Now, I'm going to ask you some questions. You're all very clever little boys and girls, aren't you?"

"Yes, miss!"

"Well, then, which of you clever little boys and girls knows the meaning of the word '*garong*'?"

Hands in the air to be the first to answer.

"One at a time, please. We'll take it in turns, going from left to right."

"It means Hero-of-Our-Nation, miss."

"It means a Very Nice Person, miss."

"Someone who's a Very Pious Person, miss."

"Someone who Lives a Good Life, miss."

But she cut them short: "That will do, children. That will do. Now listen well, all of you, to what I have to say. Listen closely. The meaning of the word '*garong*' is rob-*ber,* ban-*dit,* van-*dal.* So you see, it doesn't mean a very nice person, now, does it? A *garong*'s a Very Bad Man. When you get to be big, you're not going to be any of these, are you now? So let's have another go, shall we: What's the meaning of *garong?*"

"Rob-*ber.* Ban-*dit.* Van-*dal.* Ba-ad Ma-an."

"*Very good,* children, very very good! So when you grow up you're not going to be *garongs,* are you now?"

"No, we won't, miss," they chorused. "Yaaaeee!"

"*Aduuuh,* what clever, clever little girls and boys you all are. And *so* sweet, too. *Aduuuh,* I'm just dying to have a child as sweet and as clever. A darling little girl, a big strong boy."

One of the members of the Organizing Committee who'd said nothing all along now went up to the woman.

"Whom . . . ahem, exactly who might you be then?"

"Me? Why, a mother. To be precise, someone who ought to have been one but isn't yet."

"You mean. . . ." he countered, mystified.

"That's just what I mean."

"But, how could that have happened, *bu?*"

"Just as you see."

She thrust him aside and stepped down. Exhausted, swaying from side to side and clutching her bundle to her, she moved among the children, who applauded as they let her through. They formed up into a straight line and they filed along after her, not in the least minding the stench, as she cried out, "Sing, my darlings, sing!" And sing they did, stamping their feet:

> Here chicky chicky chicky
> Ten little chicks went out to play
> One popped off and now there were nine. . . .

Several committee members set off in hot pursuit after the column as it trooped off, bent on bringing it to a halt. The children's parents stood fixed to the spot in surprise, likewise the VIPs of the *kapubaten* capital and their wives. Out into the main road and through the courtyard the column wended its way, the children singing at the top of their voices, and at its head, cradling her infant, the unkempt woman in the worn shirt.

"Hold on there! Stop!" screamed the committee.

"Leave them be," the pensioner said.

The young clerk stepped in front of the committee members. "And who might you be, Dad?"

"Just an old pensioner."

The committee members thrust him roughly aside, but the clerk struck one of them on the temple, and he staggered off, as from behind the clerk the Calendar Kid flung stones as big as your head at them, hitting them smack in the belly. Fighting broke out, the other spectators rushing in to defend the committee. The bazaar was in mayhem when Authority showed up, carrying batons and guns. The column, still singing, continuing to wend its merry way. It was getting on toward afternoon.

The fray had now spread to the stage and to the bazaar stands. Everything was topsy-turvy. Down with all Thieves! Plates flew helter-skelter; food was trampled underfoot in the melée. One after another the stands gave way, crushed by people laying about them. Policemen were bawling, "Stop this brawl! Anybody here makes one move and we'll shoot to kill!"

Bang!—shots in the air. But nobody paid the least attention. They just carried on thumping one another, resorting to kicks and pieces of wood when fists gave out, then to using chairs and tables. Stones were flying every which way.

"Crush the Thieves!"

The police and soldiers were at their wits' end, now that the crowd had set about bringing all the stands toppling earthward. "Stop! Stop or we'll shoot!" But the shouting and firing fell on deaf ears.

A big thickset man with a mustache appeared on stage, screaming "Cease fi-i-i-re! Stop it, all of you!" into a megaphone.

The rioting, the shooting, the mayhem stopped at once, though one or two voices yelled out, "Crush the Thieves!" The police commandant grabbed hold of the megaphone.

"Now then, who're these thieves you've all been referring to?"

When the clerk replied sotto voce, he was summoned onstage by the inspector. "Up you get, sir. Best use this megaphone, they'll hear you better," he said, thrusting it at him.

Up onto the stage the latter came, to shriek into the mouthpiece, "Thieves is thieves! The guys covering for them, the ones pretending to say, 'Crush the Thieves!' *And* the ones that take bribes. *And* the ones who *steal* from thieves!"

He fell silent for a moment. The megaphone was taken back by the inspector. "Quite finished, have we, sir?"

The clerk snatched it back. "All those supporting hoarders, black marketeers, sharpers . . . "

"Garoooong!" chimed the bazaar.

"The ones that threaten decent folk with weapons! Smugglers, heavies, toll collectors . . . "

"Thieves as we-e-e-ll."

"The ones greedy for their cut . . . "

"Garoooong!"

"The ones that like to take bribes . . . "

"Thieves, every one of 'em!"

"High office, middle-management, small fry, doesn't make a bleeding bit of difference, they're all a bunch of thieves, every last one of 'em!"

"Right on!" Applause.

Erupting with laughter, the chief inspector grabbed hold of the megaphone, drawing it up close to his mouth as he guffawed, the harsh sound ricocheting round the town's walls.

"To be sure—hohoHO . . . hahaHA—to be sure. Only—" He was laughing so hard he'd started sneezing and coughing, bringing up phlegm and expelling it onto the platform, to cries of "Heeei!"

"Wanna see, do you? Really wanna know, eh? Really and truly? Sure you've got the guts for it?" he rasped into the megaphone. And with that he took off his chief inspector's shirt, service stars and all. Whipping his hat off, he unbuttoned his trousers to reveal smooth black underwear.

"Now then, here's an honest-to-goodness thief for you. The gen-u-*ine* article!"

"Right, who's got the balls? Come on, who's taking me on? You there! You?"

Snatching up a submachine gun from the floor of the stage, he cocked it and pointed it at the clerk's chest. BAM!

The clerk was blown off the stage; he rolled over three times before coming to rest spreadeagled on the ground, where he lay covered in dust and blood.

Instantly the barney resumed. Once more they went nuts brawling, stones flying every which way through the air, sticks, chair covers, kiddies' tables, strewn all about. They fell to tearing down the stands as if possessed, bullets flying all around, cartridge cases littering the school grounds.

Trembling from head to foot, gone white as a sheet, the Calendar Kid came up to the clerk, who lay there, fingers scrabbling at his shattered chest, straining to draw breath. The fracas still in full swing, the pensioner crept up close.

"Crush the Thieves!"

Bang! Bang!

The pair squatted down on the left of the young clerk. Bereft now of the power of speech, he was having difficulty breathing. His face had turned blue, his heart, lungs, innards all smashed to bits. A bit like your dish of tripe soup with blood sauce.

"Apologies, *kak,*" the kid was saying. "It was me who pinched that *kretek* this afternoon. From out of your pocket."

Half conscious as he was, the Clerk could hear nothing. It felt as if his breastbone was being got at by a thousand sawteeth. Eyes narrowed to slits, he made out vague shapes of clouds rolling up and parting. He remembered, was seeing again the woman being violated, whimpering, six men standing by, each awaiting his turn. The first one to get up adjusted his public prosecutor's rig; the magistrate took his place in the queue. Behind stood the MPs, high-ranking customs officials, the chief *khatib,* and, last but not least, the chief inspector of police. Taking it in turns, they made short in-and-out movements, mechanically, devoid of feeling. The woman lay there outstretched like a four-branched trunk of teak. The chief inspector had almost done when she gave a scream, crying out, "I'm Tini!"

The clerk was flabbergasted. Tini? Which Tini? There's Tini my wife, there's my brother-in-law's niece, there's Tini my old school-teacher, and Tini my uncle's wife's sister. *Which* Tini?

His anger boiling, he came up close to seize and pull at the chief inspector's hair, jerking the man to his feet, when, all of a sudden, the latter unsheathed a ceremonial knife and thrust it into the clerk's chest. Oh the pain, the pain! Again and again the single-edged blade plunged into the clerk's chest and belly, seemingly of its own accord. You could hear a baby crying, then a burst of submachine gun fire.

The clouds barreled up and parted. White clouds, gray, brown, red, then blue. Sad songs were wafted on the chill wind, soft songs, cold, sung by a million voices. They spread like drizzling rain across the face of the planet. The clerk tried to move, but his chest hurt so. Blood poured from his mouth and nose. Ever so slowly he opened his eyes to look at the two friends still at his side.

"Apologies, *kak,* it was me what pinched the *kretek* off you this afternoon. Fished it out of your pocket, I did."

The clerk stared at him, no longer able to speak. Blood ran down his cheek the length of your little finger, pooling in the whorls of one ear. His white face was turning blue. He fainted dead away, only to come to again. With what remained of his strength he shut his eyes, hand fumbling round in his trouser pockets, searching for something. Extracting the License to Dream, he handed the paper to the Calendar Kid. Long and wordlessly they looked at each other. The pensioner had nodded off. All at once the kid burst into tears, loud howls; he staggered to his feet and ran away weeping and yowling. The brawling was still far from over. At last the policeman raised his Sten and emptied the magazine, *rat-tat-tat-tat-tat-tat-tat!*

They all froze. The brawling ceased. The procession of kids came to a halt. Everyone stopped dead in their tracks. There was this funny-peculiar feeling in the air. The children crowded round the woman cradling her infant at the head of the line. Suddenly they burst out crying, as, wailing her head off, a little girl of ten in plaits broke away from the swarm and dashed back to the school gates. "Miss there! Her baby, it's dead!" she shrieked, gasping for breath. "And Miss, she's dead too!"

There was, that afternoon, an inert feel to the wind, which blew at ninety degrees. The *kenari* leaves, immobile, made no noise.

"That woman, what's her name?" asked the *bupati.*

"Kartini!" cried the little girl.

Together the children bore the woman's corpse upon their shoulders through the street. A Grade Six pupil had taken charge of the corpse of the dear little boy, his eyes now shut tight. The procession swerved round to the right, moving slowly, heads hanging, sobbing. The deceased woman was being borne on her back, face turned toward the sky striated into tufts of lamb's wool by a sharp wind. She'd been a good-looking woman, nose aquiline, hair long and thick. Sweat, mucus, blood—all were gone; a whiff of perfume rose from her slender form.

The wretched cortege was singing "Kartini Our Mother."

Step by step it made its way westward. The children, having now given over crying, had taken off their shoes and were walking in their white socks, their mums and dads following on behind them, unable to look up. One by one the ladies removed their shoes and flip-flops, throwing them away, their husbands following suit, flinging their own shoes into the gutter. All walked on in bare or stocking feet. A most extraordinarily quiet procession.

Soundlessly it grieved.

Dusk had begun to score its long red lines all around the base of the sky; silence to disperse itself into the town, the silence of the *kenari* trees, of the railway terminus waiting room, of fields of sugarcane, of sheepfolds. Nags yoked to their *delmans* lifted their heads up from feedbags of chopped-up tapioca and rice bran, flicking their tails this way and that. Cows rose from where they were resting, chewing their cud; vultures, *podang* birds, starlings, mynahs, scissors-birds, and swallows sat perching on every telephone wire. Their shadows, long silhouettes, were thrown along the verge of the road.

The procession shuffled along in silence, the mothers dabbing at their eyes every so often, a grade-one pupil wiping away a trail of snot with his shirtsleeve. Dusk had condensed into red stripes, red giving way into sweeps of red and gray. Three sweeps later and behold a sickle moon, in all its platinum glory.

And the Lord God caused the wind to lift out towards the clouds. *Kenari* leaves fluttering down onto the procession, a thousand bats came flapping out of the western sky, and the sun set . . . quietly.

The Kid
(Anak)

---

by Budi Darma

The transport problem's what gets to me, more than anything else. I can't believe how incredibly uncouth the government's been, flinging me here headfirst like this—and this being such a spread-out city—without bothering to give a moment's thought to the question of how you're supposed to get to work.

As was my habit, I was standing that morning under the advertisements for films, most of them obscene. When a new poster turned out to be really lewd, I'd perk up. Fact was, I had it in mind to use these pictures as a starting point for one or two uncouth plans of my own. And that's when the girl I'd been waiting for would turn up, taking up her position in front of the poster—bingo, just like that.

"Bus's taking its own sweet time arriving, isn't it, and here we are not even passing the time of day," I said, quaking inside.

As usual after my opening shot, she'd keep mum. Public transport's a pain in the arse, but it has its advantages. You do get to meet pretty girls like this one here. But since they never open their mouths after I say hello, the situation gets to be even more annoying than before.

"So, where do you work, Miss?"

No reply. Par for the course.

"Where d'you live, actually? You're here every morning waiting for the bus, same as me, only I haven't a clue where your house is."

Not a peep.

None of this came as any surprise. Not what you'd call the talkative type. That's why I had to find some other approach, a less well-mannered one. If the correct way, the polite way, doesn't do the trick, what's wrong with resorting to vulgar tricks? And if that doesn't work, well then, in the last analysis you won't have wasted your time. Something will have been achieved. Okay, you may not have succeeded in provoking a reaction, but at least you'll have spoken your mind. That's one way of getting your kicks. Which is why I simply had to do it.

"Lewd, aren't they?" It felt great to say it. "Those pictures, I mean." I pointed my little finger at a poster showing a naked woman lying on a sandy beach in the arms of a hirsute, half-undressed, well-built man. Imagine me doing that to this lovely bird—that would be something, wouldn't it?

I'd no chance to go on or to work out what she might be thinking from the look on her face, as a bus had suddenly drawn up. As usual it was packed. Another opportunity wasted! The transport problem was a major headache all right, but it paled to insignificance when this plan of mine, to be really crude with her, went into effect. I'd gone to considerable lengths, but she was acting as if I didn't exist.

We were halfway between the front and back doors. Now's your chance! Passionately I made to take hold of the girl's hand to pull her toward the back, where the bus was less crowded. What with the bus's being jam-packed, I'd have the chance to hold her close.

My hand came within inches of hers, but hers was deftly withdrawn. I had another go, only to find her breaking free again. This was no skin off my nose; I was quite used to nothing coming of it when I made a move like this. She'd carry on in this bus and I'd alight to take another. But to fail time and again, that was something I wasn't prepared to put up with—oh no. Absolutely not.

This girl looked perfectly disgusted at my having tried to hold her hand, which must explain why she started quickly moving toward the back. But I wasn't going to throw in the towel just like that. Better to behave badly than to surrender empty-handed. That's why I just plowed on in her wake, pushing up at her behind, fingers working busily.

"You *beast*!" she cried out in indignation.

Everyone turned round to stare at the girl, who was getting more and more het up. I bet it was all the attention she was getting.

"This man's a pervert. He makes a pass at me every day. This time he's really gone too far. Would you believe, he's been goosing me!"

They all roared with laughter, looking at me with undisguised contempt.

"Watch it, pal," the bus conductor said. "Make sure you're grabbing the right girl's fanny!" Leaving me to stand there as the bus went on its way. They were in stitches. I could have died.

The transport problem was bad enough. And now this!

The next day, there she was, at her usual post.

"You there! You made a fool of me yesterday. I think you ought to know that when I touched your bottom it was unintentional. But you, what do you do, you go and scream your head off, to attract attention—that's typical of your sort. You're an easy piece, all right. The bus conductor's got his paws all over you and you just stand there enjoying it."

She held her tongue. No reaction, none whatsoever. I felt driven to insult her, out of sheer pique.

"Who'd want a feel off you anyway? You look like the back of a barn. Nobody except the bus conductor would want to do that on purpose. And don't tell me you don't love it!"

I was just getting into my stride when the bus approached, packed as always to the gills, and of course they were the regular passengers, same as yesterday. Quite a few of them were looking at me with smiles of contempt.

Watch it, pal, when you're making a pass—that's what the bus conductor had said yesterday, his own hands holding the girl tight. And would you believe, today too the bus just shot past, leaving me standing there. Rude! As if getting around the city wasn't bad to begin with. Being humiliated in public's the very last thing I need.

The following day the film posters were more shocking than ever. It must have been deeply unnerving to many passers-by to see them. However, no use making a fuss, is there? There's no stopping the powers that be doing what they like. I was flabbergasted to see the girl turn up again. But though normally she didn't give a toss about what was going on round her, this time her attention seemed caught and held by the dirty pictures in blowup. Was I wrong, or did I detect the ghost of a smile? For what seemed like an age she scrutinized the crude display. I watched her, saying nothing.

I was reminded of no one so much as my wife, when she was still a young thing and I was courting her. She was very stuck-up, even, on occasion, positively insulting. She rarely troubled to conceal her annoyance, so that I was often embarrassed by her. When at last she said she'd be mine, a faint smile could be seen playing about her lips, the very smile which was now just barely discernible on the face of the girl staring intently at the dirty posters.

The same goes for my landlord's missus, at the place where I'm putting up. She was a tiger, from the word go. She'd often make me lose my cool in front of her house girl. And then the telltale sign: the ghost of a smile played on the landlady's lips. Starting then and continuing since, she's been leading me on. Which was why I didn't for a moment regret having shifted to Jakarta. My wife may have been far away—household matters meant she had to stay put—but I didn't care, I was free to have my way with my landlord's wife, albeit occasionally. That's why I'd no complaints about my living arrangements. It was transport that was proving a nuisance.

The girl was looking more blissful by the minute. That ghostly smile of hers had started to etch itself on her features. She couldn't take her eyes off the posters. It looked like they really turned her on.

That's when I became aware that she was getting her own back on me. So I said, "That's odd. Normally you don't pay any attention to these posters. But when they turn out to be as dirty as this one, you really sit up and take notice."

She pretended not to hear. She just continued to gaze at the poster with that half smile of hers. Everything about her was was getting my goat. "Isn't that just like the disgusting creature you really are," I went on. "I touch you—by accident, mind—and what happens? I get called all sorts of names. But when it comes to that bus conductor there, the guy lays his hands on you on purpose, and what do you do? Why, you just sit back and let him do it. Ordinary smut's no big deal for you, but as for the really dirty ones, *that's* when you sit up and pay attention, isn't it now? You don't fool me. Go on, admit it, you're feeling randy now, aren't you? That poster, it's making you feel fruity, isn't it? You disgust me! You think I'm keen to pester you, is that what you and your loverboy conductor think? Well, let me tell you something, I'm a married man, and my wife's a real looker—not like you!"

Quite unfazed, she turned her gaze on me. I felt myself caught in a searchlight beam. It traveled the length of my body, sweeping from head to toe and stopping at my mouth. A look that meant business. Heaven knows why, but I colored up with embarrassment. I hadn't the guts to meet her eyes. My own stayed fixed on the ground. Her voice, when she spoke, compelled attention.

"You dirty little man. Look at me—if you've got the guts, that is."

But I hadn't. I just kept my eyes on the ground. I could feel myself tremble under her gaze, and my teeth started to chatter.

"You filthy-minded little creep," she went on, "you really haven't the guts to look at me, have you? Looks like I was dead right. You like to turn your back on people, that's your attitude, isn't it? Well, if you haven't the guts to look me in the face, let's see if you've got the guts to answer me this: how can you have the heart to fool around with a married woman? Your landlord's a good egg, he helps you 'cause he feels sorry for you, you not having a place of your own. He's very good to you. Let me tell you, he feels really sorry for you because you've been married all this time and still haven't got any children. And you take up with his wife! Typical!"

I just stood there, gawping.

That night I couldn't sleep a wink. The landlord was his usual self, ditto his wife. As I said, she had this tendency to lead me on. But I couldn't get it up for my landlady, not one bit. The girl's words had really struck home; I couldn't get her off my mind.

She was smashing to look at, no doubt about it. Even if she hadn't been, it wouldn't have mattered, but since she was, I was drawn to her all the more strongly. Not quite twenty-five, and with that willowy body—I was hooked! How on earth she'd come to know about my affair with my landlord's missus I haven't the faintest. And as to how she knew about my being childless, your guess is as good as mine.

God alone knows why, but the following morning I felt so ill I couldn't have lifted a finger to flag the bus down. Could it have been on account of my not having slept a wink the previous night? But that couldn't be it; even without sleep I can usually go at it from nine to five without feeling the worse for wear. Could it have been what the girl said, coupled with her whole demeanor, which had had this oppressive effect on me? Her knowing all about my having cuckolded on a man who was helping me, and that I was childless, that must have been it. As for her rejecting my offer to have some fun, that could hardly have been the reason. A lot of other women had turned down the same offer and I hadn't fallen ill as a result. Be that as it may, the point was I was sick now.

Mercifully I managed to get some shuteye.

Waking, I received the shock of my life: who should be standing right next to my bed but someone bearing an uncanny resemblance to the girl I encountered at the bus stop each morning. "Isowandi," she said. "You'll be asking yourself what I'm doing here."

I said nothing. I just let my eyes, which I could feel grow round as saucers, rove all over her body and linger on her tummy and breasts.

"Isowandi," she went on, "you're surprised, aren't you, to find me nine months' pregnant."

Her tummy was distended all right, breasts swollen, ripe fruit ready to burst.

"When we met yesterday I was my normal self, now we meet again. ... Think of it, we've known each other for one day, no more than that, and now here I am nine months gone. You listen well: if you can't acknowledge other people's kindness you can at least show some consideration for that faithful wife of yours. Take a few days off and go visit her in Tegal tomorrow morning. Now go back to sleep and don't worry."

My mother-in-law's house seemed besieged by people. True enough, I didn't have a home of my own; after I'd married, I'd lodged here with her, my wife remaining once I had moved to Jakarta.

A whole lot of people were crowding round the place, pushing and shoving. I saw the village headman, a neighbor of ours, busy with crowd control. He was standing by the high wall yelling out orders in an attempt to get them all to settle down.

"Well, strike me dead! Look who's here," he said, catching sight of me. "It's Mas Isowandi."

Everyone turned to stare. Then the headman rushed forward to greet me, and everyone else streamed round me in a great mass. They had eyes for nothing and no one else.

The headman extended his hand; uncomprehendingly I took it.

"Well, I'll be damned!" he said.

More and more people were swarming round, trying to get close to me.

"Why?" I asked in amazement.

"Come on and see your wife!" he said, taking my arm.

The crowd scattered as we sauntered off together toward the house. The headman ordered those who remained on my mother-in-law's doorstep away and me inside, banging the door shut so that no one could follow us.

Inside, the furnishings were exactly as they'd been three months ago, when I'd left this house to move to Jakarta; everything in its proper place. Only the atmosphere had changed. My heart began to pound in my chest, the more so as we approached the door of an inner room.

When I entered, the occupants couldn't believe their eyes. My father-in-law and mother-in-law, my nephew, all looked at me questioningly and with extraordinary animosity.

"So you've decided to show your face after all, and us in this state!" said my wife, half crying.

"Just look at this!" said my father-in-law. He was pointing accusingly at a baby, and as he did so, the creature started to yelp, to struggle.

"This here's yours," my mother-in-law said.

"Can't be. I left home only three months ago, and my wife wasn't pregnant."

"It's not Daimah's, that's for sure, but it's yours all right. Can't you tell? Just look at its features!"

As I looked, it stopped its fearful row. My mother-in-law asked the headman and the nephew to leave the room. I couldn't take my eyes off the kid. He was my spitting image. There was no denying it was mine. But how to explain it?

"Now do you believe it?" my mother-in-law asked. What could I say?

It was my wife's turn. "What have you to say for yourself, *mas?* You've been screwing around in Jakarta, haven't you?"

So that was it. I was being accused of knocking up a girl a few months before I'd been transferred to Jakarta. But that couldn't be. When I have a bit on the side, it's always out of town, miles from where I live. And for the past nine months I'd been on my best behavior—well, okay, that's not *quite* true, five months ago there'd been Tamjis's wife, in Brebes. But she couldn't possibly have given birth to a child in that six-month period. It defied reason.

"I think you ought to know," my wife said, "that a girl came round here the other day. Good-looking, a bit on the tall side, shortish hair gleaming black. She had clear, saffron-colored skin and two dimples in her cheeks when she laughed. Very attractive, actually. She said she'd come from Jakarta and that you would be coming here shortly."

You could have knocked me down with a feather. The girl she'd just described was none other than the one I'd waited with at the bus stop, under those posters. But how, *how* had she managed to come all the way out here?

"Who was she?" I faltered.

"She wasn't saying. But she said you'd know her anywhere."

"What did she want?"

"To give birth to this baby—your child!"

Rubbish! I haven't had any affair in Jakarta, I said, lying through my teeth, the fact being that I'd had it off with the wife of my ever-helpful landlord. If I had an affair with this woman, where could she have given birth? I've been there now three months already, just you remember that!

They seemed every bit as surprised as I was.

"Well, maybe she's some woman you propositioned earlier someplace, long before you moved to Jakarta," my mother-in-law said accusingly.

"But I don't know anyone like the girl Daimah's just described."

"She said she was from Jakarta and she'd happened to meet my husband there. It sounded like she was telling the truth." This from my wife, half in defense of me.

"All right," I said. "It's true. I did make her acquaintance in passing; we met while waiting for the bus. But it was only once or twice. Right, now suppose *you* tell *me* what's been going on."

No one said anything, for a long time.

"She came here especially to give birth to the child," my wife volunteered at last. "Said she felt sorry for us, what with us having been married for so long and no children. She offered to give us her child, only. . . . "

"Only what?"

"It's a girl, isn't it," my mother-in-law declared.

I fondled the baby. It gurgled.

"So it is," I said.

"Every child brings good fortune, but the prospects are best with a girl."

I nodded, but this produced no response, so I asked, "Where's she gone to, anyway? Where's the mother now?"

The atmosphere underwent a sudden change. From being bloody-minded they went all fearful.

"Shut your mouth!" my mother-in-law roared.

Daimah glared at her. She went off, but not before telling the neighbors that the baby would grow up to be a whore!

My mother-in-law's face went red. "And all because of you, *you, you beast!*" she yelled, her voice rising to a shriek.

My courage surged back at the sound of these deeply wounding words. Hitherto I'd been reluctant to talk back, what with her being my mother-in-law and all, and my elder, and because she'd done me a good turn in the past. But not anymore—I was overcome by the urge to rub her nose in it.

"Daimah's been a good wife. She's been true to me, I'll say that for her. But it's time you realized that she was no blushing virgin when we got married!"

There was no chance of my taking more leave from work. But in the short time I'd been back, my neighbors' reaction had made an indelible impression on me.

As I passed Joni Marsini's house, some kids in their teens danced on ahead of me, yelling jeeringly, Dirty old man! Dirty old man! Wife's not a virgin, mother-in-law's an ex-whore, kid's gonna be one too!

Frankly I couldn't have cared less whether this was the gospel truth or a pack of lies. But where my wife and I were concerned, they were dead right. Everyone thought I'd taken my mother-in-law's scolding to heart, and went round saying so later, whereas in fact I didn't give two figs for her opinion.

Several kids came trailing behind, screaming their heads off too— Here comes the son-in-law, the ex-pimp!

You won't find me screwing around these days, not anymore. And I'm bringing the child up without the slightest doubt that whatever she grows up to be, she'll be a call girl over my dead body!

The Wallet
(Dompet)

by Putu Wijaya

The movie had ended but Kasno remained glued to his seat as the filmgoers streamed out toward the exit. It was as if he'd been bitten by a snake. "A zombie running wild in New York, threatening the world. A zombie stands for disaster: illness, war, hatred, terrorism, political conflict, corruption, you name it," he muttered to himself, seeing again the images that had poured from the silver screen and sloshed over him for almost an hour and a half.

When finally he got up to go, two or three people were still standing at the door, as the attendants started to pick up the soda bottles and paper wrappings. Kasno moved as if in a dream. "Not a great film, really, but I managed to get something out of the story of that living corpse. Must mean the old brain-box is working okay!"

Making his way along the row of seats, he happened to look down; there seemed to be a wallet lying on the floor. Black, a real beaut. Kasno quickly picked the thing up, at the same time reconnoitering the chamber. Just supposing this thing here should fall into the clutches of one of the attendants; ten to one the owner would never get it back again.

Kasno hadn't the guts to open the wallet. He just held it in his hand in full public view and sauntered out. He was a bit reluctant to hand it over to the management, as there was no guarantee that the thing would then be returned to its rightful owner.

Wallet in hand he stood at the door, but there were so many people

113

there that no one took a blind bit of notice. Kasno nonetheless hung about for a bit. He watched two men stooping down outside, then coming into the building and going out again. He held out the wallet, but neither of them paid him the least attention. They continued to stoop down, peering at the pavement.

When they came back inside he followed them into the auditorium. The two walked around it, appearing to search for something. They stopped to chat with the commissionaires, who shook their heads sadly. Kasno drew nigh, extending the wallet. But though they saw him, all right, they didn't bat an eyelash, just carried on searching.

"Looking for something, are you? Lose something?"

The two men stared in surprise as Kasno held out the wallet. Looking startled, then panic-stricken, they smiled nervously, shook their heads, and beat it.

"What were they looking for?" Kasno asked a commissionaire. The man mumbled something. "Looking for a wallet, were they?"

The attendant made no reply. He picked up an empty bottle and left. Wallet still in hand, Kasno returned to the exit. Spectators keen to enter stood there, poised to go in. Kasno continued to draw attention to the wallet, mingling with the people, expecting to come across its owner in short order. But strangely enough no one took any notice of him. A young woman even seemed to smile and whisper nervously. Maybe she thought he'd a screw loose!

Kasno began to get riled. He'd all but made up his mind to make for the manager's room when several people collided with him all at once. Reeling back, he dropped the wallet. He was bending down to retrieve it when a dainty hand suddenly snatched it up.

Kasno looked up. There, dead in front of him, stood a lovely lady, a slim young man, and a couple of what looked like big shots. Kasno was confused. But he made as if he hadn't hit upon the owner of the wallet straightaway. That important people like these could stoop to deceit didn't seem possible to him.

"Can't be too careful," said the young woman.

"What's it doing here then?" said the young man.

The fourth man went straight into the movie theater. Then Kasno inquired whether he'd really handed the wallet back to its rightful owner.

"I don't need thanking, or anything like it. But at the very least there's bound to be an ID card or some other personal document in a wallet. Lose that and you're dead meat," he said, hesitantly.

He went outside and had a *kretek,* deciding to revert to his original decision, which was to assume that, if these people were not the wallet's true owners—which didn't seem likely—certainly they would return it to its rightful owner, as requested on the Population Registration Card contained therein. The fourth man had been well-dressed and reeked of scent; impossible to think of him being driven to pinch some measly wallet.

Kasno left for home, trying not to dwell on the matter. Stopping at Cikini to buy a vegetable *martabak* for his wife, he met up with a friend of his from work. They went to a *warung* at Tegal, where Kasno recounted the story.

"Without so much as your asking whether they were the actual owners?"

Kasno blinked once or twice. "Yeah, without my asking!"

His friend shook his head. "You're the bloody limit, you are!"

"Well, I did wonder if I ought to have asked them whether it was really theirs," Kasno said apologetically.

"Not only should you have asked them, but you should have looked to see if the photo on the Poulation Registration Card was any of those men."

"But how was I to know whether it was his card that was in the wallet?"

"Had to be. And suppose there was a check in it, or cash, and the owner is searching high and low for it. Then what?"

"Sure, lots of people could point an accusing finger at me," Kasno said defensively, " 'cause almost all of them saw me taking that wallet. Damn it all!" He sat there lost in thought.

His friend then changed the subject to what was going on at the office, but deep down inside Kasno was having none of it. He kept thinking about that wallet. Black, a bit on the thick side. Containing a hundred rupiah at the least, supposing there was money in it to begin with. Might be revealing documents in it, too.

By the time he reached home, the *martabak* had gone stone cold. The wife was in filthy temper.

"Stopped somewhere first on the way home, I'll bet," she said.

Kasno made no reply. He sat there stupidly, *wallet, wallet, wallet* running through his thoughts even as his wife served up dinner.

"Wallet," he said, in a soft mellifluous voice.

His wife started.

"Wallet? What wallet?"

Kasno just shook his head. His wife, jeering at him, nagging, was shoveling *martabak* into her mouth. For one thing, she was cross because he hadn't invited her to come and see the film with him. And then the *martabak* he'd brought her had gone cold.

And thirdly, Kasno had come back late. Fourth, she had just had words with the house girl. Fifth, she still had a headache. Sixth, her child hadn't come home the livelong day. Seventh, her monthly allowance was running short, by the look of it. Eighth . . .

Kasno tried to stop up his ears. His thoughts were soldered to that wallet.

In his head he saw the woman who'd picked up the wallet in the cinema opening it, and giggling; then he left the building ever so quietly. Son of a bitch! Kasno said, inwardly.

"Just help me to find a new place to hide that wallet I put in your trousers, will you?" said his wife.

Kasno stared at her, taken aback. "What wallet?"

Mouth still crammed with *martabak,* his wife repeated what she'd just said.

"Agus has been asking for money, so I hid this wallet in your trouser pocket. Help me find somewhere to put it."

Kasno leapt up, mouth agape, thoughts awhirl. Putting two and two together, he quickly reached his conclusion; with no further thought he ran out. His wife just stood there, flummoxed.

He took a taxi back to the cinema, his heart pounding in his chest. He waited around for a bit, but soon lost patience. On the strength of some excuses dreamed up on the spot, he managed to get inside, where he walked about looking everyone up and down, searching for the man who'd taken the wallet but drawing a complete blank.

But he was not daunted. He stood in front of the door, watching the audience exit, waiting for the very last filmgoer to leave. Then he went off to the parking lot, where he again checked everyone out. But this was weird! He never met up with the man, saw no sign of him.

The cinema lights had been dimmed. Kasno stood dumbfounded, stunned, remorseful, and apprehensive. His wife would hit the ceiling when she found out. With a heavy heart he tried to go back inside to touch base with the commissionaires. He pleaded to be allowed in, saying he'd left his wallet behind. A good thing that the commissionaire was kindhearted and gave him permission. But though he searched the entire floor of the building, the wallet was nowhere to be found.

Exhausted and in despair, Kasno trudged out. He stopped in the parking lot to smoke a cigarette. His thoughts were in a tizzy. He couldn't for the life of him fathom how a wallet could possibly have fallen out of his pocket. Surely he would have checked to see that it was there in the first place.

"I'm always acting like a fool. Screwing things up. Low IQ, cursed by fate," he muttered to himself angrily, swearing under his breath.

The attendant went ahem, and Kasno realized that he would come under suspicion were he to stand there any longer. Brokenhearted, he started off in search of a *bajaj,* but hardly had he taken a few steps when he was brought up short. There was something on the pavement—a wallet. Crazy! A wallet. Looking this way and that, Kasno quickly put his foot down on it. The attendant came up to him, asking whether he was looking for a vehicle. Kasno shook his head.

"If you are, which car would it be?" the man asked, pointing to a vehicle standing by itself in the midst of the parking lot.

Kasno shook his head. He squatted down casually, quickly cramming the wallet into his bag. Then he offered a cigarette to the attendant and beat a hasty retreat.

Whistling to himself, Kasno hopped abroad a *bajaj.* He managed a stopover in Cikini, where he bought a *martabak* which was well and truly hot. But sad to say, on his return home he found that his wife had gone to bed.

Placing the wallet at the head of the bed, he stretched out beside his wife. But just as he was about to drop off, his wife rolled over and began to shake him repeatedly.

"What's the matter?"

She put her mouth close to his ear and whispered, "You're so careless, it's amazing! That wallet with money in it was in the trousers that had to be washed. A good thing I found it, and in the nick of time too. I'd have given you what for if you'd gone and lost it."

Kasno once again was floored. "Wallet? What wallet? I've got it, here. Isn't this it?"

He reached for the newly discovered wallet. But his wife had turned over and gone back to sleep again. He was flabbergasted. He weighed the wallet thoughtfully in his hand—he'd half a mind to open it. But he bore in mind what his friend had said: pick something up in the middle of the street and there's the devil to pay. Better to throw it away. *Much* better.

After bethinking himself thus for a little while, Kasno got up. Opening the window, he flung the wallet out into the street, watching it wing its way downward. It was as if he'd rid himself of his misfortune. But to calm his nerves he still needed to swig down a glass of cold water. This done, he got back in bed and was out like a light.

But the next morning as he went out the door on his way to work, there on the ground was the wallet, awaiting him, so to speak. There was nobody standing by watching. Nobody to pick it up. Curiouser and curiouser! Kasno stood looking down at it, shaking his head. At last he kicked it into the middle of the road, hopped into a *bajaj*, and was off.

Coming home from the office at lunchtime, Kasno stopped short several meters from his doorstep, checking to see whether the wallet was knocking around in the street. He went forward gingerly, shooting glances left and right. People began to give him funny looks.

"Lose something?" asked a neighbor.

But Kasno just grinned in embarrassment.

He breathed easy on gaining the fence around his house. Yes, no doubt about it, the wallet must have been picked up by one of those guys who go around collecting cigarette butts. But as he went inside pursuing these thoughts, a neighbor suddenly turned up accompanied by his child. He extended his hand, and in it was the wallet.

"Excuse me," he said, pulling the boy's ear, "this might belong to you. Just your luck that Adi here's been at it again."

Somehow or other Kasno managed to take the wallet. His mouth opened but not a sound came out. It was all he could do to nod his head in total astonishment. How the hell could that wallet have made its way back into his hands? No sooner had his neighbor taken his leave then he felt himself overtaken by disaster. It was beginning to look for all the world as if this wallet had a mind of its own. At that moment, and quite by chance, he happened upon a *bakso* seller. "You wouldn't want a wallet, would you?" he called out to him, holding the thing in his outstretched hand.

The *bakso* man was nonplussed.

"Like a wallet?" said Kasno, walking up to him. The *bakso* man went all pale, staring at it like a thief who's been caught red-handed.

"Oh please, sir, I didn't do it on purpose!" he said in a panic. And in a considerable state, he carried on pushing forward his wares. Kasno grew more and more astonished. His hands were damp with perspiration. At that point his wife appeared at the door. Hastily he shoved his the wallet into his pocket.

Kasno's thoughts were on anything but the soup his wife had specially prepared for his lunch. His head felt as if it were tucked well away in his pocket, with the wallet. But then a couple of problems which his wife brought to his attention served to make him forget about it. He got through the whole night without thinking about it, and was O.K. well into the following morning. He only recalled the wallet at the office, when he was about to order the messenger boy out to buy peppermints.

All of a sudden Kasno found himself shuddering with fear from tip to toe. He held out the wallet to the messenger boy.

"You, uh, you wouldn't fancy a wallet, would you?" he asked, his voice trembling.

The messenger to whom he'd made the offer only smiled wanly. He had no wish to touch the wallet. Laughing, he went off.

"Hey, want a wallet?" Kasno asked one of his mates at the far end of the table.

The latter shook his head indifferently.

"Like a wallet?" he asked the office secretary.

But the woman only curled her lip coquettishly.

Kasno picked up the telephone receiver. He dialed A-1 and spoke to the Director. "Afternoon, sir," he said.

The Director answered in icy tones.

"It's like this, sir," Kasno said. "I don't suppose you'd, uh, want a wallet, would you?"

"*What* did you say?" the Director asked, his voice suddenly turning rather harsh.

Kasno realized he'd gone too far. "Terribly sorry, sir, seems I've got the wrong number. I do beg your pardon, sir. It was Pak Mitro I was after. So sorry again. . . . "

He hung up in an uncertain frame of mind, still holding the wallet. Sweat bedewed his whole body. He felt as if calamity were impending. He could hardly wait for lunch break. On the stroke of twelve he went straight down into the street. In a tone of voice meant to persuade, he hailed a secondhand-goods peddler on the pavement. "Want this?" he asked, extending the wallet.

The merchant looked the wretched thing over carefully. He glanced to the left and to the right, shaking his head.

Kasno too looked left and right. He saw a police officer approaching. But what connection could there possibly be between the police and the wallet?

"Go on, take it," he urged the merchant.

The merchant shook his head without taking his nose out of his copy of the daily *Pos Kota.* "You don't have to buy it. Just take it!" Kasno said, harshly.

The merchant lifted his eyes, gazing at Kasno in astonishment. Kasno didn't hang about a second longer. He left the wallet lying on top of some other goods and took himself off.

He felt as if he'd just broken free of a tiger's embrace. To savor to the full the sense of being at ease, he bought a coconut drink at a stand beside a gas pump and downed it in one go. Then he polished off a *ketoprak,* a favorite of his since he was a kid. Still ten minutes to go. Near the cinema he had a smoke, and then, whistling to himself, he returned to the office.

Seeing that he had to pass by the sidewalk merchant, he crossed over to the other side of the road, doing his level best not to attract attention, but peering at him all the while out of the corner of his eye. The wallet, by the look of it, was no longer among the merchant's goods. The man appeared to be absorbed in reading his newspaper. But when Kasno attempted to steal another glance at him, the man quite by chance lowered his paper. They gazed at each other intently. The merchant nodded, pointing in the direction of Kasno's office. Kasno nodded back, quickly walking on.

Arriving back at his table, Kasno reeled back in fright—there was the wallet, lying on it. Why, this was nothing but an attempt to frighten the wits out of him! He could no longer contain his feelings, his thoughts, the whole shebang. For several minutes he stood there in bewilderment.

As he did so, the janitor piped up. "This must be yours, boss. It was brought here just a moment ago by the merchant across the road. He said that you'd lost it. . . . "

Kasno didn't hear the rest of his explanation; he stared goggle-eyed at the wallet, exploding with rage. Heart, chest, insides, all felt as if they had been blasted to pieces.

At last he seized the wallet with a lightning gesture, teeth chattering. Then he did an about-face and scuttled back through the office, running toward the exit door, along the pavement, headed for the crossroads, gripping the wallet, holding it at arm's length, winding up, then flinging it into the middle of the intersection.

It soared through the air like a torn sail—not, perhaps, a very good way of describing it, but that's what it looked like to the crowd of children who were on their way home from school. They saw something go fluttering through the air, something flung for no obvious reason. Something that might have been theirs. They shrieked for joy. One kid, oblivious to his surroundings, ran out ahead of his mates into the middle of the road to pick it up.

Kasno had reverted to the stage of feeling as though he'd been bitten by a snake. He saw the cars, the kids—and the wallet. Of their own accord his feet went forward one after the other, launching him out into the street, where he saved the kids from being struck by the snouts of the passing vehicles. He kicked out at them. Then everything went black.

When he opened his eyes again there in front of him stood his father, who had died some ten years earlier. "Why have you done away with yourself, Kasno?" his father asked.

Kasno heaved a long sigh. "There was no other way, Dad."

"But why? All because of a wallet?"

Kasno drew another long breath. "This was different, Dad. In your day people killed themselves out of shame at being unable to preserve their honor. But in mine, they do it on account of a wallet or a skewer of *sate*."

His father shook his head.

"Why're you shaking your head, Dad?" Kasno asked him.

"Sorry, Kasno. I've grown old. Can't keep my head straight any more. Just got to keep shaking it. . . . "

The Weirdo
(Eksentrik)

by Asnelly Luthan

She had this reputation of being one hell of a weird lady: hot-tempered, ill-favored. She had an imagination the like of which you never saw in your life, so that the curses and obscenities flung her way seemed altogether appropriate. She'd pick up the gossip, catch the queer looks coming her way. Not that any of this had managed to throw a spanner into the works, wherever she might happen to be working. People would put up with her with a sort of nervousness, a feeling that was hard to put into words. But of late her conduct, her whole way of comporting herself, was really *too* much. Every one of her colleagues, both male and female, felt themselves threatened by catastrophe on her account. She *would* go on, sixteen to the dozen. About death.

To talk about it, for her, was a bit like getting a young girl to talk about her nervousness as she'd wait round on a Saturday night for her boyfriend to turn up. Her eyes would take on this glazed look, testifying mutely to the force of her longing. You know how the bridegroom's heart goes thump-thump in his chest on his wedding night? And how hopeful and apprehensive a woman is when she's about to give birth? *That's* what it was like. Her face would be radiant, like some office girl's in the run-up to payday. Like some managing director full of piss and vinegar. Like anything you'd care to imagine that's full of hope for the future.

If this craving of hers for death, this relishing of it, could be taken as read at any given moment, it wasn't something worth noting down. Nevertheless she would go on about it all, bringing up the subject with this incredible fervor and never mind whom she'd happen to be talking to. She didn't give a fig whether people thought it worth listening or not. She'd get straight to the point.

There'd be this group of people sitting around or just talking, and she'd come over and without even asking sit right down and start off: "Death, it's something that—" but she'd scarcely got going when everyone would start to plead pressing engagements elsewhere, leaving her sitting there.

Left high and dry like that, she'd grouse to herself. "Strange. Did I say something wrong? It's only a story about death. Why shouldn't they want to hear it? I mean, I ask you, what's so odd, what's so scary about death? Either something happens, or something doesn't happen, you're suffocated and your body goes stiff as a board. Some folk'll be sad, others won't; it's all one and the same. The stiff corpse's laid out in the middle of the room—or left lying any old where covered up with a *kain*. You get people trying to do things for it. It gets washed, wrapped in a white *kain,* prayed over, then buried. So what's the big deal? Simple as ABC! Uhh, and what do you lot do, you run off. . . . " Saying which, she'd get up and stride over to her desk.

She'd come into the room and the clerical staff would hop to it. Fingers would fly across the keyboard, books would be taken down and put back. Anything to keep occupied. Anything so as to keep her from catching your eye.

Funny thing was, nobody was willing to pass up the chance to observe her smallest movement. They couldn't tear their eyes away, try though they might to appear preoccupied with other matters.

She'd sit herself down and open up a portfolio, examining its contents. Flipping through several typed pages, she would suddenly take on the look of someone struck dumb with fear. Her face would go all red, she'd smile wanly. Symptoms such as this spelled trouble and would be noted alike by friends and by office staff sitting in front of or alongside her. She'd look like it was all she could do not to give the friend beside her a nudge. But said friend would be wise to this soon enough and, wrinkling her brow, would open an encyclopedia. The woman, as a result, would keep her thoughts strictly to herself. "So this too is death. There's no getting away from it," she'd fall to muttering to herself at last. If the friend sitting next to her wasn't pretending to pore over the encyclopedia, she'd almost certainly say, "Look, get a load of this! Here's a lovely little sentence if ever there was one: who knows how long it's been lying in wait for me. It's taken me by surprise. How can I refuse, I just haven't got it in me to say no to it; no chance even to get a word in edgeways. Its such a *nifty,* such a *clever* little sentence, it's been lying in wait there for quite some time now, ready to strike in its own special way. Extraordinary! Okay, I'm hooked. I give in!"

And nobody's said one word about death, she'd think to herself.

One fine day a meeting had been in progress at the firm, for directors and department heads only. The typists, the letter openers, the sweepers especially took no part; just as well, since they much preferred talking up a storm to settling to their work. They were in no great rush to be in on the proceedings. Instead, they formed into little groups, chewing over the latest fashions. Minah's lover boy, who'd just bought a car; Titi's daughter, the one that had given birth again; Badron, who always made a beeline for the baked goods whenever there'd be a meeting—these were the hot topics. Which is how the Weirdo came to find herself seated at her table all on her own. Her mouth was busy with a cigarette and there was no disguising the fact that she'd given herself up to woolgathering, to fantasizing away to her heart's content—fantasy being her favorite way of stopping herself from talking about anything to do with death.

Already there were several butts in the ashtray. Suddenly she rose; looking straight ahead, she marched over to one of the groups. Its members suddenly stopped talking and pouted at the floor. They really clammed up when Weirdo sat down and opened fire with, "There's another way to deal with death. We—"

"Oh, go and put a sock in it, will you! We're not interested in any of your chitchat. God, you're tiresome!" said a member of the group without further ado. The others kept still as mice, shooting looks at Weirdo which said *get the hell out, why don't you?*

"Okay, have it your way!" She rose and made for another group.

"What are your thoughts about death by—"

"Shut the fuck up! And get the hell out of here. We happen to be discussing perfumes and overtime pay, not dying."

"You mean to say, you don't want to talk about death, or even to hear stories about it?"

"You can say that again!"

With a shrug, the woman had turned to leave. She'd hardly taken a few steps when she spotted the sweeper, whom she didn't know from Adam. Not to put too fine a point on it, she didn't give a damn what his name was. She did her best to make conversation, the better to find out what was the biggest headache sweepers had to deal with. What did it *feel* like, this being assigned to sweep up day in and day out? All those times he'd be sweeping up, which was the whole point of the job, but didn't he perhaps want to be doing it on a cooperative basis? And what about other characteristics of the world people like him lived in? To all of which the man's reply was "Yes, that's spot on!" or "Yes, on occasion." Or words or noises to that effect.

"You can talk all you like, but when you die, those things you've set your heart on, what's going to become of them *then,* eh?" This was for starters. Slowly but convincingly she mounted her assault. But no sooner had she settled back to listen to the man's reply than before she knew what had happened, he'd done a flit. "Hey, why's he run off?" she asked.

She couldn't see who her next target might be; the place had emptied. All those who only a minute ago had foregathered there were gone. Flummoxed by this, she was summoned—by another sweeper— to enter the conference room where the directors meeting was taking place. She went in calmly enough, giving the place the once-over before taking a seat at the invitation of none other than the Managing Director himself.

"Now then. What's all this I hear about you kicking up a fuss in the office?" he asked. He looked like someone who wasn't inclined to beat about the bush.

"You must be joking, sir," she answered him straight back, but with nary a trace of mimicry. "Fuss? What sort of fuss?"

"Just take a look round. This meeting's been interrupted. They've all been complaining to me about your raising cain, and at the drop of a hat, too."

"Who, me? At the drop of a hat?"

"Don't come the raw prawn with me. Is it or is it not you that's been busting up our talks, you and your eternal carry-on about death. If you want to be pushing up daisies, that's fine, be my guest. Just as long as you don't drag us down along with you. You—"

"Oh, about death is it?" the plaintiff interrupted the Director. She'd lost patience with him, fearsome figure though he was. "Right! Now, isn't death something very—"

"That will do!" the director roared, and the woman fell silent. "Don't you *ever* bring that up again, d'you hear? Not inside these four walls!"

"The point is, sir, we just don't want to hear another word from her. Not another single word," somebody butted in, in strangled tones and half weeping. The Weirdo glanced at him, aghast. She was bowled over. She'd not thought, never in all her born days, that any words of hers could strike as deep as all that. Not where any of the other office staff were concerned.

"Oh I *am* sorry. Please don't start crying. I didn't mean it! Really I didn't," she said slowly. She sounded sincere enough. She was to blame, she felt.

"That's enough now," said the Managing Director. He was a commanding presence, respected by all and sundry. "Look, you don't *have* to talk about death and dying, next time. I mean, what's the good of it, eh? When your time's up, it's up. No sense rattling on about it like you do."

"Right you are, sir. But there's something you ought to know—I just can't help myself! The fact that we've got to die when our time comes, that's what *pleases* me. That's what makes me go on so," she said serenely.

"But we're not prepared to put up with listening to it. It sickens us, it gives us the creeps," put in someone from amongst those who'd been "affected."

"But that's just it, you see!" was her handy retort. "If something sickens and frightens you, does that mean you've got to avoid it? Especially when it's there, and when your turn's going to come."

"But, we don't *want* to hear, and *that's* the point. We don't want you bugging us with those stories of yours, which you're deliberately trying to get us to listen to. You're just looking for a chance to off-load these irrational and mad complaints of yours."

"Irrational, did you say? Since when does death make any sense? Where's it say death's illegal? Or that it doesn't make any sense, like you said just now, sir?"

This debate, which no one was much keen on, looked liked hotting up. The Managing Director, right hand massaging his brow, was starting to get confused.

"Now look . . . "

"Just give her the boot will you, *pak!*" someone volunteered before he could get a word in edgeways. The Weirdo shot the speaker a quick glance, smiling as she did so.

"We'll sort this thing out later. Now let's get back to our work," the Managing Director said, the very words seeming to stick fast in his throat. "Director, heads of department, we'll continue next week."

On the way out she got funny looks from everyone. If it weren't for the fact that ganging up on someone at work was a no-no, they'd have overwhelmed this woman with their superior numbers. She was bad news.

"People don't want to talk about death, now why's that, I wonder," she kept asking, directing her question at anyone who happened to be walking by. No one would make any reply; all gave her the widest possible berth. Go take a running jump, that was the general attitude.

There was one occasion when the woman had been given a grilling by senior management. What the blazes did she think she was doing, going on so frankly about death and everything? She'd better clam up. Her talk was creating one hell of a stir. And if she couldn't, well then, she'd have to go, wouldn't she?!

"I can't stop talking to them about death and all its difficulties. *And* I don't want to get the sack," she said, nothing daunted and looking the managing director straight in the eye. "If that's what happens in the end, I'll go on shouting it from the rooftops."

He was not, for the first time, nonplussed. He shook his head repeatedly: this was going nowhere fast. All that had happened was that this weirdo of a woman had made her case. The point being, so long as she was seen as a bearer of bad tidings, production, far from seizing up, would actually increase, though she'd be the first to admit that this was no thanks to her nattering.

She turned out to be right. Time passed, no notice of redundancy arrived. And on she'd go. On and on and on about death. And at the most critical moments, mind you. References to dying would crop up, wouldn't you just know, in every second sentence. Now that she had started distributing leaflets, she'd really gone into overdrive. Odd, wasn't it—especially when they weren't about your last moments on earth?

Face bright with anticipation, she'd leave them lying round on every desk, for all the world as if nothing had happened between her and her colleagues. They wouldn't touch them with a barge pole. They'd just look at them, showing every sign that they were bursting with questions. Everyone had gone home, the office was empty, and no one had so much as laid a finger on the leaflets. They lay exactly where she'd put them.

When the sweeper turned up to do the cleaning, paper that had been scattered all about or thought to be scrap was put in the wastepaper bin, as per usual. Ditto these papers. He'd a shrewd idea, nonetheless, that they were from the woman everyone in the office just loved to hate. So he stopped short, picking up one of the leaflets with mixed feelings. Scanning it, he found that his misgivings were well-founded:

> On one occasion, I found myself looking at my own corpse. Nothing strange about that. Nothing to be frightened of. Certainly nothing abominable there. And yet, there was something not quite right about the corpse I was looking at. What I mean is, it wasn't your ideal corpse. Would *you* call ideal a corpse all of whose joints and limbs has been scattered every which way, or incorrectly placed? As to quite why this body of mine—which up till now had felt whole to me—should now have been dismantled, as it seemed, and so suddenly, I couldn't for the life of me say. I saw how busy people were, tending to the bits of my body. Once everything to do with my corpse that needed doing had been seen to, somebody invited me to have a talk; he was wanting to know what was to be done with this corpse of mine. It being my own, I said in all honesty that it wasn't for me to say, was it? It all depended on people other than its owner. At that point, as I watched my body being taken to pieces and examined for signs of decay, I came to. Just one of those things. A moment, if you will, of utter happiness. Ever since, I've got to thinking, to feeling, to talking about, and to keeping company with death. I started to think, you know, maybe death isn't something to be afraid of. Maybe it isn't something you're supposed to avoid, or even something you need to hash over. And why might that be, I hear you ask? Simple. Death in actual fact isn't something you'd want to keep at arm's length from Life. It's a positive pleasure. Really you want to be yearning for it. You want proof, do you? According to you gentlemen, so far as you ladies and gents know or may have heard, has anyone ever come back from the dead? There you are! *I've* never heard of such a thing. What more do you want as proof positive that death's a pleasure and really rather seductive? The essentials of death, the underlying rationale, the way leading to it, they all repay careful study. What are we waiting for then?

"Ha ha HAHAHAH"—this was the sweeper, laughing fit to bust, as she wound up.

The following morning someone else had signed up to make a song and a dance about death, dying, the whole shebang. That must have been what she'd been hoping might happen, at the very least. And sure enough, early in the morning, before work started, the place was abuzz with rumor. On the door was displayed a large poster which read COME ON, LET'S DO IT! It was signed *the sweeper.*

Without further ado the office staff started casting round in search of the instigator. Who was the culprit? Who was responsible for this infection? It was getting to be contagious! But the Weirdo just sat there calmly enough when charged and found against, as it were; and this for the millionth time. She couldn't be bothered to rebut the charge that the sweeper had acted as he did thanks to her and all those saws and sayings of hers about death. "Anyway," she replied, as the entire office sat arrayed in judgment over her, "what's wrong if something you honestly and truly believe in starts to convince someone else as well?"

"Just what on earth d'you think you're doing, by inviting all of us to cop it together?" said one of those present. "None of us want any part of it. I mean, we're not dead yet are we? Fight's not over yet!"

"But don't you think death's a sort of comfort? Or do you think that before we die we don't have to struggle for death itself?"

That set the cat among the pigeons, and not for the first time. They wanted more than anything else to spit right in her face. Once again the meeting was getting nowhere fast. This woman, who they'd been saying only recently was off her rocker, was still jabbering on about death, with the office staff not prepared even to give her the time of day. What she'd suspected might happen had indeed come to pass.

But that was at the office: what about at home? Was that how she behaved there? That's what they wanted to know. That was the big question.

Having figured out that she'd have already reached home, that's where they headed, stealthily. They slipped up close, peering through vents, through any available aperture. What they saw made their eyeballs start from their sockets. Two hours later and their hips were threatening to crack, their eyes starting to feel swollen and their feet to come unstuck from their bodies. To be honest, the odd goings-on they'd rather been hoping would take shape didn't look like doing so. Except that on the walls of the woman's house, measuring two and a half by three meters, hung all these sentences, all these words having to do with death, dying, the afterlife: PASSED PEACEFULLY AWAY. CALLED HOME. GONE TO GLORY. CLOSED ONE'S EYES FOR ETERNITY. SNUFFED IT. KICKED THE BUCKET. Et cetera.

This is what they saw. Having hung up her jacket, the woman opened her clothes in front of the mirror, inspecting her body and her facial features closely in the glass. She pursed her lips and blinked. Then, she lay down, smoking. She seemed to be reading—more precisely, to be enjoying the sentences mounted on the wall. Every so often she got up to tread on piles of paper and books scattered about on the floor. She switched on the radio, listening, mouth grimly set, to an announcement about a missing child. "Hmm, some kid gone missing. Still there isn't much that can go missing now, is there?" Then she switched off the radio. She seemed confused, as if she were on the verge of doing something but had changed her mind. She went over to the window.

"All right, you can come in now. Must be tiring, staying outside like you guys have been doing. Come on then." Opening wide the window.

This was the last thing on earth they'd been expecting. Our scarlet pimpernels simpered with embarrassment. Their urge to clap eyes on something out of the ordinary had finally been satisfied. Casting sheepish looks at one another, they stepped right in.

"Care for a drink?" asked the lady of the house.

"Thanks but no thanks," one of the would-be spies replied.

Things were getting very awkward, very confusing. Not a few of them were adjusting their seats, moving their heads about, cracking their knuckles. The others murmured polite comments, but they rang false, the words sticking in their throats, dying stillborn on their tongues. One fairly pretty girl was lightly polishing her fingernails.

"So tell me," the lady of the house began, doing her best to be hospitable, or at the very least to dispel the stiff atmosphere, "how's it with the hubby and wife and kids? Everybody well?"

"Fine," they answered in near unison. "Very well indeed."

"That's a relief."

"Indeed it's—"

"And as we're sitting here chatting"—the guests now growing restless—"what do you ladies and gentlemen think of the kid that's just gone missing? D'you share my view?"

"Hard to say," they replied in one voice.

"Ooo . . . "

Nervous tittering followed.

"Child's gone missing. So what else is new? All the same, you know that—"

"If you'll excuse us now—"

"All the same, this going missing, it can happen without your actually vanishing. I'm surprised, actually; I myself often go missing from myself. If you ask me, I think that when we go missing from ourselves, *that's* when we need to have it reported. It's no joke, you know, finding the person who can locate you and fetch you back. That's so, isn't it? I mean, you could be walking along the highway for instance. Or you've met up with a neighbor, say you've dropped in at a shirt factory or what have you, and hey presto, you're lost. Vanished. Bingo! It *can* happen, can't it?"

"Look, it's getting late, if you'll be so kind as to excuse us—"

"Sometimes you don't actually mean it to happen. But, without knowing why, what was there to start with's gone. You *can* well and truly pop off, can't you? There you are! That's death all over."

"For God's sake, stop it, will you! Look, we really must be off." You couldn't ignore the woman's chatter any longer. It was getting wilder by the minute.

"Stop what, eh? I've only just begun. Anyhow, if you've had enough, why not stay a while anyway? But go if you must. It's no skin off my nose."

The guests trooped off, all together. Left now to her own devices, she went indoors and stomped on the books and papers. "Pi-i-igs, ma-a-ngy dogs, wretches, scoundrels, *huk! . . . huuk!*" she screamed, and flopped down onto the faded and disordered sofa, heaving huge sobs.

O Lord, she longed to say, You tell me, however am I to know Thee? But a sense of profound shame supervened. She seemed to lack strength, to be unable to overcome obstacles. That was her tragedy. She felt she just *had* to give form to these stories of hers about dying, even though they might have been just that, stories and no more. Even though they might be stories her colleagues might not best pleased to hear. The tragedy was that God Himself, so she felt, had given her the go-ahead to behave as she did.

The following day, and the day after that, she carried on distributing her leaflets, talking a blue streak. It was a question of death, death, death—nothing else.

Bored with it all by now, everyone regarded her as the unhappy victim of childhood misfortune and of adult grief—this in addition to her being not quite right in the head. And this made them feel entitled to turn her into a plaything. They'd grab her by the ear and pull her hair. Her shoes would be stashed away so that they couldn't be found unless it was by the sweeper, who'd been so sympathetic and helped that daft campaign of hers. Their jeers followed her about everywhere. They'd go after her, right into the Ladies, interfering with her bottom. Up her nose they'd shove fingers which stunk from having been thrust inside her.

And as for her? She thought it was all one big joke—*they* weren't to blame. "Perhaps they want to be friends. They don't want to give me the cold shoulder," she said, doing her best to cheer herself up, though she'd often take refuge in that congenital tendency of hers mentioned earlier in this woman's tale: copious shedding of tears.

If you looked at the whole business in terms of the mayhem she'd brought about, leaving aside for the moment the direct consequences for herself, you could be forgiven for thinking she warranted being given the boot or being given notice. But no such thing ever happened. Management was at a loss to find a watertight excuse for doing so, other than all that nonsense about death that she'd been bandying about. If elections had been held for model employee, the one best at seeing to things, best at discharging his or her allotted responsibilities, she'd have come out tops, no doubt about it. Management it seems had gone over the good and the not-so-good with a fine tooth comb. She might fall into the latter category, but the Managing Director was of the view that this was insufficient reason to give her her marching orders.

"You've got to have someone like that on the premises. Why not just let her bang on about death until she packs it in herself?" And that settled it.

She's still every inch the Weirdo. But it's the sweeper who's cottoned on to the meaning of death and dying, all that stuff she blathers on about so.

Battling With Buffalo
(Bertarung Dengan Banteng)

by F. Rahardi

The clock had just struck a quarter past midnight when Umar Salim woke to find his body drenched in sweat. If memory served, he'd fallen asleep round about ten o'clock, a sleep that had been anything but sound. Mischievous dreams had disturbed it. He glanced over at his wife, who lay sleeping by his side. No sense waking her. Softly, softly, he tucked her up and left the bedroom, donning sandals outside the door. The mother of all thirsts had him by the throat. He shucked off his sandals as he approached the kitchen, where he got a jug of cold water from the icebox. He filled a glass and gulped it down in one go. Then he went into the parlor, switching the light on, and sat himself down to recall the dream he'd just had.

He'd found himself, it had transpired, in the middle of God alone knew where. The setup was not unlike some bustling town. Quite without warning, from out of all the bustle emerged a herd of buffaloes, looking terribly fierce; they ran after him as if pursuing a matador. Black as the ace of spades they were, with horns of jet. He had summoned up every ounce of strength he possessed, wanting to run for dear life to save himself from the buffaloes' stampede, but in vain—his feet felt rooted to the ground, so difficult was it proving to shift them. Umar Salim looked round to find that the buffaloes were closing in. He screamed at the top of his voice, but not a soul seemed willing to come to his aid. People, just looked on, chuckling. "Ill-mannered brutes!" he said to himself. "Just wait, when your turn comes to be chased by these buffaloes you'll know what it feels like!"

But these creatures were after him and him alone—all those people, they just sauntered by. A good job Umar Salim was in the habit of waking up at set times. And now here he was on the sofa, turning it all over in his mind. He reached for the packet of cigarettes lying on the table and shook one loose. "Crazy. Funny the things you imagine when you dream," he said to himself, to cheer himself up. He put the cigarette between his lips, set flame to it with a flick of his gas lighter, and took a deep drag. "No point losing your cool."

But inside, he'd lost it all right. You see, this was the third time he'd dreamt this particular dream. The first two times he'd also found himself pursued by buffaloes. But the street in which the event took place, the whole location differed to a degree. And in these first two dreams, the buffaloes weren't actually out to get him. All they did was snort, lower their horns, and paw the dusty earth. This latest nightmare had been the last straw. When his wife awoke and came in to find him on the sofa, Umar Salim lost no time recounting it to her. He didn't mince words.

"That's nothing out of the ordinary, *pak,*" his wife said calmly enough. "It's what you must expect if you don't sleep well."

"But this is the third time it's happened. Same dream," Umar Salim said defensively. "The third time, mind you! I mean, it's *got* to signify something. At the very least, it can't be just any old dream." His wife was willing to go along with this.

This outburst over and done with, the good woman took him back to bed, where with infinite patience she caressed her dreamer of a husband to get him to fall asleep. In fact that afternoon Umar Salim was to have attended a wedding reception organized by one of his employees. But what with him feeling out of sorts and all, he'd remained cooped up in his room all day. His wife, along with one of their children, stood in for him at the reception; a driver ferried them there. Umar Salim had fallen asleep with the twenty-four-inch TV set on, in the middle of the evening news; no problems there, he'd managed to get some shut-eye. And when his wife and child returned he managed to sleep right through. They hadn't the heart to rouse him. But getting on for two in the morning he awoke panting, his whole body dripping with sweat. As he'd jolted up in bed his wife too had awakened. She sat up looking startled and frightened.

"*Pak,* what on earth's the matter, you feeling sick or something?" she asked anxiously.

"No, it's nothing. Really."

"Why are you looking ill then? You *are* ill, aren't you?"

"No I'm not. Give over, will you? Nothing's wrong, I tell you. How was the party?" Umar Salim asked, changing the subject. His wife, not budging, just sat there massaging her husband's foot.

"Everyone was there. They asked about you."

"Thank goodness for that. Enough with the massaging, go back to sleep."

"But you're not ill, are you? How come it looked like you were? I'd rub some *minyak angin* in if I were you. Or do you want to take some medicine?"

"Just bring me a glass of cold water. Honestly it's nothing."

His wife climbed out of bed. Umar Salim leaned back against the heap of pillows. He was breathing more regularly now. When his wife returned with the glass of cold water, he drank it down greedily. His wife then stretched out beside him as Umar Salim began to describe what had taken place.

"It's happened again, love."

"Not that dream?"

"Too right. The one where I'm being chased by buffaloes. Right up to the office. Nuts, isn't it?"

"And then what happened?"

"The people at the office, they let me be chased by those blasted animals. They just stood by and made fun of me. And who am I supposed to be, after all? Their boss, that's who! I tell you, *bu,* I could have sunk into the ground!"

"Well anyway, it's just a dream isn't it, *pak.*"

"But this is the fourth time! I'd better go see a *dukun,* or a doctor. Or what d'you call him? A psychologist."

"Oh for heaven's sake, *pak,* why bother? You're far better off having a good workout just before going to bed, so that you'll sleep better and not be hassled by some old nightmare."

"Fine then. Starting tomorrow I'm going to go in for tennis more often. But I'll make sure they all know all about my difficulty down at the office. Should be interesting to see the reaction."

That afternoon, after a working lunch with the whole staff in attendance, Umar Salim recounted this business of his dream to all and sundry. The last thing on earth he'd expected was that his employees and secretarial staff should fall about, listening to him.

"Oh, you're a clever one, you are, sir," one of his secretaries said. "You sure know how to have us rolling in the aisles, that you do!"

Being managing director and all, Umar Salim felt rather hurt. But he kept his pique in check. "What makes you think I'm joking? What are you lot laughing for?"

"Sorry sir," another secretary said, a bit apprehensively. "It's just that we thought you were wanting to lighten things up a bit and stop us from nodding off."

"But I tell you this dream was for real—and it's the fourth time I've had it!"

"The fourth, sir?"

"You heard me."

"And each time you say that it's to do with buffaloes chasing you all over the place, sir?"

"Bright boy. But last night, I dreamt they were chasing me right up to this office. You lot were all here. And what do you think you did? Do you think you helped me get out of those buffaloes' way? Did you at the very least run for your own lives? Course you didn't! You just stood by and laughed yourselves silly. I ask you!"

They exchanged uneasy glances, muttering under their breath.

"And now, when I'm telling you this, what do you do? You go and laugh at me! What do you call that, eh?"

No response. Not a soul dared offer an opinion, for fear of incriminating himself. Not a soul dared look the managing director in the eye. The employees, the secretarial staff, everyone who'd come along to the meeting, they were all giving thought to the matter. They all felt bad about their behavior; they'd managed to make a laughingstock of the boss, who'd just been recounting his nightmare, poor devil.

"That will do. Don't look at me as if it's somebody's funeral," he said, breaking the silence. "I was just asking for your opinion as to the best way of confronting these mischievous dreams. Any of you have any ideas?"

"You'd better take a complete rest from work, sir. Could be you're just fagged out." Thus spake the head of marketing in tremulous tones. The others began to pluck up the courage to put in their two cents' worth.

"Better start getting more exercise, sir. Sport gets full government support, doesn't it, sir. You know what they say, 'Sports for the Community and the Community for Sports.' "

"That's just PR. Been doing it from way back, haven't I? Playing tennis."

"That you have, sir. But before it may have been only once a week—now it's got to be three times. Or with a bit of luck every day. You wanted our advice, sir; now you've got it."

"I've got an even better idea, sir. You could take up jogging."

"Can't stand the early morning air. Makes me feel sick to my stomach when it hits me. Anyhow, what's this connection between dreaming and sports? My wife's made the same suggestion, I'll have you know."

"Good for the circulation, sir. Soothes tense nerves. You'll be able to sleep well, with hardly any mischievous dreams to bother you."

"Okay then. Starting today I'm going to play tennis every morning and afternoon. After all, the people closest to me, my wife and my colleagues here at the office, they've all offered the same advice. I'd be daft not to take it."

Umar Salim was 100 percent convinced that the advice his wife and the members of his staff offered had a basis in scientific truth. So up he'd get every morning to play tennis before having his bath and breakfast. In the afternoon, coming home from work, he'd stop by again at the tennis courts. They were dead right. Once he started playing he felt himself to be in far better shape physically than he'd ever been. At night he'd be out like a light and would sleep like a log, whereas he always used to be up till the small hours and had been troubled by unruly dreams; the upshot nowadays was that he slept soundly from night till morn.

Trouble was, he'd still be visited by those nightmares about buffaloes chasing him down. And whereas before the beasts had seemed a bit hazy, these days they emerged with eerie clarity. Black buffaloes, necks rising up toward their spines, black horns poised to rip his buttocks or belly to shreds, their sharp tips glistening. Snorting, eyes wild, they charged toward him, and him running helter-skelter, in cold terror. True enough, in these dreams, intermittent as they were, none of the beasts had managed to tear him to shreds. And whenever the dream scene shifted, back he'd go to sleep. These days Umar Salim was never up nights, following such an ordeal, but the morning after would always be sheer torture.

"You know, *pak*, I'll bet you anything you wear red pajamas to bed, or a red kimono, or a red sarong," his tennis partner said one morning out on the courts.

"What are you talking about?" was Umar's unequivocal reply. "Never wear red at all."

"How about a red bedspread? Or a red pillowcase perhaps? Buffaloes at the very least don't like the color red."

"You've got a point there, I suppose. Sometimes our bedspread or pillowslip *is* red."

"Well, that's probably what's at the bottom of it all, *pak*."

Arrived home that very morning from the tennis court, Umar Salim straightaway summoned his wife. She'd been certain he'd be wanting some water, or breakfast, or a towel. Fat chance of that. In a resolute voice he instructed her to change the bedspread, pillowcase, curtain, plus anything else in their room that was red—and to be quick about it too. His wife nearly fell through the floor but didn't dare refuse her husband outright. That day everything red was carted off from Umar Salim's bedroom; that night he climbed into bed feeling victorious. The wife and kids were still out. Some of them were watching video, others listening to music, still others meeting their pals. Where the rest were the devil alone knew. Umar Salim conked out. But no sooner was he snoring comfortably away than he spotted those damn buffaloes, oh yes he did, from the corner of his eye. Straightaway they started their snorting, lowering their heads and pointing their curving, gleaming horns menacingly in his direction. They looked like creatures from hell. He tried to run for it but simply couldn't. With every ounce of his strength he opened his mouth to scream but no sound emerged.

Suddenly his wife and kids woke him up, shaking him this way and that. "Not another dream, *pak?*"

"You can say that again."

"Chased again by buffaloes, were you?"

"How'd you guess."

"And here we've gone and got rid of everything red."

"God only knows!"

The following night, toward dawn, Umar Salim fell to dreaming once again. This time there were wounds on the buffaloes' neck from which blood poured in gouts. They came up close to him, horns swaying back and forth, oddly enough, though their necks bore these marks of having been hacked about.

Ever since he'd been having this strange dream of his, Umar Salim had been prey to unholy urges. He'd give his right arm to clap eyes on a real live buffalo.

"But surely you've seen one in a zoo, *pak?*" his wife said.

"In a zoo, yes. But not the kind living in the jungle."

"You be careful or else you'll wind up well and truly gored."

"That's impossible."

"But they're wild, aren't they?"

"Yes, but when you see them it's at a distance, after all."

Umar Salim conveyed this wish of his to his staff. They nodded sagely, completely in agreement with their boss.

"If you want to know, sir," someone said, "I've also gone to the trouble of consulting a friend who just happens to be a psychologist."

"Have you now? And what was your friend's diagnosis?"

"He said, sir, that if you were to see a pair of buffaloes in the wild and with your very own eyes, then these crazy dreams of yours would cease automatically of their own accord."

"Just for the hell of it, sir," another staff member said, "I went and asked a *dukun*. I can vouch for his expertise."

"Indeed? And what did this *dukun* of yours have to say?"

"He said that your dreams will vanish if and when you taste buffalo meat."

" I see. So I'm supposed to eat the flesh of buffaloes and see them in the wild, am I?"

" 'Fraid so, sir. That's about the size of it."

"And how, may I ask, is this to be done?"

"The thing to do, sir, is to catch 'em in pairs, if you can manage. Just as long as you can afford to pay for their capture."

"That's great, just great. But there's just one small problem, isn't there. I mean, buffaloes are an endangered species, aren't they, and it's no joke capturing them in the wild. Getting there is no picnic either."

"Don't you worry, sir, it'll all be taken care of. Leave the minor details to us. The great thing is, your peace of mind shouldn't be disturbed anymore. Result: you'll be able to get on with the business, and all of us here won't be left swinging in the wind."

A lovely morning: the car barreling along on a quiet, tree-lined road. Umar Salim and several of his staff had set out for Ujung Kulon. Someone at first had suggested making for Pangandaran, in the Tasikmalaya region, or for Baluran in West Java. But the chances of coming across any buffaloes in either place were rather slim. Someone else had proposed that Umar Salim just go have himself a bit of a holiday in Bali, where he'd see the local sort of cows and get to eat dishes prepared from their flesh. The kind of cows you got on Bali were the same shape and size as buffaloes, weren't they? Umar Salim dismissed this proposal hotly. It wasn't *cows* like the kind you get in Bali that were running him down in his dreams, it was buffaloes, damn it! So it stood to reason that what he needed to see and to eat was buffaloes, not cows like the ones on bloody old Bali. The car hastened on toward Labuhan.

There in that poky town overlooking the Straits of Sunda, all had been prepared. At the offices of the Central Provincial Administration, Umar Salim's people tried to bribe their way past the officers in charge, but nothing doing. The officers stood their ground. So far as they were concerned, you could see buffalo, no problem, but slaughter them for food? No way. Save when special permission was granted. Which was only at specific times, when the buffalo herd needed to be culled.

"Fine then," Umar Salim said to his men. "The main thing is to get there. Should be plain sailing afterward."

In this hole of a place Umar Salim's party bought rice and other provisions. Word was, there was no trade store out there in the jungles of Ujung Kulon.

Chartering a motorboat, they arrived at Pulau Peucang, where they were met with a friendly enough welcome from the local forest ranger. They were given a place to sleep in the *pasanggrahan,* plus cooking fuel. Umar Salim said they should stop farting around and head straight for buffaloes, that very night, but this was given the thumbs-down by the unit responsible for looking after the forest.

"Out of the question, *pak.* For one thing, it's dangerous, leaving at night. There are still lots of savage beasts out there. And for another, it's no joke trying to sight those buffaloes. You *do* want to see buffaloes, sir, don't you?"

"Provided they can be caught and killed."

"Well, there's a bit of a problem there, sir. Actually, *pak,* we can't allow it."

"'Course you can. How much are you asking? Just say the word. The crucial thing is for me to be able to capture one such beast and slaughter it. That's the crucial thing."

"Can't be done, *pak*. Not without permission from Bogor."

"Oh, for heaven's sake, don't make such a song and a dance about it."

"We're dead serious, *pak*. It's out of the question. If all you're wanting to do is get a sighting, then please come back tomorrow."

The following morning they made the crossing from Pulau Peucang to Ujung Kulon and followed a footpath a short distance into the jungle where they happened upon an open field.

"This is where they graze, *pak*," said one of the accompanying officials.

"Where they graze? So these buffaloes, they're domesticated are they?"

"That's just a manner of speaking, *pak*. I mean, come on, they're wild."

There was a beacon to one side of the field. Under it, standing off in the distance, a group of buffaloes could be seen. Unlike those in his dreams, they looked pretty tame.

"They're not always like that, are they?"'

"Indeed they are. After all, those there are the wild cows, *pak*."

"Can I . . . can I go up close to them?"

"They'll bolt if you do, that's for sure, *pak*. Just let them get a whiff of human beings and off they'll go, you can count on it. Even before they pick up our scent you can count on the peacocks roundabout letting them know, in code. Those peacocks, you wouldn't believe their eyesight."

"That so, is it? Peacocks too, you say? Fantastic! I'm gonna try to get up close. Right, let's move!"

Slowly they crept up to a pair of buffaloes which were guarded by peacocks. The forestry officers were astonished; both the birds and the beasts seemed very tame, whereas normally once they sensed the approach of man they would quickly scatter. Umar Salim made for one of the pair, a black bull with white spots on its backside, its four legs bent all the way down. No reaction, none whatsoever.

"They can't be the same as the ones in my dream, can they?" he asked himself. The female, which was much larger and reddish-brown in color, seemed no less passive.

The officials accompanying them grew more and more surprised. "You've not got some trick up your sleeve for taming them, have you, *pak*?" they asked, from a safe distance.

Umar Salim made no reply. He crept closer still to the beasts. Once alongside them, he stroked their bellies; they just looked on, giving his hand a sniff. He ran his hand down their necks. Again they just sniffed at it. Then he took hold of those curving, pointed, black horns of theirs, but still they didn't move. Recalling the advice of his employees, what they'd said about eating buffalo meat, he signaled the accompanying officials to draw near. When they were within spitting distance, Umar Salim seized the machete that hung at one officers' waist and before you could say Jack Straw he had sliced through the buffalo's neck.

The officer's jaw dropped as a geyser of blood sprang from the animal's neck. The employees accompanying Umar Salim were as stunned as the female buffaloes and the peacocks. The bull snorted, blood gushing from its side, an enraged look in its eyes.

Frightened, Umar Salim's employees slowly back away, and the officials with them. The pack of buffaloes began to snort and to shift restlessly. The bull charged, sending the peacocks scuttling off, and the party and the officials fell over themselves making a dash for it as the animal bore down on Umar Salim. It ran him through with its horns and tossed him into the still-fresh morning air, blood spurting everywhere.

Lying there amidst the dust and dry grass, Umar Salim felt the bull's hooves piercing his backside, his belly, his chest as he rolled over and over in the dust and dry grass. There was a glittering flash of light from above, and he felt the bull's horns puncturing his head. Blood from the animal's neck gushed onto his belly. His own blood had begun to pool beneath him. This isn't happening, he thought. I'm dreaming. But the bull with the bloody neck was stamping on him, its horns goring him again and again. Every inch of him had turned crimson, the bull fastidiously trodding on him, running him through.

He lay there flat on his back, his sight growing dimmer by the minute. All of a sudden the buffalo vanished. The one that had been constantly after him in that nightmare of his had now vanished. It was as if he'd just woken from a long nightmare—a *very* long nightmare indeed.

"Your Child Is Not Your Child," Gibran Said

("Anakmu Bukanlah Anakmu," Ujar Gibran)

---

by Danarto

"Nine months pregnant and just look at her, will you, lying there so peacefully," my wife whispered, gazing at our daughter, who was almost full term.

Asleep atop the pallet, without cover or pillow, our lovely girl was like—I don't know, hard to say what exactly. A creature graced with the ability to be completely at one with its surroundings. The whole room, the furniture, the very pillars of the house seemed to watch over her protectively as she slept.

"Don't you think she's a kind of saint, lying there so calm, not a care in the world?" Mother went on to say, brow furrowed. An image so oppressive, it was enough to make the earth tremble, almost. Myself, I felt that I was merely bearing witness. I just couldn't understand the whole business to do with our elder girl, who was in final-year medicine at the University of Indonesia.

Niken's having gotten herself pregnant was a matter of concern not just to her family but to the whole faculty, seeing as she wasn't married. And she couldn't be accused of having a boyfriend; when cross-examined about it she'd say outright that she didn't have one yet. It was a bit like watching her hanging perfectly white clothes out to dry in the sun.

143

Such a capable girl, all her cleverness put to honest use, but was such honesty real? The icy wind of her voice froze the cries of her younger brothers and sisters: Lestari, Wirid, Wilujeng, and Joko. It was as if they were circling round her while we, her mother and dad, just stood by, transfixed.

Who'd got her pregnant then? Nine months had gone by, and always the same answer, every time: "I did it all by myself."

That was her constant refrain. Had there been a flood at the time, the waters would have been held in check by a heaven-sent dike. Who can withstand anything from Heaven?

"Niken, Niken, you can't be comparing yourself with Mother Mary, my sweet. Come on now!" her mother said straight off on hearing her daughter's reply.

"You said it, not me, Mum," answered Niken quick as a flash. "All I said was that I got pregnant without having sex with a man." This rejoinder was, as it were, transmitted live to the entire family when her pregnancy had entered its third month.

You can bet this came as a shock to them. The dike had cracked, there was no holding back the waters. The PWD* engineers were drenched to the skin. The wind died down, the silence that followed was met with the clink of knife and fork against plate. Then these utensils were set aside as one by one everybody left the dining room table, where the act had yet to be brought to a close. Grandpa, Grandma, Uncle, Auntie, her cousins—all were flabbergasted. The sunlight seemed so bright.

The dean of the medical faculty recommended that Niken be asked to leave; some lecturers even went so far as to recommend she be thrown out. But her classmates defended her to a man—and woman. Quite a few of them suspected that Niken had a boyfriend on the quiet, whom she'd managed to conceal so effectively that no one could possibly suspect who he might be. Was she a sort of Aphrodite, molten within but never allowing the magma of desire to erupt to the surface?

Of course she became the butt of humor, both within the family and in the faculty. "What makes you think there's anything 'moral' about what goes on below the waist?" said one lecturer, by way of rejecting faculty regulations. What's more important, another asked, the belly or the brain? A female med student with a bun in the oven, if *that* isn't a

---

*Public Works Department.

matter of moral significance, then I ask you, what is, some students volunteered. But this isn't the Psychology Department, somebody else said. "Ach, what're you all on about, she's just been carrying out a live experiment on herself," one of her friends shot back.

"Weren't you up the spout before you met me?" Grandad remarked to Grandma. You can bet it was us, the children, the grandchildren, who turned beet red with embarrassment. How come Grandma and Grandpa were talking so freely all of a sudden?

"They're high on dope! Stoned!" one of the grandchildren burst out.

"Quiet, you!" his mother retorted.

"Your child is not your child." Sounds wonderful, doesn't it, saying it like that. Which one of your friends has been spreading such gossip? Gibran? Gabran? Gubran?" my wife said, very sharply. But—and honestly, I'm not saying this just to flatter her—when she's as sharp-tongued as that, she looks prettier than ever.

"Hands down religious instructions, just as he pleases. Frivolous advice he'll have the whole community falling for, like suckers. Quick, quick, get the pharmacist, the wound's festering! He thinks the stork brought this child, or maybe it dropped from some friendly rain cloud or other or was pried loose from the mud and picked up in the rice field, we took it into the kitchen maybe to give it a good rinse together with the vegetables," she rattled on, not for one moment taking her eyes off Niken sprawled there so peacefully.

"Dad, I'd like to introduce you to your miracle worker of a friend here. What's he up to now? He's a mischief-maker and no mistake. Just like those artists. You're quite sure he's Lebanese? Not Jewish? Come on, don't lie to me. It looks like you've got no trouble with that—you'll have no trouble finding a way of making your peace with this disaster," she added, cocking an eye at me.

"It's not your child who's yours" is a quote from "Your Child Does Not Belong to You," by the Lebanese poet Kahlil Gibran. I'd cited it many a time ever since it became public knowledge that Niken was nine months' pregnant. My wife would flip hearing me say this. She would accuse me of being an irresponsible parent, foolishly committed to saving my own skin.

> *Your Children Don't Belong to You*
> They are the sons and daughters of life which yearns for
>   its own self

They are born through you, but are not from you
They are yours, but not by right.
Give them your love, but offer them not the form of your thought
For they are a world of thought unto themselves
It is fitting that you prepare a house for their bodies but not
    for their souls
For their spirits are the occupants of the *house of the future*
Which you cannot visit, even in dreams.
You do your utmost to resemble them
Nevertheless, do not make them resemble you.
For the road of life never descends downwards
Nor does it sink into days gone past.
It is you who are the bow, while your children are the
    arrows which launch forth
The Supreme Archer knoweth the target,
Eternity's choice.
He stretches you out with His power
Such that the arrow flies away, far and fast.
Joyfully embrace the Archer as he extends His hand
For He loves the arrow which flies away like lightning
Just as he loves the faithful archer.

"It's a question of conviction. Nothing to do with being responsible or not. Look," I tried to explain, "whatever we've got we have on trust, and that includes what we call these kids of ours. We can't ever really know who they are, except by means of one thing: their development, which is not in question. They come to us out of 'innermost understanding.' If they do anything to betray what we hope for them, well, it all comes from something that's not part of us two."

"If you want to think just like him, that's up to you. All I ask is that this rotten way of looking at things isn't applied to any child of ours," my wife said. "I'm really concerned about our child's future, though she's still a student and never mind how keen she might be to start a family."

"What we're talking about, dear, has nothing to do with our child," I replied.

Rays of light reflected from the sky. Clouds parted, giving way to blinding sunshine. There was an inkling of something, though something not to be fathomed. And all for what? Impelled by a kind of inarticulate comprehension, Grandma and Grandpa set out for the house of the grandchild who had caused the earthquake. Since the solemn commemoration of the seventh month of her pregnancy, Niken had been living in rented quarters, accompanied by a servant girl. She'd no sooner moved than her younger brothers and sisters set out to catch her in flagrante, on the off chance of her lover dropping round to visit.

Her grandparents were quite extraordinarily taken aback upon entering their granddaughter's digs. It wasn't because they'd come across proof positive that she'd taken up with a man, that was certainly not the case. Nor did they find Niken feeling dogged by ill-luck and wanting to put an end to it all. Oh no. Niken was busy operating on a patient! Heavens above!

"What sort of child is this, dressed up like an angel?" Grandma whispered to Grandpa, fixing her gaze upon her granddaughter, who was busy issuing orders to the friends assisting her with her surgical instruments.

Belly ajoggle with the child she was carrying, Niken had operated on a patient who'd been shot in the stomach in a firefight. Shooting had been the order of the day ever since the rioting in the Tanjung Priok district, on Jakarta's North Side; in Glodok, Kebayoran, Jatinegara, and Palmerah fighting continued round the clock. Having armed themselves to the teeth, they were regarded as rebels—disturbers of the peace, that is. The torching of buildings and other such destruction had become an everyday occurrence.

Things had got totally out of hand. Grandma and Grandpa were getting further away from their declared objective. "Niken! You've put yourself at risk!" Grandpa cried, on hearing that it was his granddaughter who'd come to the aid of one of the rebels, not least because the youth, who'd undergone surgery to remove a bullet from his stomach, was a classmate of hers.

"Come on, out with it, my sweet granddaughter. Just admit you're working hand in glove with the rebels!" Grandma snarled.

Once the operation was over and she saw fit to respond, it wasn't the old Niken who did so. She simply took her grandparents to a back door of a room and opened the door. The room was crammed with weapons and ammunition.

"You're not my granddaughter anymore!" Grandma cried, beating a hasty retreat from the house. None of it made sense any longer. There was no thread strong enough to bind it all up together, nor any steel wire. So long, be seeing you. We've each of us got to answer our own call.

Fate, probably, had decreed that a medical faculty student would turn into a protester. Could all those sessions spent cutting into bodies have supplied the main incentive for exercising control: for growing ever warier, seeing mistakes made. For being better able to take physical weaknesses into account when it came to tackling all sorts of problems. And anyway, what makes you think med faculty students are always out there fighting on the side of truth?

It could be said of Niken that she never took a moment's rest. The injured came and went, student friends or members of various rebel groups. Were the government troops so weak as to be incapable of putting down the protesters in short order? Or was it not the case that the government was so remote from things that the gradual extension of the clampdown had become a matter of the utmost importance? Ach, it's all politics!

Niken's rented quarters were more like an emergency clinic than a medical student's digs. If she was to be mixed up with the rebels, how came it that the local neighborhood-watch people couldn't arrest her? Politics again.

Or—perish the thought—could it be that the local residents were taking an active part in helping the rebels? Why else were some of them slipping through the alleyways of some kampungs and vanishing into thin air just like that? Politics!

Although the fighting raged through every district of metropolitan Jakarta, everyday life seemed to carry on unaffected. The capital continued as usual to be inundated with fruit although it wasn't the season. Rice and all sorts of good things to eat were still to be found in the godowns; it wouldn't do for this war to be *really* uncomfortable. The dining table was still the center of national defense and security.

Was this war best seen as some sort of holiday? Or could it be that this Indonesian nation of ours has a flair for the dramatic. The sort of sense of humor that lets it look upon war as a matter of course—as a joke, more or less? From this it was a short step to an awareness, not of impossibility but rather of the fact that what was hilarious and what was disastrous might well have the same significance, might in value be equal.

Niken's dress was always covered with crimson spatters; those whose lives she'd managed to save and those who died, all of them left their "calling cards" on Niken in the form of fresh blood. She looked the part of a doctor and no mistake. She worked quickly, neatly, and to a fixed schedule. She was not in the least clumsy in using the instruments to hand, insisting always that the cure had ultimately to come from the patient himself.

Opinions concerning the rebels were well and truly at variance. The rebellion had been brought about by social and economic disturbance, so one school of thought maintained. Some experts concluded that it was politics which had caused the rioting. Like rain coming down in dribs and drabs, or like spattering water become a raging torrent; whether socioeconomic or political in origin, the impact of an armed struggle between the government and this external force was similar.

I'd often hope that Niken might find a bit of time just to chat with her family. Fact was, though, she set greater store by that "social revolution" of hers. Never mind, as long as she continued to crack jokes with her younger brothers and sisters. I noticed, too, how funny it was the way her belly would be held and stroked by them, each taking it in turns. "Oh Lord, such a gentle child. She really values the simple things in life, she can joke so intimately—why should she, of all people, be so incredibly enthusiastic about heading up a rebellion?" I'd mutter, sotto voce.

Whenever I'd look long and hard at Niken, I'd feel cornered. There was little me, hard-pressed, wrestling with problems in a way that was doing me no particular credit. And there she was, this noble child whose only wish was to grapple with the great issues of the day: how to change society, how to make it more just. Her love for the poor was so great—I could read this in her expression—that all she wanted was to offer up her very spirit to them.

Niken would always steer clear of me when I tried to initiate a discussion as to why she should have chosen to abase herself. "I'm not a clever chap, Niken, but you've got to be democratic if you want me to get a discussion going," I said one fine day. She was as eager as I was, but honestly, she was just too much—she said she was prepared to be a good listener and that was all. That's not what *I* call a discussion. That's . . .

"If only you'd get sick, that way at least you'd be able to get a bit of rest," I blurted out once, seeing how exhausted she looked.

"There's no time to get sick" was her reply. And she stretched out on the pallet without cover or pillow, and conked out.

In Niken's eyes, was I anything other than a nincompoop, someone who knew zilch worth talking about? Zilch about justice, or truth, or simplicity, or struggle. Or about the millions of our fellow men who are poor as poor can be, who had to work themselves to death to rid themselves of their burden.

"Our Father who art in heaven, can this girl sitting across from me here really and truly be my child? I mean, look at her, God. She's in the thick of leading a top-secret meeting, and her with her belly all swollen up like that. Why do her friends have such confidence in her?" I whispered to God, as, softly softly, I crept into the busy rented house. From the outside it looked quiet enough. That's why the neighborhood watch people knew nothing about her, in all likelihood.

"Lord," I groaned under my breath, pretending to occupy myself with ministering to several patients who lay together on top of a bunk bed. "Wherever does she get the funds for all this here?" This was one hell of a protest, all right. "Why does my child have to take life so seriously? Something's got to be wrong with this here New Order of ours, for her to be so dead set on opposing it."

"Heavenly Father," I asked, "this child of mine, can *she* be the new generation in Indonesia?" It was as if Time itself was noting down this one-way conversation; I heard no answering voice. Probably what was called for was some sort of stiffening of the backbone. Ever touch a wet leaf in the garden? The feeling in me, you could have said, was a bit like that.

"O Lord, is my child an honest person? Has she really any idea of the issues confronting her?" Tears fell from my eyes, so desperate was I to be clear about this. All this rebelling, what's it got to do, I mean, what's it *really* got to do with my child? It was obvious that the rebels I was looking after were getting pissed off by my grumbling. Rebels— my arse. They didn't think of themselves as such, that's for sure. Bent on some sacred mission, more like.

"That's one egg smashed, for good and all," said Grandma angrily, setting the ball rolling before the assembled family. Her point was, we had to be prepared to banish Niken, to look upon her as no longer one of us. *Ilang-Ilangan endog siji:* the picture's up and vanished from its frame. A white space is all that's left. My wife wept to hear Grandma's declaration and Niken's younger siblings snuggled up to their mother, weeping as well.

"An immoral bunch of plotters, a danger not only to their families but to the whole nation!" Grandma flared, over our protests. Grandpa alone had kept quiet all the while. Another family too was complaining.

"Niken's my child," I said. "Let the final say be mine and my wife's. Her siblings are also entitled to express their opinions."

"And you're our child. Isn't it my prerogative to say what's what?" Grandma insisted, eyes ablaze. "I'm the oldest one round here and what I say goes!" she exploded, pounding the table. "Right, then, who's going to contradict me, eh? Who?"

"This meeting's certainly not going to bring about her expulsion," I said again.

"I'll do it myself, and this instant too!" Grandma threatened.

"She won't give a damn. What people think of her doesn't bother her in the slightest. We're wasting our time, meeting like this," I replied. Niken's mother and younger brothers and sisters carried on crying. A volley of knocks sounded. Everyone froze. Must've been a passing devil. But from afar, a commotion was heard; then everything went all quiet again.

"Whoever it was is no longer well disposed toward this kid and her antics."

"It's not your child who's yours."

"Still keen, aren't you, on repeating these fancy phrases over and over! Mind your step, else you might still find yourself cozying up to Miss Lebanon there!"

"Here we are, busting a gut to work out what she's thinking and there she is, at peace in a world of her own!"

A day after this meeting, her mother and I went to see her at the place she was renting. She was as involved as ever, and her with that overhanging belly of hers. She didn't give two hoots about Grandma's plan to ostracize her, had no comment about the matter whatsoever. Some things were simply beneath contempt, others noble, the feeling seemed to be. It wasn't a question of her being arrogant, she had a job to do. She examined patients and would most likely operate on one of her friends that very day.

"Before I give birth, I'm going to get married," she said flatly.

"Married!" her mother and I burst out in surprise.

"The marriage contract alone, that'll cost a pretty penny."

"Niken, just who the hell do you think you are, exactly? You'll just make up your mind on this score without seeking our agreement first? You've got a father and mother—you know that, don't you?" I said, angrily.

"No need to get excited. Here, see, for yourself; I can pay to have the marriage contract drawn up. I've got enough cash."

"Niken! You are *not* the dictator round here," her mother shot back. "This making plans without your mother and father's blessing, it's strictly forbidden. You can talk all you want. Who're you going to marry, anyway? Some bandit or other?"

"Could be. I haven't a clue. I've not yet been introduced to him. But I've said yes to his proposal."

"God in heaven. My dear girl, you've taken leave of your senses."

"Your son-in-law now, he's a dish, he is. So well-mannered, with a sense of responsibility too. Earns a good salary. I'm surprised he chose me."

"Lord, grant us strength and forgive us our trespasses, but our Niken here, she's altogether too much! What am I supposed to do faced with this child?"

"Accept his proposal. Call in the headman. Prepare the contract. And be patient," Niken added.

The wedding went off smoothly enough. It lacked nothing. Now I had a son-in-law. No more gossip. My wife and I, embracing our child, wept tears of true joy as Tomo, her husband, looked on with a sense of gratitude. Niken had spoken the truth. She and her husband didn't know each other from Adam. Rather surprisingly too, Tomo really didn't in the least mind about Niken's belly. Might it have been the wind that brought Tomo hither? Joy enveloped Niken.

"Darling, Grandma and Grandpa are excommunicating me, so I'm not allowing them to come along to the marriage contract ceremony," Niken burst out, laughing. Some of the guests were determined to come, though they hadn't been invited. They'd even brought gifts. Whereas I just wanted it to go off quietly, since in addition to being unable to afford it, Niken for her part wasn't at all keen on having a party. When I asked, what if we were rich, would she then fancy a celebration? her answer was no. Better, she said, to give it to the poor and needy.

I have no more doubts about Niken. Everything she said came out sounding informed and sensible. Anyway, what was wrong with loving the poor? What was wrong with impoverishing oneself for the sake of other people's well-being? They were noble things, the things she loved.

"Your friend came too, dear," my wife said, not really giving a toss one way or another.

"Which friend?" I replied.

"Ah, he wasn't saying. He just passed on his best wishes, handed over a present, and left. Can't think why he didn't want to meet with you."

"Who was it then?"

"Who else if not Gibran?"

"Good God—you mean he really came?"

"You better believe it, that's his gift there. Let's open it, shall we?"

Quickly I unwrapped the parcel.

"Lord above. This is really and truly his portrait," I cried as I faltered forward holding the framed black-and-white portrait. For a moment my vision grew dim. A cold sweat broke out all over my body.

"Dear? Is something wrong, dear? What ever's the matter with you?" cried my wife, taking hold of me.

"I swear I've never met him. Just read his writings. He died in 1931."

"Good God," my wife cried, and she fainted dead away. People crowded round. I meanwhile had no choice but to totter over to the door, to witness Niken being led away by several militia men.

Black Clouds Over the Isle of Gods
(Mega Hitam Pulau Kayangan)

by Putu Oka Sukanta

A t Ketapang Harbor she had gazed far out to sea, as far as the eye could see, trying to pierce the night, which hung like a jet-black silk curtain. From the other side lamplight had flickered, signs of life continuing on its own way out yonder. But she didn't know in what direction exactly the boat was to take her. To the left and to the right of her, lamps winked, a cluster of fireflies against a black surface, a hazy blur off in the clear, still distance. The coast of Bali—which side was it on? Which side? There was no way to tell.

Even supposing the night sky was somehow as clear as day, that it was at one and the same time cerulean blue and star-studded; even then, she'd have been hard pressed to make out exactly on which promontory Gilimanuk stood. A clump of hills, fortresslike, was all that could be discerned through low-lying cloud. It was at the foot of these hills that the lamps had flickered. Whether they were on sailing ships or belonged to houses on the foreshore, that was anyone's guess. The sea had spread infinitely outward, a thick, all-enveloping carpet.

She had dreaded leaving the Java coast, dreaded the slow progress toward the ship on which she was to cross the straits. The bus in which she'd traveled from Jakarta had joined the queue of vehicles boarding the ship. In it sat her mother.

How utterly alone she had felt herself to be, isolated amidst all the hustle and bustle. The passengers had shuffled forward until at last they had gained the ship's deck. Some, the majority in fact, had remained behind in the bus, yawning with fatigue, but there were not a few among them who had gone up into the lounge, or out on deck to take deep drafts of the fresh sea breezes.

She had felt herself to be utterly disconnected from everything around her, incarcerated in her solitude. A perfect stranger. She'd allowed her mind to plunge into the stillness of the quiet night, envisioning the hills lying peacefully in the twilight. Given up to such thoughts, she'd sat at the edge of an empty bench.

Then the ship had got under way. She had watched Ketapang Beach getting further and further off. She had stood, hugging her arms to herself, hair loosened by the wind, eyes cast down, tears standing in them, almost overflowing. She'd done her best to hold them back. But she'd heard her heart whisper to her in a stifled voice, *"Farewell, freedom!"* She'd glanced down at her watch. Just gone twelve.

When next she had looked, it had gone a quarter to one. The ship had berthed at Gilimanuk. An ancient Balinese Hindu temple, its gate split in two, barred the passengers' way.

Is this the gate to Pura Dalem? she'd asked herself. Pura Dalem, the place where the souls of those called to their Maker sat enthroned.

There's not a shadow of doubt, not anymore. I may as well lay me down flat on the ground. I've no strength left. I don't care if the blood is still flowing in my veins. A walking corpse, that's what I am, my heart killed stone dead. Oh heart, my poor heart! And at the very moment she stepped ashore on the island of the gods, her whole being had cried out in revolt:

Why did I ever have to be born Ida Ayu Ketut Sumartini? Why not just plain Ketut Sumartini? Why the Ida Ayu? Would someone please tell me why?

She'd boarded the passing bus, sitting down beside her mother, sinking into the padded seat, her eyes shut tight. But sleep had refused to come. As hot tears trickled from between her tightly shut eyelids, she sensed a strong arm encircling her, heard whispered endearments.

"Your mother can do what she likes to us, but there's one obstacle we and we alone have got to overcome. Everything depends on the two of us. We're one heart now. Nothing in the world can come between us."

She'd swallowed back her sobs. One bold hand had caressed her cheek, the other arm holding her in a warm embrace. She had laid her head on the man's shoulder, harboring within mingled feelings of rage and joy. She'd sensed the feeling of closeness in the gentle kisses laid upon her head.

"We're still holding all the cards. For the time being, anyway. There's no sign the *dukun* they've hired to keep us apart is having any success. So long as we put up a united front they haven't a chance. We've foiled the latest charm they've used to stop us. It's not as if we've done anything wrong, so no black magic's going to come between us."

The voice, so steady, rang still in her ear. She'd opened her eyes; how she'd ached to look up into those of her lover. But he was nowhere to be seen. Sweet memories, imparting strength to her love, were all that remained.

She'd smiled, at once amused and embittered, to recall the events that had befallen her. Ever since her family on Bali had got wind that she'd formed a tie with a man not of her own caste, practically all of them had turned against her—her mother especially, and her aunt's family. Letters from Bali had come thick and fast, and always preaching the same message: for the love of God, get back to the straight and narrow! Leave this man, they had all said, this *foreigner,* this man with no caste. For heaven's sake choose someone else, anyone, it doesn't matter who. Even someone of a lower caste than yourself would be better. But on this matter she'd been prepared to budge not one single inch. Then the fun and games had started.

On her return from lectures, she would not infrequently come upon a ritual offering placed under her bed. Her pillow would often give off a faint scent. Further investigation would reveal that a small packet of aromatic substance had been tucked under her mattress. That was when she'd tumbled to it: they'd engaged a *dukun* to lay siege to her heart!

She'd laid the whole insane business before her lover. "The minute we start believing in it, that's when it's going to have an effect on us," he told her. "But if we don't let it rattle us, if we let it be water off a duck's back, why then it's all quite meaningless."

"But just finding it scares the daylights out of me, *beli!* Anyway, just how do you propose we set about disbelieving in it? I mean, it's not as if we're not Bali folk ourselves!"

"That's a point, Tini; there's no denying we're Balinese. But you've got to remember that Ida Sang Hyang Widi Wasa is superior to black magic, and a fair sight stronger too. We've got to pray to her to give us strength. There just isn't any other way. We're the only ones who can defeat this evil. God will grant us the power, and Ida Sang Hyang Widi, she'll help us too. She's on our side."

With each passing day, she'd found it harder to ignore the impression that her whole family was giving her black looks. She was on her own now, together with *Nyoman* Astawa. Her lover came round less and less often to her house, now that her aunt had bluntly told him off to his face, saying don't make a nuisance of yourself, don't trouble Ayu Ketut Sumartini anymore. They'd arranged to meet elsewhere ever since.

It was as if the house where she was staying had undergone some sort of metamorphosis, had been magicked into a dark cave, a creepy sort of place, the very thought of which aroused in her extreme apprehension, an unbridled suspicion. There wasn't a single moment now when she felt at ease there. Often, the mere thought of entering her bedroom made her go rigid with fright. Some gargoyle squatted within, awaiting her arrival—that's what it felt like. The hair on her arms would stand on end whenever she was visited by such dread; she wouldn't dare enter, would merely rest her hand on the lintel and then retreat. She'd go into the kitchen to drink down a glass of sugar water, exactly as her lover had instructed her to do. She'd settle down to read in the parlor, trying to get a grip on herself, or busy herself with playing some cassette or other, going back in only when in full control of herself again.

Tini took the mattress to pieces: nothing. More perplexed than ever, she peered down into the space under the house, flung cupboards wide: nothing untoward there, thank God. But when she caught sight of the small parcel suspended from the top of the doorframe, an innocent-looking little white packet, her heart thundered in her chest, and she broke out in a cold sweat. She was caught up in warily returning its inanimate stare when from nowhere her aunt appeared.

"Oh that. It's just come in the post, from Bali. Don't you fret your pretty little head about it. It's there to keep you from coming to any harm," she had remarked, apropos nothing, after rabbiting on for a bit.

"Now this one here," she had gone on, "this one had two silver bracelets. Lovely, aren't they? Fit perfectly too. Go on, dear, you put on one and I'll take the other. It's meant to be worn, it's been sent as a gift after all."

Feigning affection, her aunt put on the bracelets, fastening one around Tini's wrist and one around her own. Tini noticed her aunt's lips working silently.

"I'm not mad keen on bracelets, Auntie, if you must know."

"Oh, do wear it. Take my word for it, it makes your hand look prettier than ever. Now see here, Dayu Tut, you've to wear it, no ifs ands or buts, d'you hear? The whole family wants you safe and sound."

She'd found herself put out no end at this, though she'd held back the anger that it had flared up and was seething unquenched inside. But there had been no stemming her tears, not anymore. They'd streamed from her eyes. Her breath came in gasps, her hands shook.

"I'm . . . I'm not feeling quite myself today." She'd gone and sat down on her bed, shifted her body, letting it go limp, giving her thoughts free rein to roam where they would.

"There, you see. Doesn't that just prove it, you've had a spell cast over you, Dayu Tut," was her aunt's parting shot as she quit the room, leaving her all to herself there. "I'll lay odds it's that man—he's gone and bewitched you!" She'd cried brokenly in bitter grief, mouth clenched shut, pillow pressed to her head. A wound sprinkled with vinegar; that's what it had felt like.

In no time at all word of the day's doings had reached Bali. Whence, before long, another parcel came, containing—what else? a charm against ill luck.

"This," her auntie had said, "has simply got to be kept in your brassiere. Don't you go anywhere without it, mind." She took the white packet and laid it against her chest. After saying her good-byes Tini had left the house, her mind in a storm. Yesterday night, that's when it must have been. She knew her aunt had stolen into her room, intending to give the sheets a good shake, like you do when you're keen to get rid of mosquitoes. Tears rolled down her cheeks, but still she kept her eyes sealed tight, like one asleep. Seated thus, she managed to get not one wink of sleep the whole night long. Fear, vexation, an overpowering urge to fight back, a sense of having had her face rubbed in it, on top of so many other feelings, all of them jumbling round inside, put paid to the chances of getting any rest.

She had a class that day. From a callbox she arranged an assignation with her lover. They were to rendezvous at Nyoman Astawa's house at two in the afternoon; they agreed to take to pieces the latest charm received by post. Stitch by stitch, that was how they would set about the job. The contents revealed themselves to be a few needles, five grains of rice, some refined incense, cotton, thread, and some pale material of uncertain hue.

"Don't tell me *that's* what made you scared, Tini! I can well imagine how it might have scared the wits out of someone way back when, in the days of the old kingdoms, Majapahit or Jayaprana. But nowadays, I mean, come on! These things, they're worthless, meaningless. That's to say, just as long as we're careful not to attach any meaning or value to them. Junk, that's what this is! You've no objection to my burning them, have you?" *Nyoman* Astawa had tried to rein his anger in, but there was no concealing it. His eyes were round as saucers, and bloodshot. He was holding in his breath. Tini could hardly fail to notice.

"So what are you suggesting we do, *beli?*"

"I say let's burn the thing."

"But I'm scared to death, I tell you," she said, seizing one of his hands, which had been poised to strike a match.

"Of what?" His gaze had penetrated hers, she could feel the man's courage stiffening her own wilting spirits.

"That *dukun.* He'll find out soon enough."

"How's he going to find out, eh? That's what I'd like to know. He's miles off in Bali. God's the only one who knows." And so saying he struck the match, the girl forbearing to stop him now. *Nyoman* Astawa never took his eyes from the contents of the charm as they lay charring in the ashtray, except to steal an occasional look at the face of his beloved, to assess how she was taking it. He read the terror etched into her features and saw how tense she was.

"Look, Tini," he said, taking her hands. "See for yourself. It is turning to ash, just like that. All of it except this needle." They held each other in a close embrace. The box in which the charm had come had been stuffed with cotton which they'd taken from the drawer.

But all they succeeded in doing, or so it seemed looking back, was to put off the day of separation. Tini's entire family had agreed on the matter: back to Bali she was to go, come hell or high water. They had, they felt, no other recourse if the family's honor was to be salvaged. Tini was obliged to return, in the custody of her mother, who'd come specially to fetch her. There was to be no compromising. Not where this was concerned.

The lovers managed, before splitting up, to pay a visit to the Pura, there to pray together and offer up their vows to the Goddess. Bringing flowers and incense along with them, they beseeched Ida Sang Hyang Widi Wasa to lead them out of their impasse, that they might bring their love to fruition.

"Mark my words, Tini, God's so much stronger than any old *dukun*. If you haven't lost your integrity and if you're sure in your heart, why then, you've nothing to fear from these black-magical thingummyjigs! You've got to get a hold on yourself, Tini. Try to pluck up courage. You'll need all you can get when the time comes."

At last she fell asleep in the bus. Her mother awoke, to scan her child's face intently in the haze of early morning. At five, when the eastern sky was turning a bright crimson, the bus came to a stop in front of her house. Her mother having roused her, they alighted, to be met by a welcoming party. But she could hardly believe her eyes and ears on being told that she couldn't enter the forecourt; the ritual offering which was to have been prepared against her arrival was not, it transpired, quite ready. This in itself was enough to humiliate her deeply. She couldn't imagine a thing like this ever happening to her. Hatred then had boiled up explosively inside her. The tears came cascading down.

"Patience, Dayu Tut, patience. All of us here have been praying for your well-being." Quite whose voice that had been, coming to her from among the people crowding round, she hadn't been certain. Weep was all she could do, fists screwed into her eyes. Meanwhile the ritual offerings were made ready. She did as she was told by her grandmother, who was in charge of proceedings.

The welcoming ceremony was the one specially reserved for people who'd come within an ace of being done for, people who had been taken off the critical list or who had almost copped it in a major accident. A ritual for those whom death had allowed to escape scot free. This was the one thing her family had done that was totally unforgivable. She felt so humiliated, cut to the quick: her lover was being openly likened to a menace of the first order, a living threat that had managed to get its dirty claws deeply into her.

Her heart screamed out, but she was powerless to put a stop to it. All she could do was cry, sinking deeper into the pit of sorrow until she lost touch with what was going on around her. Feeling herself grow weak, she fainted dead away.

Her family had bustled round in a tizzy. The *dukun* was summoned. She regained consciousness to find him at her side mumbling something or other. Soundlessly she cursed, wordlessly she swore.

During her first days on Bali she had had these stand-up rows with her mother. She, Tini, just couldn't get it into her head why her brother—and all because he was a man!—was free to marry outside his caste while she, a high-caste Brahmana woman, was debarred from doing likewise. What earthly reason was there for this? And here we all were, supposedly having come a long way since the bad old days.

"In a man's case, he's entitled to take to wife a woman outside his caste. We'll take the girl in as one of our own. But in yours? Adopted by this outsider and taken where, exactly? Answer me that. You'll be dragged down, Tini, dragged down, I tell you! You'll lose your status. Have you no shame? We have, even if you haven't any!"

"It isn't fair!" came her sharp retort. "And you're always going on about how we're the same in the sight of God!"

"Tini, you're Balinese. Don't you ever, ever forget that. Not Muslim. Not Christian."

"I never heard such antiquated rot in all my life!" she had said as she took leave of her mother. But the latter, her curiosity sparked, wouldn't let go.

"I beg your pardon?"

"You know those traditional *adat* clothes handed down to me by my caste? Well, they're too small for my full figure. If I'm forced to wear them, they'll tear at the seams and expose my body."

"Is that what they've taught you in school back there?"

The wound to her heart was so deep, it seemed it would never heal. She'd lived with family now for months on end, but she could never relax. Correspondence with *Nyoman* Astawa was still irregular, but not for one moment did she forget the promise made at the Jakarta temple. Ill at ease though she was with herself and with others, she managed nonetheless not to show it. In everything to do with family matters, she set to work with a will. The upshot was, her people convinced themselves that Tini had broken off her relationship with *Nyoman* Astawa, precisely as the *dukun* said she would. She was given leave to go to movies and to other shows. Her family were at pains to satisfy her every wish. She became their favorite, at last.

As luck would have it, she ran across an old school chum one fine day at the beauty parlor. Mery asked her round to her house near the market and, since their chance encounter, often called round herself. It was thanks to Mery's solicitude that the link with *Nyoman* Astawa began to firm up.

The Galungan celebrations had the whole Hindu community on Bali in a flutter, and Ida Ayu Ketut Sumartini was no exception. She was as preoccupied as any other Bali girl. At sunrise she was set to go to the temple and to the family shrine, there to offer up devout prayer. Her family, watching her out of the corners of their eyes and knowing nothing about what she was up to, couldn't have been more pleased. Ida Ayu Ketut Sumartini was taking advantage of the opportunity: she wasn't confining herself to petitioning the Goddess and spirits of departed family members to see her safely through this crisis; she was also ever so quietly seeking forgiveness and begging pardon for what she was about to do. She was seized with fear, washed through by a wave of sadness: she was standing on the verge of jettisoning everything she had loved since she was little. She let her eyes rove round the interior of the building at the family shrine. This was the world into which she had been born, in which she'd been formed, and which she was now proposing to leave behind. Sweet fragments of memory broke through the surface of her mind, recollections of the bustle during the ceremony at the family shrine, memories of having her teeth ritually filed down, of her father's death and immediate cremation.

"Oh ye gods of my father, forgive me, your servant. I shall always worship you, never mind how far away I may find myself. Soon enough I'll be on my way: if ever I should come back to perform the *sembah* here in this place, I'll know what to expect. Gods of my fathers, hear me when I call, from wherever that may be. . . . "

That night there was to have been a performance of the Arja dance at Balebanjar. A quick peek was all she had the stomach for before heading off home and going back into her room where she was overcome by anxiety.

"Have I got what it takes to up and leave? To slink off just like that from the family I love so? Can a happy life really lie in store for me if I do?" She kept tossing and turning. Indistinct sounds of laughter and of gamelan music drifted in. Toward dawn she finally fell heavily asleep, bone-tired.

That morning Tini bid farewell to her mother, saying that she was just going round to Mery's, and with that she was off. But after sunset the hour came when her mother would usually listen for visitors looking in to say hello from the door to the front gate, and still Ida Ayu Ketut Sumartini had not returned. Since afternoon Dayu Biang had been asking everybody where her girl might have disappeared to, but it never crossed her mind that that night, the very night of the Galungan celebrations, certain uninvited guests would be paying a visit.

"*Jero meduwe jero?*" Anybody in? the voice called. She hastened to open the door to the front gate. Dayu Biang's heart fair jumped out of her chest when she clapped eyes on the three men dressed in traditional garb who waited for her. Pulling herself together, she bid them enter. But when their errand was made plain to her, she fell back in a dead faint. The men had come on a mission on behalf of the family of *Nyoman* Astawa, bearing the news that Ida Ayu Ketut Sumartini had run off with her lover and was going to marry him.

It hit the family like an earthquake. One of them ran out in search of his trustworthy *dukun*. But alas, the latter hadn't been seen at home since the start of celebrations on the previous day: he was busy playing *ceki* in the gambling house.

The sun slipped down to the foot of the hills. The aircraft was waiting on the tarmac at Ngurah Rai Airfield, its crimson glare fading gradually, depositing traces of gold at the edge of the procession of black clouds throwing protective cover over the island of Bali.

"Over there, Tini, do you see those black clouds? The plane's going to fly smack through them. If you look down below you'll see the lovely island of the gods all spread out beneath you."

The Garuda plane hurled itself into space, lunging through the clumps of black cloud which soiled the sky over the isle. They parted like black fabric slashed by a small dagger. But once the plane was aloft, the clouds, floating like cotton wool, made it difficult to catch sight of the isle below.

"I shall always love you," Ketut Sumartini whispered to her heart. "But from a distance, from now on." And she rested her head on her lover's shoulder.

The Shutterbug
(Tukang Potret)

---

by Prasetyohadi

S onny Wouthuyzen—that's her name. Hard to get your tongue round.
I'd use her first name, or else just plain old Son. Fantastic build,
athlete's height, brown eyes. "Sonny's got Depok Dutch blood," our mutual friends would whisper knowingly. With their reddish-black hair and
blue eyes, that's what her mum and dad were certainly said to be.

Frankly I didn't give a tinker's cuss whether her descent was Depok
Dutch or Bugis or any of the other groups that Depok, like some ethnic
nature reserve, corrals all together. Just getting on with your job, no
bitching, no making excessive demands, that's what counts. I mean it's
not as if this here's still some little colony or other and that what
matters is who your ancestors were. It's a question of keeping up
professional standards.

When I gave her an assignment to take some photos, she fought shy
of it.

"I've promised to be home tonight, with the family, *mas.*"

"That's your own affair, Son. But I can guarantee that there's gonna
be nothing quite like it, not tomorrow night or any night after, except
maybe in three years time when the board comes to the end of its term
of office."

She'd no answer to that one. So there was nothing for it but for her
to trundle along and snap some shots of the restaurant and hotel
group's new board of directors. I was managing editor, I had to crack
the whip. If our magazine was to come out on time, every time, it was

up to me to translate the brain waves of our bosses, the shareholders, into action. Every so often the editorial board would get these strange ideas, these highfalutin notions, way above the heads of our grand armada of journalists. In all there were four of them plus one photographer, to wit, our headstrong Sonny.

The negatives of the new board of directors hadn't been developed, so Sonny said she'd do the prints after lunch. Her insisting our editorial board secretary and my PA reimburse her for taxi fare put me out even more. In actual fact, every two weeks all our reporters and photographers got money for food and transport, inclusive of operating costs. The secretary was having none of it.

"If it's kudos you're after, Son, good on you. Only don't bother to get there by taxi 'cause this office isn't reimbursing you one penny."

I set her to taking some shots of the area round the old Depok station. As luck would have it, we'd been sent this magazine article all about the Dutch folk out Depok way, describing where their descendants had spread out to. Would you believe that even over in the Hague there was a community of them. Interesting piece. Shame the accompanying pictures weren't all they might have been; an old church at the street corner, its bell decrepit with age, that was all that was featured.

Sonny lowered her head slightly when I looked in. She was cheesed off, I shouldn't wonder, at the secretary's having put his foot down. Her skin was so fair you could read each passing change of mood, just like that. Her lips trembled. She was getting her things together, banging open the table drawer. Her shoes as she moved about made a hard tap-tapping sound, and when she pushed the chair in she kicked the leg of the table. She took her leave with a curt nod and an insouciant wave of the hand.

When she'd gone, the secretary turned round to look at me.

"Ten to one she'll have collected her packet tonight. You know, *mas,* that story about the new board of management, strictly speaking we don't *have* to do it, not if you're concerned about our reputation," he observed. I nodded slightly, putting the whole thing out of my mind. I thought to myself, Who makes the decisions around here anyway about whether or not to do an article? Why, even the editorial board confined itself to putting forward ideas or just pointing us in their direction. The actual business of deciding was left entirely up to me.

But the girl would look so bushed when it came to anything having to do with admin, she wasn't above getting one of her friends to run out and buy her some lipstick. She'd prevail on them to do so many things for her that those so-called journalists of ours were finding themselves constantly being imposed upon. If she'd no compunction outside the office—and you can take my word for it she hadn't—no qualms, that's to say, about strong-arming people or pulling someone's leg, how much less so when it came to her own colleagues. All I had to do was tell them to chase up some written stuff or ask them do an interview, and before you knew it they'd be running round like chickens without their heads. Our journalists' copy, it grieves me to say, was never quite up to scratch.

But Sonny's work this time wasn't half bad. She'd found a new angle that more than passed muster: fields of *sawah* stretching out, houses falling to ruin dating from way back jumping out of the background; the old railway station was the center of the composition, the long rails forming diagonal lines. Off at its further end an abandoned railway car could be glimpsed, long *alang-alang* grass concealing part of its wheels.

"Struck it lucky that time, didn't I, *mas?* Light was perfect that afternoon. I climbed all the way up to the top of the mosque to get the shot."

My paean of praise, it seemed, had been overheard by my PA. He was reasonably good-natured, so it beats me why he always looked put out with Sonny and lost no opportunity to take her to task. I dismissed as groundless the idea that there might be something between them; that would have been only too predictable, a cliché almost. And I suppose there's no way a thing like that couldn't have ended in tears. Morning noon and night I'd get wind of rumors among the journalists. I'd pretend not to notice, swamped as I'd be with working up manuscripts, rejigging sentences and paragraphs, lending a hand with layout, with a view to keeping an eye on things, lining up the compositors, seeing that the contents of the manuscripts were just right, meeting with management or with the directors.

I was none too keen on any split taking place in our little armada. Sonny I burdened with the task of covering the carnivals held in honor of Independence Day. "It's a golden opportunity for you to get to know the meaning of *merdeka*, Son. Find out how far the Dutch were prepared to go to screw things up for us," I joked as she sloped off. The journalists and my PA had congregated in my room. They were saying things about Sonny being too stiff, too much of a skinflint, too *zakelijk*.

"We'd appreciate your having a quiet word, *mas*," said my PA, puffing out his cheeks in exasperation. "The general interests of this journal, that's what's got to be borne in mind. Not those of any one individual. That's if this publication of ours isn't going to fall apart."

"Editorial interests are what I've got at heart, not personal interests. However, if it's really going to rock the boat, I suppose we'd best make up our minds as to how we all feel about it, hadn't we? Now look here, all of you, how about just trying to hang loose when you deal with her."

As I've said, hard to get your tongue round her name. Hard to control her, hard to tell her what to do. My being well-disposed toward her backfired; turns out they all thought she was my golden girl. Her duties were light, they involved nothing more taxing than humping round the equipment and doing photographic work which the other journalists just weren't up to handling. More often than not she'd have little to say for herself in the office, or she'd go walkabout. Or else she'd be discovered catching forty winks in the library. Or you'd come upon her snoozing away on-purpose-by-accident in the editorial conference room.

The big boss too had tumbled to the fact that everything wasn't quite as it should be down in the editorial room, and he called me in specially. He was on at me to take steps.

"I shouldn't be surprised if there's an element of social envy somewhere in there, *pak*. Nothing at all to do with politics," I volunteered, having stood up for Sonny. I couldn't take my eyes off his face. Mustache and sideburns all disheveled, rash on the skin of a protruding cheekbone making it look like citron peel. He seemed to have stored up his words to find that now he just couldn't get them out. Latterly I'd found out that my PA and several journalists had lodged a report en passant about Sonny's case. I'd no problem with this. In fact, it was all to the good.

Picking up whispers here and there, and as a result of noticing who was off work when I was and of keeping my eyes peeled every morning, the penny finally dropped. Sonny was making a point of coming in only in the afternoon. But she never reported late for work, either to me or to the PA—that's what really got my goat. So I'd no choice but to haul up before me this photographer of ours with the impossible-to-pronounce name.

"We work as a team," I said, not beating round the bush. "I've got a lot of time for each new initiative, every new idea, even if nothing comes of it. But whenever there's an editorial meeting, you just sit there, Son. When push comes to shove you'll go, 'Okay, *mas,* anything you say.' But we're not in the army, Son; this isn't some battalion or other with an officer in charge."

"Yes, *mas,*" she answered, not turning a hair, for all the world as if she felt herself to be pure as the driven snow.

Sighing elaborately, I put plan B into action and invited Sonny to open up, straight talk and no holds barred. If you want the truth, I was keen to know her thoughts. Maybe they'd reveal themselves once the pressure was taken off. Whereas the journalists and my PA were convinced I was doing everything in my power to rile her, what I was really trying to do was to get Sonny to take a positive step forward.

Then she came out with it. She regarded me as somebody ready at the drop of a hat to scribble any old rubbish, just as long as readers were amused; somebody prepared to write anything so long as it had a sensational angle. I was someone who made a fetish of taking popular tastes into account. I didn't answer back, but neither could I go along with any of it. It's not a journalist's job to alter social conditions for the better. He's got no duty apart from the duty of filing circumspect reports and checking sources.

"So what you're saying is, you're not responsible for the life of our nation. You'll forgive my saying so, but here I am, me with my Dutch extraction, worried sick about how the community lives, about the state of our nation. But you, you're Javanese, the people the Dutch treated worst, the ones now suffering from structural poverty, and it's you Javanese of all people who've turned into the new oppressor. Why don't you want to try and change things, *mas?* Sorry. We're getting far off the subject, aren't we?"

So far as could be seen, it was possible her assessment was entirely in tune with current conditions and with cultural sensibilities in the country. I began to suspect this after she'd put forward as her premise the Latin American model of development. It was, she said, a miserable failure on account of its lopsided structure. What made me so sure our own country wasn't getting perilously close to becoming such a basket case?

"Come on, Son. I mean, in our country religion's the very foundation. It's not some tool of liberation theology. Indonesia's hardly Latin America."

It came as no surprise to learn that during the whole of this time

Sonny was no longer willing to go to church. I'd often ask if she still went—in jest you understand. But this was no laughing matter. To hear her tell it, the Church was "just a bunch of circus clowns masquerading as half-crazed hypocrites, *mas.*" She said the way the church elders would chat away in Dutch, not to mention the adult members of the congregation, made her sick to her stomach.

"It's their way of putting distance between themselves and the younger generation."

My fear was, she might be taking the same line with her colleagues. At regular meetings several journalists would lodge the fiercest protests against Sonny, with my PA chiming in from the sidelines, saying she was simply not able to deliver the goods when it came to seeing to work they'd put in her way, or which they'd asked ask her to take care of.

Rights, that's all she cared about. Not duties. "This here's supposed to be a professional outfit, but you, you're just an amateur, Son." As if to add insult to injury, there were all these receipts spread out on the table. For the purchase of staples and felt-tipped markers, for cab fare, motorbike lifts to the shooting location, print washing, film processing. "Actually you're supposed to send stuff like that up to the office, Son. A good thing for all of us you're not the one in charge of finances round here!"

Several others had cornered her and were giving her a hard time, wondering what her photojournalism added up to, accusing her of everything from absentmindedness to having made promises only to break them, not to mention of having temped as a model.

"Sonny's not yet fit to be called a professional photographer," our fashions and woman's page editor submitted. "I'm asking for her to be directed from now on toward fashion design. She can do some modeling for the various features. You know, accessories, beauty tips, recipes even. I mean, it saves on time and money, doesn't it? Beats paying some model for each separate occasion. She'd be willing to do each assignment on a one-off basis. This pigheadedness of hers, what must it be costing us!"

Sonny Wouthuyzen: a tough nut to crack. What a job, getting her to face up, and face up squarely, to the way people ought to live their lives. Her fate—*was* it her fate?—lay in my hands, I found out the day the boss had me on the carpet. "Whether she goes or stays is entirely up to you. If you think you still need her, that's fine by me, just carry on. I've every confidence in your being able to ease the tension among the editorial staff. It's not a big problem, after all, is it?"

Rather a small one, he should have thought, actually. Keeping up good relations on the job, now what was so very difficult about that? The point being, we had to do everything possible to stay on the safe side. We take our orders from the Department of Information. In our line of work it didn't do for anyone to be linked with or show sympathy for a banned political party. "You'll forgive my saying so, of course, I'm not accusing her of being a communist or a left-winger, or heaven forbid anything to do with G-30-S/PKI. But you've got to admit, all the signs are pointing in that direction. I don't care how you do it, but run a check on her family background. We've got to keep our noses clean if we're going to have any sort of future. God knows what sort of a fool she is, but when it comes to being idealistic she seems to want to go one better on all these young kids of ours. You know, the ones studying all about social disparities in the country."

An agonizing decision to have to make; enough to make you ill. Whether handed down in tablet form as it were, or mixed into a glass of *jamu* tonic, it could prove a bitter one to swallow. But what about the good of people in general? Was that of no account? Someone goes to the stake so that the community's integrity stays intact, so that it can carry on speaking with one voice. The way of the world, isn't it? Say you've got a violinist who's not up to scratch; why, you wouldn't think twice, would you, about slinging him out of the orchestra—unless you wanted harmony to go to pot. All of which explains how Sonny, she of the difficult-to-pronounce name, found herself forced to hand in her letter of resignation, with severance pay forfeited. She put on a brave front though inside she was all broken up.

"Photography's booming, Son," I said, in an effort to cheer her up. "There's bound to be heaps of firms in the media and on its fringe that need a photographer."

I didn't dare suggest she try her luck with any of the mass media. I was just putting the popular view, the view which held that Sonny's ideas were so advanced she deserved to set up as a broker in the intellectual marketplace, trading in abstractions before translating them into real work. If you really want to know, I felt ashamed of myself. Ashamed to find myself caught and held in Sonny's gaze with its glint of blue, the gaze she got from her Dutch mother. I'd gone and derailed somebody's passage through life, knocked her off course, and now I hadn't the guts even to see her out and say good-bye at the door. Off she went, keeping a stiff upper lip, carrying all her photographic equipment, and her heart along with it.

The daily regime took up so much time and so much energy that I hardly ever got the chance just to pass the time of day with anybody. Worse, I was managing to read hardly anything that mattered, nothing that might help to broaden my horizons and sharpen my grasp of things. At most I'd open some foreign journal to find some crock of lies about world developments, some crap about pop stars' lives or about actors having nervous breakdowns, or some blathering article by a gossip queen. I'd get this craving, sometimes, for real ideas, ideas in no way, shape, or form associated with the so-called advanced countries. What a farce all of that seemed.

The whole world was suddenly convulsed, jolted by the bullheadedness of its chief politicos, jarred by small wars you may have missed, the evening news full of gunpowder, the screen littered with corpses. The yen was overtaking the U.S. dollar, stock markets were packed with people stressed out of their tiny minds, ties askew, arms waving madly in the air. When push came to shove, I couldn't give a damn, the more so when I got a call from a woman colleague of Japanese nationality.

"Look, *mas,* it's not as if I'm wanting to defend my country, but this tragedy, it's the doing of the U.S.A. Can't you see their war debts are at the bottom of it all? What's more, they seem to think that peddling narcotics to Latin America is going to produce a breakthrough. The CIA's leading us up the garden path. On the one hand they say they want to smash the drug trade, but on the other they're using it for their own purposes, and to subsidize American standards of living."

Latin America—again. Not for the first time I'd be put in mind of Sonny Wouthuyzen, that name of hers so hard to pronounce but she herself, heaven knew, all too easy to remember. Where'd she end up, anyway? Still alive, or gone to the dogs? Somehow I couldn't bring myself to ask my PA for her address. Trust some of the journalists not to be bothered to tell me they'd run into her at the "press conference," which was the term we used for the meetings at which we discussed the allocation of finances. Instead, they set up a stir when sales reported a drop in circulation—bad news for our journal.

"Right then. No need for us to get all hot under the collar worrying about what the public wants," one of the journos put in cynically. "We've still got our niche, there's no question about where we stand.

It's not as if we haven't got a name or a market, is it now? I wouldn't go playing around with fire if I was you, to say nothing about not going in for soft porn. There's the Department of Information and its regulations to reckon with."

There wasn't much doubt that this was meant for me, in a round-about sort of way. My PA's answer to this was to shove onto the table some letters from readers, which praised the cover of our latest edition to the skies. He knew there was no stopping me when I had made up my mind, in this case to buy some slides from a freelance photographer which I thought were a value for the money. Quite a few of our readers, as it turned out, thought otherwise: the photos weren't big enough and didn't leap off the page at you. I began to suspect there was more in store when the boss called me in.

"What's all this artsy-craftsy stuff you've been doing? Don't you know artwork's only worth taking on when it's got commercial value?" I couldn't bear to look at his face with its puckered, citronlike skin. I just stood there, taking in these beginner's lessons about photography and sales. "The cover, man, that's what accounts for one-third of any magazine's drawing power. Our readers, they're busy people all right, they might not read what's in it. But a cover, now that's what busy folk or people with no money look at. When people say the cover's what matters, that the cover's got to be special, you can be sure they know what they're talking about."

Yes, boss. Right you are, boss. Very good, boss. You know the proverb, don't you, the one about how it doesn't matter who you work under, the Boss Is Always Right, whatever he says goes and screw the risks? You better believe it. He gets to dream up all the bright ideas. And the staff? They're left holding the baby. The point of their having thoughts and views of their own, is it to poke holes in any grand conception the boss might have? Not a bit of it. It's to suggest fine-tuning. And they call that a proper work ethic. I ask you. Proposals? You can make proposals till the cows come home, but if you think they'll be acted on, you've got another think coming.

"Let's not go and turn the economy or the recession or devaluation into a convenient scapegoat. Here's your chance to show how good you are at managing a journal. And don't go dragging other departments into this. Advertising, promotion, circulation, distribution— they're all doing very nicely, thank you very much. Face the facts. Subscriptions have plummeted overnight, they're the lowest ever. So, what other excuse have you got to offer me, eh? Hundreds of work-ers—no, *thousands,* if you count newsagents and delivery boys—their lives are in your hands. They're hanging on your decision.

Sonny Wouthuyzen: hell of a name to pronounce, harder to spell, but how could you forget her? Suddenly I was swept by a longing to see her, to talk about old times. I wanted to hear her describe her background, her people, the Depok Dutch. The burghers who came to Indonesia, then bought up land all over the place, in Kwitang, Kramat, Petojo, Batutulis, and just before the end, at the southern end of the Pasar Minggu district, thereafter known as Depok. There was an old lake there, a sacred site, and a church destroyed by earthquake and subsequently rebuilt. I wanted to hear about it, the better to make sense of what work might have meant to them, the better to learn where they'd got their courage from, and at the same time, where they'd found the guts to become the tinpot rajas they'd always fancied themselves.

I put my signature to the letter of resignation I'd already drawn up. The firm may have been owned and operated by human beings, but humane it wasn't. Whatever else it could lay claim to, a civilized attitude wasn't one of its qualities. Nothing mattered except advancing the company's self-interest—that and raking in the profits. Support staff had to be on the go night and day, and at the same time ready to sit up on their hind legs and wait for instructions. If you wanted to survive, let alone to make it, you had to kill off every spark of human-ity, you had to set conscience firmly to one side. Fortunately—for the firm—replacements could always be found to bring in double the profit.

"Information's big business these days, that's where the money is. You've got potential, pity to neglect it. Eat my hat if there aren't any number of outfits in the mass media that'll be out gunning for you, with your talent and reputation."

The very tone I'd used, the same way I'd put it when I'd let Sonny go, back then. Only now it was more on target, the Boss having the gall to aim a meaningful look at me as he handed over a bulging envelope, which, in some confusion, I put into my briefcase. He even saw fit to walk me out into the foyer, where a few journos were looking on cynically, the expressions plastered all over their faces saying you make me sick. If they'd an instinct for anything at all, it was for nothing so much as whining on pathetically about their sad fate, griping about their place on the duty list, or complaining about the size of their golden handshake. I believed that then, and I believe it now. I missed Sonny desperately, missed her if for no other reason than I needed someone I could have a proper heart-to-heart with. Two of a kind, we were, both having got the sack.

Fortunately—if good fortune's what you'd call it—I was still an ex-journalist, assuming that's the right expression. I could still sniff out a lead, and, following my nose, I managed after a month had passed to run Sonny to earth. Feeling suitably humbled and putting on my best face for the occasion, I paid a visit to the office where she worked—to have someone feel sorry for me; in all probability some primitive instinct of that sort was the motive. Anything to reduce stress and ease my mind. I wanted this Sonny, this Sonny whose name was so difficult to pronounce and to spell, I wanted her to give me a job. I didn't want to end up on the scrap heap.

She was looking smashing: neatly turned out, rouged lips, glittering footwear, face bright, all smiles. I found myself bowing repeatedly when she made her entrance; great play was made, by her secretary and by several of the clerical staff, of showing me a respect they most certainly didn't really feel. All at once, here in Sonny's presence, I felt very small, completely insignificant. This young woman was clearly born to be a leader. She wasn't some nobody.

"Look, *mas,* let's stop this farting around. You've simply got to get it into your head, this is a small-time operation. It *was* you, was it not, who gave me the bright idea of going into business for myself? You're right, *mas,* there's a crying need for photographers. That's how I've come to set up this little advertising outfit. Don't get me wrong; I'm not about to challenge the big boys on their own ground. They've got their international networks. But I've carved out my own market niche. *Mas,* my clients are in a class of their own."

So we're back to a class of one's own, are we? Back to the class war and the Wealth of Nations. Sorry, those aren't my hang-ups. Not my scene, intellectually speaking. Let's just suppose I pretend to go along with all of this, for the sake of being taken on by Sonny's operation. I've no doubt she'd think me perfectly capable of taking charge of the text department, supervising the copywriters, and keeping an eye on what goes into the adverts. But I'd have to work under Sonny's command, I'd have to become a cog in the kind of creative team—a team bursting with piss and vinegar—I'd once asked her to join. Is it true what they say, that life's all a muddle at times? True that you can win through eventually to some sort of self-confidence and self-respect? Where could I have left it, my self-respect? Your guess is as good as mine.

"We've got to work on broadening our horizons, *mas,* and on refreshing our thinking. Competition's fierce, and the clientele's getting choosy. What we earn depends on the satisfaction we're able to give."

Fighting talk, but necessary, for all that. At the very least you need it to help you keep your head screwed on, to teach you the value of time, and of going back and doing the work again until you get it right. I daresay I needed to hear it as well, for much the same reasons. Given time, and a growing demand for the services of advertising firms, prospects would brighten. High time for me to settle on a strategy that would do the trick. In the old days I'd managed to tumble Sonny Wouthuyzen out of the journal face flat, and I don't doubt I'll be able to elbow her out of this firm. Or at least split it in two, with part falling into my lap. Best take steps, and be quick about it too, before the firm gets to be too big to handle. Humane steps, to be sure.

In the Net

(Kena Jaring)

---

by Rahmat Ali

The minutes creep by: it's pure torture. Haven't the foggiest how I'm supposed to get to work on time. Turning up late, that's bad enough, but when your schedule's packed, all hell breaks loose. Take today. There are these guests I've promised to receive, three very important letters that need to be sent ASAP to the governor of Greater Jakarta. Plus I've got to put my signature to proposals recommending promotion for my junior colleagues. After that there's that monthly meeting to attend with head of personnel. A mountain of stuff on my desk to see to.

Not that I've made it professionally. Not by a long chalk. When it comes down to it, the perks and privileges, the little things that make all the difference, they've passed me by. So far, no official residence, just rented quarters off in some kampung. A car with red number plates? You're joking—I don't even qualify for official transport. Stuck with taking the bus to work every morning. The trysts on wheels, the funny way they get started, evolve, then peter out—there's never a dull moment. There's *that* to be said for taking the bus, at least.

I take two of them to work, day in day out. The first takes me from Ragunan to Kebayoran. No big deal. I take a sort of minivan, wine-red, the color of a mangosteen. A zippy ride, who cares if the van's crumbling to bits. A quarter of an hour and you're there. Then I change to a bigger bus. That's the second, going from Blok M to Kota, SMS; you know, the blue buses. Greyhound, made in the U.S.A.

Doesn't matter how fast they go, it still takes ages. It's a fair distance. As a rule I get off at Beos, in front of the railway station. You can walk it from there.

Kota's hugger-mugger with government offices, banks, and corporations. The clerical staff who work in there live by and large on Jakarta's South Side. Small wonder the SMS bus is crammed with them. It's the most popular line, full to bursting at the very first stop. Doesn't matter how many extra buses they lay on, it feels like the stream of passengers is never going to dry up. I should know, I'm one of them, and I've yet boarded.

Many's the time I've invited my wife to come down the office, on that crowded bus. She'll feel ill by the time she gets home. She's had it up to here, she says, with going by bus, that's the last time she's tagging along. "Mind how you go now, *mas!*" her parting words will be when I'm setting off for work. She's right, it *is* pretty awful. But then, that's life, isn't it!

First time round, four years ago, I felt like my body was being pounded to pieces. As if someone or something had grabbed hold of it and yanked it limb from limb. I'd fortify myself by drinking some *jamu* every morning and before going to bed. I can take it now, I don't feel poorly all the time, I'm not always fighting a cold.

"One at a time, please, one at a time!" goes the voice of the Jakarta municipal services officer, echoing over his loudspeaker. The bus conductor's busy at the door handing out tickets. "No need to rush, there's lots more buses after this one." The voice booms out over the loudspeaker, but do you suppose anyone's listening? All they're doing is elbowing forward with greater vigor, everyone pushing and shoving after his own fashion, keen to be the first to be seated—no, more than keen. Positively passionate. "One at a time, please!" booms the chap with the loudspeaker. And the bus is full up.

I'm not about to take any silly risks. Look at what happened the other day, when that accident happened. The bus was barreling along toward Kota when somebody tried to hop on before it had come to a complete stop. He missed his step, slipped and fell, and his foot got run over by the back wheel. You'd think this tragedy would be fresh in everyone's mind, wouldn't you. Not at all.

"Wait till the bus stops," I say. "Don't rush!"

But they've forgotten again. They're going to break the rules, again. Danger's looming.

Mind how you go now, mas, my wife's voice rings in my ear.

"'Course I will. What do you take me for?"

While all this is going on, buses done up in all colors of the rainbow are beeping and honking, their horns sounding and resounding as they jostle and fight their way into the depot at Blok M. There's this one particular bus which always come rattling and shaking in to the *dangdut* rhythm of Malay music. Party time, on wheels! But what really scares you is the sheer crassness of the drivers. The brutes will never, *ever* slow down, not even when pulling up at the terminal platform. They'll screech to a stop, then hover there, engines throbbing, for all the world like giant insects, before spewing passengers from Banteng, Grogol, Kota. Then they'll scoop up fresh victims, the people who have to take them to get to where they're wanting to go.

The minutes I'm frittering away are starting to mount up. I'm staring intently at the hands of my watch. Done for: *very* late. Sodding nuisance. All at once it's as if someone's stubbed out the fire blazing in me, when for the umpteenth time the bus just stands there throbbing. I follow along and pretty soon am one of the first to hop on board.

"Whew, we can breathe easy now!" says a man of about thirty-five, who's managed to do the same and is sitting right across the aisle from me. I've no choice except to smile wanly. City folk, they're weird. You can be on nodding terms with someone for donkey's years, but that doesn't mean you'll bother to get to know each other by name. So all we do is sit there, in stony silence. Lucky me, I thought, I've got a window seat, I can enjoy the passing view. Oh yes, it's scenic all right, except I don't know that *scenic*'s quite the word for it. At night you get all these fairy lights, at high noon everything's shimmering, and when it rains your teeth will knock. Now I was seeing Jakarta decked out in its early morning best. Later it'll get to be a furnace and in no time at all the landscape will start to go all shimmery in the heat haze. You melt in the heat. "Okay, move it!" the conductor at the back commands, and the driver steps on the gas. The bus lurches forward. That's when it starts: traveling theater!

Not too far from the front I can see some people waving like mad for the bus to stop. It brakes to a halt, but not before passengers manage to wedge themselves in the door. That's when somebody screams, and I see a woman practically go through the glass, though she catches herself and stops it happening in the nick of time. Thank heaven for that!

"What d'you mean, shoving like that! Where are your manners? Is that how you treat a woman? For crying out loud!"

" 'For crying out loud' yourself! Just take a look, will you? Can't you see all the people backed up against the door. If you don't want to be pushed, don't take the bus!"

The woman colors up with rage, while hands on hips, the youth, incensed at being accused for no good reason, is getting ready for battle.

"Tickets, who hasn't bought tickets?" the conductor calls out, forcing his way in amongst the standing passengers.

A few of them have to check. They'll have stored theirs in their bags, or else they've got them tucked under their watch straps. "If you haven't paid up," he drones on, "now's your chance. The next conductor that checks isn't gonna stand for no excuses. See if you don't get thrown off!"

Before anyone can come back at this, he goes back up to the front. "Deplu,* anyone for Deplu?"

No one's for Deplu. "Drive on!"

The driver starts to give it the gas. The wind comes whistling through the window, sweeping through my long hair.

A horn beeps, and beeps again. Up in front, over to the left, a *helicak,* a three-wheeled motorized pedicab, is refusing to budge. The conductors at the front and at the back are hopping mad.

"Son of a bitch! Fed up with it all, are you?"

"Go screw a water buffalo, why don't you!" the one at the back chimes in.

Pulling his steering wheel hard left the *helicak* driver wriggles and squirms his way out of his spot in the treacly flow of traffic.

The passengers who've caught all this are wearing looks of surprise; some, the ones who've heard the conductor wisecracking, are rolling in the aisles. As for him and his colleague at the back, they've had their fill of effing and blinding and are basking now in a warm glow of contentment.

"Half a sec. Where's me change?"

"How much did you give me just now?"

"One hundred rupiahs."

"How's it I haven't got a hundred rupiah note back from you then, ma'am?"

---

*Deplu: Acronym for Departemen Luar Negeri, or Ministry of Foreign Affairs.

"What about just now? The one you put into your tin?"

"Next time, make sure you've got the exact change ready before you get on, ma'am. Got me hands full with everyone on board now. Can't you see?"

"Fine, only don't come all innocent like, when nobody's even asked!"

Seeing as it's a woman he's up against, the conductor bites his tongue.

A mere handful of passengers gets on, climbing aboard at the Komdak bus stop. A few, tickets in hand, manage to get through the rear door. The conductor at the back clambers up the window. In no time at all his left hand's stabbing the air accusingly with his index finger: "Further up, further up, move along down inside, *pak.* Plenty of seats way down at the back. The gentleman in the check shirt. That's right, you there, *if* you wouldn't mind just moving up a bit, *mas.* Mind the ones over by the stairs. One people, one nation, ain't it now, *mas!*"

One people, one nation. That's what he calls us all. Honestly!

"Move along to where, I wonder?" an old man grumps.

"Up onto the roof's what he means, I expect," someone standing next to him replies.

"Can you beat it. Bum to bum, and still they're packing them in!" "More money, that's what they're grubbing for!" "Would you mind moving down a bit, *pak,* yes, that's it, move down." Move down? You can hardly move your foot! The ones lucky to be seated comfortably don't give a toss. There's no way the men sitting down are going to offer up their places, not even if a woman happens to be standing there, right beside them. There's still a fair way to go, and to go it you have to sit down, *if* you can. Who wants to be a martyr? I'm sitting pretty, you won't catch me playing the gentleman, any more than them. No way. God knows I try often enough to grab a seat but get beaten to it. They'll all be grabbed before you know it, the occupants laughing all the way to the bank, or looking as well they might be. I'll squirm and wriggle about. Talk about not having room to swing a cat, there won't even be room to *stand,* even if I'd wanted to. It'll be all I can do just to hold my ground on my few square centimeters of the stairwell, half of me fluttering in the breeze, the wind blasting through my body.

I'm only human, I'll groan in protest. I'll think, if only I were sitting down, at my leisure, not all keyed up like this, not staring blearily at the hard asphalt, which looks as though at any moment it's going to rasp my entire body. Splendid buildings flank Jalan Thamrin, towering upward, monstrous. Have they any inkling at all of my fate? Are they conscious of little old me, standing there on the stairwell of the bus? Their windows, watchful as eyes, look on, stirred, I fancy, to compassion and to pity, but also full of cynicism. The lights turn amber and start flashing, bidding traffic proceed with caution. A siren wails, long and loud, three police motorcycle outriders race up to the front, ahead of a black sedan bedecked with flags all gaily fluttering, a unit of armed guards at its tail. I swear, that's the life! What wouldn't I give to lead it. What wouldn't *you,* come to that. To be chauffeured round by a driver someday, lounging there in the back of the car, reading while you puff away at a cheroot. Highway heaven! A pipe dream, of course. No sense living with your head in the clouds. I'm a bureaucrat with no special entitlements coming to me.

Fine. I accept it. I'm proud to go by bus. Specially when, as so often happens, a pretty young thing will bob up out of nowhere. The acrid smells'll vanish, and what hits your nostrils is the smell of perfume from her short, see-through blouse. Wet, bee-stung lips, hair long and unkempt, sweat-pasted to her bosom. My heart will start to pound on cue, swept by a gust of erotic fantasy. Sadly for me, Miss Heart-Stopper soon gets off and it's back to breathing in the acrid fumes and feeling a loser. And then when people tread on the toe of my shoe without even saying sorry, I'll feel all the more like someone who just can't live right. My rotten luck, all over; being me's the worst of it. And I've said nothing about all those times when I'll find myself up against a real brute of a driver, the sort who goes careering round corners as sharply as he can, the bus skidding across the road. And of course when he slams on the brakes it just has to be with no warning at all. The row of standing passengers, the ones not holding on for dear life, will topple over backward, bananas lopped off the stem. Crazy, isn't it! They'll let fly a string of four-letter words, but the driver, what does he care? He'll keep the accelerator nailed to the floor. Those not used to it feel sick to their stomachs. I'll see a woman dressed like she was up from the country jackknife over, heaving up her morning's breakfast onto the floor. Well, if that's his little game he can do as he bloody well likes! Take us wherever the hell he wants. Only, please God, don't let him go crashing into a bridge. Or impaling us all on the boundary fence, like what happened last year. He went so fast the bus veered out of control, threatening to flatten itself against an iron fence, so fast it brought us to within inches of being skewered on the palings. I prayed the Lord we wouldn't all end up chicken *satay* that morning.

I've come to have a pretty good idea exactly which office workers will get off at Merdeka Square and which at Harmoni or at Gadjah Mada. I've even got to know the pickpocket working the route. He'll be more nattily dressed than your run-of-the-mill bureaucrat like me. The passengers, they won't suspect a thing. It's only when he's hopped off the bus that the ones he's fingered will raise a hue and cry. They'll find that their bags have been slashed with a razor, though of course by then he's nowhere to be found. I'll have no wish to get involved, that's for sure. It'd be more than my life's worth, knowing as I do that the thief won't be slow to use that razor on me. Anyhow, he's got a living to make just like the rest of us, hasn't he?

I come to from these daydreams when from somewhere in the vicinity of the front someone's heard crying "Fire! Fire!" There's smoke all right, I can see it billowing out quite clearly. Not even stopping to think, everyone fights to get free. Once outside and in the clear, I come upon a man whose head's been badly bruised, another whose hand's bleeding from having been caught in the squeeze, and a woman who's pale and trembling. "We'll just have to change buses," a girl observes. "Better you than me. I'm terrified!" The passengers are now down to half their number. Others are standing round, awaiting developments. "What d'you think's happened?" somebody asks. I'm dying to find out too. I go over to the front of the bus and look in at the driver's seat, around which a huddle's formed. "Blasted sacking," the driver finally yells out. "Who's the idiot that's put this on top of this cable? Seems the rubber's caught fire."

"Frigging hell!" bus conductor says. A passenger pokes his head up to shout a query over in the general direction of the driver. "This bus carrying on or what, *bang?*

"Right, let's be off!" The remaining passengers, those who've managed to retain any affection at all for the blue SMS buses, climb aboard to find themselves given the freedom of the bus, able to stretch out now that they're no longer packed together like sardines in a tin. "Kota, Kota!" tout the conductors, forward and aft. I settle down near the window. It may have been long in coming, but when it does comes, my smile is one of pure relief. O frabjous joy!

Notes and Comments on the Stories and Authors

Idrus: Three Tales from the Occupation

"The three and a half years of Japanese occupation," the historian Merle Ricklefs writes,

> constitute one of the most crucial periods in Indonesian history. Before the Japanese invasion, no serious challenge to the Dutch existed. By the time the Japanese surrendered, there had been so many changes that the Indonesian Revolution was possible. The Japanese contributed directly to these developments. Especially in Java and to a lesser extent in Sumatra, they indoctrinated, trained and armed many of the younger generation. . . . Throughout the archipelago they politicised Indonesians down to the village level both by intention and by subjecting Indonesia to the most oppressive and devastating colonial regime in its history. . . . Compulsory food requisitioning and labour recruitment along with the general chaos led to famine . . . [and] Indonesia became a land of extreme hardship, inflation, shortages, profiteering, corruption, black markets and death. (*A History of Modern Indonesia c. 1300 to the Present.* Basingstoke: Macmillan Press, 1981, pp. 187-89)

It was not meant to be so. Japanese policy was to conciliate the inhabitants of the Indies and win them over to their cause; it was designed to mobilize a subjugated populace, not just to control it. The aim was to convince Indonesians that they and the Japanese were working hand in hand to realize a new order in Asia: the Greater East Asia Co-Prosperity Sphere. For the duration, Japanese propaganda promoted the exaltation of Asians and the degradation of the white man.

This propaganda was directed not toward intellectuals but toward boys and girls between the ages of ten and twenty, and to the unlettered masses of Indonesia, and its forum was the stage, schools, radio, and the press, in that order of importance. The schools were made to conform to a Japanese pattern, and the Japanese language itself was mandatory. Radio was widely used—every kampung had its "singing tree"; the press being of little value to a population 90 percent of whom were illiterate. Direct examples of the humiliation of the European were constantly before the eyes of Indonesians, and, in place of the Dutch civil administration, Indonesian teachers and officials were installed, some as *sanyo* or advisers to the Japanese administration. In 1943 the *heiho,* or Auxiliary Forces, which was linked to the Japanese army and navy, was established: by the end of the war, more than 25,000 Indonesian youths had been recruited into the *heiho* to receive basic training. Other new youth and military groups were created: the Jawa Hokokai, or Java Service Association, was set up for all youths of fourteen and above. This organization was exploited by Sukarno to enhance his position as leader of the nationalist movement in popular eyes. At the village level, *rukun tetangga,* neighborhood associations, were created to mobilize, indoctrinate, and inform families, with headmen and low-level administrators overseeing.

But as the war in the Pacific proceeded, the early enthusiasm of the *rakyat,* the mass of petty tradesmen and craftsmen, peddlers, farmers, and kampung folk, quickly became bewilderment, disappointment, and disillusion with their new masters. Young people volunteering for the PETA (*Pembela Tanah Air,* the Defenders of the Homeland Corps), the Indonesian volunteer army which was to serve as a training ground for the Revolution, found themselves treated high-handedly by their patrons. Arrogance, occasional cruelty, and arbitrary punishment ceded to systematic maltreatment, beating, robbery, starvation, and murder. Worst of all, hundreds of thousands of Indonesians of peasant background, whom the Japanese referred to as *romushas,* were pressed into service as slave labor in Japan itself and sent to work on the construction of the infamous Thai–Burma railway. Forced rice requisitioning and food rationing led to outbreaks of famine in 1944 and 1945. It is not surprising that the early fascination with Japan turned to repulsion.

Of all this, as of its immediate aftermath, Idrus is the superb chronicler. In a handful of sketches written during the war and immediately afterward, he offers an inward view of conditions on Java during 1942–45.

These stories tell us more than any learned tome could possibly hope to achieve, about what it was like for ordinary Indonesians. "Surabaya," a long short story that reads like a telescoped novel (it has a similar depth and intensity), is his most famous tale: it deals with the bloody defense of the city against returning Allied forces in November 1946, the fiercest battle of the Revolution, which quickly became a national symbol of resistance. It exemplifies his style: terse, sardonic, darkly funny, hallucinatorily vivid. The three tales presented here are color-transparencies from the time of suffering and upheaval immediately preceding. Except in Pramoedya, they have no equal elsewhere in Indonesian literature.

These stories are not terribly profound; they are hardly more than vignettes. But what vignettes! Their language, marinated in Javanese and Malay colloquialisms, is direct and punchy. The humor is acerbic—the laughter is to keep from crying—and is promiscuous in its bitterness: no ethnic group, no social class, is spared sarcasm. Mixed with this contempt is sorrow and pity. The strong *kerakyatan,* or proletarian, feel is a function of Idrus's closeness to his material: the view is from the bottom up.

Born in Padang in Sumatra, Idrus (1921-79) is considered one of the finest prose writers of the Angkatan '45, the generation of writers who reached maturity during the war and who published their work immediately after it and during the Revolution. He had a varied career, first as an editor with Balai Pustaka, the colonial publishing house, and later with the journals *Indonesia* and *Kisah* and as an employee of Garuda Indonesian Airways. Toward the end of his life he was a postgraduate student and later lectured in modern Indonesian literature at Monash University in Australia. He died in Melbourne.

Major works: *Dari Ave Maria ke Jalan Lain ke Roma* (1948) [short stories]; *Aki* (1950) [novel]; *Dua Episode Masa Kecil* (1952) [short stories]; *Dengan Mata Terbuka* (Kuala Lumpur, 1961) [short stories]; *Hikayat Puteri Penelope* (1961) [novel]. A selection of Idrus's fiction also appears in *Menagerie III*, ed. John H. McGlynn (Jakarta: Yayasan Lontar, 1994).

Pramoedya Ananta Toer: For Hire/*Yang Menyewakan Diri*

The proclamation of Indonesian independence on 17 August 1945 unleashed five years of struggle that culminated in diplomatic recognition of Indonesia's sovereignty in December 1949. It was a time of extraordinary political turbulence as well as personal excitement, but also of tragedy in the lives of the many thousands of Indonesians who took part in that struggle. Tragedy, in that the Revolution brought in its train social collapse: not only extraordinary physical violence but internal conflict as between, for example, the former *pangreh pradja*—the indigenous civil service class created by the Dutch and drawn from the upper Javanese aristocracy—and the *rakyat* (common people) or *wong cilik* (ordinary folk); between authority and anarchy; and between the generations. Cruelty, the loss of personal integrity, the destruction of family life, egoism, and a feeling of utter helplessness—these were as much a part of the experience of Revolusi as were the fervor and exhilaration of the *perjuangan,* the struggle, against a Netherlands bent on taking up where it had been forced to leave off in 1942.

To Indonesians themselves, and above all to the Javanese, there is no better interpreter of this many-sided experience than Pramoedya Ananta Toer. This, in part, is what makes Pram what he is in the eyes of so many: the greatest writer modern Indonesia has produced. His early writings develop out of recollections of childhood, through the havoc of revolution, armed struggle, and imprisonment to the ambiguous situation of postrevolutionary life in Jakarta when cynicism, loss of idealism, and corruption seemed the order of the day. The later oeuvre is crowned by the famous quartet of novels known to English readers as *This Earth of Mankind,* the title of the first volume in the series *Bumi Manusia* translated into English by Max Lane. In it is found a penetrating analysis of the psychology and sociology of colonial subjugation around the turn of the century, carried out through the biography of Minke, an Indonesian pupil at a Dutch secondary school in Surabaya who learns to release himself from the trammels of his highborn Javanese background. These books, written under extreme duress during 1965-79 and first published in 1981, deserve their subsequent fame: the quartet is epic in scope and its bias radical; it makes sense of modern Indonesian history to Indonesians in ways that go against the grain, the New Order state having set its face against militant politics and promoted the styles and traditions of the *priyayi,* the elite stratum of ethnic Javanese society. This said, it's not, I believe, quite the best that Indonesian literature has to offer. Pram, here, is long-winded, his people seldom present in more than one dimension. The reverse holds true for his stories.

A full account of what his greatness consists of in that one dimension would touch upon his virtuoso command of the Indonesian language, which is haunted by Javanisms and therefore lost in translation. But in any assessment it must be remarked how trenchant are Pramoedya's criticisms of the culture with which, in love and in hate, he is so inward. The tales in *Cerita Dari Blora* (Stories From Blora, 1952) close with the hypocrisy and cruelty, as Pramoedya judges it to be, of Javanese mores. These are seen as a thin skin covering the fear, greed, and jealousy that lie beneath the facade of orderly everyday existence. Under the stress of war, and because the Dutch had for so long eroded their internal position, the *priyayi* code of ethics and behavior is breaking down in these stories, and with it the traditional symbiosis of gentry and peasant. Supposedly still the cultural leaders, and, so far as indigenous society was concerned, the ruling class too, the *priyayi* no longer exemplify the virtues of self-control and self-discipline in speech and in conduct. They have ceased to be honorable, and their celebrated "calm assertion of spiritual superiority," to use Clifford Geertz's phrase, is at a discount. Their "charisma," their nonrational ability to command assent, has dissipated. Indirection and dissimulation, once admired as subtle, have now acquired a sinister quality, exacerbated by "the madness of the times," as Pramoedya himself calls it in a pointed reference to earlier periods in Javanese history when, it was universally felt, the center could not hold.

All this is registered in "For Hire," through the eyes of a child, who questions and explores the limits of a partially known but menacing world, a world where murder, prostitution, betrayal are taking place, leaving no one untouched, though none dare identify them as such. The atmosphere is claustrophobic: every act is scrutinized, the imagery phantasmagoric. Fathers, older folk, nobility, all are suspect, all seen through. Whom shall I respect? Who is worth looking up to? On what grounds? These are some of the questions asked by this spare, understated narrative. Submerged beneath the chaos of war lies another subject: the complicated business of *wis jawa,* becoming Javanese, which for the Javanese is an education in emotional maturity and control and also a falling-into-the-world out of a state of untutored innocence that knows no bounds. Exactly what, in society and in its microcosm, the family, are the limits? That is a further question here. In deceptively ungarnished prose that is eloquent with the tension of unspoken things, Pramoedya's early stories vouchsafe the emotions and central attitudes of his people as no outsider could ever hope to do. This is one measure of their success, and of their allure.

The author was born in Blora in Central Java in 1925, the son of a disappointed nationalist schoolmaster disastrously given to gambling. He never finished secondary school and worked as a stenographer during the Japanese occupation, joining the Indonesian armed forces on the outbreak of revolution. In the aftermath of the 1965 coup he was arrested on grounds of his earlier leftist sympathies. He was imprisoned without trial on the remote, snake-infested island of Buru in the Moluccas and only freed in 1979. He has since been persona non grata. Publication and circulation of his books is forbidden at the time of this writing, and his movements restricted, though he is becoming known to a wider public overseas; his works have been translated into many Asian and European languages. During captivity, denied use of a typewriter, he resorted to the expedient of dictating his quartet of novels to his fellow prisoners. There has been talk of nominating Pramoedya for the Nobel Prize in Literature.

Major works: *Kranji dan Bekasi Jatuh* (1947); *Keluarga Gerilya, Perburuan* (1950), *Mereka Yang Dilumpuhkan, Bukan Pasar Malam, Dia Yang Menyerah, Korupsi* (1951), *Gulat di Jakarta* (1953), *Midah Si Manis Bergigi Emas* (1954), *Di Tepi Kali Bekasi* (1957) [novels]; *Subuh, Percikan Revolusi* (1950), *Cerita Dari Jakarta* (1957) [short stories]. Pramoedya's quartet has appeared in Penguin, and *Perburuan* has been translated as *The Fugitive* by Harry Aveling, in two of whose collections, *From Surabaya to Armageddon* (1976) and *A Heap of Ashes* (1975), other stories by him are to be found. Aveling has also translated into English Pramoedya's novel *Gadis Pantai (The Girl From the Coast* [Singapore: Select Books, 1992]). There is a thoughtful essay on Pramoedya by Benedict Anderson in Leonard S. Klein, ed., *Far Eastern Literatures in the Twentieth Century: A Guide* (New York: Ungar, 1986), pp. 67-70.

Achdiat Karta Mihardja: A Twist of Fate/*Belitan Nasib*

To Indonesian readers, Achdiat Karta Mihardja is best known for his classic novel *Atheis* (*The Atheist,* 1949), whose story pivots on the struggle between a piously Muslim world view and a skeptical Marxist outlook corrosive of received ideas. This makes the book sound duller than it is. In fact, it's anything but boring. Achdiat has a short, sharp way with a plot and a shrewd appreciation of the strains in the fabric of life in the modernizing republic. His first collection of short stories is aptly enough entitled *Keretakan dan Ketegangan* (*Fissures and Tensions,* 1956). In the tale offered here, taken from this collection, it's the rural village as distinct from the intelligentsia that finds itself at the breaking point. How it survives the test of a crisis is Achdiat's subject.

The nature of the crisis, and Achdiat's handling of it, call for two comments. First: it's a near thing. The recidivist all but succeeds in undermining a way of life far gone in torpor. His rapacity is in some ways admirable because, serving to show up the inertia of the community he energetically battens and on it, it suggests that it's long overdue for a shake-up. How long overdue be seen from the way Suarma, Misbach's prey, no longer willing to accept his *nasib,* or destiny, seizes and "twists" it in a new direction. In certain respects nothing has changed at the end; in others, everything.

Second: Achdiat's village world is, unmistakably, a Javanese one. The main form of work, *sawah,* or wet-rice cultivation on terraced hillsides, which enables two harvests per year in some areas, is one of the two agricultural methods in use in Java. The regulating social values are likewise distinctively Javanese: notice how Munah, the wife, is likened in passing to a *dalang,* or puppeteer-narrator of *wayang kulit,* Javanese shadow-puppetry, in virtue of her wit and reported way with words. Achdiat takes as read an awareness on the part of an Indonesian audience of the place occupied by the *wayang* world at the center of Javanese life. Then there is Suarma's refusal to give a *selamatan,* the ritual feast–ceremony marking significant occasions that is so crucial an element of the religion of Java, in defiance of *adat,* or local customary law: normally no laughing matter, this. And a "folk" view is taken of his tormentor: ribald censorious comment on the man's sexual appetite is projected through the compressions of *pantun,* or folk quatrain. Misbach himself is an intriguing figure. Every inch the village *jago*—literally cock-of-the-walk—or strongman, admired for his prowess, he's merely thuggish here in his need for food, sex, dominion, though under different circumstances you could see him as a "primitive rebel" or Robin Hood. Associated with the city but never quite estranged from the countryside, he remains the *village* strongman: existing at the margins of the community, he is still tied to it; his conduct nicely parodies the mercantile practicality of his more egregious victims.

The tone of the tale is warmly identificatory, reflecting the author's solidarity with and tolerance of his people, which tells you much about the work's authenticity. Achdiat's trick is to disappear into the anonymous, indeterminate voice of the people, a voice that jokes and comments from somewhere deep inside the interstices of the action. Hence the lifelikeness of the piece, alternating with affectionate caricature. Hence, too, the ambiguity of the ending. Teeuw in his survey thinks this a most accomplished story. I agree.

The author, born in 1911 in a *desa* in Tjibatu in the Sunda district of West Java, was educated in a Dutch secondary school and at university in Batavia. He has been an editor with the colonial publishing house Balai Pustaka, a senior civil servant in the Indonesian Ministry of Education, and until his recent retirement a lecturer in Indonesian language and literature at the Australian National University in Canberra. He is regarded by some as the doyen of Indonesian fiction.

Major works: *Kesan dan Kenangan* (1960) [novel]; *Debu Cinta Bertebaran* (1973) [novel]; *Pembunuh dan Anjing Hitam* (1975) [short stories].

A.A. Navis: The Helmet/*Topihelm*

Ali Akbar Navis was born in 1924 in Padangpanjang, in the Minangkabau lands of West Sumatra. During the war he worked in porcelain factories in Japan and in the Indies; after independence he served as a sitting member of the *Dewan Perwakilan Rakyat*, or People's Representative Regional Assembly. His fiction has been translated into several European languages as well as Japanese, and a novel, *Saraswati, Si Gadis Dalam Sunyi,* was awarded a UNESCO Prize for literature in 1968. *Robohnya Surau Kami* (1955), the collection from which this story is taken, is the work on which his reputation in Indonesia is founded. The title story especially has been canonized.

When it comes to proletarian realism, "The Helmet" takes some beating. The jostle and din of the rolling-stock repair yards in "Kayutanam" is most convincingly rendered, in a prose that has its sleeves rolled up and is ready to go. "Above all, I wish to make you see"—thus Joseph Conrad. Navis might have said the same. The town itself is a part that stands for a whole: it serves as a figure for innumerable smallish, semi-industrialized cities in Java and Sumatra in the first decade of independence. Here is a modernizing society remote from the metropolis and containing the residue of previous formations: the values of *desa* (village) have yet to be subsumed into those of *kota* (city). "Kayutanam," like the Minangkabau world generally, is in transition and the author's feeling for its members is both warm and melancholy.

This is as it should be. The lives and fates of *manusia yang kerdil,* the little folk, are what interest Navis here. He excels at portraying their consoling fantasies, their ethos as expressed in chaffing banter and an anti-authoritarian bloody-mindedness. As a Minangkabau, a Sumatran people remarkable both for their extroverted world view and for their social structure, which is matrilineal, and famed throughout the islands for their worldliness and practicality, he understands the meaning of *malu*—shame, embarrassment—and the correspondent desire for redress. The tragic lengths to which this desire may drive a likeable, unassuming person is a common theme in modern Malay and Indonesian literature. Navis refines it in the context of an urban working class, infusing it with a feeling for the chivvied and the powerless. About this feeling there is nothing bitter: how could there be? The tale comes out of a world where there is internal differentiation according to status and function, but where the work itself, and the relationships generated around work, are still humanly face-to-face. Class matters, but in the first instance, anyway, the story does not seem to be about class conflict, as such, so much as about a local psychology on which that conflict may act, with incendiary results.

The author lives in Medan, where as well as earning his living by his pen he is a sometime lecturer at Universitas Andalas, specializing in the culture and anthropology of the Minangkabau.

Major works: *Bianglala* (1963) [short stories]; *Hujan Panas* (1964) [short stories]; *Kemarau* (1967) [novel].

Nasjah Djamin: The Encounter/*Pertemuan*

Two remarks, one by a contemporary observer, the other by a distinguished contemporary historian, may shed some light on this story and help to place it in its proper setting. Of the period from the Japanese conquest in March 1942 to the Proklamasi Kemerdekaan, or Declaration of Independence, by Sukarno on 17 August 1945, and the ensuing battles with the returning Dutch and British forces, David Wehl writes:

> For three and a half years Japanese propaganda had been directed towards the youth of Indonesia, and for good or for ill the whole course of the Indonesian Independence movement rests upon their young shoulders. The enthusiasm, the wild excesses, the irresponsibility, the exaltation, and the eagerness to plunge forward into an unknown future, were all accents on youth. Much argument has already been expended on the state of mind of the Indonesian people at the end of the Japanese war . . . but no argument can ever reach a conclusion that does not take into consideration the fact that at the time of the Japanese surrender there were two nations in Indonesia. Not, as in England in Disraeli's time, the Rich and the Poor, but the Young and the Old. (*The Birth of Indonesia.* London: George Allen & Unwin, 1948, p. 15)

The acrimony and disappointment infusing this account ask, it seems to me, to be understood, and forgiven, in these terms.

An equally valuable insight into the dilemma of the storyteller in "The Encounter" can be gained from the classic analysis of Benedict Anderson. In his *Java in a Time of Revolution: Occupation and Resistance, 1944-1945* (Ithaca, NY: Cornell University Press, 1972), he points out that "the mutual frustration of the pemuda, who had revolutionary expectations but no revolutionary leadership, and the middle-class metropolitan intelligentsia, both collaborationist and underground, who were in a position to lead but totally inexperienced in doing so without external support, was to provide the leitmotif of the Indonesian Revolution" (p. 185).

Nasjah Djamin's story lives inside these predicaments. It trades on the knowledge that the civil war that in some respects was fought *within* the Revolution—a war between classes and generations—was far from over and done with once Holland and the world recognized a sovereign republic in 1949.

As well as one or two obscure references, this story contains a number of abbreviations from the Dutch that were in common use in the late colonial period, and which call for explanation:

> Jalan Malioboro: the main thoroughfare in the Central Javanese city of Yogyakarta. *Malioboro* is, in all likelihood, a corruption of the English "Marlborough." Yogyakarta, significantly for this story, was the provisional capital of the Indonesian government during the Revolution, after the occupation of Batavia, as Jakarta was then called, by the Dutch in 1947.

HIS: Hollandsch-Inlandsche Scholen. One of the new class of primary schools established in 1914 to cater to the needs of Indonesians and for those of non-European minorities, mainly Chinese and Arabs. Graduates could proceed to bridge schools such as MULO (Meer Uitgebreed Lager Onderwijs) to prepare for entry into three-year secondary schools. The products of this system were very much an underemployed intelligentsia, since high school training guaranteed suitable employment neither in the general civil service nor in business: insufficient opportunities existed in these fields, and those available were invariably given to Dutch and Eurasians. Those who failed to find congenial work were kept to the lower clerical levels. The frustrations inherent in this state of affairs contributed, naturally, to the politicization of the elite, who were facing a crisis of identity of peculiar intensity.

HIK: *Hollandsche Inlandsches Kweekschool.* Dutch-medium teachers training college.

KNIL: *Koninklijk Nederlandsch-Indisch Leger.* The Dutch colonial army.

RIS: Republik Indonesia Serikat. The United States of Indonesia, 1940-50; the precursor of the Indonesian Republic as such.

SR: Sekolah Rendah. Primary school.

"Unlicensed schools": *sekolah liar* (literally: "wild" schools). This refers to Malay-medium schools set up for Indonesians under nationalist auspices, or by progressive social–religious organizations such as the modernist Muslim *Muhamaddiya.* They operated outside government supervision. In general they were committed to promoting values and fostering an outlook at odds with the loyalist perspective of the official educational system. Schoolmaster Halim's fear and contempt for such *sekolah liar* requires no further explanation.

NICA: Acronym for Netherlands Indies Civil Administration, a bureaucracy-cum–military force returning with the Dutch in 1945.

Kerawang Bekasi: The title of an inspirational poem by Chairil Anwar, Indonesia's *poète maudit.* Karawang, where nationalist leaders and fighting units gathered after the occupation of Jakarta in 1945 by British troops, was a town lying on the eastern bank of the Citarum, some eighty kilometers from the capital. Bekasi is a town to the west. The atmosphere in the region lying between was at the time tense; kidnap, counterkidnap, and reprisal were commonplace, and over all hung the threat of attack by the Allies (Bekasi had been devastated on 28 November 1945 in reprisal for the murder of British Indian crew of an Allied plane downed nearby).

Time of Readiness: Literally *zaman siap;* the period of tension and practical preparation following the Proclamation of Independence on 17 August 1945 and some two months later the return of Allied forces, who were to preside over the reestablishment of the colonial state.

The author was born in Perbaungan, North Sumatra, in 1924 but was raised in the Javanese heartland of Yogyakarta. He has studied film and theater in Tokyo and today works as a choreographer and musicologist in Jakarta. His writings have won a number of literary awards in Indonesia.

Major works: *Sekelumit Nyanyian Sunda* (1959) [drama]; *Hilanglah Si Anak Hilang* (1963) [novel]; *Helai-Helai Sakura Gugur* (1964) [novel]; *Di Bawah Kaki Pak Dirman* (1967) [short stories]; *Malam Kuala Lumpur* (1968) [novel]; *Gairah Untuk Hidup dan Untuk Mati* (1968) [novel]; *Sebuah Perkawinan* (1974) [short stories].

Satyagraha Hoerip: The Last Train But One/ *Sebelum Yang Terakhir*

While the veiled and deliberately muffled circumstances vex computation of the toll, anything from 250,000 to one million people are thought to have been slaughtered on Java, Bali, and Sumatra in the four months following the assassination of six senior army generals on the night of 30 September 1965. Their attackers acting impromptu or else egged on by the military, the victims of this slaughter, almost all of whom were falsely accused, were stabbed, beheaded, or bludgeoned to death on suspicion of leftist sympathies. Often they were butchered in vengeful settlement of private scores. In the subsequent months and years, 750,000 Indonesians were imprisoned, blacklisted, or, as former *tahanan politik* (political detainees), rendered nonpersons.

The official version, much disputed, says that the murder was perpetrated by conspirators doing the bidding of the powerful and influential PKI, the Partai Komunis Indonesia; what no one disputes is that the PKI, its cadres, youth groups, and affiliated organizations were in consequence destroyed root and branch and thereafter demonized, in general recollection and discourse, as the source of all that had been evil and chaotic in national life. It was, at all events, apparent even at the time that the appalling brutality—which sundered families, divided kin, and razed entire communities—had been long in the making. The roots of the crisis are seen now to lie deep within tensions experienced in daily life and at the village level between left and right, Islam and Marxism, tenant and landlord, ABRI (the Indonesian Armed Forces) and PKI, in the twilight of Sukarno's Guided Democracy. (They are tangled roots, to be sure: the best of the many books on the subject is the collection edited by Robert Cribb and entitled *The Indonesian Killings 1965-66: Studies From Java and Bali.* Clayton: Monash Papers on Southeast Asia, no. 21, 1990.) We need only note here that a period of feverish, confrontational, and bitterly polarized mass politics, accompanied by triple-digit inflation, had come to a fiery end, Sukarno's irresponsible enthusiasms having brought civil society to the brink of collapse and anarchy. The New Order led by his successor was pledged to head off such disaster and to head off the threat of anything remotely like it ever arising. Altering the script of Indonesian public life to read not revolutionary *élan*, not ideological adventure, but stability, discipline, subordination, the new regime was interested in amnesia and in prophylaxis. Its past now edited and expurgated, the nation was to be restored to health. The program of the New Order has been more or less consciously contrived, in the words of one recent observer, "to help erase antagonistic emotions from the collective memory ... synthetic emotions [that] fanned the flames of nationalism" and that had amounted to "a collective psychosis controlled by a charismatic leader" (Michael R.J. Vatikiotis. *Indonesian Politics Under Suharto: Order, Development and Pressure for Change.* Routledge: London and New York, 1993, p. 102). In the terms in which it was conceived, and with these purposes in mind, it has been, on the whole, a successful program.

In other words, G-S-30/PKI, as it is known in the costive official parlance (or, more chillingly, GESTAPU), has been the institutionalized nightmare of modern Indonesian history. Like all trauma that doesn't bear thinking about, it must, therefore, be constantly relived. Hardly surprising that Indonesian writers have felt themselves to be at a loss to know how best to represent it. Novels pitched in a documentary vein there have undoubtedly been, and there's no lack of stories attempting a sympathetic naturalistic portrayal of events. Nonetheless, among many Indonesian writers, as among European ones in the aftershock of the European disaster of 1939-45, there is detectable all the same a feeling that a matter-of-fact treatment would betray the facts of the matter; that the enormity of the tragedy would be reduced, or rendered banal thereby. Straightforward "protest" seemed feeble, or beside the point.

Satyagraha Hoerip's choice of the uncanny is, then, a clever stratagem. The supernatural is a vehicle for his intuition of just how thin is the carapace of the normal, how easily it can and did crack. In this unearthly setting, nothing, no person or place, can be taken for granted, Satyagraha seems to be saying. Location, time, identity—all are left threateningly vague. Nevertheless, there's no mistaking the headlong descent of Indonesian society into chaos and destruction in this tale of an unscheduled transit to hell—or is it a season in purgatory? The author, on record as having been no friend of the PKI, might have been expected to point an accusatory finger. But the narrative, washed through by pity and anger, transmits a sense of a general, unspecified doom. No one is to blame for the atmosphere: spooked, premonitory, asphyxiated. This horror story was published three years after the fratricide and deals obliquely both with the events that preceded it and its aftermath. In it, you wake to perdition in eerie company. There are many ways to tell the truth about the bloodletting of 1965. This way, as befits an episode too painful perhaps to confront head on, tells it slant.

Born in 1934, Satyagraha Hoerip Soeprobo occupies a prominent place in the literary firmament of Indonesia, having been editor of the *Kami* dailies and *Sinar Harapan,* and of an influential collection of literary criticism. His stories have been widely published at home and abroad.

Major works: *Sepasang Suami Istri* (1963) [novel]; *Burung Api* (1972) [stories for children]; *Tentang Delapan Orang* (1966), *Gedono-Gedini* (1993) [short stories]; *Antologi Esai Tentang Persoalan-persoalan Sastra* (1969) [criticism].

S.N. Ratmana: Dearly Departed/*Mendiang*

S.N. Ratmana was born in 1936 in Kuningan and brought up in Pekalongan, in Central Java. He has followed a career in the district high schools, first as a teacher, later as principal. While it would be impertinent to assume that he is drawing on personal experience in choosing for his formal subject matter a schoolgirl's crush on a teacher, it seems safe nevertheless to say that the author in general knows whereof he speaks.

The *frisson* the schoolmaster derives from having skirted the dangerous edge of things is, however, interesting in more ways than one.

The interest of the story is not only in the possibility of sex between teacher and pupil, but also in the position of the Chinese in Indonesia: a position, historically speaking, that has been socially and psychologically ambiguous and at times fraught with genuine peril. The historian John Legge sums it up well:

> Small retail trade was predominantly the preserve of the Chinese, who, though not reaching the proportions which they attained in the Malay Peninsula, nonetheless came to constitute an important element in the populations of Indonesian cities and market towns. Thus foreigners seemed to maintain control of business and commerce, while the Indonesians were left to cultivate the soil. (*Indonesia*. 3d ed. Sydney: Prentice-Hall of Australia, 1980)

As a comment on the marginality of the principal non-European ethnic group in the islands, a group long resident there, this is accurate enough and may help to suggest why, like the Jews, with whom they have so often been compared, they have been the object of mingled envy and resentment. Whatever else he may have set out to do, Ratmana's storyteller, framing his account, succeeds in capturing and communicating something of this uneasy fascination with a group that stands at one and the same time inside and outside Indonesian urban life, its presence suffered rather than welcomed, eliciting suspicion, criticism, and outright attack. In 1740 there were murderous anti-Chinese riots in Makassar (Ujung Padang), and serious disturbances in 1965-67. Post-*merdeka,* their nationality and political loyalty has often been called into question, despite the comprador role they play in the Indonesian economy.

To say that the narrator is xenophobically hostile toward the people Wati marries into is undoubtedly going too far. Nevertheless, in taking a Chinese husband, Wati, on the rebound from an unhappy and unconsummated love affair, has ignored an unstated taboo—or been seen to have done so: she has departed for a world whose rituals and rules are incomprehensible to the grieving narrator. In this sense, the story is less about sex and more about strangers and strangeness.

Major works: *Sungai, Suara dan Luka* (1981) [short stories]. Ratmana has also published fiction in *Kisah, Sastra, Horison,* and *Kompas Minggu.*

Gerson Poyk: Matias Akankari

"Indonesia" has been, first and foremost, a concept: an idea espoused by an intellectual class and subsequently defended, enacted, and acted upon by patriots. It is chiefly among them that it has existed as an "imagined community," in Benedict Anderson's evocative phrase. To others, the very word has evoked not unity but difference and contention: "Indonesia" speaks not in one voice but, irreducibly, in many. Naturally enough the rhetoric of the national awakening (1908-42), like all such rhetorics, was committed willy-nilly to the invention of a tradition. It was found useful and necessary, both before and after *merdeka,* to insist on a territorial imperative inclusive of all the lands "from Sabang to Merauke" in southwestern Irian Jaya, on the argument that this marked the extent of the old Majapahit and Srivijayan empires to which Indonesia was heir. Irian Jaya, earlier known as Irian Barat, was of course the name by which Sukarno in his heyday liked to call what has since become Indonesia's enormous outlier province. He did so as part of his policy of *konfrontasi* with the vestiges of colonial power in the region—Britain in Malaya, the Netherlands in what it knew as "West Nieuw Guinea"—and in recognition of the integrationist aims of the Revolution. But the ironies surrounding this expansionist impulse have not been lost on observers: "One central similarity," Anderson remarks, as between the contemporary republic and the Netherlands East Indies, is "the isomorphism between each nationalism's territorial stretch and that of the previous imperial administrative unit." (*Imagined Communities: Reflections on the Origin and Spread of Nationalism.* 2d ed. London: Verso, 1991, p. 114)

Within the new state so sedulously mapping itself onto the old, relations between core and periphery have always been fraught, but the case to hand was arguably a special one. Irian Jaya, much of which was first charted and explored by the Dutch as late as the 1950s, a territory bisected by the snow-capped Sudirman Range, its lowlands consisting of swamp, savannah, and the densest sort of equatorial rain forest, was surrendered to the republic in 1963 and then only as a result of pressure from the United Sates and a campaign of incursion undertaken by ABRI. Thus, under the rubric of a common citizenship, were flung together (in theory at all events) members of sophisticated urban civilizations and foraging societies—Dani, Asmat, Baudi—the latter condescendingly seen from a Jakarta-centered viewpoint as living in the Stone Age. As Anderson puts it:

> The subsequent painful relations between the populations of West New Guinea and the emissaries of the independent Indonesian state can be attributed to the fact that Indonesians more or less sincerely regard these populations as "brothers and sisters," while the populations themselves, for the most part, see things very differently. (*Imagined Communities,* p. 177)

Gerson Poyk has a field day with all this: from the word go the joke is on the conqueror, not the conquered. City ways, Jakarta ways (c. late 1960s to early 1970s), are made strange, ironized by being seen through the untutored eyes of a "primitive." Set down alongside urban types, the "savage" in this account is anything but: Indonesia's Great Wen, for all its helter-skelter, which is seen and felt as if for the first time ever, turns out for him to be a rather cozy sort of place, once you get the hang of it.

There is a sense in which Poyk's story, anecdotal as it is, is also a squib, sporting with the phrase "act of free choice," the formula used by President Sukarno to characterize the referendum of 1969. This involved fractionally more than a thousand handpicked voters and was alleged to have demonstrated beyond all reasonable doubt the alacrity with which the Irianese peoples had seized the chance to integrate themselves with Java. (Votes cast for were declared to have amounted to 99 percent of the total ballot.) This fable of *pembangunan,* development, shows its author to know otherwise. The rendezvous with "civilization," where it's every man for himself and devil take the hindmost, is far from freely chosen and invites an invidious contrast both with the Indonesian state-as-amalgam, and with the state of nature that is being condescended to. Who is backward? Who advanced?

Major works: *Hari-Hari Pertama* (1968), *Sang Guru* (1971), *Cumbuan Sabana* (1979) [novels]; *Mutiara* (1968), *Matias Akankari, Oleng-kemoleng, Surat-surat Cinta Rajagukguk* (1975) [short stories].

Nh. Dini: A Journey/*Perjalanan*

A certain glamour attaches to Nurhayati Srihardini's reputation among the Indonesian reading public, on account both of her personal vicissitudes and of her feminism. Born in Semarang on the northern coast of

Central Java, she has worked as a flight attendant for the national carrier Garuda and subsequently as a radio broadcaster, before marriage to a French diplomat took her to France and Japan. She returned recently to Indonesia, following divorce and a period of residence in the United States. Her fictions reflect her cosmopolitan experience, at whose core are established questions of sexual identity. Deference and hierarchy, as the Javanese conceive them, are looked askance at, particularly as they bear on the question of women; if orthodox values are ultimately ratified, this is not before they have been called sharply into question.

Dini's stories characteristically follow a temporarily unsettled young Indonesian woman through entanglement with a foreigner, often amidst new surroundings. This makes her an honorable practitioner of the kind of romantic fiction enjoyed by consumers of such women's magazines as *Femina* or *Sarinah*. But there is more to her stories than meets the eye. Dini seeks to assess, from the inside, the predicament of a certain kind of heroine, a woman of liberal sensibilities and a quizzical temperament but one not prepared wholly to jettison received values. What is at stake, really, is the idea of order, and the concomitant threats to order, implicit in the concept of *kehalusan,* the (very Javanese) moral–behavioral notion of poise, inward restraint, refinement of comportment, adherence to what is deemed right, fitting, proper, delicate. Conscious self-definition, a tendency to dissatisfaction, a questioning outlook: how to reconcile these with an acceptance of *halus,* which is to say, with an accommodation to things as they are? That's the predicament Dini is fond of examining. Teeuw says that "in a subtle way Dini is holding up a mirror to her Indonesian sisters to show them the price they may have to pay for modernisation" (*Modern Indonesian Literature.* Vol. 2. The Hague: Martinus Nijhoff, 1975, p. 178). He is spot on.

Major works: *Dua Dunia* (1956); *Tuileries* (1982) [short stories]; *Hati yang Damai* (1961); *Pada Sebuah Kapal* (1973); *La Barka* (1975); *Keberangkatan* (1977); *Namaku Hiroko* (1977); *Orang-orang Tran* (1985); *Jalan Bandungan* (1989) [all novels].

Taufiq Ismail: Stop Thief!/*Garong Garong*

Superficially, "Garong Garong" is hardly more than a run-on joke that gets noisier and more knockabout as it proceeds. The wit is mordant and unsparing: anyone purporting to act as a mouthpiece for the powers that be is singled out as a moving target, fit to be manhandled or else mown down with raillery. Clerkly obstructionism, pigheadedness in its many forms, the pomposities of jacks-in-office, Taufiq lines them all up in his sights and lets rip.

Satire, then, and outwardly all Keystone Kops, entailing outrageous farce, capricious changes, and bungled identities, with much attempted violence. But underneath the devilment, Taufiq Ismail is otherwise engaged. The key to this story's real business—the business for which the slapstick is so much cover—is, I think, the allusion to Ibu Kartini. Javanese princess, protofeminist, and early nationalist, Raden Ajeng Kartini, born in 1879, was the daughter of a Javanese aristocrat and *bupati,* or head of a district (*kabupaten*), in the port city of Jepara on the Java Sea. Kartini died in childbirth in 1904, but her intimate letters to a Dutch woman—in Dutch, not in Indies Malay, the usual medium of intercourse between ruler and ruled in Tropical Holland—collected and published in 1911 under the title *Door Duisternis tot Licht* (*Through Darkness to Light*), soon secured her position as herald of a new age in Indonesia. She has been regarded ever since as a pioneer of progressive thinking in the colonial Indies at a time when the official aim was the maintenance of centralized rule and of *ruste en orde,* tranquillity and order. In the pantheon of the Indonesian Revolution she is celebrated as the "mother" of the modern nation.

Insofar as debate about Kartini's significance continues to rage, Taufiq's question "Which Tini?" is far from facetious. In whose keeping, he wants to know, is the destiny of Indonesia and all its hope of a better future? In whose hands the making of meaning, the monopoly of language as an instrument of control? Who sets the boundaries; who makes the definitions, and in whose interests? In the name of what generally agreed principles? In debating the importance of Kartini— both the historical figure and the nationalist institution that she has become—Indonesian editors, translators, and politicians can't but stake a claim to a potent symbol. In her brilliant essay exploring this question, Danilyn Rutherford observes that in their bid

> to appropriate Kartini for a certain nation, party, class, or gender . . . they reflect an important shift in legitimating ideologies. . . . Old Order Kartini and her New Order sister tell us much about Indonesia before and after the victory of the post-colonial state [and] . . . the languages employed by Soekarno and Soeharto, one signifying revolution, the

other motionless order. ("Unpacking a National Heroine: Two Kartinis and Their People," *Indonesia,* no. 55 [April 1993]: pp. 23-41)

On this showing, Taufiq goes along with the view that in the modern Indonesian state the fusion of nation and people, received opinion to the contrary, is still imperfect: the 1945 Revolution is in important respects unfinished, its goal of social justice yet to be realized.

On the surface, then, "Garong Garong" has a juicy albeit conventional bone to pick with *pihak berwenang*—constituted authority— with its waywardness and arbitrary character, and with the exercise of power overall in contemporary Indonesia as it impinges on family, property, religion. Underneath, and more unnervingly, it's a comedy of reference, a semantic quarrel in which nouns make mischief and verbs do the wrong sort of work. By the time it's over, not much that was there to start with and earlier thought valuable is left standing. How far is Taufiq, in provoking a disturbance, consciously adopting the role of *punakawan,* or clown–servant/retainer, à la Petruk or Semar in the plot of traditional *wayang* theater? To what extent does he see himself here as a kind of loyal opposition, licensed to cavil—often hilariously, sometimes scandalously—because committed, ultimately, to protecting the ruler whom he takes to task? The questions remain.

A devout Muslim and a committed activist since his student days, Taufiq Ismail, who was born in Bukittinggi, West Sumatra, in 1937, has a reputation as one of the more remarkable and outspoken of contemporary Indonesian poets. He has been a reporter with the daily newspaper *Kami,* a member of the editorial board of the literary journal *Horison,* and a prominent figure on the Dewan Kesenian Jakarta, the Jakarta Arts Council. He has been active, too, in Indonesian PEN,* taken part in international festivals in Rotterdam and Taipei, and attended the International Writing Program at Iowa University. He works in public relations for Unilever Corporation in Jakarta, and as an editor of *Horison.*

Major works: *Tirani* (1966); *Benteng* (1966); *Puisi-puisi Sepi* (1971); *Buku Tamu Museum Perjuangan* (1969); *Kota, Pelabuhan, Ladang, Angin dan Langit* (1971); *Sajak Ladang Jagung* (1973) [all poetry].

*International literary organization: Poets, Editors, Novelists.

Budi Darma: The Kid/*Anak*

Born in Rembang in East Java in 1937, Budi Darma is one of the best-known writers of his generation in Indonesia, and certainly one of the most productive. By profession he is a university teacher in Surabaya. Previously he spent some years in the United States, as a postgraduate student at the University of Hawaii and the University of Indiana. His earlier training was at the famous Gadjah Mada University in Yogyakarta. He is active in writer's circles and in literary journalism and takes part in debates and festivals in Indonesia and overseas.

Budi has several strings to his bow. *Olenka* (1983), which won the 1980 ASEAN Award, takes place in the United States and reveals that country's influence on the author, as well as his knack of impersonation: American characters, seen through an alien optic, are brought ventriloquistically to life. It remains, nonetheless, a stock exercise: steam realism, so to speak.

His short fiction—quite a lot of it, at any rate—is another matter. Butter wouldn't melt in these stories' mouths. Yet for all their air of innocence they spell trouble for the characters they ambush. Their plots seem to blunder into a no-man's-land where anything that can go haywire will assuredly do so. The normal rhythms of existence are comic or transfiguring, people are slightly menacing; what you see is decidedly not what you get. Effects tend to be wildly disproportionate to causes, outcomes of actions dire. Po-faced, the author sets about making his characters come a cropper. They never quite know what hit them!

In a nutshell, though an unprepossessing writer Budi is an avant-garde one, the effect of whose stories, published for the most part in *Kisah, Cerita,* and *Horison,* is to unnerve. Like those of Putu Wijaya and Satyagraha Hoerip, they make you feel in more ways than one that you are treading on eggshells.

Major works: *Orang-orang Bloomington* (1980) [short stories].

Putu Wijaya: The Wallet/*Dompet*

The mainstream in modern Indonesian fiction is a figural realism, implying belief in the efficacy and truthfulness of words. The names to conjure with here are those of the "classic writers," Armijn Pane, Sutan

Takdir Alisjahbana, Achdiat Karta Mihardja; above all, Pramoedya Ananta Toer. But there is a parallel, more recently evolved tradition, one that has rubbed up provocatively against the limits of a straightforward imitation of life. Or else it's overrun these limits into parody, expressionist distortion, extravaganza. Danarto and Yudhistira Ardi Noegraha are the writers who come to mind. Their resort to indirection, their coyness, owe much to the destruction of the literary left in Indonesia in the period from 1965 to 1970. These writers operate in the shadow of proscription and imprisonment, the fate of those who are felt to be too critical of the New Order.

Perhaps the foremost of these writers and the best-known overseas is the Balinese I Gusti Ngurah Putu Wijaya. His career has been exceptionally receptive to influence: Beckett and Camus, Javanese *ketoprak, ludruk,* and *wayang wong,* and the sophisticated "primitivism" of Balinese pictorial art. It has been, as well, an intrepid exercise in adversary dissembling. Story in Putu's hands has evolved into a mixture of lyricism, spectacle, and an unsettling general exuberance. Reading becomes a form of alert listening: theater-in-the-head. For story, here, is nothing if not a smokescreen. The name of the game, albeit unstated, is to evade the vigilant eye of a censorship that looks askance at writing allegedly projecting, or protecting, radical values. Fortunately it is a censorship that blinks leniently at writing that appears to be innocuous. "Appears" is the operative word here.

Putu's stories are allegories, whose purpose is to plumb currents of anxiety intuitively felt to run well beneath the humdrum lives of their—middle-class—readers. The apparent intention is slyly to invite those readers to ponder the source of their discontents in the social mechanism. They have been called subversive; certainly they're full of histrionic effect. These minimalist accounts are keyed to a deadpan oral delivery. They make the ordinary seem a perfidious, opaque realm: fragmentary, ungovernable, wildly funny. To put it another way, they have a wayward, refractory quality (*mbeling* is the Javanese term), a sportive, virtuoso element, designed to goad. That this is the intention can be inferred from Putu's own reference to "mental terror" as the object of the exercise. Adventures are presented in such a way as, presumably, to engender in readers anything but a complaisant attitude toward state and civil society in postrevolutionary Indonesia. "The Wallet," with its faux naif hero, is an example.

A graduate in law of Gadjah Mada University in Yogyakarta, Putu

Wijaya (born 1944) has pursued a career as an actor and director, first in W. S. Rendra's famous Bengkel Teater, or Experimental Theatre Workshop, then as founder of Teater Mandiri in Jakarta, where he works as an editor of *Tempo* magazine. His novels and stories have won prizes and, unusual for Indonesian writers, attention in the West: *Bom* (1978), a collection of short stories, has been translated by Ellen Rafferty and others and published as *Bomb!* (Madison, WI: University of Wisconsin, Center of SEA Studies, 1987). Putu's earlier novel, *Telegram,* published in 1972, is commonly seen as having taken the Indonesian fiction of the 1970s down new paths.

Major works: *Bila Malam Bertambah Malam* (1971), *Pabrik* (1976), *Stasiun, MS Tak Cukup Sedih, Ratu, Sah Keok, Perang* (1977), *Nyali* (1983) [all novels]; *Lautan Bernyanyi* (1967), *Aduh* (1975), *Dag Dig Dug* (1976) [drama]; *Es* (1980) [short stories].

Asnelly Luthan: The Weirdo/*Eksentrik*

I have been unable to discover much about the author, who lived from 1952 to 1983, other than the fact that she was born in Bukittinggi and died in Jakarta, where she had been editor of the women's magazine *Kartini.* As does Prasetyohadi's "The Shutterbug" in this anthology, "The Weirdo" suggests how real is the tension between the requirement to conform and the impulse to dissent both in the literature of Suharto's Indonesia and in the life of its middle classes. In the military–patrimonial state that is the final arbiter of what is acceptable and what beyond the pale, this tension finds expression in all sorts of ways.

At the diminishing end of the scale, for instance, there are the flamboyant, oppositionally-minded poetry and plays of W.S. Rendra, who loves to play the part of self-styled black sheep in *keluarga besar Indonesia,* the greater Indonesian family; these effusions have landed their author more than once in hot water. Further up, there is the activism of such dissidents as the group of retired generals known as *Petisi Limapuluh*, the Petition of Fifty, who were harassed and imprisoned for making so bold as to declare their unhappiness with President Suharto's succession policies. And close by, there is politics prosecuted according to the compulsory formula of *musyawarah* and *mufakat*—that's to say, by deliberation and consensus rather than through rivalry and open disagreement, in keeping with the 1985 Law on Mass Organizations. This statute decrees that all parties and bodi/

must subscribe to the state doctrine of Pancasila, the five ideological "pillars" of the Republic of Indonesia. Admirable and indeed necessary as a focus for national unity, the doctrine, as Michael Vatikiotis says, is "chiefly designed as a principle about which there can be no argument ... [and] encompass[es] all aspects of social, political and spiritual life—and rules out alternatives" (*Indonesian Politics,* pp. 107-8). To be sure, the tolerance and syncretism for which the Javanese are noted are still very much in evidence. But the traditional hierarchical tendencies of Javanese culture have been comprehensively harnessed within New Order society by those in command, and with a view to eliciting compliance and loyalty at all levels. With, moreover, mainstream socialist–nationalist secular politics blocked by the 1985 laws, the Indonesian polity has been driven into divisive religious and racial channels.

Asnelly Luthan's portrayal of a waywardness all too easily branded as lunatic and at odds with everything around it reverberates in this contemporary setting. Ostracism and persecution are the penalties certain to be incurred by the maverick, the more so perhaps where, as here, idiosyncrasy is philosophical in character.

Major works: *Topeng* (1983) [short stories]. Asnelly before her death had published stories in *Sinar Harapan, Berita Buana, Zaman,* and other Jakarta weeklies.

F. Rahardi: Battling With Buffalo/
Bertarung Dengan Banteng

Indonesia may have some way to go before it can be characterized as one of the Asian "tigers," but life at the top for the corporate or middle management type in Jakarta, or for the company director in, say, Surabaya or Bandung, can be every bit as stressful as it is for their opposite numbers in Hong Kong or Seoul, Taipei or Singapore. F. Rahardi, who earns his crust as deputy editor of the trade journal *Trubus* in Jakarta, must know this scene like the back of his hand. His story, by turns sad and droll and perceptive, is a bulletin from the front.

But there is another, very Javanese, way of understanding his predicament. Dream, symbol, clairvoyance, the contemplative life in general remain as central to Javanese cultural practice today, in town and country and among all classes, as ever they have been. *Kejawen*— "Javanese philosophy"—or as it sometimes called, *kebatinan,* from *batin,* inmost spirit, inner life—is today the most prominent form of

Javanese mysticism in Indonesia. Mixing Hindu, Buddhist, and Islamic beliefs with indigenous animism, it bases itself on the conviction of the oneness of all existence and the potency of the imperceptible world. Using meditation, ascetic exercise, withdrawal, and patient discussion, it teaches detachment, self-observation, and self-knowledge: the emphasis is on spiritual insight, progress, and correct living, in contrast to acquisitiveness and competitive performance. In *kebatinan* mysticism, the thrusting, noisy life of *nafsu*—desire, appetite—is counterindicated: How Not to Do It. Unity of inner and outer life, harmony of self and circumstance, is the goal.

Rahardi, I think, sports with these distinctions. The monsters cropping up in the story in dream and in reality are, you notice, black. It will not have been lost on his Javanese readers that black, in *kejawen* mysticism, is the color of worldly self-serving physical and material desires. Red is the shade in which Salim's bedroom is done up, and red, in this scheme and in ancient Indonesian temple art, is associated with the illusory world, in which things are separated into distinct entities, linked with death and inequality—which may be a coded way of saying that of the creatures assailing Umar Salim, much the fiercest is the demon of skewed perception and misdirected action.

This may shed light on a piece that may not, at first glance, seem particularly Indonesian. Insofar as it is "about" anything, the story concerns a career whose priorities, from the point of view of *kebatinan,* have been insufficiently pondered. Might this explain Pak Umar's coarseness of manner and his general truculence? Watching him with clinical detachment, Rahardi never loses his cool sympathy for somebody all at sea outside the stockade of villa and office; somebody knowing no alternative to a low-grade megalomania. The fate meted out to him isn't, therefore, simply bad luck or the granting of a death wish; it's the logical manifestation of a spiritual imbalance. The author doesn't moralize: no need. Psychic disturbance, as *kebatinan* understands it, must carry direct physical consequences. Here, then, is a man in pretty bad shape, in the specialized Javanese conception of what constitutes health and sickness—and he doesn't even know it.

F. Rahardi was born in Ambarawa in 1950 and writes both poetry and short fiction.

Major works: *Sumpak Wts; Catatan harian koruptor* (both poetry).

Danarto: "Your Child Is Not Your Child," Gibran Said
"Anakmu Bukanlah Anakmu," Ujar Gibran

Danarto was educated in Yogyakarta in the plastic arts, later received training in experimental theater design, and has had experience in stage production at home and abroad. These influences, together with that of *wayang* drama and Sufi mysticism, may account for the fact that his stories are anything but well behaved. Wild improbabilities, set-piece battles, shouting matches, denunciations, gestural excesses of all kinds fill them. Typically, they involve figures who seem to have wandered into the domain of the everyday out of *dongeng,* fairy tale.

From a different point of view, however, his stories are the nearest that contemporary Indonesian literature comes to fiction of the absurd, à la, say, the American writer Donald Barthelme. Realist writers seem to share pretty basic assumptions: that one thing leads to another with relative certainty; that "character" is discussable on the basis of how people behave; that it's possible for one person to understand another and even to describe him satisfactorily from the outside; that the boundary between sanity and madness is relatively clear. All these assumptions have begun to be questioned, in the West by the descendants of Kafka and Joyce, in Indonesia by Rendra, Putu Wijaya, and Danarto. And for similar reasons: when I am no longer entirely sure who are the "we" to whom I am supposed to belong, I am not entirely sure any longer who "I" am either. At the same time the story strikes me as being very Javanese, both in the intensity and complexity of intramural relationships and in its concern with questions of appearance versus reality.

This may explain why Danarto, one of several *enfants terribles* of modern Indonesian fiction, goes in for shock effects. It will also explain why he has jettisoned the four-square naturalism whose most distinguished practitioner is Pramoedya Ananta Toer. Pramoedya, a participant in anticolonial struggle, seeks to bear witness, to dramatize history. Danarto, surrounded by private affluence and public squalor in the developmental–capitalist state identified with General Suharto's New Order, wants to thumb his nose at a too-complacent Indonesian bourgeoisie. If it is sometimes taken to extremes, there is a method to the madness. The mischief done to and by his characters camouflages a thinly cloaked disenchantment with things as they are, and a protestant aim: in the immediate background of this fantasy of mass insurrection are such things as the so-called *Malari* affair, an acronym for *Malapetaka Limapuluh Januari,* the "disastrous events" of 15 January 1974, when police bloodily suppressed student-driven demonstrations by stevedores in the port district of Jakarta. Ostensibly provoked by the visit of Prime Minister Tanaka of Japan, they bespoke deeper social and political discontents. A writer like Danarto, while not "alienated" in the American or European sense, has much to be cross about. It shows here, in the uproarious goings-on.

Born in 1940 in Mojowetan, Central Java, Danarto was the recipient of the ASEAN Writer's Award in 1985 and is represented in Harry Aveling's collection of Indonesian short fiction in translation, *From Surabaya to Armageddon* (1976). He is a lecturer in fine arts and a noted theatrical director in Jakarta.

Major works: *Godlob* (1976), *Berhala* (1980) [short stories]; *Obrog Owok-owok, ebreg ewek-ewek* (1976) [drama].

Putu Oka Sukanta: Black Clouds Over the Isle of the Gods/*Mega Hitam Pulau Kayangan*

The caste system of Bali, where this story is laid, is a very complex and involved field of study: simplified, it may be thought of as a triangle whose apex is formed by three high castes known as Brahmana, Ksatria, and Wesia, to which some 5 percent of the population belong, with the remainder classed as Sudra or Jaba, outsiders, which itself comprises sundry groups, some of high ritual and social status. Balinese belief is a no less complex and specialized affair. It will be best to let a recognized authority speak in his own voice on the subject. In a stimulating essay Anthony Forge writes:

> The facts of Balinese history are well known, and nowadays much publicized: it seems almost as if this "Hindu" enclave was left behind on purpose to form a paradise for the Australian surfie, the American hippie, and the Japanese businessman. Yet, although it is doubtful if the last few hundred years of Balinese history were designed for the [contemporary] tourist trade . . . certainly their effect on the Balinese has been profound, and made them at all levels, from the raja prince to the high priest to the peasant, extremely inwardly directed, regarding the world outside Bali as containing nothing that could change Bali for the better, although possibly providing goods and services that might be

> added to Bali. . . . In fact, since the fall of Majapahit, Java, seen by the Triwangsa as the source of their legitimate claims to aristocracy, has also been transformed into the center from which threats . . . [have] come, first in the form of Islamic expansion, later in the form of Dutch Imperial power, and now, to some extent, in the form of the Indonesian Republic. ("Balinese Religion and Indonesian Identity." In *Indonesia: The Making of a Nation,* ed. James J. Fox. Canberra: ANU Press, 1990, p. 221)

Commenting further on the significance of rite and ritual in Bali, Mr. Forge goes on to call attention to "the negative side of the super-natural" and to the fact that evil spirits, the *butas* and *kalas,* "are conceived in the high theology as the negative aspect of the gods, but to the village Balinese they form a vast tribe of more or less independent workers of mischief and evil, responsible for most misfortunes and disasters." He reminds his readers of the importance, in Balinese religion, "of ancestorhood and a binding obligation on kin," rightly observing that inasmuch as these gods are very local, "deified ancestors," the creed is not for export, and he points out that participation in religious ritual is regarded as a prerequisite for membership in society, such that to neglect your obligations means the end of social existence: property and inheritance are forfeit. The danger involved is the virtual extinction of identity (pp. 223-25).

This is as succinct and as suggestive a commentary as any on the dilemma at the heart of what may otherwise seem a rather arcane tale.

The mixture of aggression and inertia characteristic of Balinese emotional life and given dramatic expression here has greatly interested ethnographers; readers wanting to know more may find it helpful to consult Gordon D. Jensen and Luh Ketut Suryani, *The Balinese People: A Reinvestigation of Character* (Singapore: Oxford University Press, 1992); or Hildred Geertz, ed., *State and Society in Bali* (Leiden: KITLV 1991); or Unni Wikan, *Managing Turbulent Hearts: A Balinese Formula for Living* (Chicago: University of Chicago Press, 1990). The latter is awkwardly written but nonetheless littered with suggestive insights.

Putu Oka Sukanta was born in 1939 in Singarajah, in north Bali, and has been active since youth in the literary world, in Bali itself as well as in Yogyakarta and, more recently, in Jakarta. He has written poetry and children's stories and taken part in theater workshops in Indonesia and overseas. With Putu Wijaya, he is probably the best-known contemporary Balinese writer, and one of the few contemporary Indonesians to have dealt directly with the experience of imprisonment in connection with GESTAPU/PKI.

Major works: *I Belog* (1980) [children's stories from Bali], *Selat Bali* (1982), *Salam* (1985), *Tembang Jalak Bali* (1986) [all poetry].

Prasetyohadi: The Shutterbug/*Tukang Potret*

On the usual tests, the economic policies of the Suharto regime since its assumption of power in 1965 have been tremendously successful. New manufacturing industries have provided additional avenues of employment, and some of the effects of economic growth have even percolated down to the poorer farmers and to the landless. Even so, it has been argued, a glaring contrast remains in levels of consumption and in disposable income, a cleavage between the mass of the population and those able to seize the rich pickings offered by the expansion of capital enterprises.

These criticisms are part of a larger debate in Indonesia today. The question they raise is not only whether foreign aid programs are part of the ideological equipment by which the West promotes its—essentially exploitative?—dealings with a country like Indonesia, but whether affluent Western society is the model for her to adopt. The whole character of New Order society has been the target of criticism, for which there is little tolerance. Dismay has been felt at the spectacle of a privileged elite devoted to conspicuous consumption enjoying opportunities for personal enrichment, thanks to the developmentalist policies of the regime. Many civil servants and bureaucrats, not to mention military leaders, have acquired an array of extracurricular business interests: even (perhaps especially) President Suharto himself, on account of his family's entrepreneurial activities, has not escaped criticism.

In addition to the social criticisms she vents, the provenance of the woman photographer herself is worth thinking about: who she is as well as what she says. As a Eurasian, of mixed Dutch and Indonesian extraction, she belongs to a community whose position in the plural society of the Indies was a notoriously difficult and sensitive one; just how difficult may be gauged from the semiderogatory or downright racist sobriquets by which *totok,* or full-blooded Dutch, referred to them in casual discourse: *mistizien* (mestizo, or half-breed), *liplaps* (literally, "in thin layers of various colors"), *inlandsche kinderen* (children of the islands), as well as the apparently neutral but faintly patronizing *Indo-European*. (The chance to draw readers' attention to an illuminating gloss on this difficult and painful subject—albeit written in Indonesian—seems too good to pass up here: see P.W. Van der Veur, *"Orang Indo-Europa: masalah dan tantangan,"* in H. Baudet and I.J. Brugmans, eds., *Politik Etis dan Revolusi Kemerdekaan.* Jakarta: Yayasan Obor Indonesia, 1987, pp. 95-119). The same position was to prove an irritant to the Indonesian nationalist movement in its early days and evoked its own reaction during and after independence. The photographer's people come from an old residential area in Jakarta's waterfront area: it was near Depok, in a small seaside village called Jakatra, that Jan Pieterszoen Coen, first Governor-General of the Indies, founded the settlement of Batavia in 1619, and it was in Depok, in November 1945, that over a thousand Dutch civilians and Eurasians were attacked and murdered by the *pemuda.*

Product, then, of the encounter between East and West (Douwes Dekker, Eurasian leader of the Indische Partij in the early years of the century, had dreamed of a multiracial society in the Indies that would fold Europeans and Indonesians into one community), the heroine of the story is on the periphery of modern Indonesia in two respects: she is marginalized, first by race and second by dint of convictions that happen to run counter to received ideas. The way in which she chooses to resolve her ambiguous position is hardly surprising: coming in from the cold is one route open to outsiders, especially outsiders who, by the accident of birth, are already half on the inside.

Prasetyohadi was born in 1954 and started professional life as a paramedic, later managing a printing press in Bandung. He has been widely published in Indonesian journals and magazines and has won several literary contests. He works as an editor in Jakarta.

Rahmat Ali: In the Net/*Kena Jaring*

Jakarta's mental hospitals are bursting with people overwhelmed by frustration, depression, and the pressures of living in one of the world's largest cities, according to the head of the Jakarta social office, one H. Rukanda. The director of the Jakarta Mental Hospital, Mr. Amin Hussein Anwar, said that most of the mentally ill are migrants who could not face the harsh competitive environment in the city. "Such people, whose beautiful dreams have been dashed, are extremely vulnerable to stress and isolation. They cannot stand the drastic change to city life. . . . Those who had suicidal tendencies were men who carry the burden of being breadwinners."

Thus, soberingly, a report by Antara, Indonesia's domestic news agency, dated 8 May 1993. For anyone who has tried to negotiate traffic in Jakarta, Rahmat Ali's diverting account will serve as a reminder that it has been so for as long as anyone cares to remember. Far from being contrived, the journey taken by his nameless commuter follows existing bus routes point for point: you could get to where you were wanting to go simply by following the stages of the speaker's journey. To make the trip from the southeastern working-class district of Blok M to the old business center known as Kota in the north— where the Jakarta Historical Museum, of which Rahmat Ali is now the director, is found—is to realize how much this city of 10,000,000 residents, packed 31,000 to every square kilometer, leaves to be desired in the way of infrastructure, and how universal is the hassle of getting around and across town by public transport. It is also to be reminded of the good humor and patience of the people, speakers of a ripe Betawi that no more lends itself to translation into English than does Cockney or Strine into Indonesian. Like the narrator, they have to put up with it all.

Rahmat Ali was born in Malang in East Java in 1939. He studied Indonesian language and literature at Airlangga University in Surabaya and served in the Indonesian navy before spending a year in America. He has written for Jakarta magazines and published stories and poetry. "In the Net" was among several entries that won the Kincir Emas Award in 1975 for the best short story of the year.

Major works: *Sang Gubernur Jendral* (1976) [novel].

Glossary

ABRI: Angkatan Bersenjata Republic Indonesia, the Indonesian Armed Forces.

Adat: Indonesian customary law.

Adik, dik: Term of address for a younger brother or sister.

Agar-agar: A kind of gelatine concocted of seaweed.

Arja: Traditional dance theater of Bali.

Atap: Thatched roof of palm leaf.

Bajaj: A dual-passenger pedicab powered by a motor-scooter engine.

Bakso: A soup made of meatballs, beans, and cabbage.

Bang, bung: Short for *abang,* brother; a revolutionary keyword, with democratic–fraternal overtones, much in use during and after the Revolution but since fallen into disuse.

Becak: Pedicab. Until outlawed in 1990, pedicabs were ubiquitous in Jakarta.

Beli: Balinese for *brother.*

BerDiKari: Acronym of *Berdiri Atas Kaki Sendiri,* standing on one's own two feet. A favorite political slogan of President Sukarno's in the 1950s, much used in his speeches and public addresses.

Bosi: The standard-issue peaked cloth cap worn by the soldiers of the Imperial Japanese Army in the field during the Second World War.

Brahmana: Brahmin.

Bu, Ibu: Javanese for *mother, mummy, ma'am.*

Bupati: Javanese for governor of regency.

Ceki: A Chinese card game.

Cingcao: A dish of fermented cassava.

Dalang: The often masterfully eloquent puppetmaster and narrator in *wayang* shadow theater.

215

Dangdut: Popular music with a strong beat, reminiscent of Hindi or Arab music.

Delman: A kind of two-wheeled ponytrap.

Desa: Javanese for rural village.

Dokar: Horse-and-carriage.

Dukun: Shaman.

Dwifungsi: The doctrine espoused by ABRI, Indonesia's armed forces, licensing its nation-building involvement in the country's civilian/political as well as military affairs.

Gado-gado: A salad consisting of vegetables tossed in a spicy peanut sauce.

Galungan: A Balinese celebration lasting 10 days and occurring once every 210 days, in keeping with the *wuku* calendar which comprises 30 seven-day "months."

GOLKAR: Acronym for *Golongan Karya,* or workers' groups. Founded in 1964 with the help of ABRI as the centralized state party, GOLKAR was designed as a means of ensuring mass assent in government policy during *pemilihan umum,* national elections. A so-called functional group, it subsumed the three secular–nationalist political parties of the Sukarno era in practice to defuse their ideologies. The military retains control over its affairs through retired officers who hold key posts on the central and regional executive boards. Membership numbers some 25 million.

Gula Pasir: Granulated refined sugar used in the preparation of confectionary.

Gusti: Javanese for *lord, master.*

Helicak: A three-wheeled motorized pedicab.

Inlander: Dutch for *native* or *indigene*; the term has faintly deprecatory or condescending overtones.

Jamu: Medicinal herbs.

Kabupaten: Administrative term for regency in Java, headed by a *bupati.*

Kain: Cloth used as an article of men's clothing, worn sarong-fashion.

Kakek, kakak: Literally, elder brother. A domestic term of endearment in Javanese and country Malay, having rather archaic overtones to modern ears.

Kebaya: A woman's blouse reaching below the midriff.

Kek, Kekek: Grandfather; grandpa; granduncle. A term of address for an old man.

Kenari: The canari tree and its nuts.

Kerei: Ceremonial bowing in the direction of the rising sun by soliders of the Japanese Imperial Army in World War II.

Keroncong: Popular Indonesian music originating in Portuguese songs.

Ketoprak: This Javanese word has two meanings: it is a kind of theater recounting historical or quasihistorical events; or a salad consisting of bean sprouts, tofu, rice noodles, and a peanut sauce.

Ketupat: A variety of rice, cooked in a very small container made of young coconut leaves plaited together.

Khatib: A preacher in a mosque.

Kretek: Indonesian clove-scented cigarettes.

Kumico: Japanese term for an officially appointed village headman.

Ladang: An unirrigated, "dry" field, as distinct from a wet one (*sawah*).

Magrib: Literally, "West" (Ar.); Prayer time at sunset for Muslims.

Martabak: Indonesian crèpe filled with spices and meat or vegetables.

Mas: Term of address meaning *sir* or *brother*.

Meneer: Dutch for *Mr.*

Merdeka: Literally, freedom; emancipation; liberty. A key catchword, greeting, and cry of solidarity during the Indonesian Revolution, uniting all social groups and reflecting its new egalitarian ethos. The historian Anton Lucas has put it thus: "It had both an ideological and a personal meaning. . . . It symbolised 'one soul, one struggle,' the essence of the struggle against the Dutch. For others, it meant the blood of the colonialists if they dared to come back, the daring of young heroes defending their country; it could also forebode revenge for the bitterness and suffering of the Japanese period." (*One Soul One Struggle: Region and Revolution in Indonesia.* Sydney: Allen and Unwin, 1991, p. 158)

Mevrouw: Dutch for *Mrs., Ma'am.*

Mie Bakso: Noodles with meatballs.

Minyak Angin: Medicinal oil sniffed or rubbed on the head and neck to relieve headaches, nausea, etc.

MPRS: Manelis Permusyawaratan Rakyat Sementara, People's Provisional Consultative Council.

Muazin: Muezzin; Muslim prayer caller.

Naga: Dragon.

Ndoro: Javanese term of address for a member of the aristocracy; literally, master.

Nek, Nenek: Grandmother; great-aunt. A term of address for an old woman.

Nyonya: Mrs., used especially for non-Indonesian or Chinese women.

Pak, Bapak: Father, Sir, Dad, Mr.

Pancasila: The five basic principles of the Republic of Indonesia, comprising belief in one God and a commitment to a just, civilized humanity, the unity of Indonesia, democracy as guided by the wisdom of representative deliberation, and social justice for all citizens.

Pancuran: A kind of waterspout in common use throughout Southeast Asia that functions as a primitive tap. Constructed of linked bamboo, it is designed to carry water to a village from a nearby source.

Pantun: A poem composed in quatrain and often secreting an item of folk wisdom; notoriously difficult to translate into English. In the original of Achdiat K. Mihardja's "A Twist of Fate" this appears as:

> *Gunting besar, gunting ketjil rambutan masak diranting/Kutjing besar, kutjing ketjil berebutan paha kambing.*

Pasanggrahan: Wayside resthouse for travelers.

Pembantu: Malay for *helper:* from *bantu,* to help.

Pemuda: Literally, "youth"; more generally, the young men and women who played a central part in the Indonesian national revolution of 1945–50.

Pendopo: Large open structure or attached open veranda serving as the reception area of the Javanese house.

Penghulu Negeri: An adviser on Islamic affairs in a Javanese civil court.

Pikulan: A bamboo carrying pole that is borne across the shoulders and has a large basket suspended from either end.

Priyayi: Belonging to the upper class/aristocracy of Javanese society.

Raden Mas: Javanese title of nobility.

Ringgit: A note or coin worth two and half rupiahs.

Sambal: Generic term for mixed spiced into which chili peppers have been ground.

Santri: One of the terms used to describe and classify Javanese society. According to Clifford Geertz, the *santri* are the devout Javanese Muslims, who follow Islamic teachings regarding such practices as daily prayer and fasting, in contradistinction to the nominal Muslims or *abangan,* who practice only a few such rituals, such as circumcision and abstention from eating pork, and who worship Hindu or Buddhist gods and observe some of the traditions of those religions. The precise meaning of the term is much disputed by students of

Indonesia; that it refers to a very real secondary identity among the Javanese is not in doubt. Tension between *santri/priyayi* and *abangan* formed in the background of the Indonesian killings of 1965-66.

Saté: Small pieces of meat roasted on a skewer.

Sawah: West rice field.

Selamatan: A ritual meal eaten collectively, in celebration of such events as birth and circumcision.

Sembah: Literally, homage, obeisance; a respectful greeting made with the palms together and fingertips touching the forehead.

Sensei: A Chinese physician.

Shalat: Ritual prayers and actions performed by Muslims five times daily.

Tante: Dutch for *aunt.* A term of address used for European, Chinese, or Westernized women of middle age.

Tape: A dish consisting of fermented cassava.

Tebelo: A term of possibly Chinese origin for a coffin or catafalque; also used in Javanese.

Titir: An alarm signal rhythmically beaten out on a drum.

Tuan: A term of address for Western and sometimes for Westernized men.

Ummat: From *umma,* the Arabic for *community;* the universal college of Muslim believers, as in *ummat Islam,* or *ummat Nahdatul Islam;* the latter refers to the orthodox Muslim party in contemporary Indonesia.

Veldpolitie: Dutch Field Security forces, deployed in operations 1946-48.

Warung: Small, often itinerant, coffeeshop-cum–food stall.

Wedana: Javanese for "district chief."

Zakelijk: Dutch for "to the point"; businesslike.

Suggested Reading

Much of the vast and vastly interesting literature about Indonesia is written not in English but in the major European languages, as well as in Indonesian itself, and much of it is highly specialized. The general reader or beginning enthusiast may nevertheless find the following books to be of use: they are exceptionally well written and make an excellent point of departure for further study.

Anderson, B.R. O'G. *Mythology and the Tolerance of the Javanese*. Modern Indonesia Project, no. 52. Ithaca, NY: Cornell University, 1965.

——. *Language and Power: Exploring Political Cultures in Indonesia*. Ithaca, NY: Cornell University Press, 1990.

The brilliant, succinct, thought-provoking writings of Benedict Anderson are widely admired well beyond his field; he is the doyen of modern Indonesian studies.

Aveling, Harry. *From Surabaya to Armageddon: Indonesian Short Stories*. Singapore: Heinemann Educational Books, 1976. One of the very few anthologies available in English. No longer in print, it is hard to find but has worn rather well.

——. *Gestapu: Indonesian Short Stories on the Abortive Communist Coup of 30 September 1965*. University of Hawaii Southeast Asian Studies Working Paper no. 6. Honolulu: 1975. Out of print but worth trying to get hold of.

Cribb, Robert. *Historical Dictionary of Indonesia*. Metuchen, NJ: Scarecrow Press, 1992. A cornucopia of information beautifully organized in short, informative entries.

R. Frederick, William H., and John H. McGlynn, eds. *Reflections on Rebellion: Stories from the Indonesian Upheavals of 1948 and 1965*. Athens, OH: Ohio University Center for International Studies, 1983.

Fox, James J., ed. *Indonesia: The Making of a Nation.* 2 vols. Canberra: ANU Press, 1980. A rich, packed survey.

Geertz, Clifford. *The Religion of Java.* Glencoe, IL: Free Press, 1960.

————. *Peddlers and Princes: Social Change and Economic Modernisation in Two Indonesian Towns.* Chicago: University of Chicago Press, 1963.

————. *The Interpretation of Cultures.* New York: Basic Books, 1977. Clifford Geertz and Indonesian studies are in many minds synonymous; he is a scintillating commentator.

Holt, Claire. *Art in Indonesia: Continuities and Change.* Ithaca, NY: Cornell University Press, 1967. A rich source of insight into all aspects of Indonesian painting, sculpture, and architecture. Engrossing and lavishly illustrated.

Indonesia. A twice-yearly journal, out of the Modern Indonesia Project at Cornell University, and the best such publication. Invariably packed with good things, and written in nontechnical language.

Johns, A.H. *Cultural Options and the Role of Tradition: A Collection of Essays on Modern Indonesian and Malaysian Literature.* Canberra: ANU Press, 1979. Provides a chart of the terrain. Completely free of jargon.

Koentjaraningrat. *Javanese Culture.* Singapore: ISEAS/Oxford University Press, 1985. The authoritative treatise in English on the subject, by a sociologist at Gajah Mada. Gratifyingly nonacademic.

Lubis, Mochtar. *Bromocorah and Other Stories.* Trans. Jeanette Lingard. Singapore: Oxford University Press, 1985.

————. *Twilight in Jakarta.* Singapore: Oxford University Press, 1972. Lubis and Pramoedya are among the few Indonesian authors whose works are easily available in English. A classic modern novel.

McDonald, Hamish. *Suharto's Indonesia.* Sydney: Fontana/Collins, 1980. A penetrating survey by an experienced journalist.

McVey, Ruth, ed. *Indonesia.* New Haven: HRAF Press, 1963. A collection of highly informative essays on most aspects of Indonesian culture.

Mulder, Neils. *Mysticism and Everyday Life in Contemporary Java: Cultural Persistence and Change.* 2d ed. Singapore: Singapore University Press, 1983. An intriguing, nontechnical account of *kejawen* mysticism and its significance, by an observer intimately acquainted with the subject.

————. *Individual and Society in Java: A Cultural Analysis.* 2d ed., rev. Yogyakarta: Gadjah Mada University Press, 1983. A short, eminently readable account.

Polomka, Peter. *Indonesia Since Sukarno.* Ringwood, Australia: Penguin, 1971. Valuable despite its antiquity.

Raffel, Burton. *The Complete Poetry and Prose of Chairil Anwar.* Athens, OH: University Press, 1993. Raffel has a tin ear at times, but his edition succeeds in conveying the flavor of one of the most passionate poets, sexually and politically, of the Indonesian Revolution.

Reid. A.J.S. *The Indonesian National Revolution 1945–50.* Hawthorn, Australia: Longman Australia, 1974. After Anderson's, the best single study of its kind.

Schwartz, Adam. *A Nation in Waiting: Indonesia in the 1990s.* Boulder, CO: Westview Press, 1994. Timely, perspicacious.

Wertheim, W. F. *Indonesian Society in Transition.* 2d. ed., rev. The Hague and Bandung: W. van Hoeve, 1964. An excellent analytical introduction to contemporary Indonesian society and history.

Zainu'ddin, Ailsa. *A Short History of Indonesia.* Cheshire, Australia: Melbourne University Press, 1980. A very accessible survey.

David M.E. Roskies was educated at the Hebrew University of Jerusalem, where he took a degree in Medieval Theology. Formerly a university teacher, he is now managing partner of an international consulting firm based in Jakarta.